SAM BLAKE

IN DEEP WATER

ZAFFRE

First published in Great Britain in 2017 by Zaffre Publishing

This paperback edition published in 2018 by
ZAFFRE PUBLISHING
80–81 Wimpole St,
London W1G 9RE
www.zaffrebooks.co.uk

A CIP catalogue record for this book is
available from the British Library.

Trade Paperback ISBN: 978-1-78576-055-6
Paperback ISBN: 978-1-78576-080-8
Ebook ISBN:978-1-78576-054-9

1 3 5 7 9 10 8 6 4 2

Typeset by IDSUK (Data Connection) Ltd
Printed and bound by Clays Ltd, St Ives Plc

Zaffre Publishing is an imprint of Bonnier Zaffre,
a Bonnier Publishing company
www.bonnierzaffre.co.uk
www.bonnierpublishing.co.uk

For Shane, Sophie and Sam.
Who put up with a lot so I can follow my dreams.
Thank you xxx

1

Cathy was expecting the left jab; it was the speed of the kick that surprised her. He was bulked up, but he was fast.

Bastard.

She came right back, caught him under the chin with an uppercut that stunned him; her left hook followed it, then an explosive push kick right into the middle of his chest guard. He was still staggering as, spinning around, her back kick sent him towards the raw brick wall where he crumpled with a grunt.

'What the fuck's going on in here?' The Boss's voice echoed around the high-ceilinged gym, drowning the bass beat of Spin 1038, the Falls Road in every vowel. 'I'm in the khazi for five minutes and all fucking hell breaks loose?'

Shaking her arms out, Cathy turned away from him, hiding her grin of satisfaction. Out of the corner of her eye, she saw the three lads who had been egging their mate to take her on shuffling nervously from side to side. *They were right to be worried.*

'Nothing, Boss.' Like choir boys. Only the lad on the floor was quiet, winded, struggling to his feet.

Turning back to them, shoving a stray corkscrew of raven hair from her face, Cathy smirked. One of them had had the cheek to leer at her cropped black Lycra top and loose wide-legged exercise pants, the waistband rolled down to her slim hips revealing the scars on her stomach that were still angry even after all these months. She would have given him the finger if she hadn't been wearing boxing gloves. *Like they'd never seen a girl in a gym before.*

Niall McIntyre drew himself up to his full height, all five foot six of it, put his hands on his hips and gave her the full sergeant major routine, complete with a look that would have made litmus bleed.

'*You*, girl, have got the semis at the end of the month. Where's your safety gear? You've enough damage done, without breaking another rib.' Turning to the lads, his pointed finger rammed home every word. 'I don't know what you've been allowed to get away with in Tallaght, but there will be no arsing about in my gym, do you hear? This isn't junior infants. You want to improve your game, it's by *my* rules. Understood?'

They nodded like five-year-olds caught on the rob. For a small man he could be pretty scary. Unshaven, a rat face cut from granite, he was a Belfast Catholic who'd spent his life in the British army. Knew how to make it sting. The lads kept their eyes on the ground. They weren't much older than seventeen, their fake tans bleached right out by the overhead fluorescents, angry tattoos battling for space on their arms and chests – Dublin's finest. They looked good, Cathy would give them that, but she was sure they were bulked up on steroids and that was a fool's game.

'You know who she is?' McIntyre's voice was sharp. They didn't look like they were going to answer, but he didn't give them a chance. '*This* is Cat Connolly.' He didn't need to add three times Women's National Full-Contact Kick-boxing champion and decorated member of An Garda Síochána. As soon as he said her name she saw the recognition in their faces, watched their expressions change like the wind, from respect to hatred, like she had some contagious disease. Where they came from it didn't matter how good you were in the ring, cops were scum, the enemy. And McIntyre knew it, would have her sparring with them before the end of the week when they'd only have one thing on their minds – drawing blood. *That was one way to get match fit.*

'Bastard . . .' Cathy muttered it under her breath, shaking her head.

'Right, if you boys can't spar without getting into shit, grab yourselves some ropes: twenty skips, twenty press-ups, nineteen skips, nineteen tucks. Keep going till you're back to one. Cat, you're with me. Where the hell's Sarah Jane? She should be here by now. She's not working in that restaurant tonight, is she?'

Cathy shook her head, 'She never does Monday evenings – even The Rookery is quiet on a Monday.' Cathy glanced at the clock high on the gym wall. It was after seven o'clock.

Where the hell *was* Sarah Jane?

It wasn't like her to be late. Sarah Jane was always early. One of the most organised people Cathy knew, Sarah Jane managed to juggle a part-time job waitressing at one of the city's swanki-est restaurants, study for her masters, fit in training and still get all her assignments in on time. Cathy put that down to her being something close to a genius. Sarah Jane denied she was bright, reckoned she got As in everything because she worked hard, that she was ordinary, just like everyone else. That had made Cathy laugh. Cathy knew *she* was the one who was ordinary; her father was a barman, her mum had worked three jobs to keep her and her brothers in shoe leather – *that* was ordinary. Sarah

Jane's dad was a Norwegian Pulitzer Prize-winning *New York Times* journalist and her mother had grown up in one of the smallest villages in Ireland, but had ended up the flame-haired poster girl for Greenpeace. That was going somewhere else well clear of ordinary.

She pressed her tongue against her gum shield. Sarah Jane *was* better organised than Cathy would ever be, which made it weird that she hadn't turned up for the best bit of their whole week – the bit when they got to have a laugh with The Boss and beat the feck out of each other. Cathy trained six days a week, but sparring with Sarah Jane gave her a chance to focus on technique rather than power. Everyone needed a training buddy, and Sarah Jane was hers. In the past few months, though, with the championships on the horizon, she'd stepped it up, and was finally feeling she'd regained her form after the explosion that had nearly killed her almost a year ago. And Sarah Jane had been brilliant, was loving improving her own fitness alongside Cathy's, keeping to her pace.

There wasn't a day that went by when Cathy didn't wish she'd curbed her curiosity all those months ago. It had been a routine break-in until she'd found those bones, the tiny grey shards a whisper of something much more ominous hidden deep within the hem of a vintage wedding dress. The story that had unravelled had gotten far bigger and more complex than any of them had ever expected, and while she might be heading towards match fitness again now, she didn't know if she'd ever be quite the same person she'd been before.

She hadn't known Sarah Jane that well then – she'd been the year below Cathy in school. It was a small school, so they'd known each other, had played on the same hockey team, but hadn't been close friends. Then Cathy had gone straight into the Guards. Actually she'd been the only girl in her year not to go to uni or college, but she hadn't been able to wait. She knew she'd learn more on the job in a day than she'd learn in a year of a degree course, and she could study at night – which was exactly what she had done.

Cathy was sure 'the accident', as half the people in her life seemed to call it, was one of the reasons she and Sarah Jane clicked when they'd bumped into each other again at the gym. There weren't many people who understood Cathy's world, and Sarah Jane had the same problem. Cathy's working class family and private girls' school education, her boxing, getting shot on the job, made her different. Sarah Jane's norm was in a place where being held at gunpoint on your tenth birthday or being evacuated by helicopter was just a thing that happened on holiday. But then she'd spent her school holidays with her dad when he was assigned to the Middle East – and as a journalist he was never really 'on holiday'. Sarah Jane found it hilarious, if ironically so, that he attracted trouble like Cathy seemed to. But she never called the bomb blast an accident.

It hadn't been a fecking accident.

A Russian mafia don called Kuteli had organised a hit on her, pure and simple; had deliberately tried to kill her and there was nothing accidental about it.

Cathy shook her head, still thinking about McIntyre's question. 'When I saw her on Friday she said she'd see me here tonight. I was working all weekend.' Cathy felt McIntyre looking at her hard as she tried to hide the flicker of concern in her voice. 'I don't know why she didn't ring if she needed to cancel.'

His tone softened fractionally. 'Well she's late, and you can't train without a sparring partner. What does she think we're running here, a holiday camp?'

'Maybe she's got car trouble . . .'

'I'll give her car trouble. I keep telling her that Micra is a heap of shite. We'll do some pad work instead. Let's see you warming up properly. Bet you didn't think of that before you belted Twinkle Toes there?'

Cathy shook her head, grinning. McIntyre was a total bastard, but he was the best in the business and he'd shaped her from a shy ten-year-old to a champion. He was her friend and mentor, a part of her family. And he'd been the one who had put in the extra time, coaching her every day, helping her to focus on getting back in the game as she fought her way back to fitness.

He didn't know the whole story, not like Dawson O'Rourke, her DI, but she'd never be able to thank McIntyre enough for his steely determination, his refusal to let her give up. The blast had left her on life support, had almost derailed her career as a detective and as a boxer, and had murdered the new life within her. Back then, before the bomb, she might have been confused, uncertain about the future, but it had been her life, her baby, and that loss would never go away. It was a pain deep inside that could still ambush her. But in the aftermath she'd learned what amazing friends she had. Between them, O'Rourke and McIntyre had shown her how to survive.

And now, after the bomb, after everything, she was heading for the top again. Recovery had taken longer than she'd ever thought it could – months and months – but she was physically ready now and she was going to take her title back. And that feeling of being in control physically was helping her mentally too. The scars ran deep, and sometimes she wondered if they would ever heal. They affected her when she least expected it, her emotions seesawing from extreme anger to the darkest despair, triggered by something she saw on TV, at work, or sometimes simply by hearing a song on the radio. One of the things she'd had to learn since it happened was how to become a very good actress, hiding how she really felt, trying to keep everything on a level, outwardly at least. At work there was no room for mistakes, and if she wanted to stay in the job she had to find ways to cope. Nobody wanted to hear her whining or to have to pick up the pieces when she flew off the handle.

It had only happened once; she'd gone back to work too early, of course. She might have been physically mended – after months of surgery and plastic surgery, physio and rehab, after running hundreds of miles, she was fit enough to persuade them she could get back out there – but her first week of nights had been a disaster. A heavily pregnant teenager had been beaten up by her boyfriend, and as she lay rolling in agony on the hall floor, waiting for the ambulance, her baby, her *wanted* baby slipping away, the boyfriend had made some smart comment and Cathy had snapped. It had taken two officers to haul her off him.

He wouldn't be hitting a woman again anytime soon.

Grabbing a skipping rope, Cathy kept one eye on the clock as she started her warm-up, her bare feet silent on the padded matting as the rope whirled. Press-ups next. Squats. Star jumps. The thick black minute hand ticked on, shaking with each increment. *Where was Sarah Jane?* She'd hardly have forgotten. They trained together every Monday night, the only exception being if Cathy was on a case and couldn't get away from work. Cathy glanced at the double swing doors leading to the changing rooms, looking for the bright flash of Sarah Jane's smile through the wired glass. *She would have phoned if she was sick, or had been delayed.*

Jumping up, Cathy started her stretches. Maybe Sarah Jane's phone was dead again.

By 7.45 p.m. she still hadn't shown up.

'Come on, girl, you're not concentrating!' McIntyre grabbed the punch bag out of Cathy's reach and slapped the side hard, the sound explosive, ricocheting off the brick walls like a car backfiring. It made her start more than McIntyre could know. But then maybe he did. He'd heard bombs go off more than once. As she tried to still her heart rate, the Tallaght boys looked up from their squats, startled. Out of the corner of her eye Cathy could see them smirking, enjoying her getting bawled at.

'You've got to focus. Remember, eyes on the prize. Let me hear it.'

'Jesus, Boss.'

'You worrying about where Sarah Jane is isn't going to get this session over any quicker. Let me hear it.'

Cathy danced backwards, her gloves beneath her chin, steadying her breathing. 'McIntyre's mantra', Sarah Jane called it . . . Well, he asked for it . . . She smashed her glove into the bag. Left, right . . .

'I *will* be national champion.'

McIntyre steadied the bag as he took the force of the punch through it. Cathy was already saturated with sweat from the session, droplets flying as she went in with a right uppercut.

'I *will* be European champion . . .'

Left uppercut. She didn't look at McIntyre, but could hear him exhale with each strike. It would be a while before she was ready for the Europeans, but he was all about positive thinking and she knew it worked. He'd taught her how to focus, taught her how to win, and that's what she was going to do.

'And the rest, girl, let me hear it, you won't be at this your whole life – what else?'

Cathy danced back again, catching her breath, punched hard 'I *will* get my masters.' Her push kick sent the bag into McIntyre's chest.

'What are you working so hard at, girl? What do you want? Let me hear it!'

Hard again with a left jab, another left jab, followed by a right. 'Forensic psychology. A first.'

'*And?*'

She said it under her breath, conscious of the audience, 'I *will* be the first female Garda profiler.'

McIntyre grunted, 'Good. That's good, girl. Put it here.' He pushed the bag towards her, bracing himself behind it, 'Just watch that right, you're dropping a bit.'

From across the gym Cathy could hear laughter, then the choir boys chimed in, their voices high pitched, 'I do believe in fairies, I do, I do.'

McIntyre turned on them, his voice echoing through the styrofoam ceiling, 'Showers. Now. All of you.'

Scattering like rats, they didn't have to be told twice. It had been a long time since Cathy had seen anyone move that fast.

'Now, girl, a couple more for me. Push kick, back kick.' Cathy caught the glint in McIntyre's eye. She danced back, smiling to herself, imagined the lippy one's face on the bag, and smashed her left foot straight at it, pivoting to kick the bag again with her right foot, putting all her weight behind it.

'Not bad, girl. Not bad.' McIntyre pursed his lips as Cathy pulled at the Velcro on her gloves with her teeth. 'Keep this up and you're in with a real shot at getting your title back. That Jordan one is your only worry.' Striding to the benches running along the wall, McIntyre picked up her towel and threw it at her. She caught it one handed, rubbing the sweat off her neck and chest, spitting out her gum shield.

'Her brother's inside for rape; she alibied him. Tried to, anyway.'

McIntyre raised his eyebrows, 'All the more reason for you to give her a pasting.'

Cathy let a glimmer of a smile creep out. McIntyre had trained all of her brothers, even Tomás, who spent more time at the poker table than in the gym, and Pete who had had to fit classes around school and the early-morning sandwich run that had grown into a restaurant empire. Aidan, the eldest, had gone into the job ahead of her, but he'd learned as much in the ring as he had in uniform on the street.

Before Cathy could answer, her phone rang.

'Bet that's Sarah Jane . . .' Dashing over to the bench where she'd tossed the phone, Cathy could feel her abs burning. Sparring partner or not, McIntyre had given her a hard time. Flipping open the cover, she was about to answer when it stopped ringing.

'Damn.'

Behind her McIntyre was tidying up, pairing the spare gloves on the shelves beside the weights, untangling the skipping ropes.

Cathy checked her missed calls. Sarah Jane's mum's number flashed up. Cathy's stomach suddenly felt hollow.

'If it's Sarah Jane, you just tell her her organisational skills are slipping.'

Cathy looked up, frowning, her blue eyes clouded, 'No, no, it wasn't her. It was her mum.'

She punched out 171 with her thumb and put the phone to her ear. The message was short, Sarah Jane's mother's voice catching at the edges like she was trying not to panic:

'Cathy, when you get this, can you call me? I've been trying Sarah Jane's phone all afternoon and her dad couldn't get hold of her yesterday. He tried to call me earlier but we got cut off – they've had some sort of row. I really need to talk to her . . . is she with you?'

McIntyre caught the look on Cathy's face.

'What's up, girl?'

'I don't know. I really don't know.'

Cathy hit instant call back. It only took seconds to connect.

Sarah Jane's mum sounded breathless as she answered. 'Cathy? Have you heard from her?'

'No.' Cathy paused, not wanting to panic Oonagh Hansen any more. 'Not yet, she didn't come to training.'

Sarah Jane's mother's intake of breath was instantaneous, the tone of her voice unmistakable, 'Oh God. You have to find her. She . . . Her dad said . . .' The words were tumbling over themselves . . . 'He said . . . Ted said . . . he spoke to her on Friday. He's stuck up a mountain in Syria and the line was really bad, but I think he said she'd got a lead on a story. He told her to leave it alone, that it was too dangerous for a student, they had a row about it . . .'

'I'll do my best. I'll call you as soon as I find her. Try not to worry, I'm sure she's buried in an essay at home and hasn't realised the time . . .'

'Please, Cathy. Please find her . . . Call me as soon as you can. I'm going to see if I can get up to Dublin in the morning, I just have to get a lift to Killarney and I'll get the train . . . but I don't know if I should stay down here where she can get hold of me . . .'

The call dropped.

For a moment Cathy looked blankly at the phone, trying to gather her thoughts. Deep inside, a feeling of worry uncurled and stretched its claws. What on earth could she be working on that she hadn't talked to Cathy about? Was it something that had only just happened? One thing she knew for sure: Sarah Jane would never miss training. No matter what. Cathy swung around to relay the conversation to McIntyre.

Something was wrong. Very wrong.

2

She might have left the gym behind, but there was a fight going on in Cathy's head as she drove towards Sarah Jane's house. One part of her was forcing herself to relax, to concentrate on the heavy traffic as she headed down the M50, tail lights blazing red through the darkness and drizzle. The other part of her was making her hands grip the steering wheel of her grey Mini so tight it hurt.

Sarah Jane was never late. That was it. That was just it. She was never late and she never didn't call. The words rolled around Cathy's head like ball bearings. Cathy knew you couldn't never not do something, but she knew what she meant, *Sarah Jane just never didn't turn up.*

And she'd had a row with her dad. On Friday. Three whole days ago.

One thing she and Sarah Jane had in common was what McIntyre called sheer bloody-mindedness. Tell either of them not to do something and it was guaranteed to have the opposite effect. Sarah Jane was striving so hard to get a really fabulous degree, to make a name for herself in her own right, to prove that her dad could be proud of her, that she was sometimes even more headstrong than Cathy – and that was saying something. But that was why they got on so well: Cathy had been known to jump in before she checked the depth too; was getting a reputation for getting herself into deep water, into situations that would have finished off most people – they understood each other.

Cathy had realised Sarah Jane idolised her dad from the first time they'd really got chatting. But this argument, over a story?

For Sarah Jane's mum, panic mode was the default response to any problem – she was infamous for getting into a total stew about everything. Perhaps it was being so far away in rural Kerry that was part of the problem, but if there was a power cut, Oonagh Hansen was on the phone to Sarah Jane in hysterics. It was entirely possible, Cathy rationalised, trying to keep calm herself, that Oonagh's interpretation of what had actually been said or not said was way off the mark. Cathy took a deep breath. But that still didn't explain where the hell Sarah Jane was.

The minute Cathy had got out of the shower at the gym she'd called all their mutual friends. Cathy knew that Sarah Jane had a pile of assignments to catch up on, that she'd been working in the restaurant covering the lunch shift yesterday. They'd talked about it on Friday morning – she remembered Sarah Jane's words as she'd raised her voice over the clamour of the canteen:

'I'm working Friday afternoon and Sunday but I told Billy I couldn't do Saturday. No way. I've got three features and another article to do and I need to research a load of stuff. I'll see you at the gym on Monday evening. I'll be in the library all day.'

Leaning on her locker, Cathy had tapped her phone on her teeth while trying to work out who to call next. Someone must have heard from her or seen her today. Even if she was spending the day in the library, why hadn't she called if she was going to miss training? Maybe her phone battery was dead, maybe her car wouldn't start, or her assignment had taken longer than she thought?

That was a lot of maybes.

If her phone was dead she could have emailed from her laptop . . .

Cathy's gut twisted again. Why did she have such a bad feeling about this? Was she jumping to conclusions? Maybe . . . There was that word again.

And if Cathy had learned anything during her six years in the job, it was that you didn't do maybe. Maybe didn't stand up in court. Maybe was about speculation, not evidence.

Sarah Jane's house didn't have a landline phone anymore, and Cathy didn't have the numbers of any of Sarah Jane's housemates . . . or did she? She didn't have their numbers in her contact list, but she did have a text from one of them, Slug. God only knew how he'd got her number, but he'd texted once looking for advice from her brother Aidan – *looking for a favour, more like . . .*

Scrolling back through her messages, Cathy prayed she hadn't deleted it. She rarely deleted anything, this was her own version of OCD, an obsession with keeping data . . . She spotted it and hit call.

Not surprisingly, Slug wasn't quite with it, and it took him a few minutes to work out who she was.

'Sarah Jane? Nope, not seen her since . . .' His pause was too long, made Cathy want to reach into the phone and grab him by the neck.

'Since?'

She'd prompted him, battling to keep the desperation out of her voice.

'I'm pretty sure she was here last night. I was on the Xbox but I think I heard the door slam. Haven't seen her since I got up.'

'When was that?'

'About three or four maybe.'

Who the feck got up at three o'clock in the afternoon? Cathy kept her thoughts to herself. 'Is she there now?'

'I think maybe she went out.'

'What time was that?'

'I dunno, she's not here now.'

Helpful.

It only took Cathy a second to decide what to do. Maybe Sarah Jane had left a note on her calendar about a meeting, or something on her desk that would provide an explanation.

'I'm coming over. If you see her, tell her I'm looking for her, will you?'

'OK.'

Cathy gripped the steering wheel more tightly. Something wasn't right, something big. Had to be. What on earth would make her miss training without getting in touch? Had she landed an interview with someone at the last minute and forgotten? Unlikely, but when she got an idea into her head she just couldn't see anything else. Which sometimes caused friction with her dad – because he was exactly the same. If anyone needed tunnel vision to get his job done, it was Ted Hansen. If he started thinking for one second about the stuff around the edges, about what might happen when he was out in the field reporting from some war-torn part of Africa or Syria, where he was now, he'd never leave his apartment overlooking Central Park.

Oh Jesus, please don't let anything have happened to her. Sarah Jane was her best friend, they had a connection. Cathy could feel cold sweat on her back. But all Cathy's instincts were telling her she should be worried, and Cathy had good reason to know her instincts were good. It was her instincts that had changed her career path one long hot summer.

The sound of Maroon 5's 'This Love', playing at full volume on someone's stereo down the terrace, the smell of sausages on a barbeque, of hot dry earth, parched by three months of real summer heat. She'd been twelve years old, sitting on the low wall outside their house, half reading her magazine. She'd looked up to see a little girl on her own, lost and lonely, vulnerable and on the verge of panic, the tears starting to fall. And a man striding purposefully across the parched green towards her, the hood of his sweatshirt pulled up to conceal his face.

Later the Guards had told her that the little girl was only four and the man had a string of previous convictions for assaults on children.

She hadn't thought about the dangers then, that the man could have been armed, that he wasn't the type a twelve-year-old should challenge. Instead she'd taken off towards the girl, shouting at her to run, yelling at her brothers to come and help. That had been the day she'd decided to follow in her big brother Aidan's footsteps and become a member of An Garda Síochána. That was the day that had changed her life.

One night over a few pints after a late shift, Aidan had told O'Rourke all about it. It had just been the three of them in the corner of the pub, the doors locked, the barman wiping down the counter further along the mahogany bar. O'Rourke had raised his eyebrows, his 'She hasn't changed' said with amusement as his eyes had met hers across the creamy head of his Guinness. She'd glared back at him, trying to mask her reaction to his stare, one that seemed to look deep inside her, the underlying tone, teasing, one he saved for her. He was right, she hadn't changed. There were times when you had to get involved, to make other people's business your business, and her gut was telling her that this was one of them.

Cathy slipped the Mini down a gear as she headed up the ramp off the M50 towards Cherrywood, the traffic lights ahead of her changing. She was getting the same feeling now that she'd had way back then on the garden wall, that same feeling that something wasn't right. She'd had it again when she'd entered the bedroom in Dalkey and seen the cream silk of a wedding dress tangled amongst Zoe Grant's clothes, a wedding dress that had turned out to have a grisly secret hidden in the hem . . . But that was history, and this was the present.

It was bizarre how she and Sarah Jane had clicked. They'd bumped into each other at the gym in Dún Laoghaire after how many years? Five? The digital locks on their lockers had both failed at the same time and Sarah Jane had gone to get one of the staff to open them. They'd got chatting while they waited for rescue, laughing about girls from school they were still in touch with, comparing notes on what they'd done since they left. Before they'd even realised they'd both be studying in DCU that September, Sarah Jane in her final year of her masters in journalism, Cathy starting her masters part-time in forensic psychology, juggling her lectures with her job, they'd arranged to train together.

The traffic lights changed to green, the vehicles in front of her sluggish as they moved off. *What was it with the bloody traffic in this city?* Sarah Jane lived on the south side of Dublin, had taken over her parents' old house when her dad moved back to New York and her mum went to find herself with her brushes and paints in rural County Kerry. It was only about ten minutes from Cathy's own shared rented house in Shankill, a stone's throw from Michael's Hospital.

Hospital. Had Sarah Jane had an accident? She was a terrible driver, but she was pretty safe – it was the other motorists she drove mad, crawling below the speed limit.

Bad news travels fast. Her housemate – although technically her landlord – Decko's favourite phrase.

Glancing in the rear-view mirror, Cathy activated the hands-free phone set integrated into her dashboard and scrolled through her most recent dialled numbers. She hit the call button.

It took Decko a few minutes to answer, the sounds of the custody office in the Bridewell Garda Station filling the void as he caught up with what she was saying, 'Slow down, Cat. Sarah Jane's missing? She'll be fine. Bad news—'

Cathy cut him off, would have laughed if she'd been feeling less sick, 'But it's not like her. Can you run her plate, see if her car's been involved in an accident?'

'Christ, Cat, you know PULSE shows every log-in. I need a better reason than that she missed training, it's not a notifiable offence.'

'Decko . . .' It came out more panicky than she'd expected.

'All right, all right. Give me a minute. What's her reg?

'It's 07 D 80305, a silver Micra. Sarah Jane Hansen, Royal Avenue, Dún Laoghaire.' Cathy reeled off the number. Car registrations were like people's names when you were in the job, were just something you remembered. The year of manufacture, the county – the Irish system made it easy. But then in this job you were trained to be highly observant. Attention to detail could save your life.

'Got it.' She could hear Decko tapping at his keyboard as he continued. 'Where are you?'

'In the car. Ring me back. I'm on my way to her house but the traffic's crap, I'm going to be at least another fifteen minutes. I know there's something wrong, Dec, I just know it.'

'OK. I'm on it. J.P.'s working tonight. I'll get him to meet you there. But honestly, Cat, bad news travels fast.'

He was right of course. Bad news always got to you before good. But knowing that didn't slow Cathy's heart rate.

As she turned into Royal Avenue, lights glowed from the elegant Georgian houses on each side of the open green. Across the far end, facing her, was a row of substantial 1930s semis; Sarah Jane's house was on the corner. There was no sign of J.P. yet. Between herself and her three housemates, their stations covered a good chunk of Dublin city from the Bridewell to Blackrock and up into the mountains. Dún Laoghaire was her and J.P.'s patch.

Cathy swung right, around the end of the green, and pulled up outside number thirty-two, yanking on the handbrake. Slamming the door of the Mini behind her, the sound ricocheting across the square, Cathy was across the broad pavement and heading through the wrought-iron gate, held permanently open, and across the lawn before the sound had died.

Pausing outside the glazed porch long enough to catch her breath, she hit the doorbell. Needle-like darts of rain headed down the back of her neck. Yanking the hood of her black sweat top up over her head, she lifted her hand to hammer on the glass, her voice raised, 'Christ, can't you hear the bell?'

Inside the porch, the front door swung open and the sounds of car wheels screeching and bullets flying reached her. Head shaven, shirt off, his tattoos on full display, Slug looked at Cathy like she'd beamed in from the planet Lunatic. Cathy banged on the glass again with the heel of her hand, 'Hurry up!'

Shoving an Xbox controller into his jeans pocket, Slug stepped reluctantly into the porch and pulled back the sliding door, opening his mouth to speak over the racket of what sounded like Grand Theft Auto coming from inside the house. But Cathy didn't wait to hear what he had to say. Instead she pushed past him and ran up the stairs two at a time, her Nikes pounding the pale green stair carpet.

'Sarah Jane?'

Calling out as she swung onto the landing, dominated by a mountain bike and piles of dirty washing, Cathy almost tripped over a skateboard abandoned at the top of the stairs. The unvarnished wooden door to Sarah Jane's room was closed. Cathy knew it was her parents' old bedroom, the big one at the front of the house. In a stride Cathy was at the door, her hand raised to knock.

But there was no need.

The door wasn't closed.

It had been pulled firmly to, to make it look like it was closed, but Cathy could see indentations in the soft wood beside the Yale lock, where it had been levered open. When Sarah Jane had started letting the other rooms in the house her dad had insisted everyone had their own door key, for privacy – and safety.

'Oh holy feck.'

Behind her, Slug arrived at the top of the stairs, the sounds from downstairs continuing like they were inside an arcade.

'What's the panic?'

Cathy glanced back at him, fighting to keep her voice level.

'It's been jemmied. Looks like a crowbar.'

3

Gloves, she needed gloves. After four years as a detective the procedure was ingrained, but it had never been this personal before. And right now Cathy didn't have time to wait. She'd used the last pair in the box she kept in her car at a forced entry yesterday. Great.

Cathy thought fast then pulled her sleeve down over her hand and gently pushed Sarah Jane's bedroom door. It didn't move. She put her forearm up against it to apply more pressure.

'Shouldn't you call her first?' Slug hovered at the top of the stairs.

Cathy shot him an acid look. 'I've tried that. Do you think you could you turn that noise down so I can think?'

Slug shrugged, not moving, focusing on the smooth wood of the door as Cathy pushed a little harder. Something behind it was stopping it from opening. She pushed again, widening the gap until it was big enough to for her to see inside.

Even through the narrow gap she could see the room had been turned over. Completely trashed. *What the . . . ?*

Deliberately keeping her body away from the door jamb, from the door itself, Cathy eased her head inside. The curtains were open, the weak light from a street lamp illuminating the rain on the window, throwing most of the room into shadow.

Every drawer had been pulled out, Sarah Jane's clothes jumbled on the floor along with notebooks and files, the sheets from her bed. There was a strong smell of perfume, rich and spicy, like a bottle had been broken. The bright strip of light from the landing cut through the mess like a blade.

Taking a sharp intake of breath, Cathy withdrew her head.

Slug was right behind her, too close, craning to look inside. She almost bumped into him.

'She's normally really tidy.'

Cathy's eyes blazed, her retort swift, 'I know. I don't think she did this herself, do you?' Then, before he could reply, 'Don't touch anything.'

She pulled her phone from her pocket. J.P. answered on the second ring, his country accent immediately reassuring. His family owned a massive cattle farm in Tipperary – he'd been taking emergencies in his stride since he was old enough to stand and hold a bottle for a new-born calf.

Cat put one finger in her ear so she could hear him properly over the sound of the video game coming from downstairs, 'I'm at Sarah Jane's, her room's been turned over. Did Decko call you?'

'I'm on my way, with you in five. Don't touch anything.'

'I have to see if she's in there.'

'Listen to me, Cat. Don't go in. Preserve the scene. You know the routine.'

'But she could be injured, unconscious . . .'

'Don't go in. We're on our way.'

Cathy drew in a shaky breath, 'OK, OK, hurry up.'

Cathy stuck the phone back in her pocket, spoke half to herself, half to Slug, 'I just need to see behind the door. She could be . . .'

'Who was that?' Cathy knew from Slug's tone, sort of non-chalant and offhand, that he already half knew the answer to that one.

'It's one of my colleagues.'

Slug's nod was exaggerated, as if he was trying to act relaxed. 'You should wait for him to get here.' *Like he was an expert on police procedure and she was a girl and couldn't handle it?*

Cathy's retort was sharp, 'Thank you, Mastermind. Did you see anyone here tonight?'

Slug took a step backwards, shrugging, defensive, 'I don't know. I was on the Xbox.'

Cathy looked at him hard. No doubt he'd been having a bit of a smoke at the same time.

'Great . . . that's just great. Have you got a torch?'

A moment later, Slug retrieved a heavy steel torch from his room across the landing. Cathy screwed up her face at the smell that hit her the moment he opened the door. Weed and sweat with a liberal dose of seriously bad socks. Sarah Jane had said he was single. She could see why.

From Sarah Jane's bedroom door, the torch's powerful beam picked out the hotchpotch colours of clothes scattered all over the floor, purples and blues merging like a bruise.

J.P. was going to kill her, but Cathy knew she couldn't wait. She'd been here a hundred times before, her DNA would be all over the place, so it wasn't like she was going to contaminate the scene.

Her heart thumping in her ears, Cathy eased the door open with the tip of her elbow.

'You should wait for him.'

Behind her, Slug's voice, even with whatever he'd been smok-ing this evening, was a lot steadier than Cathy's hand. The torch shook for a second as she gathered her thoughts. Glancing back at him defiantly, Cathy took a big step into the room, her Nikes silent on the thick cream carpet. Pivoting to swing the beam around behind the door, Cathy braced herself, suddenly realising there was a chance that whoever had done this was still here. Hiding behind the door.

Christ, J.P. was right, she should have waited for him. But what if Sarah Jane was here? What if someone had hit her over the head and she was lying in a pool of blood? Minutes could make a difference between . . . between . . . Cathy didn't let her mind go there. What was she working on that was dangerous, for God's sake? Cathy could feel her mouth going dry, sweat trickling down her spine. Sarah Jane's dad had built his reputation as a journalist covering terrorism and war zones, his idea of danger was a whole different walk in the park to your average dad. If Ted Hansen had said a story was dangerous, he wasn't joking.

Sarah Jane's double bed was a mess. The milky-white duvet and sheets had been pulled back into an angry tangle on the floor, the mattress pushed off the base into the gap between the bed and the radiator. Whoever had been here hadn't been messing about.

Cathy felt the hairs standing up on the back of her neck. Why toss the place like this? Someone had been looking for something. And wanted to find it really fast. But why the bed? Did they think she'd hidden something under the mattress? She swung the torch quickly, checking to her left, taking in the open door to the en suite bathroom, the drawers hanging open in the white painted chest opposite. Sarah Jane's minimalist desk, normally meticulously tidy, was a jumble of papers, empty files tossed on the floor. The desk chair lay on its side, a purple satin cushion beside it, the cover ripped, the stuffing spilling like entrails. *Holy, holy feck.*

'Is she there?'

Slug was at the door, his slim frame blocking the light from the landing. Throwing him a glance, Cathy shook her head.

'Keep back from the door . . . The mattress has been pulled off. I can't see down the side of the bed.'

Trying to still her heart, Cathy looked for somewhere clear to stand in the mess on the floor. The stench of Sarah Jane's favourite perfume was turning her stomach, nutmeg and cinnamon catching in the back of her throat, masking, she was sure, whatever other smells there were in the room.

Taking two big strides, desperately trying not to disturb anything, Cathy steadied herself. Leaning forward, she could just see under the upended mattress, playing the torch beam into the cavern it had created where it had been pushed off the bed. Half expecting to see Sarah Jane's foot poking out, Cathy didn't know if she was relieved or more alarmed to see the space empty except for a book lying face down on the carpet where it must have been knocked off the bedside table.

'Anything?' Slug's voice again, this time from outside the door.

'No. But someone's had a bloody good go at the place.'

Twisting around, looking for the next suitable place to step, Cathy glanced at the jumble on Sarah Jane's desk. And stopped abruptly.

'Her laptop's gone. And . . .' – in the half-light it took her a moment to work it out – 'the hard drive to her desktop's gone. The keyboard's here . . .' Cathy could see trailing cables where the tower normally lived under Sarah Jane's desk, the keyboard upside down on the floor.

There was a pause before Slug answered, 'She's probably got her laptop with her.'

Cathy paused, talking more to herself than to him. 'Did she say anything about getting the desktop fixed?'

The desktop was ancient, slow. Sarah Jane only used it to back up her laptop. Had she dropped it into the shop to be fixed? Everyone knew ancient computers were worth feck all, so it had hardly been pinched.

As if he hadn't heard her, Slug said, 'She's probably at college.'

Maybe Slug was right. Maybe she was in the students' union bar. Maybe her phone battery had died, she'd forgotten about training and someone had just broken in . . .

There was that word again. Maybe.

'She would have called, she'd never have missed training.' Cathy paused, 'She doesn't have lectures on a Monday, said she was going to be in the library all day and it's only down the road from the gym.' Then, louder, 'It closes at nine, what's the time now?'

'Ten past. Look, I'm going downstairs. How long did your mate say he'd be?'

For a moment Cathy felt like screaming at him. Slug had finally realised the cops were coming – was whatever he was smoking downstairs really more important than his housemate disappearing?

A moment later Cathy was at the en suite bathroom door. *Sarah Jane had to be at college somewhere. Had to be. There was no way she was lying dead on the bathroom floor. No way.*

Her heart was thumping so loud in her head it drowned out the sound of a car pulling up in the road outside. Cathy swung the beam into the tiny en suite, polished white tiles flashing back at her.

Empty.

Towels littered the floor. Cathy leaned inside to check the bath, at the same time catching a movement in the mirror over the sink in the corner of her eye. She started, spun around, realising at the exact same moment that the reflection was her own, her dark curly hair dragged back into a ponytail, her skin alabaster against the black of her sweat top. She took a deep breath and released it slowly. *Holy feck.* A moment later she ran the torch beam around the bathroom again.

There was nothing here. No sign of Sarah Jane, anyway. *Jesus, what the hell had happened to her?*

J.P.'s voice outside on the landing almost made Cathy drop the torch, his tone unmistakably angry. 'Jesus Christ, Cat, why the hell can't you do what you're told?'

4

The sound of the rain was relentless, like children pounding their pencils on their desks. Rebecca Ryan leaned her forehead on the glass of the shop door, the chill calming her. Running a business had its stresses on a good day, but right now her worries felt like they were off the scale.

Outside it was grey, such a miserable day that it looked like it was already starting to get dark, low cloud shrouding Enniskerry village with its picture postcard terraced Victorian shopfronts leaning into the hill. The street lights would be coming on soon, the shops that closed early on a Monday had already turned the signs on their glazed doors. Not for the first time she wondered if she should close early too. But living where she worked meant she'd only be doing her paperwork in the kitchen behind the shop or upstairs in the living room instead of down here, and it seemed silly to miss a potential customer.

Rebecca sighed. Business was better than it had been, but still tough. Trying to sell high-end Spanish and Italian designer clothes and handbags during what had felt like the deepest recession Ireland had ever known wasn't a place she honestly thought she'd end up after drama school. She'd survived it, but she felt like kicking herself sometimes. It was so obvious now that the boom had been a mirage, some sort of crazy Disney-inspired, rainbow-tinged bubble. She could feel the anger welling up inside her, deliberately fought it back. It had been a long day. Jacob was busy drawing upstairs – she'd needed to come down to get some breathing space – but she knew he could be down at any second, and soon she'd have to go up and start trying to think of something he'd actually eat for his tea all over again.

Rebecca closed her eyes, enjoying the cool glass on her forehead, consciously reaching for the positive – she *did* have her business and it provided a roof over their heads. Her village boutique was the only stockist in Ireland for the brands she carried, and she had loyal customers who came out to Wicklow to visit her – they knew what they liked and had stuck with her through the tough times. It kept ticking over, which was the main thing. She needed it to. Rebecca opened her eyes.

Everything would be fine. She was careful – that's why she was successful – and she'd worked everything out meticulously. It was all about attention to detail.

Turning away from the door, Rebecca put her hands on her hips and looked back critically at the long narrow room that formed the shop, rails of velvet-covered hangers displaying the ranges in blocks of colour, glass cases of glittering handmade jewellery refracting the lights, creating prisms on the white walls. Momentarily distracted by the sight of her reflection in one of the many mirrors, Rebecca pulled her navy blue wraparound T-shirt down over the top of her jeans and pushed a stray strand of hair into her ponytail, looking speculatively at her parting.

The strands of grey pushing through her thick strawberry-blond layers were unmistakable. Rebecca sighed. She wasn't sure if her grey hair was growing faster as she approached forty-five, or if her hairdresser's had changed their products and they just weren't doing everything they should. They charged enough. But then, she'd be mouse brown without them. Mouse brown with shades of badger. She grimaced in the mirror and immediately stopped as the movement changed the way the light fell on her face and the scar that ran from the corner of her eye to the edge of her mouth stood out, despite the layers of specialist make-up. She didn't want to start thinking about that now. Her year in the hotel resort in Spain after drama school had taught her independence and self reliance, and she'd met people and had made connections that she would never have made if she'd stayed in Ireland. She'd gained the experience she needed to set up here, but there had been a dark side, a level of violence that seemed to be completely acceptable to men who could afford a five-star life style. If they didn't get what they wanted, their patience ran thin. She'd learned her lessons the hard way.

Now it felt like a lifetime ago.

Forty-five. The figure leered at her. Almost forty-six and divorced. Single mother of an eight-year-old. Ex-wife of a philandering bastard whose main asset was his face. Rebecca sighed. She knew from the looks she got at the school gate that her private life kept the whole village in gossip, that marrying a younger man had been a bad idea from the get-go. Christ, if he'd only take his fast cars and cheap women and leave the country. But then he wouldn't be able to see Jacob so often, or have the satisfaction of annoying the hell out of her with that slow grin of his. It was almost worse when she dropped Jacob off to see him, his satisfaction that he had her boy for twenty-four hours almost tangible. And of course Jacob idolised him, but what eight-year-old wouldn't when he was given every piece of tech imaginable, allowed to stay up half the night and have chocolate for breakfast?

Rebecca turned back to the door and the empty village, fighting back the deep unease that seeped in whenever she thought about her ex. He was such a fool, took risks that could jeopardise everything in her life. His pretty face and family money had brought him everything – even her – but as she'd quickly found out, he was utterly unreliable. It had taken her a while to get used to being continually let down, but then she'd come to accept it, to expect it. Every single time she'd asked him to do anything when they were married – even put the bins out – she'd needed a back-up plan, needed to be prepared to catch the ball herself.

She'd drilled it into Jacob to call her every night before he went to sleep when he was staying with his dad, just in case – the iPhone he'd bought him had come in useful after all. Those few minutes – hearing his voice, knowing he was OK – gave her the strength to get through their time apart. Jacob might be challenging, but he was her boy and she loved every particle of his being. Everything she did was for him, to make sure he'd have all the advantages she'd never had growing up.

At least she felt they were comfortable here. She hated that her ex bought his clothes here, or at least chose what he wanted from the website and sent one of his people to collect them. If she could she'd have dropped the brand he wore, but it was one of her most popular lines and whenever he was pictured in the gossip magazines, her sales peaked. And he knew it. It gave him a feeling of control, he knew how she felt about making money, how every sale secured Jacob's future that little bit more, how important that was to her.

Had she ever loved him? Rebecca wasn't sure. He'd brought her everything she needed: a well-respected family, private school connections, a business she could develop and build on. But, in her experience, whenever there was a lot of money involved, things got messy. Now it was all about control.

And control was the one thing she needed in order to keep everything running smoothly. As if the past few days hadn't been challenging enough, today had been one big mess from the moment they'd got up. Perhaps it was because she was keyed up, on edge – Jacob always picked up on her tension instinctively. And Mondays were usually stressful after the weekend, but today . . . Rebecca didn't hear the movement behind her, but felt a sharp kick in the back of her leg. *Oh dear God.*

Behind her, Jacob was standing with a pencil in one hand, the detailed drawing he had been labouring over screwed up in the other. Shoulders hunched, glasses crooked, his face was a grimace of pure rage, his missing front teeth adding to the menace. He aimed another kick, but this time Rebecca was expecting it and managed to catch him around the shoulders and dodge the sharp toe of his runner at the same time. He fought free of her hands. 'You're stupid and smelly. And this is a stupid, smelly place.'

And Rebecca's heart broke all over again. Why the hell hadn't they told her that his class were playing tag rugby today? His teacher was normally brilliant, knew Jacob had to be prepared, talked through any change in his routine.

He'd been like a demon since she picked him up from school, all the feelings that tossed like waves inside him whenever he had to cope with new things gushing out the minute he saw her.

His teacher had been all smiles, 'He was a great boy today. No problems at all. He didn't understand that he had to throw the ball to his team, to the ones in the yellow bibs, but once we explained it, he was grand . . .'

Oh yes, grand.

Today she'd managed to steer him across the road, smiling at the other mums waiting at the school gate like she was late for an appointment, like she didn't have time to chat, and had got him safely through the shop and into the kitchen before he exploded.

'They were playing a stupid game, Mummy. They all just kept bashing into me and shouting . . .'

He'd dropped his Batman backpack on the floor with a clatter, but before Rebecca could speak, suddenly picked it up again and hurled it across the kitchen with all his might, sending the vase on the scrubbed pine table flying. Shattering as it hit the tiled floor, water and the fading yellow chrysanthemums scattered like fireworks.

A moment later he'd vanished, the sound of the kitchen door slamming reverberating through the old brick and ancient beams of the terrace. Collapsing helplessly into one of the pine carvers, water dripping onto the terracotta tiles, Rebecca had put her head in her hands. At the top of the house, she could hear him sliding the furniture across the wooden boards in his attic room, barricading the door. Then it went quiet and she knew he'd buried himself in his sleeping bag and crawled into the dark space under the bed.

He hadn't understood one minute of the rugby. Hadn't grasped that the bibs meant there were two teams, that you had to toss the ball to the guys on your team. Mind blindness, getting the gist – all the phrases that the psychologist used, were the bits he didn't get. Everyone knew that if two sets of kids were wearing different coloured bibs they were on different teams ... but not Jacob, not a child on the autistic spectrum. He just about coped in school. But it was like he was a spring, tightening up as each challenge hit him. It was when he got home that he let it all out.

Asperger's syndrome made Jacob take everything literally, made him unable to read or even recognise that people have inner thoughts; but it also made him quite quite brilliant on subjects that interested him, with a memory for detail that never failed to astound her. He only had to glance out of the window and he could draw the whole street.

'You're a smelly poo and I *hate* you.'

Jesus, what had it been that had set him off this time? She'd left him upstairs totally absorbed in his drawing, the incident at school, the vase, the meltdown completely forgotten. But now they were right back at square one.

'It's all your *fault* ... everything's spoiled now.'

What was her fault? Rebecca had reached for the drawing to see if she could work it out, but Jacob snatched it away from her, ripping it in two, sending the pieces of paper scattering over the polished floor.

'Why wasn't Daniella there on Saturday? She's always there on Saturdays. I wanted to show her my ice palace on Minecraft.' Bobbing down to his level, Rebecca tried to stay calm. This was the problem. Interruptions to his routine always caused ructions.

Saturday's disruption was still bothering him and, coming on top of today . . .

'She wasn't well, darling, I told you. Remember, Daddy told you when he called on Saturday morning.'

Why the hell he'd had to say anything to Jacob in the first place she'd never understand. He hadn't expected Jacob to answer the phone, but really?

'But he was going to take me to the zoo on Saturday. And why didn't *she* tell me she wasn't coming?'

'I don't know, darling, perhaps her phone ran out of battery. Why don't we do some stretches?' Rebecca tried to make her voice sound gentle, masking her thoughts. If she could get Jacob to do some deep-muscle exercise she knew he'd calm down, whatever the matter was. It worked like a drug.

His face didn't change; it was so contorted with anger he looked like something out of a comic, freckles hidden in the creases of a scowl so deep it had clouded his normally bright blue eyes.

'*No*. That's stupid and *smelly*.'

She just wanted to hug him. To take away the pain. But he couldn't bear being touched.

There were days when she just didn't know what to do, how to help him . . . He'd told her once, 'Sometimes it's like there's a war going on in my head, Mummy.' Mummies were supposed to fix everything, to make it better. *How the hell did you fix that?* The divorce hadn't helped, moving house. And having his father parading a constant string of women about. One day Jacob would realise that they weren't all there to play with him when he went over.

But right now she had other things to worry about. He was still wearing his Spider-Man pyjama top, had refused to take it off for school this morning, and he had a tuft of brown hair sticking up from the top of his head. He looked about as adorably cute as anyone could when they were mad as hell.

She'd rubbed the top of his arms, 'How about we watch *Top Gear*?'

'Don't touch me!'

She winced as the toe of his runner connected with her shin.

5

'What the hell are you playing at, Cat?'

Cathy could hear how mad J.P. was before she even got to the bedroom door. But how could she have waited?

She felt anger beginning to bubble, heard the challenge in her own voice, 'She's not here. I had to check . . .'

'Tell me something I don't know.'

The landing looked a lot smaller with J.P. on it. He had that effect on enclosed spaces. His midnight-blue hat and uniform bomber jacket didn't help, bulked his six-foot-two frame up even more. As she slipped out of Sarah Jane's bedroom, he frowned at her, opened his mouth to give her a lashing she was sure, but then, maybe seeing the look on her face, changed his mind. He gave an exaggerated sigh and eyed her like he was try-ing to keep his temper.

'So fill me in, Miss Marple. What's the story?'

Cathy took a deep breath, trying to steady her nerves. She could feel her heart racing, and suddenly her legs were beginning to shake.

'Her room's been turned over,' Cathy indicated the door behind her with her head, 'looks like it's been searched – and someone's taken her computer. And she didn't come to training . . .' She caught her breath again, fighting to keep her voice level.

J.P. nodded, calm now, in control. 'Dec told me.' She could feel him assessing the situation, his dark eyes taking it all in.

Cathy pulled at the silver necklace she wore hidden under her hoodie and ran the oval dog tag along its ball-link chain. The engraving 'Please return to Tiffany's' was pockmarked by shrapnel from the explosion, but still legible. O'Rourke had given it to her back in the day, one Christmas – she'd given him aftershave. Now it represented so much more – not only their bond, but her survival. He'd found it in the grass beside her when the bomb had gone off, the metal hot, and as soon as they'd taken off the first layer of bandages, he'd been there to clip it back around her neck. Now she only took it off for training in the gym.

Cathy took a deep breath and continued, her fingers worrying at the chain,

'She had a row with her dad.'

'But he doesn't live here, does he?' J.P. nodded towards the bedroom, 'He's not done this?'

'No.' Cathy shook her head, trying not to look at him. She stared at a spot on the carpet for a moment, trying to focus, to get everything sorted out in her mind. Downstairs Slug had turned off the TV, finally ending the car chase that had been echoing through her head since she arrived. Now she could hear a woman's voice – J.P.'s observer, his partner in the patrol car, talking to Slug. Asking about the stink of weed in the house and how the feck he could have been deaf to someone breaking into Sarah Jane's room. *But then if he normally played the Xbox that loud he'd have missed a bomb going off.* 'No, her dad's in Syria, he works for CNN. This is something else.' Cathy shrugged helplessly, 'Something's really wrong, I just know it. Her mum says she was working on a story – something her dad said was too dangerous for a student . . .'

'Jesus, Cat, how do these things keep happening to you?' J.P. pulled her to him, wrapped both his huge arms around her and gave her a hug. There was a good reason everyone called him the gentle giant, like the guy in the sweetcorn ads but not so green. He was the best, had kept watch over her every move when the darkness had threatened to overwhelm her after the explosion. Together with the other guys she shared the house with – Decko and Eamon – J.P. had been brilliant, giving her enough space so as not to crowd her, but she knew none of them had taken their eyes off her.

He'd carried a cloak of cold air in with him from outside, and she felt the chill now, the stiff fabric of his jacket still damp from the rain. Fighting back tears, hot in the corners of her eyes, Cathy took a shaky breath, unable to answer for a moment. *Thank God for the lads*. They'd done so much for her in the last year.

'Don't worry, we'll find her. She's probably in a pub some-where chatting up some celebrity for a feature in *Hello!*'

Cathy pulled away and play-punched him in the stomach, 'Stupid, she doesn't do that sort of stuff.'

Grinning, he reached for his radio. 'That's better . . . now let's call the troops, will we, and find out what's happened here?' He depressed the call button, 'Foxtrot Alpha One to Control . . .'

'So how long has she been missing?'

DI Dawson O'Rourke sounded relaxed. It was the Monaghan accent that did it, made him sound like a drive-time radio DJ, all soothing and calm.

But Cathy knew him better than that, and the rest of him wasn't sending out the same message.

As he stood sheltering in the porch of Sarah Jane's house, wait-ing for Cathy to reply, he slipped his phone back into the pocket of his navy pinstripe jacket, his face creased in a frown. He'd had his hair cut again, a military buzz cut. That, his broken nose and the scowl on his face made him look more like a street fighter than ever. He and Cat went way back; he'd been her first sergeant when she'd left Templemore Garda Training Academy, assigned to Pearse Street Station. Out on the beat or frozen to the core on posts outside government buildings, he'd always had a smile for her, an encouraging word when she'd got back to the station. Even then he'd been on the fast track, had been the force's youngest sergeant, just like he was the youngest inspector now. And then he'd offered her a lift home one night and their paths had become inextricably linked. But Cathy didn't have space in her head for the past right now, tonight was about Sarah Jane.

'She said she'd be at training.' Cathy said it again – she was starting to feel like a parrot.

'Which was what time?'

'Seven. At Phoenix.'

'And what time is it now?'

Cathy glanced over to J.P., who was standing with his arms folded on the step into the porch, his dark head framed by the open front door. He wiggled his fingers, five, ten.

'About ten?'

O'Rourke folded his own arms and rocked back on his heels.

'So technically she's been missing for three hours.'

'But—'

'And how old is she?' O'Rourke interrupted Cathy, switching his gaze from something on the glazed panel above her head to give her the full benefit of his winter blue eyes. But it wasn't a cold stare; it was the type of stare you saved for a five-year-old who had done the washing-up with shampoo.

'She's twenty-four. I told you.'

O'Rourke raised his eyebrows, eyeing her. He didn't have to say it. Cathy said it for him, 'She's an adult. I know. She could be anywhere. I know.' Cathy bit her lip and fixed her own deep blue eyes on his. 'I also know that it's totally out of character for her to vanish. I know she's had a row with her dad about some story she's working on that he thinks is dangerous, and her mum's having a total canary. And I know she wouldn't miss training unless something – something big – was preventing her. And . . .' O'Rourke opened his mouth to reply but Cathy didn't let him, 'her room has been turned over like someone really wanted to find something.'

'OK.' O'Rourke paused for a moment, then rubbed his chin. 'Even with all that, you know we should wait a few hours at least before we call out the cavalry.'

'Yes . . . *But* . . .'

Exasperated, Cathy felt like stamping her foot. What the hell was the point of being in the job, if you couldn't pull it out when you needed it? Now O'Rourke was here she was definitely feeling a lot better, but all of this talk was slowing them down.

'The front door was open for most of the evening because our friend here was waiting for a pizza and too lazy to get off his arse to open it.' O'Rourke drew in his breath, 'So the room could have been tossed by anyone – the local gurriers, the pizza boy . . .' He was playing devil's advocate and she knew it.

Cathy shook her head, thrusting her hands into the front pockets of her hoodie. 'Pizza boys don't search bedrooms. They might grab cash off the hall table, but they aren't going to go upstairs, are they? And this just isn't like her. I know there's something wrong, I just know it.'

Wrinkling her nose, Cathy gave him a long look with more than a hint of a glare. It was a challenge, and O'Rourke's mouth twitched into a reluctant grin.

'I've already put out a call for her car, and Thirsty's on the way to process the forensics on her room – he's just finishing up a burglary in Silchester Park and he'll be right over.'

Cathy felt some of the pressure lift. Thirsty was the best. He'd headed up the scenes-of-crime team in Dún Laoghaire for, well, just for ever. And she'd always had a suspicion that his close friendship with the Super had helped land her in the detective unit well ahead of many of her colleagues who had longer service – that and the silver Scott medal she'd been awarded for saving O'Rourke's life. Despite everything that had happened, getting out of uniform had been the best thing she'd ever done. She half smiled to herself, remembering his exasperation as he stood at her hospital bedside, *You got yourself shot in uniform, Cat, and you get out of uniform and what happens? You get yourself blown up. You might have nine lives, girl, but I haven't. And they don't let you smoke in here, you know . . .*

O'Rourke continued. 'I'll need a full description from you. What is she – five foot nine? Dark blond hair, slim.' He paused, 'Her hair still long?'

'Yep, but she got fed up with it being "boring" she said – she had it bleached. Ombre, it's called, it's sort of ash blond with purple bits underneath.'

He raised his eyebrows, 'Purple? She's got purple hair?'

'No,' Cathy shook her head despairingly, 'the lilacy bits are all underneath, it looks great.' When Sarah Jane had got back from the hairdresser's she'd looked like she'd stepped out of an all-American shampoo advert; she wasn't exactly invisible in a crowd.

'We'll need a recent photo.'

'I've got loads.' Cathy pulled her phone out of her hoodie pocket, offering it to him. He put up his hand, but she already knew he didn't need the photos this second. 'We'll find her, don't worry.' Cathy's sigh of relief was audible. She bit her lip, resisting the urge to throw her arms around him. He was right that it was early to call out the troops, and she knew how busy they were, every night stretched to the limit; J.P.'s radio had been hopping since he'd arrived.

'She got an iPhone, by any chance?'

'No, it's an android, a Samsung.'

'Let's hope she's still got it with her.'

O'Rourke paused, his eyes locking on hers like he was looking inside her. He put his hands on the tops of her arms, giving them a reassuring rub.

'We'll find her, Cat.'

He might not have J.P.'s film-star looks, but Cathy felt herself heating up. For a moment the porch became very small, like it was just the two of them, like the moment they were in had suddenly become frozen in time, the rest of the world continuing to turn around them.

Why did this keep happening?

It was at moments like this that she felt an overpowering urge to kiss him.

Cathy bit her lip again. After the blast they'd become closer than ever. It had been his face she'd seen first as she came out of the coma, his hand that had held hers when the doctor had explained her injuries. He was the only one who knew the full story, apart from the father of her baby of course, but he'd been one big mistake from the get-go. It was O'Rourke who had been there for her.

She still didn't quite understand how stuff kept happening to them. That night back in Pearse Street, her own car in for repairs, O'Rourke had been dropping her home when a Ford Astra had swerved into the path of their patrol car, the intoxicated driver too drunk to stand. Then what had been a straightforward Section 49 had become something very different when an armed gang had come barrelling out of the Power City warehouse they were stopped beside, heading for a getaway car that had made its own getaway the moment the driver had spotted their patrol car flashing down the Astra. Seeing Guards right in their path, the raiders had panicked and the bullet she'd taken had saved O'Rourke's life.

They would always be connected.

She'd just like the connection to be a whole lot more personal.

But he was her boss. He was one of her big brother's best friends, and he was thirteen years older than her. And he was dedicated to his job. And having a relationship with a junior colleague wouldn't exactly do wonders for his career prospects. Assuming he felt the same, of course.

No matter how much she felt like falling into his arms right now, maybe this wasn't the moment. O'Rourke squeezed the tops of her arms again. 'Trust me. It'll have to be unofficial for now, but we'll find her.'

6

Pulling into a space in the floodlit secure car park behind Dún Laoghaire's modern concrete and glass Garda station, Cathy fiddled with the car stereo again, looking for Lyric FM. Static, then a burst of Mozart; at least she thought it was Mozart. It sounded like one of the classical concertos Sarah Jane played on her phone when she was studying. Switching the engine off, Cathy turned it up, filling the Mini with a crescendo of violins for a moment while she gathered her thoughts. Closing her eyes, resting her hands on the steering wheel, leaning back into the headrest, Cathy ran back over everything again in her mind. There had to be something – something small she was missing that would give her a clue as to where Sarah Jane could be.

She'd given her colleagues in the district detective unit a full description – everything she could think of that could possibly be relevant – but there had to be something else . . . She tried to tune into the music – if she could think like Sarah Jane, surely she'd see it.

It was almost eleven. The car park was full, dominated by two Garda vans, the only space Cathy had been able to find tucked away in the back corner beside a Honda that looked like it had been crashed in a high-speed chase. Under the floodlights it was macabre, the bonnet crumpled, windscreen smashed. Glancing over, Cathy could see dark stains on the dash, traces of silver fingerprint dust on the steering wheel glittering in the artificial light.

Had Sarah Jane had an accident? She knew O'Rourke had had all the hospitals checked. Cathy let out a sigh and rubbed her eyes with the heels of her hands. It wasn't a traffic accident. She was sure of it. Sarah Jane would have turned up by now if it was.

Cathy knew Sarah Jane was working on an assignment about Ballymun and the tower blocks, kids with special needs. That wasn't exactly life-threatening. What else could she have stumbled on that her dad thought was dangerous?

It wasn't like they were short of possibilities in Dublin, whatever the tourist board would like you to believe. You were more likely to be mugged in the street than meet a leprechaun, that was for sure. Drugs, organised crime, and everything that went with that from armed robbery to prostitution and gangland feuds, weren't just features of the inner city, but spilled into the suburbs on a regular basis.

How could you just disappear? Cathy pulled out her phone and checked her messages. Maybe Sarah Jane had texted her and she'd missed it. *Maybe* she'd met a guy at The Rookery over the weekend, some visiting star, had fallen madly in love and had had the weekend of her life. Maybe they'd hooked up and headed off on a plane to somewhere where the sun shone and the wine flowed . . .

Cathy doubted it.

Sarah Jane was way too focused on her degree to get distracted by some casual date. She dated all right, she'd even been to the movies a couple of times with J.P., but she wasn't a clubber, wasn't a party girl. And she wasn't with anyone at the moment, although she had her eye on some guy who worked near The Rookery.

Sometimes Cathy thought Sarah Jane took life too seriously, but she knew she was just driven to succeed. Perhaps it was having parents who were passionate about causes. Cathy didn't know. It didn't matter; they understood each other. They were both focused on their careers, both loved sport. But where Cathy had three brothers, Sarah Jane was an only child, and a privileged child by her own admission. She'd been a boarder at the girls' school where Cathy's scholarship had covered her day fees, but nothing else. Their friendship was enriched by the differences though, and once they'd got chatting that day at the gym, they'd bonded like long-lost sisters. Then they realised they lived near each other and could save a fortune if they shared lifts to college.

Cathy picked up her phone from the passenger seat and hit dial. Sarah Jane's voicemail kicked in immediately. 'Hello, this is Sarah Jane Hansen, leave a message and I'll get right back to you . . .'

'It's me. If you get this, give me a call . . . please . . .' Cathy hung up – if she left too many messages the mailbox would fill up. For a moment she wondered if O'Rourke could get access to listen to the other messages in Sarah Jane's phone. Maybe there was something there that would tell them where she was, maybe someone had arranged to meet her . . .

From the moment he'd left Sarah Jane's house, Cathy knew O'Rourke would be getting things moving. Like he'd said, it was too early to declare her a missing person and they didn't have enough to start an official investigation, but he'd be calling in favours to do all he could. He'd wanted Cathy to stay at the house for a while, just in case Sarah Jane turned up, working through the rest of their friends and friends of friends, checking to see if anyone had seen her. And sitting down at the untidy kitchen table, pushing away the pizza boxes and free newspapers, Cathy had methodically checked through Sarah Jane's social media to see if she had mentioned anything about her plans for today.

Facebook, Twitter, Snapchat, Instagram.

Sarah Jane wasn't exactly glued to any of them on a good day, but they all looked quiet. She used Facebook the most, to keep up with her friends back in New York and around the world, to share photos with her dad. Even her mum used it, sending Sarah Jane pictures of her psychedelic paintings and photos jumbled with unknown faces from the knit-your-own yoghurt parties she went to.

Listening to Thirsty and his colleague chatting in the hall as they dusted for prints, Cathy had opened Sarah Jane's Facebook page and felt like she'd been slapped in the face. Sarah Jane's azure-blue eyes stared back at her from the profile picture, full of laughter, her then honey-coloured hair blowing across her face. Cathy had taken the photo last summer. They'd all gone to the Festival of Culture in Dún Laoghaire, she and Sarah Jane and Decko. J.P. had been working; they kept seeing his head bobbing above the crowd, hat on, melting in the heat. They'd listened to a Caribbean band on the stage in the People's Park, stood for ages in the queue for ice cream at Teddy's, had noodles in the international village, laughing at the little kids marvelling at the huge fairground wheel. It had been hot and sunny and a bloody great day.

Sitting in Sarah Jane's kitchen, Cathy had taken a deep breath and closed her eyes. She knew she needed to focus here. Ever since the bomb, she'd found her emotions seesawed unpredictably, and now wasn't the time to hit a dark patch. Sarah Jane needed her to use everything she could to find her.

Dragging her mind away from that day in Dún Laoghaire, she'd opened her eyes and started scrolling back through Sarah Jane's Facebook wall to Friday, going through all her posts. At ten thirty on Friday morning Sarah Jane had posted a photo of a seagull on the DART platform trying to open a chip bag. Cathy was pretty sure it was Dún Laoghaire Station – she must have been on her way into work. Saturday morning she'd commented on a cute photo of a beady-eyed owl, had a conversation with her mum, mainly about the weather. Nothing else. But she'd said she had to study all day Saturday. Sunday next. Cathy's heart rate had increased: Sarah Jane had been talking to one of their pals about a concert at the National Concert Hall the following week, her last comment, *'In work but I'm on for that. Call you when I get home.'* She checked the time on the post: 12.30. She was usually due in work at The Rookery on a Sunday around twelve.

Cathy had called the friend straight away, but Sarah Jane hadn't yet been in touch to confirm the Concert Hall arrangements.

They needed to start at the restaurant. From when she left work on Sunday. Cathy flicked off her phone and, pushing open her car door, was met by the cold salt tang of the October night. And O'Rourke's voice coming from right behind her car.

'Come on, we're heading into town. That restaurant Sarah Jane works at is just closing. The manager's hanging on for us.' Cathy swung around to look at him, her eyebrows raised. O'Rourke pulled his long navy blue wool overcoat around him, 'He says she wasn't feeling well yesterday, he put her into a cab at about eight o'clock and hasn't heard from her since.'

7

They flew into the city centre, O'Rourke's sleek blue BMW 7 series eating up tarmac still glistening from the earlier rain. Cathy crossed her arms more tightly and shifted in the soft beige leather seat. She'd run into the station to her locker and picked up her SIG, buckling the leather shoulder holster on under her black hoodie. Now she could feel it under her arm, its gentle pressure reassuring. She was sure she wouldn't need it, but that wasn't the point, she was required to carry her personal issue firearm, would be in more trouble if she was caught without it. It had become part of her when she was working, and in this job nothing was predictable.

Still in her sweatpants and trainers from the gym, her muscles were starting to stiffen up after her training session. Too much tension.

She could definitely live without anything going off tonight.

Where *was* Sarah Jane? Fear nagged at her, but Cathy pushed it away. There was nothing she could do except try and override it with positive thoughts. They were on the move, they were doing everything they could and as fast as they could.

Whatever had happened, with O'Rourke in charge there would be no lost time, no mistakes. He'd bring in all the manpower they needed, the media if necessary. He would do everything he could.

Feeling her legs starting to tighten, Cathy shifted in the seat and stretched. At least there was plenty of leg room in O'Rourke's car. Everyone thought he was mad using it for work, but the alternative was a DDU pool car that would have his dodgy back crippled after a week of nights. He reckoned he spent more hours in work than out of it, and most of those were in the car, so he needed some comfort. Life was short.

That was for sure.

The city centre was as quiet as the main road into town had been. A rare thing for Dublin. But it was a Monday night, and it was October and it was raining.

Weaving through the city centre's one-way system, down roads better designed for horses and carts, O'Rourke pulled in under an ancient brick arch that linked The Rookery restaurant to the building next door. It must have been the entrance to stables or a coach house at one time, but now security lights came on ahead of them revealing a large car park, hemmed in by a terrace of four-storey Georgian buildings, their windows lifeless, only the lights above the fire exits opening onto the car park giving any hint that they were occupied.

Cathy had the car door open before O'Rourke had unclipped his seatbelt. Glancing into the car park, empty except for several huge overflowing wheelie bins, a red Fiesta and a black Audi Sport in one corner, she turned to take in the streetscape, instinctively looking for trouble. It came automatically to everyone in the job, but Cathy's experience in the ring, the need to read body language and be constantly one step ahead of her opponent, gave her an edge that had gotten her out of trouble more than once. The different teams she'd worked with over the past six years had learned to rely on her instincts; they could all detect trouble a mile off, but she was faster. Tonight the street was quiet, light from the shopfronts and street lamps reflecting in puddles on the uneven pavement. A taxi cruised past.

Looking across the roof of the car, Cathy caught O'Rourke's eye as he pushed the driver's door closed with a gentle click. He didn't need to speak, instead jerked his head in the direction of the restaurant's on-street entrance. But before he could move his phone rang.

He rolled his eyes. As he answered, his words monosyllabic, Cathy used the time to take another look at the street, her eyes roving over the upstairs windows of the business premises. A few doors down, across the road, an all-night newsagents cum mini-market glowed welcome, its windows plastered with advertisements and notices. She caught a movement inside, the shopkeeper probably, wondering what she was doing standing in the street in the middle of the night with a man in a suit who had lined his car up neatly on a set of double-yellow lines under the stone arch to a car park.

Ignoring him, Cathy looked down the road. She'd had her tarot cards read along here somewhere – Sarah Jane had got out of work early and they'd met for coffee. It had been Sarah Jane's idea; she'd needed guidance with her love life, she said, rolling her eyes theatrically, hadn't wanted to go on her own. They had gone nervously down winding iron stairs to a cramped basement and a woman called Tiffany. It had been a bit witchy, the round table covered in a faded purple cloth with tantric symbols embroidered on it, the tiny room with its cheap carpet heavy with the scent of incense. The cards had been in silk pouches – six or seven of them, Cathy couldn't remember – all different, faded and worn through use.

Tiffany had asked her to choose a pouch, and then shuffle the cards. She'd spread them across the table so Cathy could select them in groups of threes. Cathy didn't believe in having your fortune told, but part of her was nervous. If she'd come here a year ago would this woman have been able to tell her how her life was about to change? Would she have done anything differently? That was the million-dollar question. As it turned out she'd been surprised how accurate Tiffany had been about the men in her life, about work, about where the two overlapped, about her family. But it had only been a bit of fun.

This visit was a whole lot more serious.

It had been a month or so since Cathy had last been to The Rookery to eat. Sarah Jane's dad had been over, his last visit before he went to Syria, and Sarah Jane had been keen for Cathy to meet him. She'd only been working there a few weeks then, had wanted to show him the place, and it had been a great night. The Rookery was always full of media types, journalists and TV news anchors, and of course they'd all recognised him; he'd almost been signing autographs by the time they left. Sarah Jane's manager had been agog.

Cathy had walked past the red-brick Georgian building often enough before then, though, its steep granite steps and shiny blue door guarded by two clipped bay trees making it look more like a private club than a restaurant. A very exclusive private club. South William Street had its own unique blend of hipster chic and Georgian grandeur; brightly lit bars were dotted between faceless nightclubs and adult shops, beauticians and designer boutiques that you needed an appointment to get into. The Rookery was the jewel in the crown.

O'Rourke finished his call and glanced into the car park as he triggered the central locking. 'Manager is Billy Roberts, does all the hiring and firing. He normally takes Mondays off because it's quiet, so we're lucky to catch him, apparently – he came in to catch up on his paperwork.'

Cathy nodded to herself, recognising the name. She fell in beside him as they headed out onto the narrow pavement. O'Rourke took the steps two at a time, leaning on the buzzer on the entryphone. From the pavement Cathy didn't hear a response, but O'Rourke glanced back at her as the door clicked, his coat swirling like Sherlock Holmes's cape as he pushed open the door. She half smiled. It suited him.

The hallway was narrow, with black and white tiles set at right angles to create a diamond pattern, candles on an ornate credenza backed by an enormous gilded mirror dancing with a warm glow, their reflection the only light. Adele's *Hello* album played softly in the background, the air warm with the scent of recently snuffed candles and some sort of incense. Just how Cathy remembered it from her last visit. There was something about this place that oozed sophistication.

Before Cathy could comment, a figure appeared at the end of the corridor like a dancer, tight black high-waisted trousers and a white shirt buttoned to the neck only emphasising his exaggerated movements. He swept towards them, rolling his hand in some sort of ridiculous bowing gesture, like a matador greeting his public, the light catching the oil in his dark, slicked-back hair as he inclined his head. 'Billy Roberts. At your service, Inspector. How can I be of help?'

If she had been less tense, Cathy would have laughed. Sarah Jane called him 'the host with the most', his flamboyance well known. Standing behind him, Cathy couldn't see O'Rourke's face, but she knew precisely what he was thinking, and it didn't involve Billy Roberts servicing him anytime soon.

'Thanks for seeing us – I know it's late.' O'Rourke's tone was flat, matter of fact. 'Is there somewhere where we can talk?'

Smiling broadly, Billy made an exaggerated movement with his hand, better suited to the stage. 'Of course, come this way. I'm afraid my office is below stairs, but perhaps that might suffice?'

O'Rourke's nod was curt.

As she followed them along the corridor, O'Rourke keeping a safe distance from Billy Roberts, Cathy glanced into the dining rooms on either side of the corridor. They were high ceilinged, panelled, with empty tables already set with crisp white linen and glittering silver ready for tomorrow's lunch trade. The lighting was low, candle like, polished oak floorboards and jewel-coloured flock wallpaper a stark contrast to the virgin linen. From the moment she'd arrived the last time, Cathy could see why Sarah Jane loved working here – it was a beautiful building, it held a mystery and grandeur that only came with age and impeccably good taste. The customers were generous too – the tips were awesome. Cathy could hear Sarah Jane's voice as if she was right behind her. She shivered.

Beyond the period splendour the back corridors and kitchens of The Rookery were functional and disappointingly twenty-first century. Pushing open a door hidden in the wainscoting at the end of the corridor, Cathy recoiled slightly at the brightness of the kitchen's practical strip lighting, at the dull, sand-grey lino and stainless steel doors. It was almost like a theatre – the stage dressed for a performance, and here, the backstage workings of the place.

Billy led them through the deserted kitchen, huge, industrial-sized sinks and massive stainless steel counters gleaming in the brilliant fluorescent light. Knives hung in order on the wall, and beneath the counters huge steel trays were stacked, everything spotless, military in its neatness.

'This way, folks.'

Stopping in the narrow corridor that led from the kitchens, presumably to the car park they'd just seen, Billy swung open the door to his office, gesturing them inside.

It was an ordinary office. Small, dominated by a large desk, a filing cabinet and a noticeboard that almost filled one wall, staff rosters marked out in red, blue and green marker, brilliantly coloured Post-it notes stuck all over it. Billy slipped in behind a desk covered in paperwork, invoices, more Post-its and a scattering of biros. O'Rourke sat down in the chair opposite, hard plastic. Cathy hung back, remaining standing, leaning on the white painted wall, taking it in, her eye drawn to Sarah Jane's name on the staffing rota.

She was rostered to work Friday and Sunday, it looked like she was off today and wouldn't be back in until Thursday evening. That made sense. She worked Thursday evenings if they needed her, alternated Friday and Saturday evenings and did the lunch through to evening shift on a Sunday. It was a complicated roster with what looked like up to ten staff working the floor in the restaurant at the busiest times. Below it was a kitchen roster with even more names listed.

All people who could have spoken to Sarah Jane in the days leading up to today. And they only needed one of them to know where she was, what her plans might have been.

Billy leaned forwards, all smiles, 'So how can I help you, folks? What's Sarah Jane been up to? Don't tell me she's an illegal immigrant on the run from the FBI?'

O'Rourke paused for a second before saying, 'She's disappeared. We are aware that she was working here on Sunday but she hasn't been in touch with her family or friends since Saturday. We are very concerned for her safety.'

Billy's smile turned to puzzlement as his face creased in a frown, then he leaned forward shaking his head. 'Are you sure? This is terrible, I can't believe it. We all love Sarah Jane here, the staff and the customers. She's very popular.'

O'Rourke's tone was curt. 'Can you just run through the last time you saw her for us? Take us through Sunday from when she arrived.'

'Goodness, of course—'

O'Rourke cut in, 'Did she appear agitated at all, upset?'

Billy opened his eyes wide and, shaking his head, reached to straighten the already perfectly aligned pot of pens on his desk, 'Not at all. She was a bit under the weather when she got here actually, at what . . .' his eyes searched the ceiling for the answer, 'about eleven forty-five in the morning? She's always a bit early for her shift, starts at twelve.' He paused, 'We had a party booked in for five o'clock so we were really busy, but around four I could tell she was really starting to flag. She looked peaky, you know?' Billy pursed his lips like he didn't approve, 'She kept telling me she was fine, but she wasn't.' He was emphatic, 'I could see she wasn't feeling well, sometimes I just *know*.'

Cathy pulled her chain from inside the neck of her hoodie and ran the oval silver dog tag along it. It would be just like Sarah Jane to come into work if she wasn't feeling well, her sense of duty overriding common sense. She hated letting people down.

Billy continued, 'She's fabulous, but nobody can work if they're not feeling the best – it's tough out there, you have to keep smiling. She looked pale so I pulled her off the floor. She kept saying she'd be OK in a bit, so I got her to sort out the linen room, then she did some paperwork, but even sitting in my office she seemed to be struggling. So then I said I'd get her a cab. She needed to be in bed, not serving aperitifs.' Billy stopped as if that was the end of the story.

There was a pause. Cathy got there before O'Rourke. 'And . . .'

She felt like rolling her hands for emphasis but instead raised her eyebrows and tried hard not to sound like she was talking to a child.

'Oh.' Billy looked surprised that there might be any more to the story, 'Well, I gave the driver her address in Dún Laoghaire, and off they went. I haven't heard from her since.'

'You didn't think to check that she'd arrived home OK?'

Billy shrugged, slightly affronted, 'She's a big girl, she has a mobile phone – I didn't think she needed a babysitter. And with one body down we were pushed here. Like I said, it was busy.'

'So what time precisely did you put her in the cab?' O'Rourke's turn. He still had his coat on, had shoved his hands deep in the pockets – probably, Cathy thought, to stop himself leaning forward and grabbing Billy Roberts by his strangely tanned neck.

'Eight thirty.'

'What company do you use?'

'We use a limo service for clients but I flagged this one down, it's quicker than calling one. Dublin's awash with taxis these days.'

'So you don't know who the driver was or what company he worked for?' O'Rourke's tone was clipped, a sure sign he wasn't impressed.

Billy shrugged, 'I've got a receipt – presumably it has his number on it. It was the end of the roll, though, the ink's really faded.' Before he could continue Cathy cut in, pushing herself off the wall with her foot, 'Have you got CCTV cameras on the street? If there's a clear shot we can run the plate and find the driver.'

8

The Rookery CCTV wasn't nearly as revealing as Cathy and O'Rourke would have liked – the picture was great but the angle was wrong and the camera was trained on the front door. In a state-of-the-art CCTV viewing room that rivalled any of the Garda stations, Billy Roberts switched on a bank of flat TV screens and fiddled with a remote control.

The system seemed to be pretty full on for the size of the building, but as Billy had explained as they'd come in, The Rookery had a lot of very high-profile customers, and couldn't risk anyone getting their pocket picked or paparazzi taking sneaky under-the-table shots. The cameras were a discouragement.

Standing behind Billy's chair, Cathy and O'Rourke stood side by side, straining to see the images of the street. The shot was focused on the front-door steps and part of the pavement, with a slither of road showing in the periphery. People walked past, their faces picked up by the arc lights that lit the front of the building. A group of three lads went by, jostling and joking, then two Gardaí, their fluorescent jackets bright in the early evening darkness. Cathy recognised one of them from a Taser course she'd been on.

'Just run it again.' She could feel O'Rourke tensing beside her. 'The picture's so clear you can see the reflection on the door and the door plate . . . look, you can see the taxi draw up.' Cathy bit her lip as, peering into the screen, two figures appeared on the pavement partially reflected, hazy like ghosts. Even in the yellow of the brass Cathy caught a flash of blond hair.

'This confirms your timing.' O'Rourke glanced at Billy, 'We'll see if there's more CCTV on the street and cross-reference. Can we take this? Our people may be able to get more if they blow it up.'

Billy held out his hands, 'Of course, whatever you need.'

Cathy dragged her eyes away from the image on the screen. 'Can we have a look in her locker, please? I presume you've a master key?'

Billy pursed his lips for a moment, his forehead creased in a frown. 'I'm sure we do. Give me a minute and I'll look in the office.'

It took Roberts more than a minute to find the key, but when he reappeared he directed them down the corridor to what appeared to be a staff changing room. He flicked on the over-head fluorescent lights. Tall grey steel lockers lined the walls, two high, reminding Cathy of the ones they'd had in school. A long mirror separated the banks of lockers opposite the entrance, and there were staff toilets at the far end of the room.

'Now, here we are . . .' A bunch of keys in one hand, a scruffy piece of A4 paper in the other, Roberts scanned the numbers on the doors looking for Sarah Jane's. 'This is it. Fourteen.' Cathy stood right behind him as he slipped in the key and turned the lock, pulling the door wide.

It wasn't exactly overflowing. A clean white shirt hung from a pole, its tails brushing a pair of trainers and a bright pink make-up bag. Unmistakably Sarah Jane's.

'That hers?' O'Rourke came up behind her to take a look.

'It is.' Cathy turned to him and he produced a pair of blue latex gloves from his jacket pocket like a magician. Pulling them on, Cathy reached inside to slide the shirt across, lifted out the trainers to see if there was anything behind them. The back of the locker was empty. She glanced at the soles. Clean. 'That's her back-up make-up bag – she uses a different one for every day.'

'No handbag or keys?'

Cathy shook her head, 'Nope, or laptop.'

Outside on the pavement O'Rourke checked his watch. It was almost midnight.

'Let's see if we can identify some cameras pointing this way and we'll check their tapes first thing. We're not going to get anything else until the morning.'

Cathy thrust her hands into her hoodie pockets, staring at the spot where the taxi had pulled up in front of The Rookery. Deep in thought, she hardly heard him. She pursed her lips and looked up, scanning the buildings, then looked across the road.

'The newsagent's. It's twenty-four hours.' She indicated the shop about four doors down on the other side of the road. 'Bet they've got CCTV. Must have. They do MoneyGram transfers, they're a target.'

'Well spotted.' O'Rourke followed the direction of her gaze. The lights were dimmed but definitely on, an illuminated OPEN sign prominently displayed in the window. There were shops like this dotted all over Dublin city, everything stores that provided money transfer services like Western Union or Ria. Not everyone worked nine to five, or had a bank account. Night shift workers needed coffee and sandwiches and services just like their day shift counterparts. Her voice sounded loud in the quiet street, 'Come on.'

Stepping into the road he was ahead of her, across it in three strides. Behind her the front door of The Rookery rattled as if it was being locked from the inside.

Outside the newsagent's Cathy silently pointed to two cameras that criss-crossed the front door. The one on the left was angled more out into the road. 'I think we could be in luck.'

O'Rourke pushed the door open, holding it wide for her to enter, 'After you.'

The shop's interior was cramped, every available space taken up with the type of things you run out of and need in a hurry – everything from sandwiches to washing powder, tins of coconut cream, kidney beans, bags of rice piled beside toilet rolls and spices. The man behind the counter was young, Asian, had a pile of text books open beside the till. He looked up as they entered, smiled, nodding a greeting. O'Rourke pulled out his warrant card.

'We'd like to see your CCTV for yesterday evening, around eight thirty?'

'No problem, what are you looking for?' The man had movie-star looks: tall, clean shaven, jet-black hair cropped short, wearing a navy sweater over a white button-down shirt. *Very nice.* He was wearing jeans, but looked too smart somehow for an all-night grocery store.

'A cab pulled up here last night, collected one of the staff from The Rookery and took her home. She's disappeared. We want to see if you've got a shot of the cab and the registration plate.'

The man's mouth fell open. 'Not Sarah Jane?'

It might have been because it was so late but O'Rourke looked at the man blankly for a minute. Cathy mentally shook her head.

What did they say about Ireland, about everyone knowing each other? He had to be the guy Sarah Jane had been going on about that she fancied who worked near The Rookery. She'd said he worked in one of the shops, but not which one. Cathy took a step forward. 'Do you know her?'

The man nodded, 'She works over there part-time, she's studying journalism at DCU. Always comes in here for Polos. I'm in the College of Surgeons,' he added, indicating the books. 'Vijay Khan – nice to meet you.' He held out his hand. O'Rourke returned his handshake. Cathy leaned forward and followed suit as Vijay continued, 'I studied in New York for a year. Heard her accent and we started chatting.'

'You're Anadin?' Cathy smiled. Ever since she'd met him, Sarah Jane had been full of this gorgeous guy she'd bumped into who was studying medicine, had thought his nickname was hilarious. He'd told her it had started as an autocorrect in one of his friends' texts, and had stuck, bearing in mind his choice of career. Although you'd need more than Anadin for pain relief if you were under Vijay Khan's care; he was specialising in surgery.

Vijay looked surprised, 'Yes, how do you know?'

'She mentioned you.'

His blush was hot, 'Really?' Then, embarrassed, he glanced out of the window, 'I was here last night. I was busy, but I saw the manager over there putting someone into a cab. I didn't realise it was her. Is she OK?'

'We don't know.' O'Rourke's tone was serious, 'She's disappeared.'

His mouth dropped open, 'You serious? You'd better look at the tapes. She's always in here, was in on Friday too.'

Cathy smiled, 'You've got a good memory.'

He blushed again, 'She's pretty easy to remember.'

'Did you speak to her on Friday?' O'Rourke's tone was probing.

'She was on her way into work – she usually says hello if she sees me. I work part-time too so I'm not always here. I hadn't seen her for a few weeks, but it was busy when she called in, we were stocktaking, so I didn't get a chance to chat for long.' He paused, 'I was hoping she'd drop in again when she had her break. Come through to the back and I'll show you the security tapes. I can keep an eye on the door from inside. The video is an old system, but the recording is pretty clear. My uncle's just got a quote for a new digital system – he's finally realised videos are obsolete.' Vijay held the door open for Cathy, 'The camera angles are pretty comprehensive, though – he's fanatical about shoplifters.'

'There she is.' Cathy felt a jolt, like a bullet hitting her right in the gut. They were huddled around a dated TV in the back room of the shop. It was a tiny space – part store room, part office – and smelled strongly of aromatic spices. Vijay had pinned the door open so he could keep one eye on the street door. He scrolled back to 8.25 p.m. on Sunday. The time stamp glowed orange in the top corner of a four-way split screen giving four different camera angles criss-crossing the shop's interior and the street outside. The images were black and white and a bit fuzzy, but clear enough to see what was happening.

In the bottom right of the screen on the external camera, they watched a figure who could only be The Rookery's manager, Billy Roberts, come out from under the arch. Walking around the side of The Rookery, he waved down a taxi which drew up alongside the pavement. He spoke to the driver for a second and went back in under the arch into the car park. A few moments later two figures could be seen coming back around the corner. Billy had his arm around Sarah Jane's shoulders. Her head was bowed, her distinctive hand-knitted cowl scarf wrapped around her hair and neck, keeping the night chill out. They couldn't see her face, but from her walk Cathy could see something was wrong. Sarah Jane was tall, held herself like a dancer, but on the camera she was hunched, like she had a bad stomach cramp. They watched as Billy Roberts pulled the back door of the taxi open and she climbed inside. He closed the door and a movement on the other side of the vehicle suggested that he was speaking to the driver for a moment. Then he stood back and tapped the roof of the vehicle, glancing into the back window as it pulled away, the rear registration plate clearly visible. O'Rourke had his phone out before Cathy could speak. Squeezing past Cathy back out into the empty shop, O'Rourke relayed the information to base.

Cathy turned to Vijay. 'Can we see the tape from Friday?' Part of her wanted to see Sarah Jane again acting normally, to remind herself of what that looked like. Vijay picked up a video tape from the pile he'd taken off a shelf above their heads. A white strip down the side was marked with the date in felt pen. 'Here we are, she came in about eleven thirty, I think.' He slipped the tape into the machine and rolled the footage, watching the time stamp scroll as he fast-forwarded. 'I was having a cup of coffee out the back . . .'

At eleven forty a guy in his twenties in a safety vest and hard hat came in and grabbed a sandwich and a bottle of Coke from the fridge. He spoke briefly to an older man behind the till. Vijay paused the recording, 'That's my uncle, he owns this place. I just help out.'

'I hope he pays you.'

Cathy half smiled at Vijay's shrug. 'It's family.'

The builder moved to the door, opening it to let a girl in a denim jacket into the shop, her blond hair knotted on the top of her head. She was followed closely by a pumped-up looking guy in a black leather jacket. The builder had a quick glance at the girl's butt and, nodding to Vijay's uncle, threw him a grin and slipped out the door.

'I think she comes in next.' Vijay sat patiently as the digital clock on the screen flickered through tenth-of-a-second increments. 'Here she is.'

On the external screen, Sarah Jane came into view walking along the pavement. Inside the shop, the guy in the leather jacket rubbed his face and Cathy saw prison tattoos across his knuckles. They were unmistakable – in any language they meant gurrier. If he had those tattoos, he had a record.

They watched as the guy in the jacket appeared on another camera in a different corner of the screen, browsing the magazine shelves. Then, in the top right-hand corner of the screen, Sarah Jane walked in.

Cathy started, her focus now fully on the interior of the shop, on the video as it played out in each corner of the screen. The girl already in the shop said something to Vijay's uncle, and put a light-coloured suede fringed bag on the counter, pulling out a pile of papers from it and passing them to him with a thick envelope. Standing behind her, waiting, Cathy could see Sarah Jane was wearing her long black coat, the ultra-fluffy pink scarf her mum had made wrapped around her neck, her plait snaking out from under it. *She was always cold.* Behind the counter Vijay suddenly appeared from the back room. Cathy kept her face straight – he'd obviously spotted Sarah Jane on the live camera footage being relayed into the stockroom.

Cathy knew Sarah Jane well enough to see that the smile she threw at him was special. It lit up her face.

On screen, Sarah Jane came up to the counter, standing just behind the other girl, and reached for a packet of Polos from the display stand that dominated the counter, throwing them playfully to Vijay to scan into the till. She pulled her wallet from her coat pocket, paid him and stood for a moment saying something to him.

Vijay paused the tape, answering Cathy's unspoken question, 'She was slagging me, I just got my hair cut.'

Cathy smiled to herself. She could see the chemistry between them even on the tape – Sarah Jane's confidence, Vijay's shyness. He hit the play button again and Cathy watched as his uncle nudged him, passing him the paperwork and envelope. Vijay rolled his eyes to Sarah Jane and vanished through the door to the stockroom just as the girl at the counter straightened and passed whatever she had been writing on to Vijay's uncle. As he was looking at it, she glanced quickly behind her and placed her hand on Sarah Jane's arm. Obviously surprised, Sarah Jane turned to her, smiling. As Cathy watched the screen, the girl said something quickly that made Sarah Jane frown.

Whatever she had said, Sarah Jane didn't get a chance to reply. Cathy leaned nearer to the screen, watching closely as Vijay's uncle interrupted them. It looked like there was some problem with the paperwork the girl had given him.

Sarah Jane reached for a lottery slip from the pile on the counter, used the pen that was attached to the stand by a long piece of hairy string to scribble something on it, folding and slipping it under the girl's fringed bag. The girl glanced anxiously behind her, checking what the guy in the jacket was doing, but he was absorbed in one of the magazines from the top shelf, and was slowly flicking through the pages. The girl glanced quickly at Sarah Jane, flashed her a smile and stuffed the lottery slip into her handbag.

What the . . .?

In that second, on the screen, Vijay reappeared from the stockroom and Sarah Jane smiled at him and jerked her head towards the door. Cathy glanced at him, looking for clarification.

'Sarah Jane said she was late for work, that she'd be back later.'

'Did she come back in?' He froze the screen, capturing her in the doorway, and shook his head. His eyes were fixed on Sarah Jane's back, her pale hair caught back in its loose plait. 'No, I didn't see her again until Sunday, when she got into that cab.'

'Who's the girl she spoke to, have you seen her before?'

Vijay nodded, 'She's Russian maybe, I'm not sure. She came in about a week ago to do some MoneyGram transfers. She must have been doing them for friends or something.'

Cathy turned back to the screen. In the bottom left corner, the external camera trained on the door showed Sarah Jane standing outside the shop reading the notices in the window. A moment later the girl inside concluded her business, pushing the receipts Vijay's uncle had given her into her bag, looking around for the guy in the jacket. He put the magazine back and joined her, turning left out of the shop door, his arm protectively around her shoulders as they headed across the road. The other external camera picked Sarah Jane up again as she apparently finished whatever she was reading in the shop window, and turned to cross the road, heading for the arch beside The Rookery where O'Rourke had parked this evening.

'We've a hit on the cab.' Cathy jumped at the sound of O'Rourke's voice behind her, 'It's a city centre company. He's just dropped a fare to James's Hospital, will meet us here in ten. Come on, we can wait in the car.' O'Rourke held out his hand to Vijay. 'Thank you for your cooperation, we may need to take a statement from you and send someone over for these tapes in the morning.'

'No problem, anything I can do to help. You'll keep me in the loop when you find her?' Vijay's face was troubled, his forehead creased in a frown.

Cathy reached out and touched his elbow, 'We will, don't worry, we will.'

9

When they found her. When they found her. Cathy kept Vijay's words circulating in her mind. They would find her. They couldn't not find her. Cathy didn't do failure. And nor did O'Rourke.

'Jump in, cabbie shouldn't be long.' O'Rourke hit the central locking on his key fob and his car flashed them a welcome. He slipped into the driver's seat as Cathy pulled her door closed. She shivered involuntarily and, glancing at her, he stuck the key in the ignition and fiddled with the dials on the dashboard. A moment later hot air was pumping out over her feet.

'Better?'

She nodded, her eyes meeting his. He was looking at her intently, his eyes full of concern. She drew in a shaky breath and glanced away; she wasn't up to deep conversation now, the image of Sarah Jane in the shop was too strongly imprinted in her mind.

Reaching out, he put his hand on her knee, giving her a reassuring rub. Before she'd thought about it she'd put her hand on top of his, his skin warm, and linked their fingers.

'Your hands are cold.' His voice was soft.

'My hands are always cold.' Avoiding his eye she gave his hand a gentle squeeze, 'You know what they say about cold hands . . .'

Out of the corner of her eye she caught him smile. Breaking the union of their fingers, he picked up her hand and held it in both of his, rubbing it to get it warm. 'Better?'

She shot him a shy grin. But her movement broke the moment, if it had been a moment at all, and he put her hand down gently, patting it, sitting up straight in his seat, the leather creaking as he pushed his shoulders back, wincing as he straightened. He glanced over at her. 'So what do you think?'

Cathy bit her lip and ran her hand into her hair, pushing a dark curl back out of her face. *She thought a lot of things, none of which she was going to blurt out right now, even if they were on their own in a dark car park in the middle of the night. Too much was happening.* She paused before speaking, 'Vijay's straight up. He likes her a lot, he's a good witness.'

There was a pause. Expecting O'Rourke to respond, she glanced across at him. He was staring out of the window into the middle distance, his broken nose in profile. He looked tired, the shadow of stubble already forming along his jawline. He was worrying about Sarah Jane, she could see it in the creases in his face. He knew Cathy was as worried as hell too, but where she found it hard to hide, he internalised everything. Always had done. He was impossible to read, which, she had realised a long time ago, was why he was so damn good in the interview room. She was sure he'd be good at poker too, but he'd resisted all her brother Tomás's efforts to bring him to the tables.

Needing to draw him out, to bring him back from wherever he had gone, Cathy swung around in the seat, drawing her knees up, catching a familiar blast of his aftershave over the scent of the car's leather interior.

'Who's the cab driver?'

Back to business.

He snapped out of it and focused on the steering wheel, running his hand over the soft leather covering.

'Nigerian guy. Dispatcher says he's very reliable, no complaints. Family man.'

Before Cathy could answer there was the sound of a car drawing up behind them. She looked over her shoulder out the back window. A silver Ford Mondeo had parked across the entrance to the car park. 'This looks like him.'

O'Rourke glanced into the rear-view mirror. 'Let's roll.'

Ade Adebayo had arrived from Nigeria some eighteen months previously, borrowing the money to buy his taxi, and the licence, from his brother-in-law, who had been in Ireland almost five years. He had been sending money home to his wife and six children from the moment he'd arrived. Adebayo swung the driver's door open and got out to talk to them, leaning with his back on the car, his arms crossed. Cathy ran her eye over the interior of the Mondeo as O'Rourke introduced them. It was spotless, as clean as O'Rourke's meticulously kept BMW. He was a nice guy, round faced, slightly overweight, his smile broad, genuine. His English was so heavily accented Cathy struggled to understand him, but he was keen to help.

O'Rourke took the lead. That worked for Cathy. Some men responded better to men, and they had an unwritten agreement about stuff like this.

Standing on the pavement outside The Rookery, O'Rourke had his hands in the pockets of his overcoat, the navy wool almost black in the reduced light. When Billy had locked up The Rookery he'd turned off the outside floodlights, their stark white light now replaced by the soft glow of the street lamps.

Steam rose from O'Rourke's breath as he spoke, 'You picked up a girl here last night?'

'Yes, boss, took her to Dún Laoghaire – long way, big money.' Adebayo held up his thumb and forefinger and rubbed them together. Despite his strong accent, Cathy understood that this trip had made his week, 'The boss man gave me sixty euro up front. I told him too much, but he insisted.'

Cathy frowned. Sixty euro was a lot. She usually paid thirty-five; she'd once paid fifty to get out of town, but that had been after midnight. At least it was a sign that Billy had wanted to get Sarah Jane home safe.

O'Rourke pursed his lips, 'And you dropped her where?'

'The man here give me address, I put it into my phone.' He reached for a Samsung S5, tapping the screen, 'Thirty-two Royal Avenue.'

'Tell me about her. Did she talk to you?' O'Rourke adjusted his stance on the pavement – more friendly, relaxed. He kicked an imaginary stone with the toe of his shoe, the leather grating on the wet paving stones.

Adebayo shook his head emphatically, 'Not well, boss, she didn't speak at all, just huddled into corner, curled up, like. I was listening to the game on the radio, not my job to talk.'

Cathy studied him as he spoke. Sarah Jane was normally chatty, particularly with cab drivers; perhaps it was the journalist in her, but she was deeply curious – nosey, as she put it herself. She always talked to cabbies, was fascinated by their stories, of the window on the world that they had, meeting so many people each day. She'd told Cathy that she'd caught a cab once in London on the morning of a Tube strike and the driver had collected a friend on the way. She's been transfixed with their conversation about a man in a white suit being arrested for murder – mistaken identity, apparently – and something about a vintage American car that was worth thousands hidden away in a lock-up in east London. Cathy could hear her now, *'I couldn't believe it, it was baking hot and I was on the way to an exam, I should have been reading over my notes and it was like I was sitting in a film set. One day I'm going to write that into a book!'*

Cathy knew if Sarah Jane hadn't spoken to Adebayo at all she must have been feeling *really* ill.

'So you dropped her to her house?'

'Yes, boss.'

'Did you see her go inside?'

Adebayo frowned, thinking hard, 'Not sure, boss. Know she got out but I didn't see her go inside. The game was on, I didn't see.' He pulled a face, shrugging. 'Sorry, boss.'

10

Despite all the planning and the strategies recommended by his psychologist, half the time Rebecca had no idea what caused Jacob's meltdowns. She had to spend hours tracking back through his day, trying to find out where it had all gone wrong. Sometimes it was as simple as a boy on his table telling him he'd coloured something in the wrong colour. Or a fire alarm going off. Once it had been a man on the TV saying something about the atmosphere, like there was only one layer. Sometimes it was someone using a well-known phrase like 'What's your taste in music?' that totally confused him. How could you eat music?

This evening, thankfully, he'd calmed down and had spent the time before bed absorbed in Minecraft, lying on the sofa with her laptop balanced on his tummy, his fingers flying over the keys. Which had given her a few moments to catch up with her paperwork.

'Ah, a mutant creeper just blew up my house!'

'I thought you were on creative?' Her eye still on the invoices spread out on the coffee table in front of her, Rebecca had been only half listening to him.

'There's creepers in creative and survival. And hard core.'

'Hard core?' He had her attention now, 'What's hard core?'

'It's where you have one life and if you die the world gets deleted.' His eyes still on the screen, he continued, 'It's really really fun, it makes the game better.'

'Right. What are you on now?'

'Survival. Stormblade282 is showing me how to make a TNT cannon.'

Rebecca had rolled her eyes. Jacob was obsessed with Minecraft, but it was better than some of the things he'd been obsessed with. Like insects – she shivered at the memory of the jars of earwigs on the kitchen table – or the Winsor & Newton colour chart, which had seemed harmless enough until he'd used every drop of ink in the printer to produce A4 pages of solid colour, and then had a meltdown because he only had the blues done. Eventually she'd persuaded him to print small squares of colour, but it had still cost her a fortune in ink. At least with Minecraft he was learning spatial awareness and it was stretching his creativity, or at least she hoped it was – but TNT cannons?

He was fast asleep upstairs now. Rebecca swirled the chilled white wine around her glass, enjoying the dying embers of the fire. She'd turned the TV off when she'd taken him up for his bath, and now had a CD on, gentle jazz reaching out to the parts of her mind normally busy with a hundred different things. This was the only time of the day she got to relax. Not that it was day – it was well after midnight. Rebecca took a sip of her wine, thinking about today. She needed to spend more time with Jacob, try and free up some afternoons so she could organise play dates. But there was just so much to do.

Immediately she began feeling guilty all over again that she let him play Minecraft too much. He should be out playing with friends, they should be out doing things together. She sighed inwardly. In all his eight years she hadn't worked out how you were supposed to balance motherhood and working, especially working for yourself, which seemed to take up every waking minute. But it wouldn't be for ever. Her one aim in life was to earn enough money to make sure he would always be comfortable and so she could stop working – while she was still young enough to enjoy it – and spend time with Jacob. Take him to the zoo, to exotic beaches, show him New York and Paris. Earn enough that she could employ someone else to do the worrying.

Rebecca took a sip of her wine and reached for the book lying on the coffee table, pulling it onto her knee. *The Five-Minute Journal.* Cloth bound in cream hessian, it was something one of her customers had mentioned. An astute business woman, she said she used it every day to record her successes, to focus on the things she was grateful for. Ordering it from the States hadn't been cheap, and she rarely had the time to be diligent with it, but on days when Jacob was struggling with life, or she was struggling with the business, this little book gave her a few moments to unwind and think. The inspirational quotes at the top of each page were like her guilty pleasure. She knew when she did get a chance to switch off from the shop and everything, her mind was always so much clearer. Having the journal, feeling its pull when times were tough, almost gave her permission to dream again.

The only way to get what you want in this life is to know where you are going, and that means making a plan. She'd had that phrase in her head ever since she'd read it in a teen music magazine when she was twelve.

And she'd used it from then on. Writing her goals down helped crystallise them – six-month goals, five-year goals; the plan itself, the how to get there, usually fell into place once you knew what the end game was. Sometimes it was just about getting through tomorrow or this week, but right now, cosy in her own space, the music freeing her mind, she had space to look forward.

When she'd been studying for her Leaving Cert she'd created a mood board of where she wanted to go – photos of the Gaiety School of Acting leading towards an iconic panoramic shot of the Hollywood hills she'd torn from *Vogue*. Blu-tacked onto the textured pink floral wallpaper of her box bedroom alongside posters of her heroines, Marilyn Monroe and Audrey Hepburn, women with poise and class and timeless beauty, she'd positioned it so it was the first thing she saw every morning when she woke up.

She hadn't made it to Hollywood, but that board had been more about getting herself out of a north-side council estate where the view from her bedroom window was an expanse of waste ground surrounding the skeleton of a burnt-out car than anything else. At night as she leaned on the window sill and looked out, she'd pretend the car was a modern art sculpture, closing her eyes and imagining she was in New York or Los Angeles, that the sirens she could hear were like the ones on *Hill Street Blues*.

She had gone on to study drama, and disguising her inner-city Dublin accent had been crucial in getting her the job in the hotel in Spain. That year had been one long performance, had shown her what a five-star lifestyle was really all about.

A glimpse of a whole new world. And it hadn't been what she'd expected at all. When money was no problem, the value system changed; drugs were like chocolate, people became disposable. That year had opened her eyes to a lot of things. Some of them things she didn't want to remember. Like the Russian guest who had wanted a lot more than she was prepared to offer personally, a man who had been unable to understand that she didn't come as an added benefit to renting a suite.

Rebecca abruptly tried to curtail that line of thought, reaching for the bottle on the floor beside the sofa and topping up her glass, but it wasn't something she could forget: the excitement at being invited to a private party with some of the hotel's wealthiest guests, of choosing what to wear, the sound of laughter and the chink of glasses from the balcony. The heat of early August had been solid, even long after the sun had set, and as the party had begun to wind down she'd felt his hand around her waist, breathed in the cloying smell of his aftershave. And then, as she pulled away, suddenly realising what was happening, the impact of his hand across her face and the sound of the glass breaking as she'd fallen through the partly open first-floor window had merged into one moment of shock, like a high note on a violin as the bow was drawn roughly across. Thank God the suite had been immediately above the pool. Her silver evening dress had suffered, but that was the least of her problems.

Whether it was deliberate or some sort of inbuilt coping mechanism, she'd blanked out most of the details. She remembered one of the groundsmen pulling her from the water, and the bright lights of the emergency room but not much more.

Thank God.

That night had changed the plan, though; the scar on her face would have made movie auditions tricky, not that she'd ever wanted to play dopey women in romantic leads, but even so . . . She'd come back to Dublin to sort herself out, had thought she'd only be here for a few weeks, regrouping, getting back on track, working out the next step. But then one night, sipping gin cocktails in Lillie's Bordello she'd met Jacob's dad, and a world of opportunity had opened up. A world of opportunity that came with a few less than tasteful caveats, but his weirdness in the bedroom was a small price to pay for the access it gave her to an established business and ready cash flow. Being pushed through a window hadn't been her idea of an ideal way to change her course in life, but it had brought her to where she was now. And whatever about the stresses and strains of being a single working mum, of having a child on the spectrum, of the long hours and the worry, there was nothing better than being your own boss.

Rebecca took another sip of her wine and opened the journal. One of the things she liked about it was that the pages weren't dated, so she didn't feel a failure if she didn't get to write in it regularly. Smiling, she scanned the quote at the top of the page, from Einstein, 'It's not that I'm smart. It's that I stay with problems longer.' Below it there was a space for her to write, 'I am grateful for . . .' In every single entry she wrote Jacob's name here. She chewed the pen for a moment, and then, under 'What would make today great . . .' she wrote, 'Everything going to plan.' There wasn't a space for it, but at the top of each page she often wrote a word that she wanted her day to be guided by. Someone had told her she should come up with a word at the start of each year, but she found that a daily word could be incredibly powerful. She chewed the end of the pen again for a moment and then wrote SUCCESS in capital letters across the top of the page.

The success she'd had was nothing like the success that, if she played her cards right, lay before her. She just had to take one step at a time.

11

The pool was empty when Cathy arrived at six the next morning, the gym she and Sarah Jane were members of in Dún Laoghaire only just open. The staff were used to her being their first visitor of the day, understood her training regime and left her alone to focus on a hard workout, whether that was with the weights in the gym itself or in the pool. This morning, as she rolled up her black polo neck sweater and camouflage combats, stuffing them into her kitbag, she could feel the worry of yesterday weighing heavily. She pulled on her black Lycra swimsuit and dragged her hair back tight into a ponytail.

The last thing she felt like right now was a thirty-minute hard swim. She'd prefer to be heading straight for the station to see if any news had come in overnight, talk to O'Rourke, find out what his plan was, review the leads, go back over the CCTV footage they had. But she knew she'd feel so much better after training, she'd be fresher and energised, her head would be clear and she'd be a whole lot more useful. Getting match fit for the national heats would normally be top of her agenda right now, but since last night that had become the least of her problems. Jordan Paige might be her only serious opponent, but winning was as much about focus as fitness, and right now she couldn't focus on anything except finding Sarah Jane – the only win she was interested in at the moment.

And she knew O'Rourke was as worried as she was. She was pretending to him that it was all fine, that she was fine. She wasn't fooling anyone, least of all herself, but she knew that keeping everything moving forward as fast as possible was the only way they could keep their minds busy and not think about the alternative – about what might be happening, or might have happened, to Sarah Jane. They had both been in this job a long time, had seen more than anyone who lived in Normal Street could imagine in their worst nightmares. That was just the way it was. You coped.

Until it got personal.

She felt a gnawing in her stomach. When she was a child she hadn't known what this feeling was, this feeling of sickness. Then one day out of the blue she'd realised it was worry – she had no idea how it could be a physical thing, but it was, and right now it was real.

Cathy sat down heavily to pull on her swim hat, trying to cram her hair into it. It had been about one in the morning when they'd got back to Dún Laoghaire. O'Rourke had given her a hug as they parted in the station car park, resting his chin on her head for a moment, telling her to go home and get some sleep. He was right, they were both more use to Sarah Jane rested, but as she'd pulled out of the car park, the heater in the car on full, she'd seen the light go on in his office.

The pool area smelled strongly of chlorine as Cathy padded through the showers, the water undulating to its own beat, lit from below the waterline by hundreds of concealed bulbs. As she stood ready to dive, one of the staff switched on the sound system and Katy Perry's 'Firework' burst into the heavy, centrally-heated air.

Cathy could feel tears, pricking at the back of her eyes. This was Sarah Jane's song. It was like it was written for her. She was the spark, she *was* original. She shone like the Fourth of July.

Cathy dived, cutting cleanly through the water, powering into the butterfly. She needed to clear her head, to get the adrenaline pumping, to stay on top. Sarah Jane needed her to hold it together. Like O'Rourke had said last night as he'd wrapped her in his arms, they'd find Sarah Jane – if it was the last thing they did.

Cathy's hair was still wet as she walked into the station, punching her pass code into the key pad on the internal door and taking the steps two at a time towards O'Rourke's office. Her phone rang as she swung around the top of the stairs: Sarah Jane's mum, Oonagh. She sounded breathless, the line bad.

'Cathy, I got your messages. I'm sorry the mobile reception's terrible here, it's better to call this number, my landline ... Have you found her?'

Leaning against the banister Cathy chose her words carefully, 'Not yet, but ...' How could she put this tactfully without sending Oonagh into a total spiral of panic? 'My DI is on it now. He's doing me a favour – it's too early to classify her as missing – she's an adult and there's every chance that she's bumped into an old friend and just hasn't thought to call anyone because there's absolutely nothing wrong. But ...' Cathy paused, 'he knows her too and he's very concerned. We're talking to the people who saw her last.'

'And you said she went home in a taxi on Sunday, so that's good. She can't be far from home, can she?'

Cathy stuck her hand into the pocket of her combats, 'That's what we're working on. I'll let you know as soon as we know anything, I promise.'

Cathy could hear Oonagh Hansen's voice crack, 'I know you will. I'm going to stay by the phone here in case she calls. And I've left messages all over the place for Ted to call. If we could find out what they were talking about I'd be less worried.'

That was for sure. 'I'll keep in touch. Don't worry, you'll be the first person I call when I know anything.'

Cathy tapped the edge of her phone on her teeth as she headed down the corridor to O'Rourke's office.

Pushing the door open, Cathy hesitated for a moment. J.P. was already there, leaning on the window sill, the fluorescent light reflecting off the silver numbers on the epaulettes on his pale-blue shirt. His hands stuck in the pockets of his navy trousers, he threw her a rueful smile. There was no need for words. She threw her kitbag into the corner as O'Rourke walked in behind her.

'You should dry that hair before you come in, you'll get pneumonia.' He headed for his desk, a pile of printouts in his hand. He had his shirtsleeves rolled up, his pale pink shirt crumpled, tie abandoned somewhere. He'd obviously been here all night.

Behind his back, Cathy pulled a face at the hair comment. He wasn't her mother. 'Anything new?'

Throwing the pile of paper onto his desk O'Rourke put his hands in his trouser pockets and turned to her, 'I've had our taxi driver checked out – no previous, seems reliable. Popular guy.

Not the brightest button, but a hard worker.' Pursing his lips, he scowled at the wall for a moment, 'We'll get the rest of the security footage from the shops and business premises around The Rookery this morning.' He rattled the change in his pocket as Cathy crossed to sit next to J.P. on the window sill. She hopped up and tucked her hands under her thighs, 'So now we need to establish whether Sarah Jane actually went into her house when she was dropped home or not. And whether she was present when her room was broken into.'

O'Rourke transferred his gaze to a spot on the floor and nodded slowly, 'I've got uniform checking with the neighbours this morning. We'll try and catch them before they leave for work.' He grimaced, 'It was Sunday evening, dark, there's no guarantee anyone was looking out of their windows, but you never know.' He turned to look at Cathy, 'A media release has gone out, though, so we might get some feedback from this morning's news reports.'

Cathy shifted to get more comfortable, 'We need to find her car.'

'We do. Her registration plate has been circulated. If it's in the city it should turn up.'

A soft knock at the door announced the arrival of Detective Sergeant Frank Gallagher and Detective Garda Jamie Fanning, both from Dún Laoghaire's district detective unit, both looking worried.

'You wanted us, Cig?' The Irish term for inspector.

'Thanks, gentlemen.' O'Rourke invited them in with a sweeping movement of his hand, 'This is still unofficial, so we're keeping it close, but we've got a possible missing person, Cat's friend Sarah Jane Hansen.'

Gallagher nodded curtly and Cathy could see he'd heard. Nothing stayed under wraps for long in the station.

Gallagher and Fanning were a strange double act – looked more like father and son than colleagues, but perhaps that's why it worked. Tall and wiry, his grey hair cropped short, Frank Gallagher had been married for more years than Cathy had been on the planet, his wife a local councillor. Despite so many years in the job, he always looked to Cathy like a bank manager about to go for a game of golf. He was one of those guys who took everything in his stride, which was why his expression today made her bite her lip. Jamie Fanning, known as 007, was the complete opposite – early twenties, hair an expensive blond, most of the time he looked like he'd stepped out of a Ted Baker ad. He reckoned he was a player – as far as Cathy was concerned the jury was definitely still out on that – but he was OK, when he wasn't being a twat. He'd earned his nickname from his jackrabbit tendencies, trying to bed every girl he ever met. He'd been trying to score with Sarah Jane from the first time he'd met her, but his reputation preceded him. He just wasn't the type to cotton on to the fact that he didn't have a chance.

'What's the latest?' Frank Gallagher exchanged glances with O'Rourke as Fanning came into the office and play-punched Cathy on her shoulder. His blue eyes were concerned, she had to give him that. She flashed him a smile.

'That's better, champ.' He pretended to shadow-box with her, his fists under his chin, reaching for a hook.

'Feck off, you eejit.' Cathy didn't even rise to it, knew she'd have him KO'd on the floor in less than sixty seconds. And she was sure he wouldn't appreciate a broken nose.

Fanning grinned, about to say something else when O'Rourke's phone rang. Cathy pushed him out of the way so she could see O'Rourke's face, but he wasn't giving anything away as he listened to the caller, his frown deep.

'Thanks, we'll get someone down there.'

Cathy slid off the window ledge, 'What?'

O'Rourke slipped the phone back into his shirt pocket, 'Her car's in the Drury Street car park. Attendant has just called it in to Pearse Street. Do you and Frank want to get over there, Cat? Thirsty will be over to process it as soon as he's free. Call in as soon as you have news.'

They made good time into town, the unmarked Vectra's blue strobe headlights clearing the bus lane. Cathy jumped out of the car before Frank Gallagher had even had a chance to turn off the lights. The third floor of Drury Street's modern car park was well lit, Sarah Jane's car parked in a central bay.

Frank reached into the glove compartment for a box of latex gloves and passed Cathy a pair through the open window, 'Here, put these on. Thirsty will be here in a minute.' Glad to be out of the car, stinking of stale coffee and vinegar, the floor in the back littered with fast-food wrappers and styrofoam cups, a by-product of too many hours on surveillance, Cathy snapped the gloves on and rolled her eyes at him.

Her shoulders hunched against the morning chill, Cathy threw up her hood, pulling her leather jacket around her. It was a padded motorcycle jacket, a gift from the team when her last one had been destroyed by the explosion, the thick leather taking the brunt of the flying glass and shards of metal and, she was sure, saving her life. When she'd left the pool this morning she'd thrown a hoodie over her roll neck sweater, but the extra layer didn't seem to be helping a whole lot.

But Cathy realised that she wasn't just shivering because of the weather. What would they find inside the car? Sarah Jane's laptop, her diary? Or worse?

Glancing at Frank for reassurance, Cathy could feel her stomach clenching as she walked towards Sarah Jane's Micra. As she got close enough to take a look inside, Gallagher switched on the powerful torch he'd pulled from the boot, shining it into the tiny car's interior. The inside of the car was in shadow. It was hard to see, their own images looming in the window glass like Dementors.

One thing was for sure – Sarah Jane wasn't in the car. *That was good*. Was that good?

'Try the door?' Gallagher held the torch up, shining it into the back seat. 'I'd need a warrant to open it, and we'll never get that.' Cathy could feel her stomach turning as she walked around to the driver's side. He was right, even the Guards couldn't go around breaking into people's cars on a hunch. But a friend could try a friend's car door. Cathy pulled the handle, expecting it to be locked.

It wasn't.

Cathy glanced back at Gallagher as she swung the door open. On the other side of the car, Gallagher opened the passenger door and pulled open the glove compartment.

'That her phone?'

Cathy grimaced and leaned in to take a better look – a phone in a bright pink case lay on top of a pile of car manuals and a paperback book, its spine hidden, well thumbed pages facing them.

'Yep.' Her voice came out louder than she expected, croaky. She cleared her throat self-consciously, thinking for a moment.

The black hole of worry that had opened as she'd stood at the side of the pool this morning suddenly yawned wide and flashed its teeth. Sarah Jane always felt lost without her phone, even if the battery was low, which it usually was. Maybe she'd been late and had forgotten it – it wouldn't be the first time – but why hadn't she locked the car? What had she been thinking about as she'd parked to make her forget basic stuff like this?

'Her phone's always running out of battery, but if she'd forgotten it, why didn't she get the cab driver to swing past here on the way home? It's only a few minutes from the restaurant, and the manager had already paid him.' Cathy spoke as the sound of wheels on the ramp beside them announced Thirsty's arrival in the scenes-of-crime van. He pulled up across the end of the car and climbed out of the van, his thick-soled boots sucking on the damp concrete of the car park. A life-long Pioneer, Dún Laoghaire's main Scenes of Crime officer had renounced alcohol long before his four now grown-up daughters had arrived, and was nicknamed for his affinity to orange juice. Now nearing his thirty years' service and retirement, his dark hair was peppered grey, his lungs constantly protesting against his fifty-a-day habit. He'd looked out for Cathy from her very first day in Dún Laoghaire.

'Hand it over here, lass. I've got a friend in headquarters who'll be able to download her call activity directly from the phone. Until this is a case on the radar with just cause we can't be looking for a warrant for call records.' Thirsty held open a brown paper evidence bag for her to drop Sarah Jane's phone into.

Cathy nodded, 'You going to give everything the once over?'

'That's for sure.' Thirsty turned to Gallagher, 'You have a word with them to make sure it's not towed? We can't take it back to the station in case she comes back for it and her parking's going to have expired by now.'

Gallagher nodded curtly, his face puzzled, 'Doesn't make any sense does it? Leaving it unlocked?'

'Just as well she did, though.' Thirsty turned to open the back doors of his van.

Watching Thirsty approach the car, suited up in his white paper overall, made Cathy feel sick. He flashed her a sympathetic smile as he paused for a second before reaching to pull open the boot.

It gaped wide and black. And empty.

Thank God. Standing back, giving him space, Cathy pulled out her necklace. It wasn't like she hadn't seen him at work a thousand times before, but this was different.

Cathy knew she just needed to focus, to see if there was something she'd forgotten, some tiny detail that would come back to her if she could lighten up a bit and allow all the areas of her mind to synchronise. She needed to use all her experience to help Sarah Jane. For feck's sake, it wasn't like she was a receptionist in a call centre. This is what she did, this was her world, and Sarah Jane was her friend. Sarah Jane would know one hundred per cent that Cathy was pulling out all the stops to find her. That's what friends did, that was the way Cathy was made. Behind her, Cathy suddenly tuned into Gallagher giving O'Rourke an update over the phone. He was back in the driver's seat in the front of the DDU car, had the engine running and the heater on despite having the window open. Realising that she was really cold, Cathy pulled open the passenger door and climbed in. But her head was too full to worry about being cold now. She knew there had to be something they were missing here. Women were randomly attacked, granted, but in the vast majority of cases they knew their attackers. Had Sarah Jane been attacked, or had she vanished deliberately because something had frightened her? What had she been working on that her dad had thought was dangerous?

Sarah Jane disappearing voluntarily didn't make any sense, Cathy knew, and she discounted the thought almost immediately. If something or someone had frightened her, she would have called Cathy straight away, wouldn't she?

Cathy shifted in the car, pulling her still damp ponytail away from the back of her neck. She needed to get her act together and use the stuff she was learning studying for her masters in forensic psychology, as well as the experience on the street, both personal and professional.

Cathy had always been fascinated by motivation, by what made people act in the way they did, and by body language, the unspoken ways people communicated. What made a lad watch women through their windows at night? How did a gang member sleep knowing he'd killed, knowing that he could be next on a hit list? It was as much about psychology as it was about criminality, and the lecturers on her course had little idea of what it was like out at the sharp end, what it was like to spend endless nights out in a patrol car where you never knew what could happen next.

Beside her Gallagher shifted, his olive-green waterproof jacket crackling, plain-clothes regulation issue. He was just as worried as Cathy; she could see it in his face as he glanced at her.

Cathy smiled quickly. They were all in the same boat here. Her colleagues all knew Sarah Jane. Cops hung out with cops; maybe it was the hours – it was definitely the nature of the job that few people understood it – and outsiders were treated with caution. But Sarah Jane understood, knew what they could and couldn't talk about, had slipped right into the gang when Cathy had first introduced her one night in the pub at the end of a tough shift. At this stage she had met them all – Thirsty, O'Rourke, her housemates.

Thirsty had been here for thirty minutes now, pulling the huge steel box that contained the tools of his trade out of the back of his van. Hairs, fibres, prints, endless photographs; he'd catalogue everything as if this was a full-scale investigation.

But why had Sarah Jane left the car unlocked? The question kept nagging at her. And left her phone behind? The battery was dead – maybe she'd forgotten her charger so there was no point in taking it into work. Thirsty would make sure it was recharged in controlled conditions so they could check her calls.

'You going back to base now?' Cathy asked, looking across at Gallagher. 'Not much more we can do here until we can check out her call log.'

He nodded, 'I'll get the car park CCTV – her ticket will give us her entry time. We'll see if she was on her own.'

Cathy pulled out her phone and hit dial. O'Rourke answered immediately.

Her voice caught as she spoke, 'Thirsty's here – he's almost finished. Frank's heading back in. I want to go back to The Rookery, talk to Billy Roberts and Vijay again, see if they've remembered anything . . .'

Cathy wasn't sure why she was being drawn back to the restaurant, but something was niggling her.

'Grand, keep me posted.'

As Thirsty and Gallagher left, the tail lights of their cars bright in the dim car park, Cathy headed for the lift, the heels of her boots echoing on the concrete. She ran through the footage they'd seen on the CCTV cameras so far in her mind. Billy Roberts hailing the cab, it pulling up, him helping Sarah Jane into the back. *There had definitely been something up with her.*

As she arrived at ground level Cathy tried to think of all the times she could remember Sarah Jane being ill. She was fit and healthy, still glowed from her long summers spent abroad as she was growing up. But she was allergic to mussels – had she eaten something at the restaurant? And if she'd gone home to bed, what had happened then? Slug, her housemate, was in his own world, and it wasn't one orbiting this planet, so he was worse than useless, had no idea of her movements. The other two they shared the house with were away at the moment, probably didn't even know she was missing. Well they would by tonight; O'Rourke's press release would be on all stations, appealing for anyone who might be able to help to come forward.

So Sarah Jane had come home Sunday night, and then what? Had she gone out again? Had someone called to the door? Had she been there when her room was turned over? It was as if, by taking her computer, someone wanted to silence her, but why?

As Cathy walked around the corner opposite the Break for the Border pub, she wondered if she could be more useful in Dún Laoghaire, in the station, rather than here. But the key with any missing persons investigation was to try to establish who the last person was that the misper had had contact with. And at the moment it was looking like the taxi driver.

Had he done something? Had he pulled over and attacked Sarah Jane? It wouldn't be the first time a woman had been assaulted by a cabbie.

Sarah Jane was gorgeous. As all-American as could be, pure white teeth and thick now ash blonde hair with the body of an athlete. Thanks to her dad's Norwegian heritage she was all ice-blue fjords and fresh air. She attracted attention wherever she went. She was outgoing and confident – good at hiding her personal insecurities, her fears that she'd never be able to live up to her father's reputation as a journalist, that all her relationships would go the same way as her parents' marriage. Not that that stopped her looking for the perfect man, but as she admitted herself, she was picky – perfect was a hard role to fill.

Cathy knew O'Rourke was pulling Traffic's surveillance tapes on the route to Dún Laoghaire. It would take a while, but they should be able to track the taxi on its way out of the city and into Dún Laoghaire and make sure there were no stops.

There had to be something they were missing, though, Cathy was sure of it. Perhaps if she chatted to Billy Roberts and Vijay again there would be something else, anything, they could tell her that would help.

Arriving in South William Street, Cathy could have kicked herself. It was probably too early for The Rookery to be open or for any of the staff to be on the premises. She should have called Billy to find out when he'd be coming into work and arranged a time to talk to him.

She tried the bell anyway. No answer. Standing at the top of The Rookery's steps, Cathy leaned on the ornate iron railings, looking up and down the road. It was just after ten o'clock, and delivery trucks were already parked in the narrow street, a street-cleaning vehicle, brushes revolving, cleaning the gutters. Across the street Cathy could see the newsagent's was busy.

Sticking her hands into the pockets of her jacket, Cathy turned again, looking up at the buildings on either side of the street, checking out the security cameras. The team would be calling into every premises as soon as they were open to find the footage from Friday onwards.

A seagull flew down from a roof opposite, powerful wings outstretched. Riding the breeze it vanished under the arch of the car park that opened out behind the restaurant. Cathy watched him as, huge yellow webbed feet out in front of him, he landed on the flat casing of a camera positioned above a fire exit on one of the buildings backing onto the car park. She leaned over the balustrade to take a better look – it was pointing in this direction and looked very hi-tech.

Skipping down the steps Cathy glanced into the car park. It was surrounded on all sides by tall Georgian buildings, some of whose front doors she guessed had to be on the street running parallel to this one. She walked under the arch to take a better look. Looking up, she could see there was a camera over what appeared to be the back door to The Rookery itself. She scanned the car park. The vehicles that had been parked there last night hadn't moved.

Pulling out her phone she opened Google Maps, looking to see which premises backed onto the car park. It only took her a moment to work out that the one with the camera over the back door was a nightclub. She'd never been there as a punter, but The Paradise Club was one of Dublin's few casinos and lap-dancing clubs. They didn't need to advertise – they were one of the 'in' places, a bit like The Rookery, that were always busy. Cathy frowned. They had a reputation for running a clean house, no drugs. Whether that was true or not, Cathy wasn't sure, but she could find out easily enough.

The seagull squawked and took off again. Cathy checked out the angle of the camera it had been sitting on. It was trained on the door, but if it had a wide angle it might have picked up Billy Roberts helping Sarah Jane to the taxi on Sunday night.

Turning around, Cathy walked briskly out to the street and around the block. The pavements were still glistening with the night's rain, and a man on a bicycle wobbled past her.

A moment later she'd reached the spot indicated by the cursor on her screen. It was a tall red-brick Georgian townhouse, its windows shuttered, a similar set of steps to those at The Rookery running up to a firmly closed door, paint gleaming gloss black, a brass plate beside the bell the only clue as to what the business of the building was. Cathy leaned forward, straining her eyes to read the neat Times New Roman script etched into the plaque.

The Paradise Club. Cathy rang the bell. She was sure it was far too early for anyone to be about, but it was worth a shot. She turned around on the step, pulling out her phone, and was about to dial O'Rourke when she heard a sound behind her and the door swung open.

12

Turning around on the top step of The Paradise Club, Cathy's eyebrows shot up as she was greeted by the guy she'd seen only last night on Vijay's security tape, the hunk in the leather jacket who had been looking at the men's magazines while Sarah Jane had been waiting in the shop. Casual, in a tight-fitted black T-shirt, a wide black leather-studded belt through the loops of his jeans, both arms heavily tattooed. He wasn't the type you forgot.

'Gardaí.' Keeping her face friendly, Cathy flipped open her warrant card.

His eyes were stony as he looked at it carefully. *Charming.*

'How can I help you?' His accent was heavy, Eastern European, Cathy wasn't sure where from.

'I'm investigating a missing persons case, I wondered if you'd seen this girl in the last twenty-four hours?' Cathy held up her phone, a photo of Sarah Jane laughing. It had only been taken last week in the college canteen.

Showing no hint of recognition, the man shrugged, 'Maybe, I'm not sure. What's happened to her?'

'She works at The Rookery restaurant around the corner, she disappeared sometime between Sunday evening and Monday evening. We're tracing her last known movements.'

He shrugged again, 'I don't know how I can help.'

'Perhaps you could start with telling me your name?'

'Nacek, Piotr Nacek.'

'And you work here?'

'I run the security.'

It was a bit like pulling teeth. Nacek, one hand in the pocket of his jeans, leaned the other hand high on the doorframe and Cathy caught sight of his knuckles, the prison tattoos. The vast majority of Eastern Europeans still had to do national service, which made them perfect for a role in security, but Cathy wondered if he had been up front about his criminal record with his employers.

'We'd like to have a look at your security recordings. Sarah Jane Hansen, the missing woman, got into a cab last night outside The Rookery, and I believe one of your cameras covers the car park at the rear of the building.'

'It's broken.' He shrugged, 'I'm waiting for the security company to come and fix it.' He paused, 'Don't you need a warrant?'

Helpful.

'We can get a warrant if we need it, but businesses are usually quite forthcoming in this type of situation. Unless they've got something to hide.'

He shrugged, the muscles under his T-shirt rippling, 'Nothing to hide here. I'll check with the boss but that camera's not working at the moment.'

'Good of you. Here's my card. Some of my colleagues will be along a bit later asking as well, so if you could get an answer by then it would be useful.' She paused, 'I believe you visited the newsgent's on South William Street on Friday?"

He shrugged, 'I'm in there a lot, it's around the corner.'

'You were with a girl on Friday, a blond girl who was making a money transfer?'

The shrug again, his face disinterested, 'I know a lot of people, I might have been, I can't remember.' Cathy paused, wishing she'd taken a photo of the screen in Vijay's shop, that she had a still of the girl to show him. It might help jog his memory.

Cathy had a feeling from what she'd seen on the tape, from the girl's body language, her anxious glance at him, that she had been nervous of him for some reason. She knew she needed to tread carefully but knowing what the girl had said to Sarah Jane was starting to gnaw away at her. Perhaps it wasn't important, but she just needed to find out, and the only person who could tell her was the girl.

'I might need to come back to talk to you again—'

Nacek interrupted her, 'I'm here most of that time,' and with that he closed the door, leaving Cathy standing on the step. *Nice.*

Cathy pulled her phone out of her pocket, heading back down the steps and around the corner. Pausing to lean on a rough brick wall between two shopfronts, she crossed her arms and waited for O'Rourke to answer. This time it took him a few rings.

'I've found the guy on the tape, the one in Vijay's shop on Friday when Sarah Jane was in there.'

'How did you manage that?' O'Rourke sounded surprised,

'He runs the security at The Paradise Club. It backs onto the car park behind The Rookery. I just called in looking for their CCTV footage.'

'Helpful?'

'Not exactly.' She could almost hear O'Rourke nodding as she continued, 'He doesn't remember being in the shop on Friday. Can we lift a photo of the girl from Vijay's tape? I really want to know who she is and have a chat with her. If he works this close, maybe she does too, someone else around here might recognise her.'

'No problem, I'll organise that. Although I'm not sure what she'll be able to tell you, she was probably asking Sarah Jane the time or something.'

'But Sarah Jane wrote something down for her. It might have been a bus number or the name of her mascara, but they spoke.'

'True.'

Cathy persisted, 'I want to know a bit more about that Money-Gram transfer she was making.'

'Don't spend too long on that, it's unlikely Sarah Jane's going to turn up in Outer Mongolia or wherever she was sending the money.'

'I know, I'll be quick. I'll see if Vijay's there now.'

Cathy hung up and headed across the road.

13

'So what do we know?'

Sitting behind the desk in his office, O'Rourke steepled his fingers, his eyes on a photograph attached to the noticeboard on the opposite side of the room. That had been another missing persons case, the one that wouldn't let him go. Cathy knew it helped him think, to focus. The day he'd arrived in Dún Laoghaire he'd stripped off the cellophane from the pristine cork board and pinned the photo of a teenage girl in the top right-hand corner. The whole station had been talking about it.

It was a cold case. Unsolved. Cathy hadn't said it to anyone but the case was one from their time in uniform in Pearse Street when Cathy was only a student.

Lucy Reynolds had been sixteen, her long mahogany hair clipped up at the sides, the rest almost reaching her waistband. She'd gone to a concert in Marley Park and had never come back.

Cathy knew that somehow having Lucy looking at him from across the office drove O'Rourke on; even when the shit was hitting the fan, Lucy kept the fire alive. One day, Cathy knew, O'Rourke would get to the bottom of her disappearance. Even if he was retired he'd do it, he'd find out what happened to her, why there was no body. And when he found the perpetrator, Lucy's killer, he'd absolutely nail them. Of this Cathy was quite sure.

But she couldn't think about that now, about old cases and girls not coming back. It wasn't an option. Sarah Jane was missing now and they were going to find her. There wasn't room for failure. She shifted her bum on the window sill of his office, focused on her black leather boots, her hands stuck in the pockets of her camouflage combats. Her hair was taking so long to dry today she'd taken it down.

'Last sighting is the taxi driver dropping her home Sunday night – no further contact, or social media updates after that. Her mum was trying to reach her yesterday, Monday, and couldn't, she failed to turn up at the gym last night.' She could hear herself, matter of fact, the bones of what they knew.

'How are we doing on getting her previous movements mapped?' O'Rourke knew the answers, but from experience Cathy was aware it helped to talk these things through. Batting the facts around they might spot a hole or make a connection that was glaringly obvious when you put two apparently unrelated pieces of information side by side. It wasn't the way everyone worked, but it was a routine that worked for them.

'I saw her Thursday, and from then on we're pretty sure where she was – up to Sunday night. Between social media posts and witness statements we know she was at The Rookery most of Friday, and several people saw her in the library at various times during Saturday. She was there all day – it would be characteristic for her to get stuck in and not leave. Sometimes she doesn't even stop for lunch.'

'Saturday evening?'

'We've a gap there. Looks like she went home and didn't leave the house until she went into work on Sunday, but we're still checking. It's on house to house's list.'

'So Friday she gets the DART to work but Sunday she drives in?'

'The traffic is horrific on a Friday, she usually gets the DART in and the bus home from Kildare Street. Town can be a bit dodgy at night – that's the safest bus stop in the city, it's about a hundred yards from government buildings.'

'Where there's a twenty-four-hour protection post,' O'Rourke interrupted; it had been in his district when he was a sergeant.

'Exactly. She listens to podcasts on the way or works on her laptop. She loves the peace and quiet, and it saves on parking. She drives on Sunday because there's no traffic, so it's faster to get in and the DART and buses aren't as regular. Sunday pay justifies the parking. By the end of the weekend she's too knackered to mess about with buses.'

'But this Sunday she didn't drive home or get the bus, she felt ill and the manager, Billy Roberts, put her into the taxi.'

'And she didn't go back to her car to get her phone, which is a bit weird.'

'Maybe she thought it was in her bag, was too sick to realise she didn't have it?'

'Maybe.' There was that word again. Cathy grimaced.

'Anything else on Vijay's tapes?'

Cathy shook her head. After their encounter on Friday, Sarah Jane had only appeared again on the newsagent's security footage getting into the cab.

'Vijay's uncle wasn't sure about showing me the MoneyGram dockets.'

'Understandably.' O'Rourke rolled his eyes, 'We'd have some fun trying to get a warrant to look at them.'

Cathy scowled at him. She knew he thought she was wasting her time, but they had to look at *everything*, and she wasn't about to be put off. She continued, 'There's money going all over the place – to Belarus, Romania, Moldova, Nigeria, Brazil.'

'Big spread.'

'I . . .' Cathy started to say she'd taken a photo of the Money-Gram docket that Vijay's uncle had told her the girl had signed when Sarah Jane was in the shop, but thought better of it. He didn't want her wasting time chasing down that line of enquiry. The money was being wired to a mobile phone account in Belarus, so until she found someone who spoke Belarusian, assuming that's what they spoke there, and was prepared to stick their neck out to try and contact the receiver, there wasn't a whole lot she could do. Cathy wasn't even sure where Belarus was, let alone if the person at the other end would talk to them but Cathy just had a feeling.

There seemed to be a lot of money leaving the country through these companies. Vijay's uncle had said they got all sorts of people in, that they'd stopped taking transactions unless they felt the sender actually knew the person receiving the money personally. They'd had too many men coming in to ask about sending money to girls in the Philippines or Russia, who they only knew online. He'd shaken his head as he'd explained to Cathy, astounded that it had never occurred to these men that the stories they were being told might not actually be true. But online fraud wasn't Cathy's problem right now, she had other things to worry about, like where the hell Sarah Jane was.

'So what do we think Sarah Jane was working on that her dad thought was dangerous? He still out of comms?'

Cathy shifted on the window sill, pulling at her necklace. She stuck her free hand in the pocket of her combats. 'Yes, his boss at CNN said he's investigating something to do with jihadi brides, they're trying to reach him but they can't expose his position – ISIS are monitoring all transmissions, so they can't just ring him up.'

'And what do we know about what Sarah Jane was working on?'

'Last time we spoke about it, she said she was writing an article on the urban cowboys that hang out around Ballymun, near college. She wanted to develop it and do her thesis on them.' O'Rourke raised an eyebrow as Cathy continued, 'She was asking about the kids that keep the horses. She was always talking about the cycle of poverty and education, reckoned if kids had hope they wouldn't offend. That's one of the reasons McIntyre opened the Phoenix gym there – he teaches loads of the inner city kids to focus on fighting in the ring instead of on the street.' Cathy hesitated, thinking, 'Sarah Jane was fascinated with the horses.' She spoke slowly, reaching into her memory for their conversation. The last time they had discussed it had been a week ago at least. Cathy had been delayed getting to the canteen, had been checking something with her lecturer. As she'd arrived, dumping her files onto the table they always sat at, right in the corner, Sarah Jane had been packing up for her next lecture. Typically working while she was eating, her laptop had been open – she'd been googling images of boys riding bareback in Ballymun, across Keane's Field between the flats.

'Keeping horses? Abusing, more like.'

Cathy snapped back to O'Rourke, to his office, to the gold fountain pen he was fiddling with. 'That as well. You'd think a dog would be an easier pet to keep, wouldn't you?'

O'Rourke sat back in his chair, 'You have to feed dogs, pay for dog food. Horses eat grass. Plenty of that for free. I don't understand why the council haven't impounded them. It's open ground.'

'McIntyre says it's private land. Some developer who was brought up in Ballymun owns it, lets the lads keep their horses on it. He's built them some sort of stable, apparently, down at the bottom corner.'

Cathy started playing with her pendant again, 'If we had her laptop we'd be able to see who she'd interviewed. She's a detail person, makes lists of everything.' Cathy paused, 'Can the lads check to see if she backed up her files? I think she told me she used a cloud server, Carbonite? We'll probably need a US warrant but they might be able to help?'

O'Rourke nodded, 'Will do. Can take a while but we'll give it a go.'

Cathy continued, 'God knows how we'll find out who she was talking to though – those lads aren't exactly chatty. The minute they see us coming they'll clam up.'

'Can McIntyre help?'

Cathy nodded, 'I'm sure he could – they trust him, he's part of the scenery up there, knows everyone.'

'So give him a call, see what he can dig up. I've got the technical guys up at headquarters to see if they can access her email, might give us a lead.' O'Rourke put his pen down.

'Don't they need her password?'

'Gmail's pretty secure, but they have their ways. Do you know it?'

Cathy shook her head, 'She used an encryption site for everything – for her Gmail, websites and stuff, she has this notebook she keeps them all in, changes them regularly. And before you ask, it's not in her room, I checked.'

'Handy. Do you think she actually talked to any of the kids, the lads with the horses?'

'She wanted to. I'll see what The Boss can find out.' Cathy moved from the window to the chair on the other side of O'Rourke's desk, perching on the edge of it. O'Rourke rolled his eyes.

'Could you stop fidgeting? You're starting to wind me up now.'

'Sorry.' Cathy put her elbows on the edge of the desk, rubbed her face with her hands. She felt like a spring that had been pushed down flat, all pent-up energy. She needed to get back into the gym. Cathy sat back in the chair, 'A lot of those kids are working for dealers, collecting and delivering.' Cathy frowned, 'Sarah Jane's a journalist and is downright nosey. She could have asked too many questions in the wrong place.'

O'Rourke rolled his eyes again.

'Feck off, I'm not that bad. Sarah Jane ferrets around all sorts of stories, I stick to . . .'

'Murders?'

'Well maybe.'

O'Rourke's tone was serious, his look searching. Cathy shifted sideways in the chair, uncomfortable under his gaze, 'Sarah Jane's really sharp. You know she is.' She paused, screwing up her face, looking out of the window. The rain was running in streams down it now. Cathy spoke slowly, half to herself, 'If we only knew who she'd been talking to . . .' She closed her eyes and ran her hand into the roots of her hair, pulling the curls.

O'Rourke's voice cut through her thoughts, 'I think you need to give McIntyre a call, then get out to Ballymun and talk to those kids, show her photo around, see what gives.'

14

'So when is the next shipment due?' Rebecca Ryan pulled a biro out of the pot beside the till and scribbled a note on the pad beside her. 'I hope everything was checked this time, I'm not paying for damaged goods.' She paused. 'Grand. Cash on delivery as normal.' She smiled into the phone, 'Nice doing business as always.' She hung up and shuddered. Her supplier was pretty unpleasant to deal with on a good day, but at least she didn't have to meet him very often. He stank of cigars and hair oil, could never understand that she was the one in charge, that she called the shots, that she wasn't just some bossy manager. Not that she cared much about that once everything ran smoothly – he was reliable, that was the important thing.

Sometimes she wished she'd applied that logic to her marriage. Jacob's dad was an idiot, one of the worst kinds, who had never cottoned on to the fact that it wasn't his level of intelligence that had made things happen for him.

Putting the pen down, Rebecca looked critically at the rails beside the till, her mind whirring. With every shipment she needed to focus on where the cash was going, making sure the books balanced. Running a business looked glamorous from the outside but it was all about keeping the balls in the air, all of them, and sometimes that was exhausting. Today her word in her journal had been 'organisation'. She had yet to persuade Jacob to tackle his bedroom but she was optimistic. Moving anything in his room required intense negotiation unless he took it into his head to reorganise the space, and then she'd walk in to see what he was doing, to find his toy cars lined up in size order at a thirty-degree angle on his dresser and the clothes that usually populated the floor in a big pile on the top landing.

Rebecca smiled to herself at the thought and stretched; it had been a long day, and a busy one. One of the mums from school had been in and – Rebecca couldn't resist another smile – had ended up struggling out of the door laden with turquoise paper bags. She'd come in looking for something to wear with her jeans at some corporate weekend away and had ended up with the top plus new jeans and a couple of outfits for the evenings. It was some business event her husband was involved in, and she needed to make an impression. Rebecca knew the value in making her customers look amazing, and this mum *had* looked incredible. Her husband would get a shock when he saw the credit card bill, but Rebecca knew he'd be showing his wife off and *she'd* be telling people where she shopped. This might be a tiny boutique in a village in County Wicklow, but Rebecca had achieved a national reputation – partly due to her ex-husband being a society darling and her poster boy, but also because she knew who to dress, and a few free outfits on the right people when she was starting out had gone a long way.

Rebecca twirled the biro through her hair. One thing she loved more than anything else in this world was making money. Money gave her strength, it bought power and opportunities. It opened doors and would ensure Jacob never had anything to worry about.

Her year in Spain had taught her an appreciation for the finer things in life, and that being the one in control was key; not to mention the contacts she had made and the knowledge she had gained to set up on her own. She often laughed to herself at her *naiveté* when she'd gone to Spain. Her plan had been to earn a bit of cash to set her up when she moved to LA to find her way into film or TV, and she could earn more from a summer on the Costa del Sol, getting a tan into the bargain, than she could working for minimum wage in Quinnsworth. Times had been tough in Ireland then – even finding bar work was difficult, especially when you were overqualified and had no intention of staying. She'd seen the ad for English-speaking staff at a five-star resort outside Puerto Banus, the type of resort where the super-rich hung out in the security of an enclosed environment where there were no paparazzi and a guarantee of discretion.

She'd started as a waitress, and within weeks was a hostess in guest services, efficiency quickly promoting her to manager. She'd seized the moment and ensured her guests wanted for nothing. The tips had been incredible and she'd ended up staying much longer than one summer, just over a year in fact, and had made some powerful friends and connections.

Rebecca knew that she was stronger now than she'd ever been – her driving force was wanting to give Jacob everything she'd never had as a child. The estate she'd grown up on had been tough. Their three-bedroom semi had had an outside toilet and a back boiler – the hot water generated by the fire her mother lit every morning in the living room hearth. It was like something out of the 1950s.

She'd worked hard in school, got all the As she needed to attain her goal: getting out.

Leaning on the counter, layers of turquoise tissue paper cushioning her elbows, Rebecca looked out at the village. Despite the gossips, this was exactly the type of place she'd dreamed of growing up, out in the country where you could leave the house and find woodland and mountains literally on the doorstep – not waste ground, burned-out cars and discarded needles. Where the air was clean and your neighbours were bankers and artists, not dealers and junkies.

And Jacob loved it here. She'd never taken him back to his grandparents' house, to the place she grew up in, but she would one day. Both her parents were dead now, had been killed in a car crash soon after she'd got back from Spain. She'd stood at their graveside, the wind whipping her hair across her face, chilling the straggle of mourners to the bone, and she knew that now she really needed to make it on her own, and exactly how she was going to do it.

'Mummy.' A voice behind her interrupted her. 'It's 5.21, what's for tea?'

Turning around, Rebecca smiled. 'It's 5.21 is it? Are you hungry already? What would you like, my darling?'

Jacob grinned and shoved his hands in his pockets, his eyes fixed on her, big, round and deliberately innocent, 'Pizza?'

Rebecca looked at him knowingly; he was some chancer, she wondered where he got that from. 'You know we only do takeaway at the weekends.'

'It's not takeaway, they deliver it, you don't have to go and get it, you just have to call them.' He held up the cordless landline, the gap in his teeth appearing as he smiled.

Rebecca looked at him, wavering for a second. She was hopeless where he was concerned.

'Please, Mummy.'

She grabbed the phone from him playfully. It had been a good day, and it wouldn't hurt this once.

Upstairs, TV on, the pizza box open on the low oak coffee table in front of them, Rebecca reached for her glass of wine. Jacob liked the lights turned down low, so apart from a brass lamp over in the far corner, the fire was the only source of light, the flames jumping over the Farrow & Ball 'New White' walls of the living room. She'd kicked off her shoes onto the African tribal rug beside the coffee table and was now curled up on the sofa next to him. Munching pizza, his eyes were fixed on the TV and he was distracted enough to lean back on her, to let her cuddle him.

She knew he saw things differently to everyone else, that the colours and sounds of the programme caught his attention sometimes more than the content. When he was much smaller she'd taken him to a birthday party – it hadn't been her best idea, the noise and craziness had been overwhelming, but he'd focused on counting the balloons, on the number of each of the colours. His perception of things was so different to hers, but that's what made him amazing, gave him his brilliant memory, his ability to draw, to remember facts like they were his friends' names. They'd been in the supermarket the other day and he'd started telling her about eggs, about how chickens produced extra bones to provide calcium for their eggs but crocodiles didn't. Or people. Then he'd looked speculatively at a toddler having a meltdown, 'a moment' as Rebecca thought of them – they'd had a lot of those – and he'd said, 'Why do people have children when you can adopt them pre-made without having any vitamin deficiencies?'

When she'd finished laughing she hadn't really had an answer to that one. She smiled again now, remembering it. He could be absolutely hilarious with some of the things he came out with.

Jacob reached for another slice of pizza as the *Six One News* came on, a Garda call for assistance in a missing persons case the first item.

'Irish American Sarah Jane Hansen is a journalism student at DCU and works at The Rookery restaurant on South William Street. She got a taxi home to Dún Laoghaire on Sunday night and . . .'

Jacob stirred beside her as the missing girl's photo was flashed onto the screen.

'That's wrong. She had her hair tied back. Like Daniella does, in a plait.'

Her glass halfway to her mouth, Rebecca froze, stunned. 'How do you know that, honey bun?'

Jacob munched on his pizza, his eyes trained on the screen. He spoke with his mouth full, 'I told you. On Sunday I was on single player and my battery ran out. I was coming in to tell you.'

'I remember that bit, darling, but how do you know about the girl's plait?'

Jacob took another bite. 'She was in the car park where you parked. She got into a Discovery with an army man. She had a long long plait like Danni, the one like a fish tail. She said it's hard to do. I was getting out of the car to go in and tell you about the battery but they came past really close, so I waited cos I didn't want to get flattened.'

Rebecca's mind whirred, but keeping outwardly calm she took another sip of her wine. Jacob told the truth without wavering, so there was no doubt in her mind that if he said he'd seen the girl, then he had. And he wouldn't have any hesitation in telling other people. He didn't have internal brakes, the natural sense to know when to speak and when to keep quiet, often piping up in completely inappropriate circumstances. She still cringed at the memory of walking around the supermarket – he'd seen an overweight lady with a basket full of ready meals and started on a long explanation of the calorific content of prepared food and the symptoms of diabetes at the top of his voice.

So if this missing girl came up in conversation at school, or anywhere, he'd be totally straight about telling people he'd seen her, and he'd end up being the centre of attention, and he *hated* that.

Rebecca flinched at the very thought – the other kids would be asking questions, no doubt fascinated that he could be a crucial witness in a national news story, one that had actually been on the TV. She could see him surrounded in the playground, faces looming all around him, voices probing, drowning him in a cacophony of sound. He'd be trapped, unable to tell them to give him space, to communicate that he couldn't cope with being crowded, unable to answer the questions, to even filter the questions in order to answer them. The noise and the jostling and the excitement would be a sensory overload and he'd have a total meltdown.

And this was Enniskerry, the village where an American girl, Annie McCarrick, had vanished in 1993. The minute it was out that he'd seen the girl who had disappeared, the gossips would have a field day, and everyone would be cross-examining him, even the teachers, she was sure. He wouldn't understand it at all. Here, of all places, a missing American girl could end up being the sole topic of conversation for weeks. Her mind worked fast, assessing the options, running over the possibilities. She couldn't bear for him to be upset, and something like this could be catastrophic. It had taken so long to settle him in school, something like this could blow that sky high – school refusal was an ongoing problem for parents with children on the spectrum. Unable to verbalise the issues, to understand, let alone explain what was upsetting them, school became just too scary and unmanageable for kids who were often extremely intelligent, and gifted in so many ways.

'Are you *sure* it's the same girl, Jacob? Absolutely sure?'

His eyes on the TV, totally absorbed now in a story about golden eagles being reintroduced to Ireland, Jacob nodded. Rebecca put her glass down on the coffee table with a crack. How on earth was she going to manage this one? Rebecca's mind worked fast.

'We need to tell the Gardaí – the people who are looking for her. Would you do that, will you talk to them tomorrow for me?' If the Gardaí told Jacob he'd been a good boy and to forget about it, maybe he wouldn't say anything in school? It was inevitable it would get back to them if they didn't report it – the local sergeant's twins were in his class – but if he spoke to them first, perhaps he'd let it go? Jacob was too focused on the eagles to reply; Rebecca doubted he'd even heard her. She'd have to try again in the morning.

15

Cathy pulled out a pine chair from the round kitchen table and sat down heavily. She hadn't the energy to change back into her combats after training, had stripped off her sweat-soaked vest and jumped into the shower, pulling on her spare set of workout gear – a T-shirt and sweatpants – from the bottom of her kitbag. Resting her elbows on the smooth, pine-effect table, she ran her fingers over her temples and into her hair. The house was quiet. Eamon was working nights, and Decko was on a late shift. He was on his way, though, had been given a detailed list to pick up from the Indian takeaway.

'Wine?' Across the brightly lit modern kitchen, arty spotlights reflecting off black polished granite, J.P. was looking into the fridge. He'd changed into a holey old loose-knit jumper of indeterminate colour, one Cathy was sure his mum had knitted when he was about fifteen. Together with his faded jeans, he looked like he'd stepped straight in from the farmyard.

'I'd love a glass, but I'd better stick with water.' Cathy knew there was a danger alcohol would go straight to her head in her present mood, and the last thing she wanted to be doing tomorrow was nursing a hangover.

J.P. nodded sagely like it was a sensible decision and pulled a bottle out of the fridge, holding it up and looking speculatively at the label, 'Posh fizzy, do? I think this could be stolen property, but I'm sure it'll taste OK. There's even a lemon in here. You'd think you're in Finnegan's pub.'

Cathy smiled, 'I think you've missed your vocation as a barman, John Paul Morgan.' He grinned at her over his shoulder and closed the fridge door as she continued, 'How long did Decko say he'd be? I'm starving.'

'Ten minutes, tops. Eamon won't be impressed he missed out, we'd better save some for him for when he gets back in the morning.'

Takeaway curry wasn't everyone's idea of the perfect break-fast, but when you were on a week of nights your schedule got turned on its head. After a tough night it was quite normal for the team – the girls and the lads – to go to an early house when they knocked off and unwind over a few pints. Eamon would be delighted to find they'd saved his for him.

Cathy smothered a yawn, 'Is he still in Ronanstown?' She'd lost track over the past few days; so much was happening that the reality of her daily life felt like it was slipping away.

'He's hanging in there. Only a few more days to go. The van got rammed last night and some scrote took a baseball bat to the windscreen.'

'Sure that was worth the effort.'

J.P. grimaced, 'He wasn't expecting bulletproof glass, that's for sure. Think he got whiplash from the recoil.' Before J.P. could go on, a clattering at the front door announced Decko's arrival.

'At last.'

'So bring me up to speed, what's the latest?' Decko reached for the silver foil container of basmati rice and piled a second help-ing onto his plate. Cathy had put Eamon's portion safely on the counter to cool, knowing what her other housemates were like. She knew she ate a lot during training, but she had no idea where these lads put their food. The fridge seemed to be permanently empty. The house kitty covered the essentials – bread, butter, bacon, eggs and sausages. The consensus was that if you had the makings of a fry you wouldn't starve, day or night. In fact some of their best meals were huge fry-ups the morning after the night before, when the scent of bacon was the only thing that would wake them. Cathy's strict diet when she was training meant that she couldn't let rip like the others, and she usually ended up laughing at them looking at her detox shakes like they were contagious.

As Decko helped himself to more curry, Cathy put her knife and fork together on her empty plate and answered his question.

'O'Rourke's TV appeal went out tonight. On the *Six One* and the late news.' She leaned forward to check the time on her phone – it was well after 11 p.m. 'With a bit of luck there will be a few calls by now. We've got CCTV of her getting into the taxi taken from the shop across the road, so we've got a time frame and something they could show with the report. Plus her photo, obviously.'

Reaching into a brown paper bag for another onion bhaji, Decko nodded. He was usually the comedian, but not tonight, 'What's the feeling?'

'Still no idea, really. O'Rourke was talking to Aidan – Niamh wants us to keep an eye on the fact that it could be a random abduction, maybe some guy was watching her and followed her home, or was watching the house.' Cathy reached for her water, her mouth alight from the curry. She'd never thought that having her brother Aidan married to the Assistant Commissioner would have any direct impact on a case she was working on, but since Sarah Jane had disappeared, knowing that Niamh was there in the background was a relief. Until they had credible evidence that there had been foul play, that Sarah Jane was in danger, they couldn't launch an official investigation; Niamh still had to balance her budgets, but at least O'Rourke wasn't worried about picking up the phone and keeping her briefed. Cathy put her glass down, twirling it around carefully on the table as she spoke, 'She's right about keeping every avenue open, but the burglary seems to indicate that someone was interested in Sarah Jane's computers, and what she was working on.'

'Which was?'

'A load of stuff, but the lads with the horses in Ballymun seems to be the most likely to ruffle feathers. I had a chat to The Boss earlier when I was out at the gym, he's going to find out exactly who she was talking to, what their connections might be. He'll have more luck than our lads, everyone talks to him.'

J.P., silent until now, stood and picked up his and Cathy's plates to take to the dishwasher, 'Reckon she could have been getting too close to something without realising it?'

Cathy shrugged. 'Half the criminal activity in the city is orchestrated from around there. Everything from fencing fags to phones, drugs, the whole lot.'

'Maybe someone saw her talking to some of the runners and thought she was asking about the horses as some sort of cover?' J.P. stood hovering beside the dishwasher, the door open, his face thoughtful.

'God only knows.' Cathy stared into her empty glass, swishing the slice of lemon around, and she was right back in St Pancras station in London, sitting outside a French restaurant in the main part of the station. She'd ordered a latte as she waited for Sarah Jane, and it had been delivered by a very attractive waiter together with a glass of iced water and lemon and a compliment about her hair. She smiled at the memory. He hadn't known where to look when Sarah Jane had arrived pushing her bright pink suitcase, her leather jacket slung over an equally bright pink ankle-length summer dress, the colour setting off her tan and the amethyst bracelet she always wore. She looked like she was about to shoot a magazine ad, all her accessories colour coordinated.

St Pancras was a place they both loved, from the converted Victorian station with its beautiful curved steel and glass roof to the wide marble concourse and gorgeous shops. It felt like a meeting point, a fulcrum in time and place where stories and lives met and intersected. Early, Cathy had sat mesmerised by the constant flow of people, by the pianos strategically placed along the concourse that anyone could sit down and play. As she'd sipped her coffee a black guy had started playing something classical. Beethoven, Sarah Jane had announced as she arrived moments later in a rush of people disembarking the Eurostar.

'My God, he's good – he should be getting paid for playing.' Pushing her suitcase under the marble topped table, Sarah Jane had leaned over to hug her, 'Sorry, have you been waiting long? I had—'

Cathy had interrupted her, 'A problem?' She'd almost laughed. Despite travelling halfway around the world on her own before she was sixteen, Sarah Jane seemed to have a catastrophic relationship with anything that moved. When she caught a plane her bags went one way while she went the other, when she caught a train there was a bomb scare or sheep on the line, or worse a human fatality, an 'incident' as the London Transport Police termed it. The last time she'd been on a coach it had caught fire on the motorway and she'd been stuck in a bus station somewhere outside Madrid for hours. It was like the transport companies, whether they were Ryanair or Virgin Trains they could see her coming and were playing some sort of elaborate game. Between that and her non-existent sense of direction, she really needed a minder when she travelled. Even when she was using Google Maps she walked in the wrong direction.

'So what happened this time?' Cathy smothered a grin as her best friend slumped down into the rustic-looking wooden chair, pulling her ponytail over the shoulder of her pale tan leather jacket. Her dad had given it to her for her birthday in New York, the leather so soft it looked like butter. And her hair was almost the same colour as the jacket and ramrod straight. How many times had Cathy wished she could swap her crinkly raven curls for something a whole lot more manageable?

'It was OK – Dad got me a cab, and that was fine, it just got a flat on the way to the station. I had to run to get the train.' Sarah Jane looked for the waiter, her eyes lighting up when she spotted him, 'Hmm, the day is looking up.' Flashing her brilliant smile at him she'd ordered lemon tea.

Cathy had never seen anything arrive so fast.

But Sarah Jane's attention was back on Cathy, 'And then, when I got here, they got all shirty at passport control. Apparently I might be undesirable on a US passport but I'm totally fine with an Irish one. Fortunately,' she paused, 'I had both.' She grinned, 'How was your anti-terrorism course? What's the talent like in the London Metropolitan Police?'

Behind them an announcement had echoed around the station, drowning the chink of cutlery and the chatter of excited travellers.

Decko put his hand on Cathy's arm, bringing her back to the kitchen, the middle of the night, and Sarah Jane's absence. 'You'll find her. Anyone who's checked up on her will know she trains with you, that she's under McIntyre's wing – he's known those families since they were kids, they won't want to mess with him. Maybe some goon is using her as a pawn in one of the feuds – they want to show who is strongest and they'll let her go in a day or so. The power politics between the gangs is nuts.'

'Maybe she had a row with the cabbie and he dropped her at a petrol station and she got lost trying to find the way back? You know what she's like, she could be walking around Cabinteely Park in circles and we're all overreacting.' J.P. switched on the dishwasher as he spoke.

Cathy smiled. They were both trying to make her feel better, she knew. 'I hope you're right.'

Upstairs Cathy leaned on her bedroom door and crossed her arms. Decko and J.P. had decided to have a game on the Play-Station before they hit the hay, and she could hear them roaring through the floorboards as they destroyed an army of zombies. At least she thought they were zombies; it was hard to tell, but she was pretty sure they were winning.

Her single room wasn't the most welcoming nook at the best of times, and right now it was the last place she wanted to be. Sparse was the way Sarah Jane described it, but as Cathy was always saying, it was comfortable, had everything she needed and she was hardly ever here. She didn't do fancy, didn't need a palace to live in, and she loved sharing with the lads, even if she did have the smallest room. When her compensation had come through after the explosion she'd thought about using it for a deposit on an apartment, but she wasn't ready to be on her own yet. It was too soon. She needed to know she had company, that the solid things she was used to were all still there. The explosion had shaken her but she felt safe coming home to this house and the lads. Instead of a deposit, she'd used part of the money for a new car and put the rest in the bank. It still felt like dirty money, and would do for a long time. When she was ready she'd decide what to do with it.

But tonight she was in a dark mood – even the single rail for her clothes looked lonely, her Bagpuss hot water bottle cover looked positively miserable, and the pile of dirty washing under the window wasn't exactly motivating. It only took her a moment to decide what to do. Tonight she needed to be in her own bed at home, to be fussed over by her mother, and she needed to get her washing done or she'd have nothing to wear to work tomorrow.

Pulling her kitbag out from under the bed, she threw in her toothbrush, make-up and a change of clothes and scooped up the laundry, stuffing it into a pillow case. At the bottom of the stairs she stuck her head around the living room door, raising her voice over the sounds of explosions. 'I think I'm going to stay at my parents tonight, I can get this lot done and find out if Niamh's heard anything O'Rourke isn't telling me.'

16

Cathy rolled over in bed and opened one eye, groggy, hauling herself from a deep sleep. The digital alarm clock beside her bed said 6.30 a.m. She hadn't arrived at her parents' house until about 1 a.m., her mum the only person still up, her head buried in a book as she sat curled up on the sofa beside the dying embers of the fire in the living room. Cathy had given her a hug, loaded her mum's washer-dryer and gone straight to bed, only to find herself tossing and turning all night. She'd ended up getting up to check her washing, padding around the silent house trying to switch her mind off. She'd gone back to bed and she must have fallen asleep just after she last looked at the clock at five.

Exhaustion clouded her mind, and it took a moment for her to realise why her brain needed her to wake up so urgently.

Sarah Jane.

Darkness seeped from somewhere in her middle outwards, engulfing her for a moment, making it hard to breathe, like a pressure in her chest that was pushing the oxygen from her lungs.

Cathy stared up at the ceiling of her childhood bedroom. She'd come here last night with her washing, but really she knew she needed the comforts of home, of solid walls, of her mum telling her everything would be fine.

It would be – it would be fine. *Christ, she hoped so.*

It was still dark outside, the phosphorescent plastic stars she had stuck around the central light when she was nine years old glowing gently in the light seeping around her door from the landing.

Downstairs Cathy could hear voices – her mum's, and then the deep rumble of male voices. She picked out her dad, her brother Aidan. . . and O'Rourke. *What the hell was he doing here?*

Swinging her legs out of bed, Cathy was down the stairs and had swung around the door jamb of the kitchen before she realised she was wearing a firehouse-red NYFD T-shirt – and nothing else.

'Have you found her?'

'Don't you think you should put some clothes on, love?' Turning from the sandwich she was making at the counter, Cathy's mum, Theresa, looked at her over the rim of her glasses.

Ignoring her, and the heat she could feel of her blush rising as O'Rourke's blue eyes took in the full picture, Cathy wrenched a handful of dark curls out of her face, still wild from the pillow. A small part of her would always look back on this moment and be thankful that she had shaved her legs.

'Well? Have you found her?'

'No, Cat, we haven't.' Niamh Connolly, Cathy's sister-in-law, recently appointed as An Garda Síochána's first female Assistant Commissioner, shook her head.

Aidan kept his voice low, met her eyes as he spoke, 'Dawson's here to give Niamh an update. Get some clothes on and come join us.'

'Right. Right.'

Not wanting to go, to miss anything, Cathy hesitated, her eyes meeting Niamh's for a moment. Niamh was sitting at the head of the table, her dark bob effortlessly sleek even at this hour of the morning, her pale-blue uniform shirt emphasising her eyes. She and Aidan had moved back in with Cathy's parents temporarily while their new house was being renovated. Little had they expected to be holding a briefing meeting in the kitchen.

Aidan raised his eyebrows in that 'well, what are you waiting for, go to it' way that applied to little sisters. A second later she was heading back up the stairs, two at a time.

'You really must have something to eat.'

Back in the kitchen, after the world's fastest shower, now in khaki combats and a black polo neck, Cathy was about to shake her head when her mum slipped a plate of toast and marmalade down in front of her. The smell made her stomach growl. She must be burning calories with nervous energy, she hadn't realised she was hungry at all after eating so late last night.

'Thanks.' Cathy fired her mum a grateful smile. Her mum had pulled her greying hair back in a ponytail, and was wearing one of Cathy's dad's BBQ aprons over her yoga gear, the slogan *007: Licence to Grill* totally at odds with her glasses and slippers.

'So, what's happening?'

Cathy had hardly got the words out when her mum interrupted. 'Eat.'

It was a command delivered in exactly the way her mum had spoken to her when she was at school. Across the table she could see O'Rourke fighting a smile. *Bastard.*

'I am.' Cathy stuffed a piece of toast into her mouth, 'See, eating . . .'

O'Rourke nursed his coffee. He looked like he'd had about as much sleep as she'd had. But he'd obviously been home to shower and had changed into a new crisp pale pink shirt. This one had delicate white stripes. He didn't address anyone in particular when he spoke.

'We're collating the information that came in last night from the media release and starting call backs this morning.'

Niamh turned to Cathy, her voice calm, 'Sarah Jane's been missing since Sunday. It's now Wednesday. There's been no contact at all with any of her family or friends, and it's totally out of character. Her room's been broken into. Too many women have gone missing over the past few years for us to sit back and wait to see if she turns up.' She paused, 'We're making this official.'

Hearing Niamh say Sarah Jane's name made Cathy suddenly want to cry. For about thirty seconds. Then she just wanted to hit someone. She chewed hard for a minute, struggling to stay focused, and not to let the anger building inside her spill over. Maybe she was just exhausted, but Sarah Jane needed her to stay in control. She worked well when she was mad – she won medals when she was mad – and right now she needed to take in all the available information so she could process it. She swallowed as Niamh spoke again. 'I know it's not news, but we're treating this as an abduction.'

She was right. Cathy knew Niamh was right. She'd known it from the moment she'd gone inside Sarah Jane's room and seen all the mess. Sarah Jane just wouldn't have vanished off the face of the earth without saying anything. Not voluntarily. And she wouldn't have smashed her room up first.

'Why on earth would someone want to abduct Sarah Jane?' Cathy's mum peered over her glasses, a tea towel in her hand, her tone innocent. When Cathy had called her to ask if she'd seen Sarah Jane, a tiny part of her had been praying Sarah Jane was having a bad day and had gone to have a cup of tea with her. It had happened before; Theresa seemed to be the go-to person for most of her children's friends to confide in. Perhaps it was because she never judged. She was one of the world's positive thinkers, could find the good in any situation. Almost.

There was an uncomfortable pause as everyone at the table – Niamh, Aidan, O'Rourke and Cathy's dad – turned to look at her mum. *Holy, holy feck.*

Cathy knew the answer, could see from their stony faces exactly what they were thinking. The vast majority of assaults and abductions were sexually motivated. It had to considered fairly high up on the list of possibilities, couldn't be ruled out. Sarah Jane wasn't exactly invisible in a crowd.

Before anyone said it, Cathy cut in, 'Why turn over her room? And take her computer? Surely it's more likely to be related to that than a random attack?' Cathy could hear the impatience in her own voice.

Niamh studied her empty plate, the knife lying precisely across the centre, 'We have to look at every possibility. She's come into contact with someone who has taken her away from her family and friends, who may mean her harm – for whatever reason. You know the stats. Six women have gone missing in the Dublin mountains alone.'

Niamh was right. Of course she was, that's why she was so good at her job she'd made it through the ranks to the top in an organisation that was only twenty-five per cent female. 'If that's a possibility, we have to review all those cases, and any serious assaults in and around the south city and Shankill.' Cathy could hear her lecturer's voice echoing in her head as she spoke, 'Offenders usually work in familiar territory. If there are any similarities, it's highly likely that the assailant knows the area where she lives, where she was last seen. They might not live there – maybe they work there. The key is that they feel comfortable in that area.' She paused, 'That's only about half a million people we have to worry about.'

Her mum put a fresh pot of coffee gently onto the long pine table, the aroma already filling the kitchen, and pulled out a chair, sitting down between Cathy's dad and Aidan, giving Cathy her full attention. 'Is someone who is going to commit an assault really going to be the same type of person who is going to abduct? That's a steep level of escalation.'

Cathy would have smiled if her cheeks hadn't been colouring. For someone who had left school at sixteen, her mum had more qualifications than all of them put together, had been studying at night since before Aidan was born, was the powerhouse behind Team Connolly. Even so, this wasn't the type of thing you discussed with your parents. But this wasn't about her. This was about Sarah Jane.

Cathy considered her words, 'Sex offenders don't start at abduction. They work up to it. Some of them begin as peeping toms, but then that gets boring, doesn't give them the thrill. They have to step it up a bit, stealing women's underwear off their washing lines, trying to get into their houses, graduating to serious sexual assaults.' Cathy paused, shifting in her seat uncomfortably, 'The next step is rape, and/or abduction. They don't all get there – some of them get caught before that, but it's a classic pattern.' Theresa opened her mouth to speak, but Cathy hadn't finished, 'There's been a load of studies done on serial offenders in the US. One suggests that the average number of a rapist's victims is seven, another one says eleven; in each case the violence escalates.' Cathy's mum was nodding. O'Rourke's eyes met Cathy's – serious, no agenda, his voice gravelly, 'We'll see who's known in the area – complaints and convictions – and we'll find out where they were on Sunday evening.' It was a procedure Cathy knew, but she needed to hear him say it.

It took a moment for Cathy to pull her eyes away from his as she said, 'Abduction takes planning. Whoever did this was organised, had to be. Sarah Jane's really fit – she beats the feck out of me, for goodness' sake. Even if she was really sick, like Billy Roberts was saying, she's not going to be tricked into going anywhere unless she trusts whoever she was with, and she'd put up some fight if someone tried to grab her off the street.'

'Previous assaults and convictions will be a starting point. We're working through all the staff in The Rookery too.' O'Rourke eyed her over the rim of his cup.

'Wasn't there a strong suspect in the missing women cases – could he be involved?' Theresa leaned forward, looking at Niamh at the head of the table.

'He was convicted of a serious assault and kidnapping, did ten years, but he's out of the jurisdiction now. We have to rely on other forces for information. We can only watch him while he's here.' Niamh sounded worried, 'But we have to be open to all possibilities.'

Cathy's mind whirred. The women who had vanished in Wicklow and Kildare had haunted her as she'd recovered from her injuries after the bomb. Unable to get back to boxing straight away, she'd needed to get her fitness back, as well as find space in her head to deal with it all, so she had started running. Perhaps she'd been running away from everything that had happened, she wasn't sure, but the mountains had been the perfect place.

Empty and silent, with only sheep for company, long tracks criss-crossed the hills, took her around the edges of silent lakes, and as she'd pounded the peaty ground she'd half expected to stumble over a body, to see the white of bone shining against the heather.

'We really need to know who Sarah Jane has come into contact with in the last few weeks.'

'Thirsty's got her phone log now, so we can go through it.' Cathy couldn't read O'Rourke's expression as he spoke – he was keeping his face deliberately blank.

Jesus, what had happened to her? She could be lying half dead somewhere in a bog up in the mountains right now . . .

Cathy took a slow breath, trying to still her heart. Sarah Jane needed them to be methodical now, to be professional. She needed them to find the strands, the threads that would lead back to her. Panicking wouldn't help anyone.

'This isn't a random thing, though – someone went to the trouble of taking her computer. They had her address.' It was the one thing they were absolutely sure of, and in her gut Cathy was certain they needed to work from there outwards.

Her mum leaned forward to check the milk jug, 'Perhaps it was someone she met online, on one of those dating sites, someone who was worried the computer would link him to her?'

Cathy sighed, thinking back to her last college essay. 'Maybe. Maybe someone was stalking her online, had befriended her.' She paused. It was a real possibility. 'The type of offender who does that is going to be very careful, a planner. And that type of person is not necessarily going to be acting out of character immediately after the event, or beforehand for that matter. They will be a habitual liar, could easily be a psychopath who finds it easy to kill.' Cathy stopped abruptly as she realised what she'd said.

Theresa reached across the table for Cathy's arm, squeezing it hard. Cathy's blurry eyes fixed on her mother's engagement ring, a cabochon ruby set in a nest of diamonds. Her dad had sold his first car to buy it. 'It could be nothing like that. You know what Sarah Jane's like. She's very highly strung, and she's *always* getting lost. Maybe she just needed some time out.'

Cathy threw her mum a glance. *Really?*

'Is there *anyone* you can think of that Sarah Jane's mentioned recently? Someone new on her radar? A JDLR, someone who gave her the creeps?' O'Rourke had asked her the same question at least a hundred times over the previous days. Cathy shook her head, running her hand across her eyes.

Cathy's mum cut in, 'JDLR?'

O'Rourke clarified, 'Just doesn't look right. Cop's rule of thumb.'

17

Cathy drew in a sharp breath, dizzy for a moment as reality collided with everything whirling inside her head. This whole situation was utterly surreal.

Blocking out the voices of the others sitting around her parents' kitchen table – O'Rourke crunching manpower numbers with Niamh, Aidan explaining the stages of a missing persons investigation to her mum and dad, Cathy picked up her coffee. The cup was almost empty but she needed to do something with her hands as the thoughts collided, her stomach churning.

'Sick with worry' just about nailed it. She always felt hyped up and anxious before a fight, but this was different, she felt like something was creeping up on her like a shadow that made half of her want to curl up into a ball in a dark place and cry, and made the other half of her want to get her gloves on and to draw blood.

How could someone just disappear? How could her friend just disappear? After everything that happened to her in remote parts of the world, after living in New York when she was younger – spending her school holidays there, for goodness' sake – she came to Dublin, one of the safest cities in the world, and this thing happens.

Cathy's sigh was ragged. But she didn't have time to let the dark part of her get stupid and miserable. Cathy looked around the table, searching for something positive. And there it was: *if*

Sarah Jane had had the power to pick the team to help find her, Cathy knew she would have chosen these guys. People who knew her, who had a personal reason for wanting her found.

Then something else struck her, like Sarah Jane was whispering in her ear, like she was bringing Cathy back, centring her, and she could hear Sarah Jane's laughter like a breath of wind stirring the tall pines beyond the French windows at the end of the garden. *None of the various scenarios in which Cathy had imagined herself having breakfast with O'Rourke had included her parents being at the table.*

Cathy sighed, the flicker of a smile warming her. O'Rourke was leaning over to talk to Aidan now, his voice hushed, his blue eyes earnest.

Oh heck.

Cathy tuned out – over O'Rourke's shoulder she could see it was beginning to get light outside, a bird lifting from the leafless branches of the old apple tree standing like a wizened crone in the middle of the lawn. The bright lights inside the kitchen made the garden look darker than it really was. Cathy strained to see out. If she just glanced at the French windows, all she could see was her own reflection, the scene at the kitchen table; but if she concentrated, if she looked really hard, she could see the garden, could see the apple tree. She shut her eyes for a second. If she concentrated hard enough, would she be able to see Sarah Jane, see where she was right now?

Abduction cases vied for attention in her mind: Jaycee Lee Dugard, Josef Fritzl. Jesus – she just prayed whoever had Sarah Jane, whatever the reason was, was keeping her alive; prayed that they could get to her in time. Before she went mad. Before the bastard killed her.

The odds might be against it, but Cathy knew that Sarah Jane would know she'd come for her. And she'd bring the might of the entire Garda Síochána when she did – all Sarah Jane had to do was to hang on, to stay alive long enough for Cathy to find her.

If Sarah Jane had been abducted, whether it was sexually motivated or not, she was a witness the perpetrator couldn't afford to let go. From burglary to abduction, they'd taken a lot of risk, which had to mean that whatever this was about, the stakes were higher.

O'Rourke interrupted Cathy's thoughts, sliding his chair back, the sound explosive on the terracotta floor tiles. He stood up, 'We're going to expand the team. I've got Paul Dobbyn in as bookman – he's good, he'll keep track of all the interviews and reports. We'll draw the rest of the team from Shankill and Cabo. And we've got J.P. in buckshee.' Cathy almost smiled. O'Rourke co-opting J.P. temporarily to the detective unit from uniform for the duration of the investigation was a good decision. J.P. knew Sarah Jane almost as well as she did. Leaning on the back of his chair, O'Rourke continued, 'I think the planning has to be key here. Sarah Jane's bright, she wouldn't be taken in by a stranger.'

Cathy's mum stood up to refill the coffee pot, and Cathy became conscious of the sound of the percolator as it started to bubble frantically behind them. Cathy held her cup out, the smell of the coffee kick-starting her brain. Adrenaline had her wide awake now, but she knew she'd need caffeine to last the day.

'I think we need to focus on who would take her computer – and why. Your mum could be right, it could be an online dating thing. Was Sarah Jane hooked up to any of those sites, was she writing a story on one of them? Maybe that's what her dad meant when he said it was a stupid thing for a student to do?' O'Rourke's face creased in a frown, 'If we could get hold of him, it would be a major step forward. CNN are doing their best, but it might take a while.'

They all knew Syria was a war zone.

Cathy shifted in her chair, 'If it was someone she met online there's no way an abduction is going to be his first offence. Like I was saying, a sexual predator's behaviour escalates to something like this, and planning is all part of that.' Cathy reached for the sugar, heaping the spoon high, and took a sip of her coffee, her college assignments flicking through her memory. Cathy pulled at her chain, running the scratched silver dog-tag pendant along it. 'Sarah Jane must have a connection to whoever has taken her, or how would they even know where she lived, about what she might be working on? This didn't happen by accident – we've got that on our side.'

'We'll talk to everyone she knows,' O'Rourke said.

'There has to be some link, something we're missing.' She paused, 'That fact alone gives us way more to go on than a lot of cases, we just have to work out what it is.'

'We need to hit the road, get this thing moving.' O'Rourke shouldered on his coat and started to head for the door. 'We've a full day ahead of us.'

18

The interior of the shop was warm, the soft lighting making it cosy, bright spot lights highlighting opulent 'buy me' displays. Cathy pushed off her hood as she closed the door behind her, shutting out the dull greyness of the afternoon. She'd wanted to get here sooner, but O'Rourke had said the boy was at school and his mum had insisted his routine couldn't be altered when she'd called the station this morning. Cathy had looked quizzically at O'Rourke – then he'd said that the boy had Asperger's syndrome and it had all made sense. And it wasn't like Cathy hadn't had plenty to do, reviewing the house to house statements, watching and rewatching the CCTV they had, but she'd been itching to get here all day.

J.P. arrived separately, and as she'd waited for him to park Cathy tapped her fingers on her steering wheel, unable to keep still. From what O'Rourke had said, it sounded like eight-year-old Jacob might have some valuable information on Sarah Jane's movements before she got into the cab on Sunday evening.

Now they were both here, Cathy looked around her, wondering if anyone was minding the shop. There didn't seem to be anyone here. She glanced at J.P. and thrust her hands in her pockets, trying to stifle her excitement – she needed to keep a lid on it. It was like any lead, it was more likely to blow out than turn into something worthwhile.

The clothes crowding the rails in the shop were gorgeous, well out of the range of her pay packet, she was sure. Even the pot crammed with pens beside the cash till looked like it would cost her a month's salary. Before she could speculate more, an attractive woman appeared from somewhere at the back of the shop, high cheekbones accentuated by her hair pulled off her face and twisted in a knot behind her head. She was elegantly dressed in tailored black trousers and a black silk blouse, the sleeves rolled up to reveal an armful of gold bracelets. She looked like she found looking good easy, like it was second nature.

'Can I help you or would you like to look around?'

Cathy pulled her warrant card out of her jacket pocket, 'Gardaí. A Rebecca Ryan contacted us about a missing persons inquiry? I'm Garda Cathy Connolly. This is my colleague, Garda Morgan.'

The woman's switch from a shop owner chatting to a potential customer to a worried mum was seamless, the strain suddenly showing. 'Thanks so much for coming. I hope I haven't wasted your time. He definitely saw the girl on TV, but he's had such a bad day at school, I'm not sure how much he'll be able to tell you.' She paused, shaking her head, 'He told someone in the playground he'd seen the girl on the news, that he had to talk to the Gardaí. They didn't believe him.' She held out her hands in a helpless gesture, 'I was afraid this might happen. He doesn't lie, you see, it's just something that makes no sense to him, he can't understand why people would suggest he might.'

Cathy smiled sympathetically, 'One of my brother's friends has Asperger's, I'm familiar with some of the issues. I know no two people are the same, but I get it.'

Rebecca looked relieved, 'Come upstairs. Jacob's in his room. I hope you don't mind waiting, but I'll have to get him out first so you can talk to him.'

Upstairs, Rebecca ducked under the edge of Jacob's single bed, trying to see him in the gloom.

'Please come down, Jacob, the nice lady I told you about is here. She's waiting in the living room. She just wants to talk to you about the girl you saw on TV.' The only light on in the room was his lava lamp, red wax blobs moving languorously in ink-blue liquid, throwing amorphous shadows over the pale-blue walls. Under the bed, the corner Jacob had rolled into beside the far wall was in almost total darkness. And he'd curled up behind a pillow so Rebecca couldn't even grab him.

'Not coming. I don't want to talk to her. She won't believe me either.' Jacob's voice was muffled, as much by the pillow as his location.

Rebecca sat back on her haunches and ran her hands over her face, her bracelets rattling down her arm, taking a deep breath. She knew if she slid the heavy pine bed out from the wall she'd be able to catch him – assuming he didn't bolt when he realised what she was doing – and bring him physically downstairs. But if she did that, she knew he wouldn't say a word – he'd bring a new definition to the phrase 'hostile witness'. She wasn't going to win this unless she came up with a brilliant idea. And just now she was right out of brilliant ideas.

Shifting her knees on the hard wooden floor, her wool trousers and Jacob's fire-engine-shaped rug too thin to make kneeling comfortable, she bent over and tried again.

'The lady needs to talk to you. The girl on the television has got lost and her mummy is really worried about her. If you got lost and I was worried about you, you'd want someone to help, wouldn't you?'

'No. I don't get lost. That's a stupid thing to do. Why didn't she have a map?'

Rebecca took a deep breath, trying to hold on to the ragged fluttering ribbon that was her patience; some days it was hard. Sometimes there were parts of her life that felt like a series of constant battles.

'Not everyone can read maps, darling, and maybe she forgot it. We aren't going to know until we find her. The lady just needs to know what you saw.'

'I told you, her hair was wrong on the TV. They got it all wrong.'

Rebecca fought to keep her voice steady, 'Yes I know, darling, but they need to hear it from you so they can get it right. It's like homework, sometimes you need to make mistakes to learn how to do things right.'

'They're adults, they should get it right.' Rebecca put her hands on the side of the bed and rested her forehead on it. The duvet smelled comforting, of the non-bio washing powder she used for his things.

'But that's the whole point, darling, they don't know how to get it right unless a really clever little boy who knows what *is* right can tell them.'

'I'm not little. I'm the tallest in my class.' She shook her head, would have smiled if this hadn't been so serious and she wasn't feeling so desperate. He *was* the tallest, she'd walked right into that one.

Rebecca paused. *How* was she going to get him to talk to them? She kept her tone level, light. 'I'm sorry – I know, darling. I meant that the adults need help, the Guards need you to help.'

'No.'

It was a very final sounding 'no'.

A gentle knock at the door made Rebecca start. The door opened a crack and Rebecca leaned back on her heels to see the detective – Cathy, did she say her name was? – peeping though the gap.

'I'm really sorry, he won't come out.'

Cathy stayed outside the door, 'Jacob, can I come in?'

There was a movement under the bed, but no response. Rebecca mimed a shrug. They really didn't have anything to lose. She gestured to show Cathy that Jacob was under the bed.

Cathy came in and hunkered down beside it.

'My name's Cathy, Jacob – except most people call me Cat.'

Before she could say more, Jacob interrupted, 'Have you got a tail?'

'Eh, no.'

'So that's a stupid name, isn't it?'

'It's a nickname. My real name's *really* long . . .'

'What is it?'

Cathy glanced at Rebecca, her face amused. Rebecca shook her head in mock despair and rolled her eyes. She'd explained downstairs that Jacob said what he thought, that he could sound cheeky, but he was actually just saying what everyone was thinking but had learned not to say out loud.

'OK, so my full name is Catherina Anna Maria Connolly. My mum wanted to call me Catherina Maria but my grandmother insisted on adding the Anna, after the Empress of Russia – she had high hopes for me.'

There was a pause. Then Jacob said, 'There was a Catherina Maria who was a composer. Are you a composer?'

'No, I'm with the Gardaí, I'm a detective.'

There was a pause, 'Just as well you're not called Maria Catherina then, she was a Dutch serial killer. She killed twenty-eight people.'

Cathy fought the laughter bubbling up inside her. 'How on earth do you know that, Jacob?'

'Google, obviously.'

'Obviously.' Cathy paused. Rebecca tapped her on the sleeve and mimed him playing with a smart phone. Cathy grinned. He was a bright kid. 'Are you good at finding things out, Jacob?'

'I like facts. What sort of car do you have? My mum's got a red Golf GTI 161-D-2. It was the second car made last year.'

'I've got a Mini Cooper. It's new too, but not that new. It's eclipse grey and it's really fast – a Mini like mine did nought to sixty faster than a Bugatti.'

There was silence for a moment, 'It was made faster – that wasn't a standard model.'

He'd Googled it. Cathy smiled to herself, 'That's very true. You're good at facts, aren't you? I like them too – it's my job to find things out. That's what we have to do in the Gardaí, we have to look at the facts to find answers.' She glanced sideways at Rebecca, 'Can you tell me any more facts about Sarah Jane? The girl we're looking for? Your mum says you saw her on the TV.'

'They got it all wrong. I keep telling you. Her hair was wrong.'

'Will you come down and talk to me about it? The photo they used on TV was one of mine, Sarah Jane had her hair down the day I took it. But I think you might have seen more than that – could we make a list?'

'I'm busy.'

'Jacob, please . . .' Rebecca put her head under the bed.

'No.' It was very definite. 'I've told you already.'

Rebecca pulled her head out and glanced at Cathy, shaking her head – *what could they do?* Then she said loudly,

'OK, I'm going to go and make Cathy and the other police-man a cup of tea and I'll talk to them. I don't want them to be cross.' Rebecca stood up stiffly, brushing her head off the pirate bunting criss-crossing the room, her bracelets rattling down her arm. With the lava lamp and all Jacob's pirate bits, sometimes his room felt like it really was under the sea. Which was a good thing. It calmed him. When things were getting crazy in the real world, this was where he came to sort them all out.

Cathy stood up beside her.

'Don't let them have my chocolate biscuits.' His voice was clear this time. *Nothing like getting your priorities right*, Rebecca through wryly.

'I won't. If you came down you could have a chocolate biscuit.'

Silence.

Rebecca gestured to Cathy with her head, leaning forward to whisper in her ear, 'Maybe if we leave him alone he'll come down on his own.' Pulling open the door of the attic bedroom, Rebecca followed Cathy down the narrow stairs.

Downstairs, the living room above the shop was calming and comfortable, in creams and oatmeal, but Cathy wasn't looking at the décor. She was sure Jacob had seen something, but how could they get him to talk to them?

Cathy glanced at J.P. He was sitting forward, too big for the space, uncomfortable in his grey pinstripe jacket and striped tie.

He never looked comfortable unless he was wearing his jeans and an old sweater. Fanning, with his crisp chinos and suede shoes, was always winding him up about how you could take the farmer out of the farm but you couldn't take the farm out of the farmer. Right now she was glad of that. There was a quiet strength and calmness about J.P. that made him a great interview partner.

Cathy turned to Rebecca, tried her best to sound calm, 'Can you tell us what happened from your point of view, how Jacob saw Sarah Jane?'

The soft glow from the fire lit Rebecca's face as she sat at right angles to them, her knees butting up against a chunky low oak coffee table. Jacob grinned at them cheekily from a jumble of photos on the mantelpiece, a row of brass shell casings sitting like Russian dolls beside them, picking up the lights of the room. Cathy pulled her pendant out from the neck of her sweater and ran it along the chain as Rebecca formulated her thoughts,

'We were in town, we did our shopping and went to McDonald's – the usual. We'd got back into the car when I remembered that I'd said I'd drop off my Saturday girl's sister's CV to The Rookery. Amy's sister is in London at the moment, but she'll be coming home soon and wants a job in town – she wants to get into modelling and TV and The Rookery has a reputation for launching the careers of its staff. I've known the manager for years.' Rebecca paused, pushing her hair behind her ear. 'I swung around there before we came home. Jacob was on his computer and I was only going to be a minute, so I left him in the car while I popped in.'

'Who did you talk to in there?' The sofa's vanilla leather creaked as Cathy moved forward. J.P. was silent beside her, but he was taking it all in, she could feel him watching everything.

'The manager. Billy Roberts. But he was a bit busy so I didn't hang about.'

'What time was it?'

Rebecca screwed up her face, thinking, 'About three, three thirty? I'm not totally sure, but about then.'

'So what happened next?'

'Well I got back to the car and Jacob was trying to get out. I'd told him to stay put, but his battery had run out so he was trying to come in to tell me.' Rebecca rolled her eyes, 'I should never have left him, anything could have happened if he'd gotten out of the car.'

'But he was fine, and you were only a minute,' J.P. cut in, his voice soothing, encouraging her to continue. Cathy kept her thoughts about leaving children on their own in cars to herself.

Rebecca grimaced, 'Yes, I suppose so.'

'So when did you find out Jacob had seen Sarah Jane? Did he tell you when you got back into the car?' Cathy tried to sound casual, to keep Rebecca relaxed.

Rebecca shook her head, 'No, he didn't say anything – he was focused on his battery going dead. I've got this inverter thing that runs the computer from the cigarette lighter so I rigged that up and we came home.'

'And everything was fine until . . .'

'Until the news last night. I'd had a good day in the shop and he wanted pizza.' Rebecca paused, 'Sorry, you don't need to know any of that. So we were sitting watching the news and the girl's photo flashed up, and he said the picture was wrong, that her hair was different. I was just so surprised. I asked him where he'd seen her and he said she'd been in the car park on Sunday. He'd looked up when his computer stopped and there she was with an army man he said – I think he just meant someone in combats – and that the man was helping her into a car. She had her hair tied into a fishtail plait. Jacob knows a girl who does hers like that and he's fascinated by it.'

'How does he know it was Sarah Jane?'

'He's got a brilliant memory, some things just stick. He recognised her.'

'Did he see them leave? Say what make of car it was?'

Rebecca shrugged, 'He said they drove past our car really close. I'm sorry, I think he might have mentioned the make but it didn't mean anything to me and I was just so surprised I didn't take it on board.'

'Perhaps you can ask him again when he's feeling better?'

'Of course. I'm so sorry.' Rebecca ran her hand into her hair, her face pained.

Cathy shifted on the soft sofa. Despite Rebecca's distress, she could feel the knots that had been gripping her shoulders from the moment she'd realised Sarah Jane was missing beginning to loosen. Only slightly, but she could feel an adjustment in the tension, hope slowly seeping through her like dye. *They were on to something, had to be*. She knew kids like Jacob, knew how bright they could be, how observant they were of stuff that other people took for granted or didn't even see. As Tomás's friend had explained to her, they looked at the world through different eyes. And they didn't lie.

'It's a huge help, don't worry. It's vital that we piece together her movements before she disappeared.'

Rebecca smiled weakly, 'Her parents must be distraught, I can't imagine anything worse.'

Cathy nodded, her mind temporarily with Sarah Jane's mum, Oonagh. Distraught was one way of putting it, hysterical closer.

Cathy had been keeping her updated, had suggested several times that she come up to Dublin, but Oonagh wanted to stay put. As she'd told Cathy, Sarah Jane knew where to find her and how to contact her if she stayed in Kerry. Cathy was sure Oonagh was trying to keep sane by telling herself that Sarah Jane just needed some space, that she would walk in the front door when she was ready. Cathy sure as hell hoped she was right. It was a nightmare for all of them. And they still hadn't been able to get hold of her dad.

'Does she have brothers and sisters?'

'No, she's an only child.'

Rebecca winced, 'I couldn't bear it if anything happened to Jacob . . . He's a handful, but I can't even cope when he goes to his dad's. I spend half the night worrying he's letting him have too much computer time or has forgotten to brush his teeth.'

Cathy leaned forward and pulled her card from her back pocket, 'If Jacob can tell you anything else or you can persuade him to talk to us, can you give me a call?'

'Of course. I'm sorry to drag you out for nothing . . .'

'Not at all. We'll check the CCTV in the area near the restaurant and find the car. You've been really helpful.'

19

Downstairs in Rebecca Ryan's shop J.P.'s phone had started to ring before they'd even got to the door. He checked the screen. 'Better take this. It's Bray again, that case is in court tomorrow.'

'Go on. You head off, I'll catch you later.'

He smiled politely to Rebecca and headed for the door, the phone clamped to his ear. Cathy turned to her, 'Your clothes are gorgeous.'

'Thank you. Come in one day when you're not working and I'll look after you.'

Cathy was about to reply when the door opened and a man walked in. Turning to acknowledge him, Cathy tried not to stare. He was drop-dead gorgeous. Over six foot, late twenties by Cathy's reckoning, shoulders broad under a plain khaki combat jacket, blond hair cropped close. And he looked vaguely familiar. *Where had she seen him before?*

Rebecca smiled at him, 'Can I help you?'

'I'm collecting some suits for my boss?' His voice was friendly, heavily accented, Eastern European ... Eastern European ... Cathy remembered where she'd seen him before – in Pearse Street Garda Station, he had acted for the Gardaí as an interpreter. She'd only seen him for a moment, but the girls in Pearse Street had been full of him.

'I have them here.' Rebecca slipped behind the counter and picked up three huge turquoise paper bags. The man let the door close behind him and Rebecca came around the counter and passed the bags to him. As he turned his back to Cathy, getting a grip on the silken rope handles, Cathy could see he had a tattoo of a clock on the back of his neck. A very strong-looking neck. He looked like he worked out. *Nice.* She could see what the Pearse Street girls had been talking about. Then her brain caught up. *He might be able to help her with those MoneyGram transfers, or know someone who could.*

Cathy suddenly realised she was staring. She hauled her eyes away but not before, swinging around with the bags in his hand, he'd caught her eye. She could feel her face colouring.

He flashed her a smile and, not quite knowing where to look, she half returned it.

'Have we met before?' He looked at her, amused, blue eyes dancing with mischief. *Christ, he thought she was trying to pick him up.* She added hastily, 'You're an interpreter, aren't you? I'm with the Gardaí.'

'Ah, yes I am. I'm not sure if we've met, I think I would have remembered. I'm Aleksy.'

Cathy almost laughed – he was smooth, she had to give him that. 'Cat Connolly. Have you got time for a quick chat?'

The bar in the Enniskerry Inn was empty when they walked in, a fire roaring in the grate. He pushed the door open for her, following her in, the turquoise bags still in his hand.

'What can I do you for?' The barman appeared, his black shirt rolled up at the sleeves, bald pate reflecting the lights above the recently refurbished bar. All mahogany and chrome, it was slick and trendy, but comfortable. Cathy opened her mouth to reply but Aleksy cut in,

'Are you serving food?' He turned to her, smiling, 'Do you mind? Will you join me? I know it's early, but it's my day off and I'm starving. I don't want to head back into the city yet.'

She hesitated. She wanted to go over what Rebecca had told her, but something was really niggling her about the girl she'd seen speaking to Sarah Jane in the shop. Cathy had looked through the MoneyGram dockets, and with the help of Vijay's uncle, found the one the girl had signed herself. The only problem was that her name was illegible and the address she'd given was an office building in the city centre with about two thousand staff. Cathy had tried the phone number she'd listed as her own, but it rang out. The money was being wired to a mobile phone account, and she knew it was a shot in the dark, but maybe, if Aleksy could talk to the person who owned the phone, they would be able to tell her who the girl was. Then Cathy might have half a chance of finding her . . .

Cathy could smell something delicious. She wasn't sure what it was, but her stomach was reminding her that she hadn't eaten since breakfast.

'I don't have much time but . . .'

'We've a bar menu in here or,' the barman jerked his head behind him, indicating a raised area separate from the bar, 'there's a better choice in the restaurant.'

'Restaurant would be great, thanks.'

Heading through the main bar to the cosy, dimly lit restaurant above, Cathy was impressed by the leather bucket chairs surrounding highly polished tables, tea lights flickering in the middle of each one. The last time she'd been here it had been stuck in a 1970s time warp – she had an overwhelming memory of everything being yellow.

Aleksy headed for a table in the corner out of sight of the main bar and shrugged off his khaki jacket, slinging it around the back of the chair. He was wearing a bright white T-shirt underneath it. A very fitted T-shirt. He definitely worked out.

'Come and join me.'

Cathy drew in a sharp breath. *The way he said it. Was he hitting on her? How out of practice at this dating thing was she?* 'Thank you.'

She pulled out the chair opposite him, unzipped her jacket and slung it around the back of the chair. When they'd left the shop she'd only intended to stop for fifteen minutes, to have a quick drink and see if he could help her, but maybe taking her mind off the investigation for half an hour was what she needed to get her thoughts straight, *like when you've forgotten someone's name but it comes straight back to you when you start thinking about something else.* She reached for her phone. 'Sorry, I just need to . . .'

She quickly texted J.P.: *Will b a bit longer. Can u update O'R? C u later.*

A waitress appeared and placed menus on the table as he said, 'So how can I help you, you wanted a chat?'

How much could she say? Cathy kept her voice low, choosing her words carefully, 'I'm working on a case – a girl who has gone missing, Sarah Jane Hansen. She was seen in town, in Dublin city, in a newsagents that's an agent for MoneyGram. She spoke to a girl in the shop who was transferring money to a mobile account in Belarus, and I want to find out who that girl is. The MoneyGram form she filled in isn't giving me any clues, so I thought if we could contact the people she's sending the money to, they might be able to help.'

Aleksy's face creased in a frown. She could see from the expression on his face that he understood how tricky the legal issues around getting that information were. 'It will help your investigation?'

Cathy grimaced, 'Sort of. My inspector thinks I'm wasting my time, but there's something . . .' She continued quickly, 'I want to get a full picture of all Sarah Jane's movements before she disappeared, to make sure we've got all the information.'

'Your inspector isn't ready to bring in an interpreter?'

He was quick, but perhaps she had it written all over her face. 'Not exactly. I'm sort of looking for a favour, really.'

'So have something to eat with me and I will owe you a favour.'

An hour later they were still the only people in the restaurant, although the bar below was beginning to fill, the sounds of a football match on Sky Sports and the low rumble of men talking reaching them at their corner table. Their conversation had been easy.

'So I have been in Ireland for just over six months and all I have seen is Dublin airport, the Phoenix Park, several Garda stations and here, Enniskerry, with the terrible roads. I only get out of the city when I'm running an errand like collecting these suits – I'm working as much as I can while the work is there, but that doesn't leave room for pleasure.' Aleksy took a sip of his coffee, the cup small in his strong and broad hand. *He wasn't wearing any rings.* Cathy deliberately looked at her own coffee, swirling the froth with a spoon. She'd hardly noticed the time pass. It turned out he was Polish, but spoke fluent Russian and several other Slavic languages, which was why he was so useful as an interpreter. They'd chatted about university, his military service, about life in Poland, about how he could work for a year in Ireland and earn enough for a deposit on an apartment back home. He was bright and interesting and very good company. As well as being very good to look at.

But right now she had a case to focus on. She needed him to agree to help her and see if finding the girl in the shop would bring her a step closer to finding Sarah Jane.

'Enniskerry is a very nice village – it feels like it's right out in the country but it's much closer to the city than I expected.'

'They call the road up here from the motorway the twenty-one bends.' She looked up, catching him looking at her.

He said quickly, 'I didn't count them, I was too busy trying to stay out of the hedge.'

'Ditch.' Cathy put her spoon down in her saucer and took a sip of her coffee.

Aleksy's forehead crumpled as he shook his head, confused, 'I don't remember a ditch, just a very thick hedge.'

'The Irish call a hedge a ditch. In Wicklow, anyway.'

'Oh, I see,' he said, nodding his head like that made perfect sense. 'But I thought a ditch was a gully in the ground, a trench for drainage, like in Holland.'

'Well that's a dyke, but in Ireland a hedge is a ditch. A ditch is a ditch too, but sometimes it's a drain.' She fought to keep her face straight. He was looking really confused now. He shook his head.

'Your language is different from the English they taught in school at home. I have a lot to learn if I want to be a good interpreter.' His smile was genuine, warm. 'So where else should I see while I am in Ireland? I need to work as much as I can while I'm here, so I need to make the most of my time off when I have it. I heard the highest pub in Ireland is near here?'

'It is.' Cathy turned to look over her shoulder. Beside the restaurant's main street door was a rack of tourist guides. Pushing her chair out she stood up stiffly, the muscles stretched in her training session this morning starting to tighten. Heading over to it, browsing for a moment, she selected a handful and, returning to the table, fanned them out.

'These are all fairly local and good places to visit. The pub is called Johnny Fox's, but next time you have a day off you should go to Powerscourt House – it was destroyed in a fire, but the gardens are gorgeous.'

'There seem to be a lot of things around here that are gorgeous.'

Cathy felt her face heat instantly, opened her mouth to say something, but Aleksy was already looking at the brochures as if delivering high-voltage compliments was the most natural thing in the world to him.

'And is this Johnny Fox's really the highest pub in Ireland?'

Cathy smiled, in part thankful that the conversation had moved on.

'Supposedly. It's years since I've been there, but they're famous for their Irish shows, and they have musicians in the bar most evenings playing traditional music.'

'I have never heard proper Irish traditional music. Is it good? Do they have leprechauns too?'

Now he was teasing her, his eye meeting hers with a wicked twinkle. She shook her head, laughing. 'No, of course not. I'm not mad about traditional music, but in the right place with a fire lit and a few pints, it's great.'

'Show me?' *Show him what?* 'Now, will we go up to Johnny Fox's? It's still early.' He glanced over at his phone, checking the time. It was only just six o'clock. 'How far is it?'

Cathy hid her surprise. She really wasn't in the mood for a date with a complete stranger, she'd too much on her mind, and she was due back at the station at some stage. *Although he was totally gorgeous, and they'd established that they knew people in common, people they'd both worked with, so he wasn't really a total stranger but still . . .*

Cathy opened her mouth, waiting for her brain to work out how to refuse without offending him, but a voice interrupted her, 'Can I get you anything else?' Another waitress appeared behind her, her accent different from the one who had served them earlier.

'The bill would be great.' Aleksy got there first, speaking as Cathy turned around, smiling. But her smile didn't last long.

'Two bills, please.' Working hard not to react, the words stuck in her throat.

This woman was pregnant. Very pregnant. Glowing and cheerful and expecting a baby. Cathy felt her stomach fall. Most of the time she could cope with seeing other women pregnant, but she'd had a tough few days, and when she was tired and emotional her own loss became physical, tangible.

Unaware of the impact she was having on Cathy, the waitress reached awkwardly over to collect their plates, her voice warm, friendly, 'Are you going into the bar?'

'No, no. We're heading up to Johnny Fox's.' Cathy's tone was definite. He might have said he'd owe her a favour if she kept him company in the restaurant, but he hadn't agreed to help her yet. This could be the break she needed, and right now she wasn't in the mood to let that chance slip. *There had been too many lost chances in her life already.*

Cathy stood up and grabbed her jacket.

'Where are you parked? You can follow me up.'

Cathy had forgotten how narrow the road up to Johnny Fox's pub was. With only the cat's eyes as guidance, she drove carefully as the road twisted steeply up into the mountains, hairpinning twice around an ancient granite garden wall that leaned drunkenly into the road. *You'd know the Romans were never in Ireland.*

Taking it slowly, she glanced into her rear-view mirror to see that Aleksy was following. She needn't have worried, behind her his headlights were glued to her tail, the Audi he was driving was jet black, new and sporty. *It probably wasn't his, but it was exactly the kind of car she'd have expected him to drive.*

A moment later she was bumping into the field across the road, a stiff wind buffeting the Mini as it gathered momentum crossing the open hillside.

The overflow car park was literally a field and unlit. With only a few cars parked in it, Cathy pulled in close to the gate, hopping out as Aleksy pulled in beside her. Her arms crossed tightly against the chill, she leaned on the side of her car, waiting as he swung open his door, reaching into the passenger seat for his heavy combat jacket.

'My God, it's freezing up here – quick, let's get inside.' Her dark corkscrew curls whipping across her face, Cathy pulled her hair out of her mouth as she spoke.

'Show me the way.'

Even in the dark she could feel the heat from his smile. *Maybe this wasn't the best idea she'd ever had.* She didn't want to lead him on – well … but she did need his help, and she wanted to find out more about him. *Purely professionally, of course.* She really couldn't think about starting a relationship now.

But Cathy knew what she was telling herself in her head and what her heart was saying were two very different things. She felt like she was being physically tugged in two different directions between finding Sarah Jane and getting to know Aleksy. Well three, if she was honest. O'Rourke was never far from the centre of her world either. *Christ, why was she such an emotional wreck?*

Across the road, possibly the most famous pub in Ireland looked warm and welcoming, an old bicycle leaning against the wall, an even older car parked near the door, battered tin signs for Gold Flake cigarettes between every glowing window. Cathy glanced at Aleksy from under her eyelashes as they headed across the narrow road. He had his hands thrust into his jeans pockets, shoulders hunched against the wind, looking her way. She quickly averted her eyes, but felt the warmth of his gaze on her. After everything that had happened this week, this year, his attention felt like the glow from the evening summer sun, unexpectedly warm. But she couldn't let him distract her from the job. Not now. This was about Sarah Jane. She needed him to help her with the case, with contacting whoever was receiving the money transfers.

Skirting a milk churn, Cathy pushed open the split stable door of the porch and was hit with a wave of wood smoke-scented heat as a woman pulled open the glazed inner door of the pub. The woman was too busy talking to her friend over her shoulder to notice Cathy, who stopped suddenly to allow her through. Behind her Aleksy bumped into her, his hand automatically moving to her waist, his body hard against hers.

20

Sitting behind his desk, the morning light chill, Dawson O'Rourke leaned back in his chair and twirled his gold Cross pen through his fingers, staring intently at it.

Cathy shifted position, easing the tired muscles in her butt off the sharp edge of the window sill, and stifled a yawn. Her movement seemed to bring him back to the here and now.

'Late night? You couldn't sleep?'

Cathy could feel a blush rising before she could stop it. *Why the feck did she blush so much? It wasn't like she had red hair or anything. She must have a red hair gene somewhere; that would be about right, McIntyre was always telling her she was too hot headed.*

It hadn't been a late night as it turned out, just a bit unexpected. The memory of Aleksy catching her as she had slipped in the mud on the way back to the car came back with a jolt – that and the feel of his arms around her and the softness of his lips as he'd kissed her. Well maybe she'd kissed him, she wasn't entirely sure.

Cathy cleared her throat, self-consciously rubbing her nose, hoping the layers of make-up she'd lashed on after her swim this morning hid the stubble burn. The kiss had gone on a bit longer than it should have done before she came to her senses.

'Not too late. I went up to Johnny Fox's.'

There was no point in pretending she hadn't, O'Rourke seemed to have an uncanny knack for knowing more about her life than she did. If she didn't mention it he'd find out and then he'd give her the third degree. Not that she had anything to hide – well not much anyway. He'd told her to leave the translation thing alone. But she wasn't good at leaving stuff that was niggling her. Aleksy had explained that they spoke both Polish and Russian in Belarus, plus Belarusian and a Polish Belarusian dialect – he reckoned he shouldn't have a problem speaking to whoever was receiving the money. But whether they'd talk to him or not was a different matter.

'Johnny Fox's was the last place Annie McCarrick was purportedly seen.' O'Rourke interrupted her thoughts, his tone speculative, surprised, 'You don't think her case has anything to do with Sarah Jane's?'

He sounded like he thought she'd been up there getting a feel for the place, was checking every avenue. Cathy was good with that. If her hunch about the girl played out she'd explain everything. But he had a point. She thought about it for a moment.

'They were similar in age and both American, but it was over twenty years ago. Hard to know, with zero leads in the McCarrick case.'

They had to consider every possibility, but unfortunately it wasn't like they were the only two twenty-somethings who had disappeared in Ireland in the last thirty years.

As she'd driven up into the hills last night Annie McCarrick had been on her mind – she and the other women who had gone missing in the Dublin mountains. But each of those disappearances had been apparently random, had occurred late at night in lonely, out-of-the-way places. Sarah Jane had vanished in a highly populated area. *Someone must have seen something.*

Aleksy had been dubious about contacting the people in Belarus, didn't want to get arrested for data protection violation but had finally agreed to give it a go. And then he'd kissed her. And she'd kissed him back. That had been a really bad idea. All the way home Cathy had had flashbacks to a fire escape in a nightclub and a short red dress and too much champagne and another misjudged moment that had left her with a lot more than stubble burn.

At least last night she'd stopped it – she'd ended up saying she was sorry, and pretty much left him standing there. Head down, she'd slipped into her car and had headed off down the road before she'd realised she still needed to get his email address to send him the photo of the MoneyGram form that she'd taken – just in case he could read the girl's name. She'd given him her phone number, and he'd given her his, but then when she'd looked this morning she'd realised that it hadn't saved properly. Would he call after she left him standing there? She knew she'd be able to track him down through the interpreter services list, it was just a matter of getting Pearse Street to have a discreet look and then getting over her acute embarrassment to speak to him. At least she knew she hadn't led him on. He'd been the one making all the moves. *Was that a good thing?*

'You need to try and get more sleep, you keep drifting off.'

Holy feck, O'Rourke must have been talking to her all this time and she'd totally tuned out.

'Sorry, what were you saying?'

'Run through with me what the boy, Jacob, saw again.'

In a moment Cathy was back with it, 'Jacob couldn't tell us much himself, I need to go back to talk to him if I can – he's had a bit of a meltdown though over the whole thing, so it's quite possible we won't get anything else out of him.'

O'Rourke rolled his hand, indicating she should get on with it. 'Did he see her?'

'Apparently, yes, she was getting into a vehicle with someone Jacob described as an army man – Rebecca, his mum, thought that meant someone in combats – between three and three thirty Sunday afternoon.'

'So presumably she was feeling OK then? What did our friend Billy have to say about that?'

Cathy shrugged, 'I rang him late last night as he was closing up – we need to get a proper statement from him – but he said Sarah Jane had a half-hour break at that time and usually went out for a sandwich.'

'And she started feeling ill when she got back?'

'Apparently so. The boys are going over the restaurant CCTV this morning and the ones we've pulled from the other premises on South William Street to see if we can find the car. Shouldn't take long. She's on the internal restaurant tapes up to three o'clock all right, then she's a bit of a blur on one of the cameras just before she left the building. Billy said she started feeling ill when she got back, and she was in parts of the building with no cameras afterwards – the linen room and his office.'

'So this army character might be able to shed some light on what made her ill? We need to find him.'

*

Irina let the tepid water of the shower play over her face. She knew she should get out, but her body ached. Her soul ached. And for these few seconds every morning when she shut her eyes, it was like she was back home again, like her alarm clock had just gone off and the house was waking up and she was getting ready for college. In the kitchen her mum would have the radio on, coffee on the stove and toast on the grill, the smell working its way around the tiny apartment, summoning her brother from his bed, rubbing his chest as he headed, yawning, down the hall, his hair sticking up in every direction.

But when she was in the shower at home, Irina had been bright and breezy, looking forward to her lectures, to seeing Meti. Now she was exhausted from working all night. Work that required her to strip for and have sex with men she didn't know, men who repulsed her, whose demands were warped and way beyond anything she had ever imagined possible.

The water ran cold and Irina jumped back against the shower curtain, a cry slipping out. There was never enough hot water for all of them. Dog Face, the woman who had brought them here, said they spent too long in the shower, that was the problem, that they had to be quicker if they all wanted it hot. Irina pulled the cold ragged cloth of the shower curtain away from her legs and reached for her towel, rubbing it hard over her skin, trying to shift the smell, the dirt. Would she ever feel clean? The shower would never be long enough or hot enough to shift the memory of fifteen men every night.

Slipping her feet, blistered from her stilettos, into a pair of cheap plastic flip-flops, Irina wrapped the towel around herself. It wasn't long enough, of course, barely covered her backside.

But for these few minutes at least, she was alone. The other girls – eight of them now the Slovakian one had gone – had gone up ahead of her to their tiny separate bedrooms, would be crashing out on the narrow single beds, getting a few hours sleep before they had to get up again and get their make-up on, ready for the early-morning punters, the ones who came before work.

Crossing the wet tiled floor, covered with strands of hair from the others, Irina bobbed down to look in the mirror above the single washbasin. It was flecked with toothpaste, smeared where someone had tried to rub it clean. But she could just see her face, bare now of the heavy make-up they all wore, her blonde hair hanging damp over her shoulders. She pulled her hair away from her face, tugging at the roots, testing to see if she could still feel it, to see if she was still human. She could.

The pain set her teeth on edge.

She was going to get out, was going to get home, was going to see Meti's face again, feel his soft breath on her face, feel him wrap her in his love like a feather duvet. She didn't have any choice, she was going to get out or she was going to die here, in the hell hole of a five star brothel in a foreign country.

And when she did get out she was going to take all her scraps of paper with her, the registration plates, the men's names, the names of the shops she'd been able to see out of the window of the apartments they'd been in. She'd written them all down in the dialect her family spoke at home, in what looked like poetry, in a sort of code. She shivered.

Upstairs, Irina could hear doors slamming, raised voices, bickering. Luisa, the Brazilian girl, crying. Luisa had been crying since they'd arrived, and it was getting on everyone's nerves.

Irina ran the phone number through her head again. It was like a rhyme now. And there was no way she was going to forget it.

She wished she could trust the other girls to help her, but she'd realised very quickly that that wasn't the way this worked. Control was about keeping them isolated, about having favourites, about playing the girls off against each other so they knew they could trust no one. Lonely and isolated, they were even more vulnerable. Irina thanked God again that her passport was Russian, that the address on it was the apartment they'd left when she was fourteen. It meant the men who held her couldn't find her family – they threatened all the girls that their families were in danger if they didn't comply, if they attempted to escape. As if beating them up and raping them wasn't enough. Her only option was to get a mobile phone, a safe one. The girl knew where they were, if Irina could talk to her, explain that they had been duped, that they had thought that they were coming to work as waitresses, chamber maids, supervisors . . . Irina shook her head at her own stupidity. The girl would help, Irina was sure she would help.

She just needed to get hold of a phone. And fast. They'd already been here longer than the other places – who knew when they would be moved again?

She *had* tried to get a phone already. The guys at the birthday party had been drunk when they'd arrived even though it was still early, had started buying champagne, heading straight for the private rooms to get the girls to dance. The rules were that the punters could watch the floor show, could get them to dance, but couldn't touch them.

'*They don't touch, you understand. You take them to the private room and dance and they get a taster. Then you get them into a bedroom.*' The voice of the man with the cowboy boots filled Irina's head again. He'd arrived in the huge living-cum-dining room at the top of the house that first day, his arms full of thongs and lace basques that looked like they came from the wardrobe department of a porn film.

He'd flung open their bedroom doors, calling everyone together. Some of the girls had been getting dressed, and had shrieked as he'd looked them up and down as they struggled to pull on their jeans. When they were all in the living room he'd explained the way things would work. 'Here you get paid for the number of drinks they buy you, twenty-five per cent of each one. They get a two-minute dance for free with every bottle of champagne. Show them what you've got. They can pay for up to an hour there. You get a bonus for every one of them you get into a bedroom. This is a classy joint, five star. You give the punters a good time and we'll look after you. When you've covered your board and lodging, you get the balance.'

He'd looked after them all right. They were fed and clothed and locked up, forbidden from speaking to anyone else working in the club. Most of the girls couldn't speak English anyway, and they were all different nationalities – Brazilian, Nigerian, Bulgarian, Romanian. They could hardly speak to each other, let alone anyone else. She'd pretended she only had a few words of school girl English – between that and the bits of Russian some of the others had, it was enough to get by.

But in reality her English was a bit better than school girl, it was degree level, and from the moment she'd realised what was going on, Irina had been listening, had started to make notes whenever she could. She'd found it hard, at first, to understand the accents here, there were many different ones, but she'd been sure they were in Ireland. All the buses she'd seen as they headed for the club had been blue and yellow, with Dublin Bus written across the front and down the side.

She just needed to get a phone. The guys at the birthday party hadn't been much older than her, all designer jeans and designer bum fluff. The one who had honed in on Irina, and had gestured that he wanted a private dance, hadn't been too bad looking, stubble concealing acne scars, hair thick with gel.

And he had his phone stuck in the pocket of his jeans.

Her heart had jumped when he'd pulled it out, tossing it on the table as he sat down, leaning back in the black leatherette chair in the booth, its chrome arms reflecting the soft red lighting, the deep plush burgundy carpet, stains and cigarette burns invisible in the muted light.

Inside the room, not much bigger than a broom cupboard, Irina had started dancing. Smiling like she enjoyed it, gyrating and running her hands over her body, making him want her. When he looked like he was going to explode, she had flicked her hair back and climbed onto his lap, arching her back, stretching the sequined bra over her breasts, rocking to the bass beat that filled the club. He'd been mesmerised, his mouth hanging open like a dog, had gripped her thighs so hard she could feel the bruises forming as he tried to hold her over his cock, rock hard inside his jeans.

Twisting, she'd leaned in to him. Pushing her long hair up over her head so it covered him too, she put the other hand onto the sticky table like she was using it for support as she worked her breasts close to his face, panting like she was enjoying it. Rubbing herself up and down his jeans, she'd tried to knock the phone onto the floor. She reckoned if she could keep him focused, get him upstairs and keep him pissed, he might forget the phone, and no one would see it in here in the dark. Maybe she could kick it to the side of the room when they stood up and, pretending she'd lost an earring, come back and get it later.

Irina turned on the tap and splashed her face with cold water. It had been a stupid plan, hadn't been a plan at all. If it had rung while another girl was using the room they would have found it straight away, and where would she have hidden it in the gear she was wearing? She'd have had to shove it inside her to get it upstairs or into the bathroom.

It had all gone wrong anyway. One of the others in the group had tried to take photos of the girl dancing for him and everyone's phones had been taken. She hadn't even managed to get the guy's phone onto the floor.

And then the bastard she'd made such an effort with had said he and his mate wanted two girls. They wanted to pay extra so they could both fuck both of them and then watch the girls go down on each other. Irina felt her stomach roll. They'd seen it in a movie, he'd said, laughing, looking at her thinking she couldn't understand his bullshit man talk.

When they'd got upstairs to the mirrored bedroom, the one with the red satin sheets, they'd said they wanted a floor show first, wanted to see the girls play. Then this boy and his mate had dragged her onto the bed, and both tried to fuck her at the same time, laughing when she cried out . . .

Irina shivered. When they'd finished she thought that was the end of it, but the first one had pushed her to her knees on the shag pile carpet, shoving her face into the other girl's crotch, rank with their cum and lubricant and massage oil, then climbed onto her like a dog, and made her lick until both of them came. Irina gagged again, just like she had then, turned the tap on full and washed out her mouth, the freezing spray from the tap splattering her breasts.

Irina rested her hands on either side of the basin and took a shaky breath. She couldn't take much more of this. She had to get hold of a phone.

'Come on, get a move on. I need to lock up.'

Behind her the door opened and Irina jumped, straightening up quickly, pulling the towel down behind her, her breasts exposed as she wrestled with it. The rules were no sex with the staff, but that didn't stop the guards taking every opportunity they could. And they were rougher than some of the customers.

*

Cathy bit down on her gum shield and hit the punch bag as hard as she could. Left jab, right jab, right hook, axe kick. The sounds reverberated around the empty gym like gun shots, the chains holding the bag rattling. It was early evening, and for once, thankfully, there was no one around. She'd hit the off button on the stereo as soon as she'd arrived, needing the quiet after an intense day at the station, going through statements and security tapes until she was seeing double.

Finally she was starting to feel more centred, having spent the last half hour training: skipping, press-ups, roll-ups, more skipping; pushing her body as far as it would go. Now she was soaked in sweat. Dancing backwards, she hit the bag again with an uppercut, grunting with the effort, with the impact of the punch.

'Hey lass, take it easy.'

At the other end of the gym McIntyre had materialised through the double doors. She'd known he was around, had seen movement in his office out of the corner of her eye. She'd been sure he was watching her through the etched glass, but she'd needed some time on her own, knew he'd understand. Normally if he wasn't already in the gym, she'd stick her head around the office door as soon as she arrived. But not today. Today she needed to get her head clear.

From the doorway, McIntyre called out, 'So what's the story? Anything new?'

Cathy couldn't look at him, danced back instead and threw a roundhouse kick at the bag, the sound of the thud echoing off the raw brick walls, the chain holding the bag rattling again.

'Nothing after she got out of the cab. The driver said he dropped her home but didn't see her go inside. Slug, her house-mate, is a total waster, has no idea whether she came in or not. Or when someone trashed her room, for that matter.'

Cathy let out a sharp breath, bit down on the gum shield again and tensed for another punch.

The next moment McIntyre was holding the bag. It was his military training, she knew, but it never ceased to amaze her how a man of his age could move so swiftly and silently across the gym. From his tattoos anyone could see he'd been in the Paras, but she'd heard that he'd been an instructor at the end of his career, training special forces. He was like a bloody shadow, invariably appearing when she was doing something she shouldn't be, like walloping that little prat before training on Monday. Jesus, Monday felt like a lifetime ago.

'Take it slow, if you get too tense you'll do yourself an injury. Try and relax.'

'Relax?' She almost spat it out.

He ignored her. 'Lift that right a bit, keep your elbow up.' She rammed her fist into the bag, 'That's better, that's better. Now fill me in.'

Cathy danced back, her gloves tight in under her chin, then went in with a left jab, and another. 'The bit that's really worrying me is this story she was working on, the one she'd had a row with her dad about.'

'The one about the lads and the horses?'

Cathy shrugged, 'Maybe. If that was it. Did you hear anything yet?'

She threw a glance at McIntyre. His face was thoughtful as he slowly shook his head. He would have called the minute he'd heard anything, Cathy knew.

'You're so alike, you two. Sarah Jane's just as headstrong and driven as you, and she's a fighter, she's hung on in every match to the bitter end. Telling her not to do something is – well . . . Her dad said it was dangerous, did he?'

'Yep.' Cathy planted a left in the bag, 'According to her mum, but you know what her mum's like. It's quite possible that she got that bit arseways.'

'Hmm.'

Another glance at McIntyre's sceptical face stopped Cathy in her tracks. 'What?'

'Ted Hansen's a war reporter, isn't he?'

'Yep. He's based in New York, but he's in Syria at the moment. That's why Oonagh panicked. He Skyped her to say that they'd had a row, but the connection dropped. She couldn't get hold of him again to see what they were arguing about, and then she couldn't get hold of Sarah Jane. O'Rourke's got half of CNN trying to reach him now, but he's out of comms, chasing a story in the desert.'

McIntyre didn't say anything, just stood looking thoughtful. Cathy shook out her arms and headed for the bench. She needed water. Opening the Velcro on her gloves with her teeth, she bent down to grab her towel, rubbing her face and neck before reaching for her water bottle. Still holding the bag, McIntyre watched her, then finally spoke.

'Have you got any idea what else she was working on? Apart from the horses?'

Unscrewing the top of the bottle, Cathy shook her head and spat out her gum shield. It was a lot easier to talk with it out. 'That's the sixty-four-million-dollar question isn't it? I wondered if it had something to do with drugs. Some of the lads are runners, aren't they?'

McIntyre nodded silently, then said, 'I've put the word out. Won't be long, I'm sure. But it sounds like you need to get hold of her dad. His judgement of a perceived threat is a bit different to everyone else's. If he reckoned it was dangerous . . .'

'That's what worries me.'

Cathy rubbed her eyes with the heel of her hand. This whole thing had been off the scale since she'd got that call from Oonagh Hansen. Could it get any worse? Cathy took a swig of her water, feeling her emotions welling up inside her. She had tried again to persuade Oonagh to come to Dublin, but she was insistent she stayed put in case Sarah Jane tried to contact her at home. Mobile reception was poor in that part of Kerry, and it made her feel more connected being close to the landline.

Walking over to the bench that ran down the side of the gym, McIntyre sat down and patted the polished wood next to him. 'Come here, girl, sit down. You need to conserve your energy.'

Cathy plumped down beside him, leaning forward, her elbows resting on her knees.

'You knew her best, girl, you need to keep on top of this. If she said anything that could give you a hint, it'll come to you. I know it will.'

Cathy felt him pat her shoulder. She still couldn't look at him.

The sob escaped from Cathy's mouth before she could hold it back.

'Ah come here, girl. Sarah Jane's a fighter, she's fit and she's focused. Whatever's happened, she'll be hanging in there.'

A moment later Cathy had buried her head in McIntyre's shoulder, as hard as stone, the tears flowing freely. He put his arms around her and rocked her, didn't say anything, just let her cry.

21

Cathy felt a whole lot better when she got out of the shower at Phoenix. Her muscles were still aching from her workout and her heart was still aching, but she'd turned the shower up as hot as it would go and spent a few moments just concentrating on the feeling of the water massaging the back of her neck. She'd read something on Facebook about mindfulness, about how it was good for your soul to clear your head and just be in the moment. This was the first time she'd tried it and it seemed to work wonders. After ten minutes in the shower, she felt stronger than she had done all day.

Wrapped in a towel, her hair pulled back, Cathy was reaching for a bottle of moisturiser when her phone pipped with a message. It was buried in the bottom of her kitbag and it took a moment for her to find it, her anxiety growing the longer she searched.

But it wasn't O'Rourke.

She couldn't resist a smile as she opened the message.

It was from Aleksy. He'd been called into Pearse Street Station to translate for a suspect, was she anywhere nearby?

Her thumb hovering over the keys for a moment, Cathy paused. She wanted to meet him, without question, but it was late and her plan had been to go home and try and get some sleep, ready for tomorrow. But she still wanted to give Aleksy the info on the account that the girl in the newsagent's had been sending money to.

She checked the time again and made her decision, texting back: *There in 20 mins. Meet you in the public office?*

Seconds later a smiley face appeared on her screen.

Pearse Street Station was busy day and night. A huge granite-clad building, just over one hundred years old, it had been the very first Garda station to welcome female officers. Whenever she came here Cathy thought about that, about the shock that must have reverberated into the very corners of the building when it was realised that ladies' loos would be needed.

Pushing open the heavy public front door, Cathy saw Aleksy immediately. He had his back to her, was ostensibly working his way through the notices pinned to the wall. Wearing jeans and a leather jacket, his hands in his back pockets, Cathy couldn't help notice that he had a very nice bum.

'Hiya. Sorry, were you waiting long?' Cathy hung slightly back from him deliberately. Feeling awkward.

He turned to her, the smile already on his face. Relaxed, friendly. 'No, just finished. Were you working?'

If she spoke fast she'd get past the whole awkward thing, 'No, I was at the gym. Phoenix, out in Ballymun. It's out on the north side of the city, but my coach runs it so I'm there about six times a week.'

He raised his eyebrows, obviously impressed. She'd told him a bit about her boxing when they'd been in Johnny Fox's, but modesty had prevented her from going into any great detail.

'Six times a week? That's very dedicated, you must be very good at boxing.' He spoke as if she had been keeping something back from him; technically she had, sort of. *Not that it was all that interesting.* 'You must tell me more. Where's good to get a drink around here?'

'Flannery's is nice. It's not far, and they do craft beers.'

A moment later he was holding the door open for her.

Flannery's was a Garda pub, its cheerful fire engine-red front opening onto an interior that was all dark wood and dim lighting, vintage signs hanging on the walls. Still busy after the 9 p.m. shift change, its clientele was predominantly male and unmistakable even in civvies. The tourists Flannery's attracted had no idea how well protected they were.

Following Aleksy in, Cathy was suddenly self conscious. Several heads turned in her direction, checking out who had come in, recognising her, checking who she was with, what their business might be. Cathy winced inwardly. By the morning the whole of Pearse Street Station would be gossiping about them having a drink together. So much had happened in her life that out of choice she felt more comfortable in Garda pubs, where everyone spoke her language, but maybe tonight it wasn't the best decision she'd ever made. She took a mental deep breath – why was she worried? They weren't dating, and even if they were, was it anyone's business but hers? Cathy mentally shook herself. Before the blast she wouldn't have given a damn what people thought, it was only now that she found her emotions on a knife edge. She needed to get a grip, that was all there was to it.

Aleksy headed for the bar as Cathy chose a small round table at the back in an alcove, out of the way so they could chat without being overheard. Sitting down on the bench seat, her back to the wall, she pulled out her phone, pretending she hadn't noticed the curious looks she was getting from across the room. She was known for her boxing and the bravery award that had got her into the detective unit so young, but then being targeted with a bomb on the job sort of made you stand out a bit. There were definitely days when she wished no one knew who she was. This was one of them.

She watched Aleksy discreetly as he leaned on the counter chatting to the barman, saw him nod to a couple of guys as he waited for their order. Obviously he was well known too. *Damn.* As the barman passed him a pint of Guinness and Cathy's bottle of Torpedo, a man Cathy didn't recognise touched him on the arm and said something quietly in his ear. Aleksy shrugged. In his fifties, the man was wearing a dark tweed jacket and looked more like an accountant than a copper. Cathy tried to get a better look at him as he moved away and headed for the Gents. *What was that about?*

'Who was that?' Cathy asked as he reached the table, her curiosity getting the better of her.

'Not sure. He thought he recognised me.' Aleksy took a sip of his pint.

'But you know a few of the lads here?'

Aleksy shrugged again. 'I haven't been working for the Gardaí that long, it sort of happened by accident. But I've spoken to a few of them, of course.'

'And what did the guy in the jacket say?'

Aleksy smiled, 'You have been in the detectives too long, Cat Connolly. It was a mistake, he doesn't know me. Now tell me about this number you want me to call.'

He'd neatly sidestepped her question. *Why?* But it didn't worry Cathy, someone here would know exactly who he was if she asked. That was if she had the energy. Cathy could feel her day catching up with her, she was getting tired and she had other priorities.

For one she wanted to get the bigger picture on these money transfers.

And she wanted to get to know Aleksy better. Seeing him again now, that was one thing she was very sure of.

She glanced across the table at him. He had the most amazing eyes.

She took a swing of her beer. Ice cold. She needed it. *Why do you always meet gorgeous guys when you have so much on your mind there isn't space for more?*

'OK, so I told you about Sarah Jane, my friend that's gone missing, and the girl she spoke to in the newsagent's.' Cathy pulled out her phone and searched for the photo of the Money-Gram docket to show him again. A moment later she found it and enlarged the image so he could see it more clearly.

Even allowing for the poor lighting in their corner, it was hard to read. Frowning, Aleksy picked up her phone and angled it to get more light on it.

'Can you email it and I can enlarge it and print it, see if I can make her name more legible before I ring?'

'Of course.'

'There's an Irish telephone number here.' He pointed to the sender's number listed on the docket, just above the amount and country it was going to, 'Have you tried it?'

Cathy nodded, 'It just rings out. Perhaps she's run out of credit. And the address isn't much more use, it's a huge office. There are so many Eastern Europeans living in Dublin now that without a name, they can't help.' She sighed, 'Two of my colleagues have been to talk to the guy she was with in the shop, but when he finally remembered he'd been there, he reckoned he didn't know her. He said he'd bumped into her in the street and was trying to get her phone number.' Cathy hesitated, 'I know it's going to be tricky. They might not talk to you at all – I wouldn't give out information over the phone to some total stranger.' It *did* sound mad now as she was saying it again. O'Rourke was probably right that it was a waste of time. He was usually right, but she needed to be sure herself.

'I'll do my best'. Aleksy reached out and rubbed the back of her hand, his touch hot.

Holy cow, she needed to concentrate. *She was sure his best would be pretty damn good.* Cathy knew if the information proved valuable, it was going to be tricky to explain how she got it to O'Rourke, but that was the least of her problems at this particular moment.

His touch had sent a super-charged bolt of something straight through her, which would have been manageable if her imagination hadn't taken over and her head gone into over-drive. He had the top buttons of his shirt undone. It was a heavy white cotton shirt with a denim panel on the inside of the collar that ran around his muscular neck. The lack of buttons only revealed a hint of what was underneath, but it was enough for her mind to fill in the gaps. She could feel her cheeks heating. Cathy shifted uncomfortably, pushing her back into the wall, trying to ground herself. This was a Garda pub, for God's sake, nothing she did would go unnoticed.

There were times in her life when she definitely needed to plan things better. This was one of them.

It was a long time since she'd reacted to anyone like this, but it was a long time since anyone she'd been vaguely interested in had been interested in her. For a moment her confidence faltered – was he interested or was it all in her head? Then she remembered the car park in Johnny Fox's. That had been very real. Very real and very fecking amazing.

And she knew now why she'd had to stop it.

Cathy drew in a sharp breath, trying to get back on track. She wasn't in a place right now where she could take on anything extra emotionally. Every spare particle of her was focused on finding Sarah Jane, on visualising her walking right back into her life, on working on all the information they had so they could identify the thing that they were missing.

Aleksy picked up his pint. He took a swig and, in doing so, moved his knee under the table to touch hers. And the fireworks went off all over again.

'I will make this call tomorrow and find out all I can. I'll say I bumped into her and she dropped her purse, and I found the number. Will that be a good idea?'

Jerked back to the pub, to the tiny table, to him sitting so close to her, Cathy took a swig from her beer, the bottle still chilled, the glass cold and damp in her hand. She cleared her throat, 'Yes, better not to mention the Gardaí, we don't want to frighten them – she might not have a work permit or something. If you can get her name, then I can try and track her down.'

'OK, but you know this might not give you the answer? Even if you find her, the chances of her knowing who your friend is, remembering their conversation, could be small.'

'I know, I just have a feeling . . .' Cathy couldn't explain. She looked down at the docket, a surge of emotion overwhelming her. There had to be one strand in all of this that they had missed, and if they could pick it up and follow it to its conclusion it would give them all the answers.

Aleksy picked up his pint again and his eyes locked with hers over the creamy head.

'Good evening. What are you doing here?'

O'Rourke's voice made Cathy jump more than she thought was even possible. Had she physically reacted? Christ, she hoped not. She felt like she'd lifted about six inches out of her seat, but she prayed that was all in her head. Turning to look at him, her face fixed in a relaxed, easy smile, she tried to slow her heart down. *What the feck was he doing here?*

Her response was accompanied with a wide-eyed, *what the feck's it got to do with you* look. 'Having a drink. You?'

O'Rourke's face was stony, 'Something similar.' O'Rourke turned to Aleksy, his eyebrows raised. 'Who's this?'

'Aleksy Janosik.' Before Cathy could respond, Aleksy put out his hand as if he was completely unaware of any tension radiating from O'Rourke.

'O'Rourke, Dawson O'Rourke. Cat's on my team, and we've an early start tomorrow.'

Aleksy shrugged, 'Good to meet you. Cat said she couldn't stay long.' He smiled, 'Don't worry, I'll make sure she's safely tucked up and gets her beauty sleep.'

Oh holy fecking God. Cathy grabbed her bottle of beer. Where was she supposed to look now? She could almost feel the steam coming off O'Rourke.

'Glad to hear it. I'll see you in the morning, Cat.'

She smiled weakly, and with a swish of his coat he was heading to the bar, the man with him someone she didn't recognise, but from the way the crowd parted in front of the bar, he was as senior, if not more so, than O'Rourke.

'He doesn't seem very happy that you are out.' Aleksy pulled a face, 'Are you not allowed a social life?'

Cathy shrugged. Her relationship with O'Rourke was complicated on a good day and it wasn't something she was going to even try to explain, especially with him in the same room. He was standing with his back to her now, but she knew him too well. He would be watching her in the mirror, she was sure. She couldn't blame him, really – when it came to relationships she had made some monumentally bad decisions in the past.

'I'm really sorry, I think I'm going to have to go. We do have an early start.'

Aleksy shrugged, his knee bumping off hers under the table. His smile was warm, understanding, 'It's fine, I understand. You need to find your friend. I will call when I have news from Belarus.' He got up from the table.

Cathy felt like hugging him, 'Thank you. Really. Thank you.'

Aleksy shrugged again, 'It's no problem, we'll talk tomorrow.' He leaned over and his lips brushed her cheek. 'I'll call you.'

As he turned to leave she could feel her face heating up, was one hundred per cent sure O'Rourke was watching. She picked up her phone and pretended to look busy, praying the blush would subside.

22

The station was relatively quiet when Cathy arrived. It was early, and she was ahead of everyone else.

After her chat with McIntyre last night, and the drink with Aleksy, however brief, her head felt clearer. As if all the emotion she'd been trying to hold in had been dulling her senses. Aleksy had already texted her this morning as she'd left the gym, *How r u doing lovely lady? I hope we can have another drink soon*, followed by a row of smiley face emojis. She'd texted back: *Me too, but now I have to work!!*

Aleksy was attractive and intelligent and easy to talk to. As they'd walked to the pub he'd told her his degree was in mechanical engineering – hence the clock tattoo – but for now he was working several part-time jobs – painting and decorating and translating while he looked for something permanent in his field. He planned to stay in Ireland for a few years, get a good job and buy a place in Poland that he could rent out so he'd be on the property ladder when he moved back permanently. He was like Sarah Jane, had a plan all worked out.

Not that vanishing off the face of the earth had been in Sarah Jane's plan.

McIntyre had given her a long look as she'd headed out of the gym.

'Keep me posted, girl. Everything, do you hear? I'll see if I can turn anything up.'

'Thanks, Boss.' She'd wanted to hug him again, to thank him for being there, to thank him for . . . well, everything. With his contacts, if there was a rumour on the street, McIntyre would hear it. She'd flashed a smile at him – it had been enough.

'That's better. Now you go talk to O'Rourke. He's a good one, he'll get this sorted, trust me.'

Now, looking around the empty recreation room that doubled as an incident room, Cathy felt like O'Rourke was here, some sort of ghost in his steel grey Louis Copeland suit and pale-blue shirt, unbuttoned at the neck, and Cathy felt a surge of thankfulness that this was his case.

He might get bolshie about her social life, but thank God this was still his patch, that he hadn't been promoted again. Cathy knew it would come, and a small part of her was dreading it. He could end up anywhere, posted to somewhere at the opposite end of the country. He'd become an integral part of her life since the blast, had been there to keep her spirits up when she hit the dark patches, the times when the shadows were blacker than black and threatened to subsume every glimmer of light.

It had been O'Rourke who had sorted out the incident when she first went back to work, when she'd lost it altogether and assaulted the bastard who had just beaten up his pregnant girlfriend. On the report sheet his broken jaw had been attributed to him tripping over his feet coming down the apartment steps, the paramedics attending substantiating their report. He'd tried to press charges, but hadn't got very far – she'd heard on the grapevine that Dún Laoghaire's busiest legal aid solicitor had laughed in his face when he'd turned up to make a complaint.

Then apparently a few words had been whispered in the guy's ear about backing right off by someone who definitely wasn't on their team, but who no one wanted to mess with. She put that one down to McIntyre.

It made her well up to think how so many people had closed ranks to protect her. Like they were helping her now, pulling out everything to find Sarah Jane.

The night she belted the girl's boyfriend O'Rourke had taken her home and sat with her while she'd cried. Cried for her baby and for what was left of her sanity. How could she be operational if she was likely to fly off the handle whenever they got a call about something personal? And if she didn't have her job, what did she have? Despite her natural positivity, she knew she'd go nuts if she spent any more time at home. It had been the next day, just after she'd got back from the gym, when O'Rourke had shown up at her door with the leaflets for Dublin City University. Something new to focus on that would keep her mind busy while she switched to light duties for a bit, found her feet again.

She was amazed he'd remembered. During one of their first night shifts together in Pearse Street, when she'd just come out of the Templemore Garda Training Academy, he'd asked her where she saw herself in ten years, what she wanted from the job. She'd told him how ridiculous it was that a national police force didn't have its own in-house profiler, that she was fascinated by what made people tick, that it was an area she'd always wanted to go into. But with all the other stuff going on in her life she'd lost sight of it.

Until that day. And it had all made perfect sense. The lecturers in DCU had been delighted to have her in the class, had agreed that she could work her tutorials around her shifts and training, and with something to keep her mind occupied she'd slipped back into the unit and had been fully operational again within weeks.

Cathy's sigh was jagged. She felt her jaw tighten, anger pulsating, giving her strength. They would find Sarah Jane, and then they would unleash the full might of An Garda Síochána on the perpetrators.

Cathy leaned back on the edge of the snooker table, a layer of plywood converting it into a passable conference table. In front of her a huge whiteboard had been set up on the back wall.

The incident board.

Photographs of The Rookery, of Sarah Jane, of her bedroom at home, were joined by arrows with times written in, in marker, caps sloping slightly to the right. Close-ups of her bedroom. *What had they been looking for? Who had been looking?*

Nothing made sense. But Cathy felt if she looked at these maps, diagrams and photographs long enough, she would see what they were missing.

Cathy knew the rest of the team would be coming in soon and the incident room would start to hum again. It wasn't that they weren't working 24/7 on Sarah Jane, but everyone needed sleep. Down the corridor in the detective office the early shift were busy processing statements, logging every call, every tiny detail that had been thrown up overnight by the reports on the news.

Behind her she heard the swing doors open. It was O'Rourke.

'You're in early.'

'Couldn't sleep.' Swinging around to face him, Cathy came to an abrupt halt. He was standing as if fixed in the doorway, hands in his trouser pockets jiggling his change. His face was pale, his eyes focused on a distant point on the floor. Avoiding hers.

'What is it?'

She could read him. They'd known each other too long, been through too much for him to be able to hide his thoughts from her. Something bad had happened, and he didn't know how to tell her.

'What?' Turning fully around, she suddenly felt faint, her stomach swirling. She leaned back against the snooker table for support. 'Spit it out.'

'A call came in, a few minutes ago. Guy walking his dog in the mountains, up beyond Johnny Fox's, has found a woman's body.'

Cathy opened her mouth to speak but no words came out.

'It might not be her, Cat. It might not be her.' He looked straight at her, his blue eyes filled with pain. He sounded like he was trying to persuade himself as much as her.

'We need to get up there.' Cathy moved so fast she caught herself by surprise, had closed the gap between them and was pushing past him to get out the door before she realised that he hadn't moved. He stopped her, catching her firmly by the shoulders.

'The lads are on the way up. There's no hurry, let them secure the scene first.'

'What do you mean there's no hurry? It could be Sarah Jane, I need to know.' Cathy's thoughts were tumbling around her head. Then she knew what he meant. There was no hurry because the body wasn't going anywhere. She took a deep, deliberate breath, trying to slow her heart, which was beating so hard she thought it would jump out of her chest. *Focus, she needed to focus.* Like those few seconds before she went into the ring for a fight. She needed to blank out everything else and to try and keep calm. But this wasn't like before she went into a fight. This was different. And she wasn't doing a good job of keeping calm.

'Do they think it's Sarah Jane?'

His hands were still on her shoulders, heavy now – it felt like he was resting them as much as preventing her from rushing out of the incident room. 'It's not clear. It's a white female around the right age. That's all we have until the team get up there. The witness was very distressed, his statement is confused.'

'Holy God.' Cathy's hand flew to her mouth. She could feel herself pale several shades and for a split second she thought she was going to vomit.

A moment later O'Rourke's arms were around her, holding her tight. She leaned her forehead into his chest, intensely grateful to him for holding her. She'd read somewhere that human touch was vital in times of crisis, it did things to your brainwaves – calmed them, like nothing else could. It had worked for her before, he'd been there for her then too, his voice and the touch of his hand a constant while she'd been in hospital. Right now, her brainwaves were on overload, and touch was what she needed. She wanted to stay here for ever.

He didn't move, rested his chin on the top of her head for a moment.

'It might not be her, Cat.' His voice was low, she could hardly hear him. He paused, 'Look at me.' Rubbing the tops of her arms, he pushed her away from him so he could look in her eyes. He spoke slowly, his voice low, in control.

'Take a deep breath and we'll head up. I need you to keep it together on this one. I need to know about distinguishing marks, tattoos, piercings.'

Cathy took a ragged breath and looked at him blindly, her eyes clouded with tears, not fully understanding. 'Why?'

'Parts of the body are missing. It's possible it was animal activity, but it's looking deliberate. We'll know more after the PM, but it's going to make identification harder.'

'What bits are missing?' The words caught in her throat. Tears were rolling down her face now.

'Her head, and her hands.'

Oh Holy God. Sniffing, Cathy looked at him hard, processing the information. And the cop in her kicked in, 'Clothes?'

'That's more like it.' O'Rourke squeezed her shoulders, 'She was partially dressed, but I don't have clear information. And we don't know for sure what Sarah Jane was wearing when she disappeared.'

'But I'd know. I'd recognise her clothes. I'd know if it was her.'

'Exactly.' He looked at her hard, 'You sure you're ready for this?'

'Yes. Yes of course I'm ready.' She closed her eyes and took a deep breath, counted to three. When she opened them again his eyes were fixed on hers. 'What are we waiting for?'

The road up into the Dublin mountains was narrow and winding, low walls preventing the car from slipping sideways into the fields and farmland that tumbled away steeply to their left. Cathy had only been half concentrating as O'Rourke swung up beside the little blue wooden church in Kilternan, her mind on Sarah Jane, on holding on to the tea and toast and peanut butter she'd had before she'd gone to training this morning.

She needed something else to focus on, to banish the pictures of Sarah Jane's headless, handless body lying in the undergrowth on the side of a mountain. She'd seen enough bodies to know exactly what it would look like. Hypostasis, post-mortem lividity, would leave even Sarah Jane's skin pale, her blood drained to the lowest point. And as to the rest, Cathy wasn't even going to go there.

Then they passed Johnny Fox's pub. And the memory of Aleksy's kiss shot straight back into her head. *As if there wasn't already enough going on in her life.*

It was all starting to merge together, like she was on one giant emotional rollercoaster. Cathy could feel her head beginning to pound. It was like the sands were moving, like things that had once been fixed in her life were all changing. All at once. Sarah Jane's disappearance, O'Rourke, meeting Aleksy, and now this – finding a body. Cathy dug her nails into the palm of her hand. *Please don't let it be Sarah Jane, please don't let it be Sarah Jane . . .*

She summoned a picture of Aleksy back into her mind, holding it in her head, trying to get back in the moment, trying to get out of this moment. He said he'd call today to tell her if he'd found out anything about the cash transfers. Maybe O'Rourke was right and the girl in the shop had only been asking Sarah Jane the time, but Cathy needed to be sure, and the only way to find out what she'd said was to ask her personally. And to do that, she needed to find her.

O'Rourke slowed at the lights. 'You OK?'

At the sound of O'Rourke's voice the image of Aleksy vanished. Cathy didn't answer, instead she pulled her necklace out of her sweater and ran it quickly up and down its chain.

'Watch it, you'll wear that out.'

'Sorry.' She didn't even know why she was sorry. Cathy dropped the pendant, unsure what to do with her hands.

Clasping her fingers together she pushed them between her thighs.

'Where are we going, exactly?'

'It's about ten minutes straight up here, just beyond civili-sation on the edge of the forest.' O'Rourke slowed behind an ancient dark green Fiat that was struggling with the incline, tapped out a tattoo on the steering wheel with his fingers. She could feel his tension, radiating like white heat.

'And the dog walker who found her?'

'The dog actually. It's a wolfhound, needs masses of exercise so he takes it out every morning before he goes to work, and then again in the evening. Apparently they walked the same trail Monday night.' He rubbed his hand over his face, 'I'm losing track of time. There was nothing there then – he reckoned – he was there pretty late too, he works shifts. So that narrows the window of opportunity a bit.'

Cathy felt O'Rourke glance at her. They were as tense as each other, it was like the atmosphere in the car was supercharged. And not in a good way.

The Fiat ahead lazily indicated left and slowly pulled between low granite pillars into a drive. O'Rourke had had enough.

'Sit tight.' Flipping the switch on the mobile blue light suction cupped to the dashboard, he put his foot to the floor, the BMW taking off. Driving a beautiful high-performance car had its definite advantages when you wanted to be some-where fast.

O'Rourke was an incredible driver, had ridden police motor-bikes when he'd started in the job. To survive on a motorbike you had to be three steps ahead, anticipating the unexpected and understanding your limitations. He brought that skill to the car, and was one of the few people she felt completely safe with driving at speed.

As the houses dotting the side of the road became less frequent, Cathy could feel they were getting closer. The road narrowed and O'Rourke slowed, the blue light still pulsating on the dash. Right now she was torn between desperately wanting to get to the scene and desperately *not* wanting to get to the scene. She didn't want to know, but she had to. *Please don't let it be Sarah Jane.* She was feeling physically sick again, like she had in the station.

O'Rourke slowed again, then around a bend she saw them up ahead. The technical bureau van had been wedged up on a slight incline that led off the road, like the entrance to someone's drive. But this wasn't a drive; a signpost indicated it was the start of a forest path.

A Guard in a fluorescent jacket was standing in the middle of the road directing traffic, reduced to a one-lane stop/go system, so approaching motorists could safely get around the row of Garda vehicles pulled in to the right. It couldn't have been a worse spot; a sign warned motorists to beware of their car slipping off the road for five hundred metres. O'Rourke flipped his indicator on and, recognising him, the Guard flagged him over. He pulled up across the front of the technical bureau van. They wouldn't be going anywhere for a while.

Checking the wing mirror as she swung open the door, Cathy felt the keen freshness of the air before she registered the cold. It was definitely chillier up here than in Dún Laoghaire, those couple of hundred feet making all the difference. Johnny Fox's was supposed to be the highest pub in Ireland; she doubted that, but there was no question it was colder up here than at sea level. *And Sarah Jane hated the cold.*

Taking a deep breath, Cathy reached into the back seat and pulled out her leather jacket, slipping it on as O'Rourke popped the boot open. He pulled out two white forensic suits, folded flat in clear plastic bags. He handed her one. As she ripped open the plastic and pulled it on, he reached in for blue foot covers.

'OK?'

'No.' Cathy paused, leaning on the back of the car to pull the foot covers on over her boots. 'Let's get this done.'

23

The body was hidden in a shallow grave, well off the path. In an effort to conceal it, a trench had been dug in the peat and loam under dense, overhanging laurel bushes, the leaves glossy, dark green, twisted with briars.

But whoever had gone to all the trouble of bringing her into the mountains hadn't bargained for a dog the size of a bear catching the scent and hauling her out by her ankle.

Squeezing past the white tech van, Cathy felt her heels sinking into the soft ground as she weaved between two mossy granite boulders marking the start of the forest track. To her right, hidden from view by foliage but very close, she could hear voices, recognised the Kerry accent of one of the forensics lads from the Phoenix Park. A moment later a flash of white revealed their exact location. The scent of pine blended with rotting leaves caught in her throat.

A branch had fallen across the path and Cathy paused, her hand on the cold lichen-covered bark. She ducked under it, unable to look in the direction of the white overalls, instead focused on the path in front of her; on the sound of the paper suit she was wearing, rustling as she moved; on the shapes of fallen leaves, dry and brittle; on the carpet of pine needles on either side of the narrow path; on an impression in the mud that looked like a huge paw print. She took a deep breath. She felt like she was going to lose the contents of her stomach at any moment.

'You *sure* you're ready for this?' Ahead of her on the path O'Rourke had stopped and turned.

Cathy took another deep breath, trying to still her heart. It felt like it was exploding in her chest. Emotion swirled inside her, common sense and experience mixing with a hollow feeling of dread that was worse than anything she'd ever experienced. She'd been in some pretty awful situations in the past, but she hadn't seen any of those coming.

This time, she knew exactly what she was in for. A headless corpse missing its hands. The corpse of a girl about the same age as Sarah Jane.

She had seen plenty of dead bodies and had attended PMs with guys bigger and tougher than her who had lost their breakfasts or faded away so that by the end, she'd been the last one standing. She'd got through up to now by distancing herself emotionally from those bodies, from the victims – it was just something you had to do in this job or you'd never sleep. But this time it was different. This time she was walking into a situation that had one of two definite outcomes. And one of those outcomes was that her best friend, someone she loved most in the world, the girl who perhaps knew her the best, was lying dead on the side of a mountain, and that someone had hacked off her head and her hands.

Cathy gagged. Closing her eyes she tried to centre herself, reached for the echo of The Boss's words of wisdom as he stood beside her just before a fight, his voice barely a growl in her ear. Blocking out all the sounds around her, she reached for his Belfast accent, felt his presence beside her, willing her on. *She could do this. She could do anything she put her mind to.*

Then she felt O'Rourke's hand on her shoulder. It was warm and firm and strong.

Looking up, she met his steely blue eyes, his face creased with concern.

'It's OK, I'm ready.' She paused, 'I'm ready. Just stay close to me.'

He put his arm around her, squeezing her shoulder. A few steps on they reached a break in the foliage, a tributary from the main path twisting back parallel to the way they had come. It was hardly a path at all, more an animal track, hidden from the road entirely, cut into the edge of the hill. Where the soil had eroded, knotted tree roots were exposed like clawing fingers.

Fallen branches cracking beneath her plastic-covered feet, the track wasn't wide enough for both of them, and dropping his arm O'Rourke took the lead again. Cathy felt overwhelmingly grateful. *She really wasn't ready to go first.*

Another few yards and the track opened into a tiny clearing, the path blocked by crime scene tape. To their left, above them, the hillside was sheer, reaching up to what looked like the ruin of a stone cottage. But that wasn't what drew Cathy's eye. Ahead of her, on the other side of O'Rourke, two white-suited techs were stooped under an overhanging bush. Hearing them arrive, one of them turned. He flashed her a sympathetic smile, the brief nod of his head acknowledging how difficult they all knew this was.

'Stick to the markers.' The tech pointed to a series of stepping stone-like discs that had been placed across the clearing, leading from the path to where he was standing. O'Rourke had stopped at the tape. She took a step to stand beside him.

This was it. Nobody could do it for her.

Summoning courage from she didn't know where, Cathy ducked under the tape and took a tentative step forward. She felt as if the forest had fallen silent around her. All she could hear was the sound of her own breathing and the beat of her heart. Another step and another, and the second tech who had been bending over the body turned and took a step back.

Cathy's cry was involuntary. Under the overhanging branches she could see a bare leg, long and slim. It still had smudges of dirt along its length where it had been pulled free from the loose, loamy soil around it. The foot she could see was bare, nails painted bright red. Cathy took another step forward, her eyes following the leg upwards. The girl was wearing a black T-shirt and not much else. Her underwear had been removed, her legs falling slightly apart, bruising around her thighs livid against her bloodless skin. She was lying on her back, one arm thrown above her head, the other trapped beneath her. Her T-shirt had been ripped open, a black bra pulled down to reveal generous breasts, even in death the nipples pink. Lying slightly downhill, Cathy couldn't see anything beyond the girl's shoulders, which vanished into the dense foliage. *Thank God.*

Cathy released her breath like a balloon exploding, 'It's not her. It's not her. Oh holy God, it's not her.' She clamped a hand over her mouth to stop herself from screaming.

'Absolutely sure?' O'Rourke's voice was loud beside her. She turned and buried her head in his shoulder. She could feel his arms around her as she fought back the sobs escaping from inside. It took her a moment before she could speak. Then she pulled back from him, looking up into his face.

'Yes. Totally. She hates nail polish and would never have a Hollywood – she's allergic to the wax.'

24

Cathy pummelled the punch bag like she'd never hit anything before, pounding it until her muscles burnt, until she reached the wall, and then went beyond it. The gym was empty, the strip lighting reflecting off the polished pine floor, one of McIntyre's mixes on the stereo, 'Eye of the Tiger'.

Left hook, right hook, snap kick. Her foot hit the red and white vinyl bag squarely, sending it flying in a broad arc, the chains attaching it to the ceiling rattling.

But it was stopped dead halfway, caught in mid swing by The Boss.

Taut as piano wire, Cathy was poised, ready to send the bag on a reverse axis as soon as it came back to her. But it wasn't coming back. She bent double at the waist, panting, sweat pouring off her.

'Hey, girl.' Niall McIntyre took a step towards her, steadying the bag.

Cathy tried to catch her breath, 'Hey Boss.'

Their fists met in a salute.

'What's the news?'

Cathy grimaced, avoided his eye, still bent over again, her gloves on her thighs. Her heart was pounding, thundering in her ears.

'Easy does it, take your time.' He let the bag swing free. Rubbed her shoulder.

She didn't know how to say it. Paused, grappling with the emotion inside her.

She spat her gum shield into her glove.

'We found a body.'

Her voice wasn't much more than a whisper. Still bending over at the waist she didn't see him pale. He didn't speak, gave Cathy the time she needed.

'In the mountains. I had to go up to the mountains and identify her, to see if it was Sarah Jane.' She took a deep breath and straightened up, but the next sentence came out in a sob, 'It wasn't her. Thank God it wasn't her.'

He threw his arm around her shoulders, 'Thank God.'

She barely heard him as he guided her to the low bench that ran around the edge of the gym. Sitting down, Cathy pressed her shoulders to the cold brick wall and stared blindly at the raised ring in the middle of the gym, red and white ropes connecting the padded corners of the square like sentences in a story.

'Tell me.'

McIntyre was leaning forward beside her, his elbows on his knees, his navy-blue vest revealing his tattooed, muscular arms. He might be pushing seventy but he was the wiriest, fittest person Cathy knew, had a core of pure steel. She took a deep breath, her breathing calming.

'It was someone else. Similar age, the pathologist thinks, it's hard to tell . . . But anyway, it wasn't her.'

McIntyre took it in, 'Do they know what happened to her, the girl?'

Cathy shook her head, 'PM is today. She was pretty badly beaten and her head and hands had been hacked off.' Cathy paused, 'Well not hacked – pretty cleanly removed, actually.'

McIntyre nodded, getting it. 'So someone doesn't want anyone to know who she is.' He paused for a moment. 'That's a gang thing, you know, Eastern European. It's their way of keeping order. Remember that guy in the canal?'

'The guy in the suitcase?' The investigating team had ruled out gang involvement early on, but the press had continued to speculate. 'They thought for ages that that was a gang feud.' She paused, 'They're checking missing persons now. Unless she was an illegal there should be some trace of her. Pathologist doesn't think she'd been there long, maybe a day or so.'

'Well that's good. Harder when the body's decomposed. Still, taking off her hands and head is pretty definite.'

'Prof Saunders said it was like the guy knew what he was doing. I mean not that he regularly went around chopping people up, but that maybe he was trained as a butcher or something.' Cathy grimaced. 'He removed a piece of skin on her ankle too that could have been a tattoo, but the good news is that her blood group is AB negative. It's really rare – only found in one per cent of the population. Doesn't tell us who she is, but the guys are going through the European missing persons lists so we might get a hit.'

'Lucky to find her at all. Those mountains keep their secrets.'

After her workout Cathy felt more able to tackle the incident room. Dragging her hair back into its messy ponytail she shoved her spare training gear back into the bag she kept permanently in her boot. She'd come straight from the station in Dún Laoghaire. O'Rourke had dropped her – silent, unable to speak – back to her car, and she'd hit the M50, heading straight for the gym.

Now her muscles ached almost as much as her heart, and she was grateful that the changing room was empty – rare around lunch time. Despite the shower and the lightweight black V-neck T-shirt and stretch pants she'd changed into, she was still sweating. She paused for a moment, resting her head against the cold steel of the locker, her eyes closed, grateful for the moment.

Reaching for her phone she turned her back to the locker door and checked her messages to see if she'd missed anything. A tiny part of her, the eternally positive bit of her psyche that found the upside in everything, kept thinking maybe, just maybe, Sarah Jane would text.

She hadn't.

But Aleksy had. *Tried several times but getting voicemail. Don't want to leave a message. Will keep trying xx*

Damn. At least he'd keep trying. And he'd signed it with two kisses.

Part of Cathy smiled to herself while the other part sighed. Even her eternally positive side was struggling with this, was boxing with the shadows, ducking and diving and trying not to get beaten down. And right now she really didn't think she had the emotional capacity to start a relationship, no matter how much her body was telling her it wanted to.

Shoving her phone in her pocket, Cathy headed out of the locker room to her car. There was something about mindlessly beating the shit out of a punch bag that helped her sort things out in her head, reorganise them so she could think clearly, and she'd really needed that today. Not that it had brought any solutions, but it had made her feel better. She'd spent a lot of time in the gym after the bomb blast, trying to come to terms with everything that had happened. The FBI case against Kuteli, the Russian who had orchestrated the attempt on her life, might have been a massive success and had landed Kuteli behind bars, but Cathy knew she'd never be completely satisfied until she knew he was a dead man. As well as the bit of her psyche that found something good in everything – the bit that had got her through all the shit that had happened – there was another part that didn't forgive. She was quite sure Kuteli was continuing his operations from inside prison, and until he'd lost everything that meant anything to him, like she had done, a little bit of her would still be after him. Some things you never forgot.

The tech guys reckoned the only reason she wasn't dead was because the two gougers who had booby-trapped her car had only been able to get their hands on a small amount of Semtex at such short notice. They'd probably reckoned on her filling her near-empty petrol tank as well – but she'd had so much on her mind that day, petrol had been the last thing she'd been thinking about. The car had been running on fumes.

Sometimes she wondered if she'd ever get back to the place she had been in mentally before Pete's party – that still felt like the start of it all – when her biggest problem had been staying away from chocolate right before a fight or having the hots for her boss. The pregnancy, losing her baby, almost losing her life, they had all become mixed up into something that had changed her, had made her more vulnerable on the inside, but harder on the outside. She couldn't let anything else hurt her now. It would take her too close to the edge.

She couldn't lose Sarah Jane. It was that simple. They were going to find her, and when they did, when they caught up with whoever had taken her, Cathy was going to make personally sure he or they knew exactly how it felt to lose something precious.

25

'This it?' Cathy's heart was thumping as 007 pulled the DDU car up outside a low-rise apartment block. She had literally just left the gym and hit the M50 when O'Rourke had called to say they might have a breakthrough. She'd headed straight to Dún Laoghaire, collected her firearm and dashed out to Fanning who was already waiting for her, the Vectra's engine running.

A call had come in from Ballymun Garda Station about a missing girl. A missing girl who was about the same age and height as their Jane Doe. Who lived in *Ballymun*. What were the chances of it being unconnected to Sarah Jane's disappearance? As she had listened to O'Rourke on speakerphone, Cathy's mouth had gone dry.

As Fanning had pulled out of the station car park, she'd got straight on the phone, willing McIntyre to pick up. He had the gym phone on divert to his mobile, and thankfully it hadn't rung for long. 'I need the low down on the O'Connors . . .'

Fanning turned off the engine and the unmarked Vectra's headlights, checking Google Maps on his phone. He took a look out of the window. 'Looks like it, and the lights are on. What did that coach of yours say about the family?'

'Well respected, keep out of trouble. Eithne O'Connor runs that flower stall at the top of Grafton Street. The missing girl is her granddaughter, her brother reported it.'

'Parents?'

'Boy said their mother was dead, overdose. Grandmother brought them up.'

It took a few minutes for Eithne O'Connor to open the front door, a few minutes in which Fanning had paced across the landing to the huge floor-to-ceiling window on the fourth floor and had a good look up and down the road, a few minutes in which Cathy had felt her heart beat so hard she could hear it.

As the glossed council blue door opened an inch, the rattling safety chain restricting its movement, Cathy could see the face of an attractive older woman, heavily made up, her bleached hair swept back in a complicated up-do, her fringe heavy. She looked like a sixties film star.

'Eithne O'Connor?' Cathy tried to keep her voice level, unemotional.

'Who's asking?'

'Gardaí,' Cathy flipped open her warrant card. 'We had a call from your grandson Jazz, he's very concerned about his sister Daniella.'

'He's not here.'

'Perhaps we could talk to you? We believe Daniella may have been missing for a few days?'

'She's not here but that doesn't mean she's missing.'

'Could we come in, perhaps? We'd like to chat to yourself and to Jazz.'

Eithne O'Connor didn't move, 'Like I said, he's not here.'

'Would you be able to call him? Or perhaps I could?'

Eithne O'Connor unhooked the chain and opened the door, 'Reported Daniella missing, did he? Well he would have been the last to see her. She's strong willed, that one, like her mother. Hardly ever here.' She shook her head, 'She works in that swanky restaurant, The Rookery. Reckons she'll get a job in TV or modelling if she plays her cards right. They all do, the girls who work there.' She paused, 'Sure they have to do a bit more than take orders to make that happen.'

Cathy worked hard to keep her face deadpan. *Daniella O'Connor worked at The Rookery.* When the boy, Jazz, had called into the station he'd been nervous and anxious, anxiety that had got much worse when they'd taken him into an interview room. According to the Garda who had logged the report he'd been upset and confused, unable to remember the name of the place she'd worked or where it was exactly. But from the weight of concern in Eithne O'Connor's face, the sadness in her eyes, Cathy had a feeling she'd reached her own conclusions. It was more than likely that she'd seen the news about Sarah Jane going missing from The Rookery, heard the reports of the body they'd found in the mountains that had ended up on the lunchtime news. She already suspected the body was Daniella's, Cathy was sure of it.

'Can we come in, please?'

Walking up the hill towards Keane's Field, the wind whipping the stray curls from her ponytail across her face, Cathy was still reeling from her conversation with Jazz's grandmother. Her stomach had been churning going into the flat. She'd had to break bad news before, had seen relatives hysterical with grief, some silenced, almost catatonic with shock. Eithne O'Connor had been neither, had listened to Cathy explain that they'd found a body, quietly, calmly. Standing in the middle of her living room, her arms crossed tightly, she'd lit a cigarette, the tremble in her hand the only sign that she was affected by the news. She'd wanted to be on her own, had refused when Cathy had offered to call a friend or relative.

'No point, is there, it might not be her. No point in getting upset about something that hasn't happened, is there?'

She'd given Cathy one of Daniella's hairbrushes, long blond hairs entwined in the bristles. The DNA contained in the root follicles would give them an answer. If this were a movie they'd have a result, whether positive or negative, in hours. In the real world, Cathy knew, it would take much longer. Then she'd asked where Daniella's brother Jazz was, and the pieces had come together suddenly like someone had punched her hard in the head. 'He's up by Keane's Field with that mad horse. Krypton he calls it. It's wild but he reckons he can tame it. Doesn't talk about anything else.'

Sarah Jane was writing an article about urban cowboys, and both she and Daniella had worked at The Rookery. Now they were both missing.

And in the missing persons report, Jazz had said that Daniella had a tattoo on her ankle – exactly where the PM had identified a piece of skin missing from body of the girl they'd found in the mountains. They wouldn't know until they had a DNA match, but the circumstantial evidence that the body they had found was Daniella O'Connor's was piling up.

Cathy wasn't ready to think about what that could mean for Sarah Jane.

Had they chatted in work and Daniella mentioned to Sarah Jane that her little brother was into horses? Had Sarah Jane spoken to him?

Whatever had happened, Jazz O'Connor could be the key to it all. *Sarah Jane couldn't be lying in the forest somewhere, or hidden in the mountains in a bog. It wasn't going to happen like that. Cathy wouldn't let it.*

Cathy shivered. The wind up here was biting, the fields lit only by glimpses of moonlight shining through the clouds. But she knew it wasn't the wind that was chilling her. O'Rourke was already waiting for Daniella's medical records to check her blood group, but the timing of her disappearance and the discovery of the body, the efforts to prevent them from identifying it, all raised red flags. And Daniella's photo, sitting on the mantelpiece in her grandmother's flat, had made Cathy start when she spotted it. If the same guy was involved here and was into tall slim young girls with long blond hair, he'd certainly found them.

Cathy needed to talk to Jazz.

She was probably mad to try and find him now, but every hour was another hour Sarah Jane was missing, another hour when . . . Cathy curtailed that line of thought abruptly.

Cathy had tried Jazz's mobile number but it had gone straight to voicemail. She looked around the empty hillside now – how on earth was she supposed to find him up here? She'd told Fanning to stay in the car, reckoned he had Gardaí written all over him; and whatever chance she had of getting these lads to talk to her, they'd run a mile if they saw him. Now she was beginning to wonder if she should have gotten him to drive further around, to start looking on the other side of the hill.

Ahead of her Cathy could see a path worn in the mud, dark against the dark of the grass, vanishing over the crest of the hill. Pulling her jacket around her she could feel her boot heels sinking into the soft ground. She was mad, one hundred per cent certifiable, but she knew she wouldn't sleep unless she tried to find him tonight. How far could he have gone? How long would he stay out here?

Cathy wondered whether Sarah Jane had walked along this path, had she come up here? This is where the lads from the flats hung out, where the horses grazed – you could see them on the crest of the hill from the motorway.

Then Cathy saw them. As she reached the top of the ridge, below her a herd of horses had gathered around an old plastic bath full of water. The horses shifted, and in their midst she could see a boy brushing down a piebald stallion. It was a huge horse, bigger than all the others, looked like it was part cart horse. Even from this distance, in the half-light she could see the long white hair over his hooves. The other horses, piebald and black, their thick coats shaggy and flecked with mud, stirred, and the boy looked up fast, like he'd been caught at something.

Cathy stayed where she was, waited for him to take her in. She lifted her hand in a half wave. He went back to brushing the horse. She couldn't see his expression from this distance but his body language was pure scowl. Tentatively Cathy started to head down the gentle slope towards him, stopping about fifty yards away – close enough to be heard but not close enough to spook him. Cathy pulled her warrant card out of her pocket.

'You Jazz O'Connor?'

'Who's asking?'

'My name's Cat Connolly, I'm with the Gardaí. You reported your sister missing and I need you to tell me a bit more about her. We want to find her.'

Jazz glanced up at her, his face hostile, 'I told them before, I don't know where she is, she's not answering her phone.'

'I know.' Cathy paused, sensing she might not have much time here, that she needed to build his trust but she needed some answers fast. 'When did you last see her?'

'I told them. She went to work on Friday night and didn't come back.'

'Can I buy you a burger? It's freezing up here. And I'm dying for a coffee.'

She hadn't thought he'd say yes, but Jazz had looked at her for a minute, and then turning back to the horse had put his arm around its neck and rested his head on its flank for a few moments. The horse had responded, turning its huge head to nuzzle him. Cathy didn't know if he was speaking to the horse, but then he patted it and turned to Cathy. As if the horse understood it had whinnied and tossing its head, trotted off to another part of the field to crop the tight grass. And as the stallion moved the rest of the herd scattered, re-forming closer to him.

Jazz watched it go and then, as if he was dragging his feet through quicksand, headed in Cathy's direction.

Fifteen minutes later they were sitting in McDonald's, a Big Mac and fries and chocolate milkshake in front of Jazz, a skinny latte in front of Cathy. The food might have dubious nutritional value, but they made great coffee. Out in the car Fanning was tucking into a quarter pounder with cheese, twisty fries and a side order of chicken nuggets. At least one of them was happy.

As Jazz emptied his chips into the lid of the Big Mac box, Cathy took him in. He looked younger than fifteen, skinny and pale, his hair cropped short, one ear pierced. His hoodie was flimsy; she wondered how he kept warm out there up on the hill.

She took a sip of her coffee. *Start with the easy stuff*, she could hear O'Rourke saying inside her head.

'Is the horse yours? He's absolutely huge.'

Jazz paused for a moment, a chip inches from his mouth, 'Sort of. He's wild, really. The others belong to different people, but no one can get near him.'

'He seems to trust you.'

A glimmer of a smile. Jazz didn't say anything. Cathy tried again, 'Do you ride him bareback like the others?'

Jazz shook his head. 'Not yet. No one can ride him. Last lad that did got thrown and got trampled.' Cathy could feel her eyes opening as she tried not to react. *Nice*. 'He hit him, the lad, had a whip and tried to race him. He's not that sort of horse.' Cathy took a sip of her coffee. 'I need to build his trust before he'll let me ride him. I've got a halter, though. I think he's nearly ready.'

Jazz nodded half to himself, stuffing chips into his mouth and speaking with it full. 'The guy who owns the land had a stable block built for when the weather gets really bad. It's over on the other side. He's got loads of money, keeps an eye on the horses.' He paused, 'So are you going to find Daniella?'

Cathy hesitated. Eithne O'Connor had asked her not to say anything to Jazz about their suspicions that the body could be Daniella's. She would do that in her own time. *'He's already lost his mum. They fought all the time, but Daniella looked out for him, they were close. He's been pining since she went. I'll tell him when you know for sure.'*

'I hope so.' Cathy left it there, 'I'm working on another case as well – Sarah Jane Hansen. She works with your sister at The Rookery.' She paused, 'She's my best friend.'

Jazz stopped chewing for a moment and something passed unspoken between them. 'I saw it on the news, that's what made me go to the station. It's weird, them working in the same place and both going missing.'

'That's for sure.'

'She came to see the horses.'

Cathy stopped breathing for a moment, 'Sarah Jane did?'

Jazz nodded. 'She had her break with Daniella one day and she said she was in DCU. They started talking and she said she was writing a thing about urban cowboys. Daniella said she needed to talk to me cos I was one.' He said it with a note of pride in his voice. Then, 'What does urban mean?'

Cathy took a slow sip of her coffee. 'Means town, like you live in the city – it means cowboys who live in towns.' Jazz took this in. 'What did Sarah Jane ask you about?'

Jazz shrugged, 'Just about how many lads kept horses, did we race them, like. And about school and stuff, and drugs – that sort of stuff.'

Drugs?

Was that what connected these disappearances? Dealers? Or was it customers? Did The Rookery's clientele look for more than food when they were ordering?

Cathy knew Fanning was working through the customers who had been in when Sarah Jane was working on Friday and Sunday. In his statement to the Gardaí in Ballymun Jazz had said he'd last seen Daniella on Friday night; did someone come into the restaurant on Friday who was involved in serious crime? Had Sarah Jane stumbled on a connection? The Rookery took contact details with each booking, it was just a matter of working through them all. And Cathy knew they'd be able to cross-reference who served which table that night and look for patterns in the weeks before the girls went missing. Restaurants all used digital systems these days. There would be a digital trail, and there were guys up in the Park, in headquarters, who loved nothing better than putting all the data together to create a clear picture.

'So tell me about Daniella. She wants to be a model?'

'That's why she's working there. Lofty, he's my friend, says she should be on Page Three. He wants to be a photographer, is always taking pictures of her.' He chewed for a minute, 'And because of the tips. The tips are only mighty.' Sarah Jane had said the same thing.

'Can you tell me about the last time you saw her?'

Jazz's face paled . . . *He'd heard the front door of the flat slam shut before he realised it had been opened.* Lying on his stomach across his bed, his comic in his hand, he'd frozen. His nan couldn't be back from the flower stall, could she? He'd glanced at the clock radio on the floor beside his mattress. Twelve o'clock. Jesus H. Christ, she'd only murder him if she caught him bunking off school.

But it couldn't be his nan. No way. Eithne O'Connor stuck at her pitch rain and shine, had never missed a day sick. Her stall was renowned for staying open longer than some of the shops on Grafton Street, she was always saying the best punters were the suits rushing home who had some apologising to do. That with the right chat a fella would take a bouquet twice as big as anything he'd buy at lunchtime and she could get rid of all the flowers that wouldn't keep.

But if it wasn't her, who was it?

He looked over his shoulder and a moment later a blond head had appeared around his bedroom door.

'What the fuck are you doing here? You're supposed to be at school.'

His heart pounding, Jazz had glared at Daniella, opened his mouth to say, 'And you're supposed to be at work . . .' but wasn't quick enough. She hardly drew breath, 'And what the fuck's that smell? Jesus it's rotten – you can smell it in the hall, what've you been at?'

Jazz had turned back to his comic, could already feel his cheeks colouring. If she saw him blushing she'd go on about it for a week. But there was no ignoring Daniella.

A moment later he could feel her presence at the end of the mattress, towering over him, his box bedroom filling with new perfume, doing battle with the more normal aroma of socks, and today, mud.

He'd tried to pretend she wasn't there, but it hadn't worked.

'Look at the state of this place. And why can't you take your fecking mucky jeans off before you go near the bed?' Daniella had sniffed the air noisily, making her point. 'Is that horse shit? Christ on a bike, how can you come in here covered in horse shit?'

Trying to keep his flushed face turned away from her, Jazz looked over his shoulder, speculatively, at his socks. They had once been red and white, and were now caked in mud around the ankles where his jeans didn't quite get down as far as his runners.

'It was raining. I was cleaning him up . . .'

'That horse? Have you been up on Keane's Field again? Jesus, never mind clean him up, why can't you clean y'self up? You look like something that crawled out of the Liffey.'

Jazz had screwed up his face and turned to glare at her. He wasn't any good at arguments, could never find the words as fast as she could. His silence didn't stop her, though. It never did.

'What on earth were you cleaning him with anyway? He's a mad one, don't you ever listen to Nan?'

'I got an old brush. I need a proper one. A curry comb.' The last part came out slowly, the new words hard to say, not nearly as confident as he'd heard the other lads saying it, talking about tack and hoof picks and stuff.

'Nan's going to fucking kill you. She told you to stay away from Keane's Field – that stallion will kill you if you try to ride it.'

What the hell did she know? Jazz had felt himself turning into one giant scowl. And why wasn't Daniella at work? Why the hell did she have to turn up and muck up his day? Lofty would be here in a minute – Jazz had been planning to take him up and show him Krypton while it was quiet. He'd brushed the horse's mane specially.

Well that had been the plan, but if Lofty knew Daniella was around he wouldn't want to go anywhere near Keane's Field.

From behind him, Jazz heard Daniella opening the wardrobe. Hers was so full she kept half her clothes in his room. Wire coat hangers screeched along the metal rail as she sorted through the dresses and tops.

'What are y'doing?' He turned over to see her pulling a sequinned jacket out of the wardrobe. 'None of your damn business, horse boy.'

'You going out?'

'Maybe.'

'Where?'

'To see a friend.'

Jazz looked at her, his head on one side. What the hell was she up to this time? 'So how long are you going for?' He'd wanted to get money off of her for the brush for Krypton; this wasn't good news.

'Never you mind.'

'I'm going to tell Nan. Tell her you went out in that skirt. She says it's too short, that you look like you're a working girl in that.'

'No you fucking aren't.' Daniella spun around as her tone changed abruptly. Jazz fought to keep the smile off his face. He'd hit a nerve.

'You're a toerag, horse boy. I'll leave her a note, tell her I've got an early shift in the morning, that I'm going to stay in town with one of the girls tonight so I don't have to get up at the crack of dawn to get into work.'

'In those clothes?' Jazz raised his eyebrows nonchalantly.

'Ah shut the fuck up. Don't you dare tell her . . .'

'Or what? You won't be here to know . . .'

'Or I'll fucking kill you myself.'

Jazz had rolled over and pulled himself up into a sitting position on the bed. 'No you won't. Nan really wouldn't like that.' He paused, making his face look thoughtful. For added emphasis he put his finger to his chin. 'I could be persuaded, though. Twenty should cover it.'

Daniella narrowed her eyes and glared at him. 'What you going to do with it? Buy pony nuts?'

'Maybe.' He had her now.

Reaching into the back pocket of her skirt, Daniella pulled out a wad of notes. Jazz's eyes grew wide as she rolled off a twenty and threw it over to him. Then, looking at him, she pursed her lips and peeled off another one.

'Here, don't spend it all at once . . . and don't say a fucking word to Nan, or anyone. You haven't seen me, right?'

Jazz had lunged for the money before she changed her mind.

Cathy's voice interrupted his thoughts, 'We checked with Daniella's manager this evening. He said he last saw Daniella on Friday night. He said she said goodnight to everyone and headed off as normal when her shift finished. How did she normally get home?'

'Bus usually. But she didn't get home. She said she was going out, but she didn't come home the next day either.'

'Exactly, so we need to find out where she did go. We're going back over the CCTV tapes to see if we can pick her up walking out of work.'

'When she's going out, she gets a lift home with her boss after work on Friday. She thinks I don't know she's seeing him, always tells Nan she's going to her friend's house.'

Cathy crooked an eyebrow, 'Daniella was seeing Billy Roberts?'

Jazz shook his head, 'No, her boss is this guy Richard Farrell, he owns the restaurant. He's always in the magazines, drives an Aston Martin. I think she said he lived in Foxrock.'

26

'We're on the way to Farrell's home address now.' Cathy spoke into her phone as Fanning spun the car around. 'Should be there in about thirty minutes tops.'

Without rushing him, Cathy had managed to get Jazz to finish eating and they'd dropped him back to his nan's. Now they were heading over to Foxrock. Fast.

As 007 accelerated out of Ballymun to head south on the M50, Cathy had the phone clamped to her ear, filling O'Rourke in, 'Sarah Jane knew Daniella, she came up here and spoke to Jazz about the horses for her article.'

'Jazz give any hints about why Sarah Jane's dad might think that was dangerous?'

'He said she was asking about drugs and his school and stuff. I wasn't getting a vibe that he was hiding anything.'

'And Daniella was dating this Richard Farrell?'

'Apparently. Jazz said he thought she'd gone home with Farrell on Friday night – she often did, apparently. But he hasn't seen her since she went to work Friday lunchtime.'

There was a pause while O'Rourke thought about this. 'Farrell's happy to talk now?'

'More than happy. He sounded really concerned, said he had no idea Daniella was missing.'

'Two young blondes who both worked in his restaurant disappearing within a few days of each other is a bit of a coincidence whether he claims he knows about it or not.' O'Rourke said it half to himself. 'Call in as soon as you can, the team are going through the CCTV tapes of the surrounding premises. The camera that covers that car park behind the restaurant is out of action, apparently.'

'Another coincidence.'

'I was just thinking that.'

Foxrock was the Dublin equivalent of millionaires' row, huge houses with even huger gardens set back off a broad road – high, solid gates hiding the treasures inside each house. Cathy had been inside a couple of these properties before, had been stunned by the luxury – black and white tiled halls scattered with ancient marble busts, original oils on every wall.

'It's this way, if Google's right. Roscrea Close.' Fanning hit the indicator and pulled left between two narrow granite gate pillars.

'You sure? This looks like someone's drive.'

'I think it was, once.' Fanning slowed as they passed an imposing three-storey manor house on their left. 'Must have sold the land.'

Driving carefully down the narrow lane, wooded heavily on both sides, Fanning had his headlights on full beam. It was pitch dark. The headlights picked up movement and Cathy jumped as a fox shot across the road. 'Holy feck.' Her hand flew to her mouth. 'My heart.'

Fanning shot her a grin, about to comment, but she gave him a look. She wasn't in the mood.

A moment later Fanning swung around to the left and a security light blazed on, illuminating huge electric gates set into high, rough stone walls, a tiled driveway meeting the lane.

'Obviously he's doing OK. Must be a lot of money in posh food.' Fanning ducked to look out of the windscreen and get a better look at the property.

'More than you'd think . . .' Cathy trailed off as the gate began to roll open. Fanning accelerated up the incline. The driveway curled around landscaped gardens to the porticoed front door of a mock Tudor mansion, walls built from aged red brick, roof tiles designed to look uneven, handmade. Lights glowed like jewels around the front door.

Inside, the house was just as palatial.

Relaxed in designer jeans, tooled cowboy boots and a navy cashmere sweater pulled over a white T-shirt, Farrell greeted them at the front door, the sound of barking coming from somewhere behind him. He was younger than Cathy had expected, late thirties or early forties maybe, his deceptively natural-looking sandy hair tousled. Opening the door wide he ushered them into a massive marble-floored hallway, a huge staircase rising to a mezzanine level. Cathy looked up to see a balcony that ran around the whole hallway.

'Come in, please. This is really terrible, I had no idea Daniella was missing, what's happened?'

Leading them into a living room, Fanning's mouth almost fell open. It looked like something out of a *Hello!* shoot. Two huge black leather sofas seemed to float in a room that was bigger than huge, floor to ceiling windows along one wall looking out over an Olympic-sized indoor pool lit only by star lights under the rippling water. The lighting was low in the living room too, chart music playing through some hidden sound system in the background. There was definitely money in the restaurant business.

Farrell collapsed onto one of the sofas, pulling one leg underneath him, then leaning forward, his face anxious, said, 'I'm sorry, can I get you a drink? Tea maybe?'

'No thanks, we won't keep you long.' Cathy sat down on the other sofa, Fanning beside her.

'Nice pool.' He nodded towards the window.

Farrell looked at it vaguely, 'Thanks. Need to keep fit, you know how it is.'

Cathy wasn't so sure about that. He was good looking, trim but soft. His idea of fit was different to hers.

'So can you tell us when you last saw Daniella?' Cathy wasn't in the mood to pussyfoot about.

Farrell shook his head, 'This really is awful. I picked her up after work on Friday night and dropped her to the bus stop on the main road on Saturday morning. I had a business meeting in Gorey later that afternoon, so she said she'd get the bus back. That's the last time I saw her.'

Cathy paused, waiting to see if he followed it up, filled in the blanks. *Like why one of his staff was staying overnight.* He didn't. 'So you and Daniella are in a relationship?'

Farrell ran his hand through his hair, pulling at it slightly like he was worried. He picked up a heavy crystal glass from the table beside the sofa and swished the amber contents around before he answered. He took a sip and grimaced, 'Sort of . . . Well, yes. Nothing formal, and it doesn't really do to be dating your employees, so we needed to keep it quiet.'

Cathy was sure Daniella hadn't been impressed with that arrangement. Maybe dating a working class girl from inner city Ballymun was the problem, even a stunning one.

'You know she's only seventeen?'

At least he had the decency to look a bit sheepish, 'Eh, yes. She's almost eighteen, though, and she's very mature. We have a lot in common.'

Cathy raised her eyebrows slightly. *She bet they did.* 'Have you been seeing her long?'

'A couple of months. Like I said, it wasn't formal.' He paused as Cathy looked at him. *Not formal? What the feck did that mean? He just had a quick shag when he felt like it?*

'I thought she'd started seeing someone else, actually. She usually calls during the week, but I haven't heard from her since I saw her at the weekend.'

'Did you try to call her?'

He shrugged, reaching for his glass, 'Her phone went straight to voicemail. I thought she'd blown me out.' *And why would she have done that, exactly?* Cathy didn't say it out loud, instead said, 'So just run through what happened on Saturday, did she say she was meeting anyone on the way home?'

He shook his head, 'No, she just said she wanted to go shopping in town on the way back – I gave her some cash. She usually gets the bus.' He paused, 'Her grandmother's a bit of a dragon, and I don't think Daniella told her that we had a thing. She was never keen on me dropping her back to Ballymun in case someone saw us.' He paused, his face strained, 'I shouldn't have listened to her. I should have dropped her home. Do you think someone followed her from the bus?'

Fanning sat forward on the sofa, his voice hard, 'At this stage we've no idea what happened to her, we're keeping all lines of inquiry open.' *He didn't like Farrell.* Cathy smirked to herself, *Perhaps 007 wasn't all bad.*

'We're also investigating the disappearance of Sarah Jane Hansen, a student at DCU who also works at The Rookery.'

'I know, that's terrible, I saw it on the news. And then the *Daily Mail* called. They are always the first out of the blocks.' He grimaced, 'She'd only just started though, was part-time. I don't think I ever met her.'

'She's a waitress, like Daniella. She started at the end of the summer. In fact we've reason to believe Sarah Jane and Daniella worked together and knew each other quite well. Billy Roberts didn't think to mention it?' Cathy's voice was sharp.

'No. No, he didn't. But I've been out of the loop a bit the last few days . . .'

Out of the loop? Avoiding the press more like. Cathy was getting the disctinct impression that he was far more more worried about the bad publicity than what had actually happened to Daniella and Sarah Jane. Cathy took a deep breath, fighting her temper. Right now she wanted to grab Richard fecking Farrell by the neck and make a mess of his pretty face. And from the tension she could feel radiating off 007, he wouldn't be far behind her.

Instead she smiled at him sweetly, 'We're going to need to take a DNA sample, for elimination purposes, if you don't mind.'

27

The yard was packed when Fanning drove under the security barrier and swung around behind Dún Laoghaire Garda Station. The night shift was out, preparing for the bars to close, their personal cars filling the car park, punctuated with a row of riot vans and, today, a huge sailing boat. Cathy didn't even have the headspace to work out why that was here – drug seizure, probably; she was used to seeing the unexpected, but a double-masted yacht resting on a trailer was something she hadn't anticipated. Beyond it, Cathy's Mini was tucked in the back corner of the car park where it would be less likely to get damaged by colleagues flinging open car doors when the shift changed at 3 a.m.

Above them, Cathy could see O'Rourke's light was on in his office.

Fanning unclipped his safety belt, 'I'll get the coffee.'

Cathy glanced at the clock on the dash – it was well past eleven, 'Sounds like a plan.'

Upstairs, O'Rourke was pacing. She wasn't even through the door when he started firing questions at her, 'So what have we got? Start with the young lad, let's see how the pieces fit.' He obviously wasn't in the mood for preliminaries.

She took a moment to get everything straight in her head. She was still reeling from meeting Richard Farrell and his apparent ignorance of what went on in his restaurant. Fanning had managed to get them out of the house without her hitting him, but only just. She hadn't spoken all the way here, fighting her need to break something.

Pushing the door closed behind her, Cathy headed for her usual perch on the window sill. The cold night air had done her good, and she was feeling a bit calmer now, but there was something about all this that didn't quite tally in her head. If she was less tired she was sure she'd see it, but right now she felt like it was blurred and in the distance. If she ran through everything maybe they'd get there.

'The last time Jazz O'Connor saw his sister was before she went to work on Friday. Jazz told me Daniella regularly went home to Foxrock with Richard Farrell after work on a Friday. He owns The Rookery, is Billy Roberts's boss. There must be some serious money in food though – his house is incredible – he's got an indoor heated swimming pool.' O'Rourke pursed his lips, acknowledging her point as Cathy continued, 'Farrell claims he last saw Daniella when he took her to the bus stop on the N11 on Saturday morning.'

'He see her get on it?'

'He parked at the stop and she waited in the car with him until it arrived, then got straight on.'

'There are traffic cams all the way along the N11 and they have CCTV on all the buses.'

'They sure do.'

'Time?'

'He reckoned around ten in the morning.'

'I'll talk to Dublin Bus. The team are already checking all the tapes from around The Rookery for three thirty on Sunday, to see if we can find this car the young lad – Jacob, is it? – saw. Be handy if we knew what we were looking for, of course. We'll get them to look for Daniella leaving on Friday evening too.'

Cathy sighed, 'His mum reckoned Jacob might have said what sort of car it was but the make didn't register with her as something she recognised or she thinks she would have remembered. She's working on getting him to tell her again.'

O'Rourke rolled his eyes, causing Cathy to bristle, 'Don't go there. It's not Jacob's fault. We'll get it. Without him we'd have no idea this had happened at all.'

He pursed his lips, 'Next move?'

Cathy pulled her phone out from her back pocket and glanced at the time. It was almost eleven thirty, 'Actually I want to go talk to Billy Roberts again.' As she looked at the screen, her brain sifted the information they had so far. Billy Roberts had been helpful, but . . . 'He should be shutting up shop shortly. I want to see what he can tell us about Farrell's relationship with Daniella. I know the team are working their way through questioning the staff, but I think he knows a lot more than he told us the last time. And I know we've asked him before but I want to see if he's remembered anything about where Sarah Jane usually went for her break, see if anyone's mentioned seeing her leave the building at three thirty.'

At that moment the door opened and Fanning backed in carrying three mugs.

'Timing is everything in life. I never thought I'd be pleased to see you, 007.'

O'Rourke grinned as Fanning put the mugs down on his desk, passing O'Rourke one, before turning to Cathy, 'And sugar for you, Cat, although—'

'Don't even think it, Fanning. I'm not sweet at all.'

He opened his eyes wide, 'Got it.' Picking up his own mug he stood cradling it in his hand as Cathy moved to the visitors' chair in front of O'Rourke's desk and took a sip of her coffee. She caught O'Rourke exchanging an amused glance with Fanning. *Fecking men.* She wasn't in the mood for backchat right now.

Ignoring them, Cathy opened her phone, hitting dial. A moment later someone in The Rookery picked up.

'I need to speak to Billy Roberts. It's Detective Garda Cathy Connolly.'

Cathy could feel O'Rourke and Fanning watching her. A few moments later she heard a familiar voice.

'Billy? Hello, this is Garda Cathy Connolly, we've got a few things we need to follow up with you this evening. Can you hang on for us?' Her tone didn't give him an opportunity to say no. Hearing his reply she glanced at the clock on her phone again. 'We can be with you in twenty minutes.' She paused as he replied, then, 'I think it needs to be tonight. We won't keep you.' She glanced at O'Rourke. 'Great, we're on the way.'

'He not keen?'

Cathy shrugged. 'Would you be? Long shift and then we call.'

'Two of his employees have gone missing.' O'Rourke's voice was steel edged.

He didn't need to tell her. Cathy stood up, taking another swig of her coffee, 'Any news on the girl's body?'

O'Rourke shook his head, 'Early days. Saunders reckons she died of asphyxiation: he's found semen in her oesophagus.'

'Sex game gone wrong?'

O'Rourke rolled his eyes again, 'Can't speculate at this stage, but it gives us a DNA profile to work off when we have a suspect. And he's sure she wasn't dismembered in the mountains where we found her.' He grimaced, 'Not enough blood. Saunders reckons she's been dead about four days and the decapitation was post mortem.'

'And the rest of her?'

'No sign yet.' A moment of silence fell between them. Cathy knew he was thinking the same thing as her: the last time a headless corpse had been found – in a suitcase in the canal – the head had never turned up, despite the Garda investigation and then the Trojan efforts of one of Ireland's best investigative journalists to uncover the truth – she'd almost got there, but not quite. They both knew that with no dental records or even an opportunity for facial reconstruction, identifying the body could turn out to be a waiting game. The circumstantial evidence might be strong, and when they got Daniella's medical records and checked her blood group that could bring them a step closer, but they couldn't assume it was Daniella O'Connor until they had a DNA match, which could take a while. It was entirely possible this girl was totally unrelated to their case; although no one else had been reported missing, it had to be said. And as Cathy had said to Fanning earlier, you'd think someone would miss a girl of that age, that she'd be top of the list of missing persons. It never ceased to amaze her how some people seemed to fall through the cracks of society.

Could you be missing if no one had lost you?

Cathy fought back the images of a girl's violated body lying partially concealed by fallen branches and overhanging bushes on a cold lonely hillside.

She put her mug down on O'Rourke's desk, getting ready to leave, when Fanning said, 'Any news on Sarah Jane's dad?'

'CNN still haven't found him. I'm not sure how you can just disappear in this world of modern technology.'

'Sarah Jane has.' Cathy hesitated, 'The disappearances couldn't be connected, could they?' She tried to keep the note of panic out of her voice.

O'Rourke grimaced, 'Let's hope not. Her dad won the Pulitzer for an investigation into the links between organised crime and terrorism, didn't he?' He paused, 'But apparently this trip he's doing something on jihadi brides, so unless ISIS have kidnapped Sarah Jane it's unlikely. And they are exhibitionists. We'd have had a statement or a video by now if they were involved.' He said it matter of factly, but his eyes were far from calm as they met hers across the room, connecting them for a moment.

'Christ.' Cathy shivered, breaking his gaze and pulling her pendant from the neck of her sweater, running its chain across the bridge of her nose, 'Ted disappeared before, in Afghanistan. He wasn't captured, but his cameraman was. They were filming for Channel 4 and something went wrong. Sarah Jane couldn't say much about it.' Cathy paused, 'He's always in the middle of something. She told me he was filming the British army and almost got blown up in Sierra Leone.'

'I think it's an occupational hazard.'

Cathy rolled her eyes, 'Some occupations are definitely more hazardous than others.'

28

Fanning swung into the car park behind The Rookery and pulled on the handbrake. It took them several minutes in the dark to find the door Billy Roberts had directed them to, concealed between several industrial-sized wheelie bins. It wasn't marked, had no outside handle, was plain and almost invisible, its navy paint blending with the dark brickwork in the shadows. Only an entryphone beside it indicated there was anything on the other side.

Cathy took a step back to look around the car park, at the camera locations here and at the back of The Paradise Club, while Fanning buzzed.

Seconds later the door opened; Billy Roberts had obviously been waiting for them. He looked tired and annoyed.

The narrow corridor that led into the back of the kitchens was as brightly lit as the working area itself, and had the same grey lino on the floor. To their right, a door to the locker room was standing open, the long mirror inside catching Cathy's pale face against her black polo neck as she passed. The next door on the left was closed but Cathy knew it was the CCTV viewing room Billy had taken herself and O'Rourke into. Billy led them into his office. The table light was on, illuminating his desk which was scattered with long rolls of till receipts, bags of coins and a form of some sort he was filling in. A huge calculator sat beside it.

'I'm just finishing the cash.' Sitting down behind his desk he moved the calculator and the till rolls to one side, 'So how can I help?'

This time Cathy sat in the visitors' chair, Fanning hanging back leaning against the wall. She wanted to see Billy Roberts's face and reactions as she ran everything past him. She didn't mess about with a preamble. They were all tired.

'We've a witness who suggests that Sarah Jane got into a car in the car park here between three and three thirty on the afternoon of the day she disappeared. Can you shed any light on that?'

Billy shrugged, 'Like I told you on the phone, she had her break around then. Three fifteen, I think, she often goes out to get some fresh air in the afternoon.'

'Have you any idea who she could have been meeting?' Cathy watched him as he shook his head. From the expression on his face, he seemed very sure he didn't know. Cathy was about to push it but changed her mind. Instead she asked, 'How long is her break?'

'That one is thirty minutes. Gives everyone a chance to sit down and get something to eat. They get a longer one too but it's later, depending what time they start work.'

'Did she speak to you before she left?'

Billy indicated his desk, 'I was stuck in here. It was only when she came back and I saw her in the locker room I thought she looked sick. She said she was fine, though. I pulled her off the floor and told her to sit down in here. She kept saying she'd be OK. But she really didn't look great.'

'Did you have any indication that she was unwell before she went out for her break?' Cathy leaned forward in the chair. *What had happened during those thirty minutes? Who had she met?*

'None at all.' Billy shrugged again. He was getting good at it.

Cathy tried a different tack, 'Did you have any customers on Sunday who could have been described as looking like they were in the army? Maybe in fatigues or combats?'

Billy's brows knitted in thought, but he shook his head, 'I'm sorry, I don't think so. We're pretty formal here so I think I would have noticed. Maybe she arranged to meet whoever it was. Have you checked her phone records?'

'We will do.'

They had already, but Cathy wasn't about to tell Billy Roberts that. Sarah Jane hadn't made any calls on Sunday afternoon at all. They were combing her phone records looking for calls made to unexplained numbers on previous days, but so far had drawn a blank.

'And tell me a bit about Daniella O'Connor, I believe she works here too.'

Billy raised his eyebrows, surprised, 'She did work here. If she shows her face here again I'll be firing her. She's not shown up for work all week and isn't answering her phone. Little madam has left me right in the lurch.'

'You don't think there's anything strange about that?'

'What, her not coming to work? She's a lovely girl, but she's north side, you know. Not exactly university material like Sarah Jane. She's very popular with the customers, though – pretty.'

'Popular with the boss too, from what we hear.'

Billy looked at her archly, 'I don't know what you've heard, but I wouldn't know anything about that.'

'Does Richard Farrell normally date his employees or was this the first time?'

Billy pursed his lips and didn't answer. Fanning snorted behind her. Billy Roberts was obviously starting to get on his nerves too. For someone who was supposed to be managing a restaurant he didn't seem to keep a very close eye on his team.

She tried again, 'Does he?'

'He's young, he's good looking and he's loaded. We have some very ambitious young ladies working here. Some very attractive young ladies. These things happen.'

'How long had they been dating?'

Billy was about to shrug again when he caught Cathy's eyes. 'A couple of months, I don't know. Daniella started getting a bit mouthy around then, complaining if her shifts didn't suit her, wanting Friday nights off. It's usually a sign.'

'And is Richard Farrell around much?' Cathy was beginning to wonder why Sarah Jane hadn't mentioned him, but then she wasn't impressed by money, would have had a different perspective to Daniella O'Connor.

Billy yawned. 'He's in and out. I call him every night with the figures. He trusts me to run the place right so he doesn't have to be in every day.' He continued before Cathy could comment, 'I really don't know what else I can tell you.' He opened his hands in an expansive gesture. 'If I think of anything important, I'll be straight in touch.'

'Tell me how you know Rebecca Ryan.'

Billy's look of surprise changed to puzzlement. His voice was guarded as he replied, 'We worked together years ago – in the hotel business in Spain. I went there after the Leaving Cert and we both ended up working in a five-star resort near Puerto Banus. Pop stars and millionaires. No paparazzi, very private. Her parents were killed you know, tragic. It was in all the papers. I went to the funeral and we hooked up again. We meet up every now and again for a drink. She's very busy, runs a nice little business in Enniskerry. I send any customers I can her way and she recommends The Rookery . . .'

As Billy closed the back door to The Rookery firmly behind them, Cathy pulled her jacket around her. The night had turned cold. Fanning was at the car before she'd gathered her thoughts. He pipped the central locking and jumped into the driver's seat, waiting for her.

But Cathy's mind was whirring, digesting the information – or lack of it – that Billy had given them. She needed a few minutes to think.

She thrust her hands into her pockets and tried to visualise Sarah Jane walking to a parked car. Who had she been meeting and why?

She walked forward a few paces to get a sightline from under the archway where Rebecca had said her car had been parked. Pivoting on her heel, Cathy looked back into the car park. It had been the middle of the afternoon, and assuming the wheelie bins were in the same places now as last Sunday, Jacob would have been able to see about a third of the car park. The back door of the restaurant was hidden from view, but he'd have seen Sarah Jane quite clearly as she walked across to any of the marked parking bays in the centre of the enclosed yard.

It looked like they had a clear half-hour window to check on the tapes. One of the restaurants across the road must have picked up the vehicles entering and leaving. And Cathy wanted to get back to that security guy, Nacek, to find out if he'd seen the girl from the shop before or since. He'd told Gallagher and Fanning that he didn't know her, but Cathy really wasn't sure. Her first impression when she'd seen the tape of the shop was that she was his girlfriend, why had she acted so anxiously otherwise?

Perhaps he *was* telling the truth about not knowing her, but he'd actually seen her around a few times and the super friendly act was his way of getting her number?

Perhaps she was acting worried because her real boyfriend was outside the shop and she knew he wouldn't be impressed if he saw her talking to Nacek?

Cathy knew from experience there could be hundreds of variations on interpreting behaviour, none of which came close to the truth. They'd done an exercise in college on it, on how experience and prejudice can lead to assumptions that are just plain wrong.

Tracking down the girl via Nacek had to be a damn sight easier though, than tracking her via Aleksy and some unknown party in Belarus, assuming he ever got an answer to his calls.

As the thought formed in her head Cathy turned and walked out towards the road, under the archway. It had rained while they were inside and puddles gleamed in the orange glow from the street lights, the road and the pavements wet. To her left the lights were on in the shop across the road, the MoneyGram Money Transfer sign bright in the darkness.

Something really wasn't adding up in Cathy's head. Sarah Jane fancied the pants off Vijay. She'd told Cathy she didn't get to see him much or chat to him properly because his uncle was always there, but whenever he was in the shop she tried to pop in as often as possible. Cathy could hear her laughing about how she'd found every possible excuse to drop in over the road when she was working, had been willing Vijay to ask her for a coffee, hoping that one day their breaks might coincide. She was sure he was interested, but he was so shy, and his shifts in the shop were so random, fitting in around his studies, that she never knew whether he was going to be there or not. The last time she'd mentioned him she'd said something about getting his phone number and asking him for coffee; she'd been determined to try the next time she saw him.

So why hadn't she gone into the shop on Sunday? Had she been late for work and not had time? If she had known that Vijay was working, Cathy was sure she would have done. Cathy knew Sarah Jane, knew her insecurities about relationships. Sometimes being attractive was a nightmare because everyone assumed you were taken and you never got asked out. How important could the meeting have been that she'd gone to see this guy instead of popping over to the shop for a chat? Why had she met anyone at all on a day that *she* was working? It was really easy for her to pop into town – if it was someone she needed to talk to about a story, why hadn't she fixed a time when she wasn't due back at the restaurant in thirty minutes? So much of this didn't make sense.

More questions than answers were forming in Cathy's head, but she knew you couldn't find the answers unless you knew the questions.

Behind her she heard Fanning reversing the car. He stopped in the middle of the car park, the headlights illuminating the cobbles under the archway.

Sarah Jane had to be back in work in thirty minutes. So that meant that the man Jacob had seen her with had to drive to wherever they were going in under fifteen to give her a chance to get back on time – ten, probably, to allow whatever was happening at their destination to happen. Was he taking her to meet someone? Was this what her dad had meant by something dangerous?

Where could you go from here in ten minutes? The streets weren't gridlocked on a Sunday afternoon, but all the shops were open, and it was busy enough. Where could you go in ten minutes that you couldn't get to on foot a whole lot faster?

Cathy thought back to the restaurant, to Billy's office ... to the locker room.

She dialled O'Rourke.

'It's me. We're done, he didn't know anything.'

'Really?'

Cathy ignored the sarcastic tone in his voice, continued, 'Listen, I know we've checked Sarah Jane's locker at The Rookery, but I was wondering if she or Daniella could have left something in a different locker that could point us in the right direction. I'm not getting how or why Sarah Jane would have left the restaurant with some random bloke when she only had a half-hour break. It just doesn't make sense. Something links Daniella and Sarah Jane, and at the moment it's The Rookery. I think we need to go back again and have a really good look around.'

'We don't know categorically that the body we have is Daniella O'Connor until we get a DNA match, but I hear you.

We've got two young women missing from the same premises. We don't have grounds for a warrant until we get a positive ID, but I don't see why Farrell would object to us searching the place, unless he's got something to hide. I'll have a chat to him. Get home and get some sleep, I'll call everyone in for nine.'

'Billy will be pleased, we'll be interrupting his lunchtime trade.'

'Worse things have happened.' *He was right there.*

Turning and heading towards the parked car, its engine running, she opened the door to find Fanning had had the heater on full blast. She got in gratefully.

'O'Rourke's going to get permission for a search of The Rookery. Something's not adding up here. We've a team briefing at nine.'

29

The phone lay on the rich pink carpet just beyond her fingertips.

Irina eased the guy's unconscious head a little further across her chest, his floppy dark hair tickling her breast, and stretched her left arm out as far as it would go. Further than it should go. The muscles in her shoulder screamed at her, the bones in her spine sounded like they were grinding on each other.

Could she reach it without waking him up?

She didn't know how long the drug would work for – she'd only had a half of one of the tiny blue and grey capsules left over from the blister strip the new maintenance man had given her.

What would she have done without him? He hadn't been working here long either he'd said. He'd been sent upstairs one morning to fix a light and she'd seen the pain in his face as she'd limped from the bathroom up to the bedroom. He'd stopped her as they were passing on the lino-covered stairs, whispered to ask her if she was OK. He must have heard her talking to Dog Face – he spoke Russian too, although she'd hadn't found out yet what part he was from. She'd hesitated, but his face had been so concerned, his eyes so understanding.

She hardly dared speak to him in case they caught her, but she'd told him. About the client they called The Whale. About the champagne bottle and how he had hurt her with it. He'd kept his face straight, his big blue eyes fixed on the hole worn in the lino on the first step. But he'd paled a shade she was sure, and when he'd looked back at her, unconsciously reaching out to run his hand over the top of her arm, his eyes had been steely hard.

He'd slipped her the capsules the next day, told her if they were taken with alcohol they'd knock The Whale out and with luck he wouldn't remember anything, wouldn't know he'd been fast asleep while she polished her nails.

She just wished she was brave enough to ask him to help her get a phone, but she knew she couldn't. You couldn't trust anyone here. She'd have to explain about the girl in the shop. She couldn't risk it.

Irina had split the capsules, terrified a whole one might give The Whale a heart attack; she'd only used a tiny bit at a time, slipping the powder into his glass when he was distracted.

Just as well – even half a capsule had made him sleep well into the hour. And it hadn't taken too much when he'd finally woken up to persuade him that he'd had a great time. And needed to pay the extra. Which kept everyone happy, except possibly The Whale's bank manager, but what did Irina care about him?

Of course if The Whale had had a phone with him all her Christmases would have come together. But that would have been too easy. He probably left it in his car in case his wife was tracking his location.

Gritting her teeth against the pain of overextending her arm, Irina reached a little further, the muscles in her shoulder and neck protesting as she tried to slide out from under the man's head. His open mouth was around her nipple, drool sliding down her side. All she needed was for him to wake up with a fright and bite her. Another fraction closer and she felt the cold metal of the edge of the phone.

It had rung earlier – he'd stopped to answer it and then turned back to her for a moment before having second thoughts about something – and reached for the phone to send a text. She couldnt believe that he had the simplest pin code imaginable, 2580, straight down the middle of the key pad. The second he had his back turned – talking to his wife, girlfriend, whoever – she'd slipped her hand under the pillow for the remains of the last capsule and had slipped it into what was left of his drink, praying it would dissolve before he noticed it.

If she could get the phone, if she could make the call, she could cope with anything.

Irina could feel her heart thumping in her chest, her mouth dry. Was this her chance? *Please, God, don't let him wake.* She glanced down at him. His eyes were shut. He was a lot younger than The Whale, and she'd only had half a capsule; would it be enough to keep him knocked out? Her fingers were so close. Holding her breath, she caught the very edge of the phone, her nail on the metal ridge running around it. *Christ.* Her fingernail flicked off it. It wasn't quite deep enough to give her purchase.

The man groaned and Irina's stomach went into freefall. *He couldn't wake up, couldn't, she was too close.* She lay paralysed, her eyes closed. Praying like she'd never prayed before.

And he rolled off her.

She held her breath. She didn't dare look. Then he snored. Irina closed her eyes, relief coursing through her. A moment later she took a furtive glance from under her eyelashes. He was sound asleep. But she wasn't taking any risks. She eased her body to the edge of the mattress, conscious that a sudden movement might wake him. Anything might wake him.

This time her fingers closed around the cold case of the phone. She held it so tightly the edges cut into her hand. She drew in a slow deep breath, trying to still her heart. She couldn't afford for her nerves to take over; if her hands were shaking too much she wouldn't be able to dial.

But how could she call without waking him?

It didn't matter. If she got that far, she might only have seconds but she was going to use them. She'd been over this so many times in her head. He snored again, sleeping like a child. *If his mother could see him now . . .*

Then he stirred in his sleep, and started to roll further away from her. Like a cat reacting to his movement, Irina rolled the other way, over the edge of the bed, used her knee to break her fall, one elbow, lowering herself down onto the thick carpet. She hardly dared breathe. Resting on her elbows, she typed in his PIN. The green call icon flashed in front of her.

She punched in the number.

The phone clamped to her ear, she heard the call click through and start to ring.

30

Cathy pulled off her glove and reached for her water bottle just as her phone began to ring.

'You on the way in?' The sense of urgency in O'Rourke's voice was unmistakable.

'I'm up at . . . hang on.' She spat out her gum shield, 'Phoenix.' Cathy glanced at the clock on the wall: it was just 8 a.m. She'd hardly slept the night before, had got home at about one and got up again at five. Seemed stupid to be tossing and turning. Now she was just finishing up, having had a really good session trying to focus on the image of Sarah Jane getting into a car with an unidentified male. Why had she done that? The question had been revolving in her head as she had lain awake.

'What's up? I'm just heading for the shower, will be in for nine.' Tucking the phone to her shoulder she sat down on the low bench that ran around the edge of the gym and pulled back the Velcro on the cuff of her other glove. From the noises in the background she could tell he was in the incident room, could hear him muttering to someone like he'd just been asked a question. Then he was back to her.

'We've had a development.' He paused. Cathy felt like reaching into the phone and grabbing him by his designer tie and pulling hard, 'What?'

'Sarah Jane got a call about ten minutes ago. Thirsty's mate up at the lab, the one who is working on her phone, heard it ring. He didn't answer it, obviously, but a girl left a message.' He paused again like he was trying to focus – he was obviously trying to do too many things at once. 'She said her name was Irina. We think she's Eastern European, she's been trafficked. From what she said we think she's in the city centre. We're tracing the owner of the phone she used – whoever it is must know where she is. Sounds like there are a bunch of them in there, all different nationalities.'

'Jesus.'

Her heart, already beating hard from her training session, began thumping. She knew every nuance of his voice, knew what he was thinking without him having to say it.

Sarah Jane's dad had said that whatever she was working on was dangerous. It didn't come much more dangerous than the scrotes who were involved in human trafficking. Innocent people were the sharp end of a business that involved organised crime, drugs, the whole lot. But what had it got to do with Ballymun and the horses? Were drugs the connection? And the guy in the combats?

Someone had tried to contact Sarah Jane. It had to be connected.

Cathy tried to take it in. Leaning back against the wall of the gym, she yanked her hair out of her face. Way across the other side, in the office, she could see The Boss leaning over his desk making notes on her fitness sheets. O'Rourke continued, 'The girl on the phone thought she was leaving a message for Sarah Jane. She said she needed help. Then she rang off. She referred to the place they were in as "the club". She was talking like Sarah Jane would know who she was and where she was.'

'A nightclub?'

'Or lap-dancing club. We'll know for sure pretty quickly.'

'And she thought she was talking to Sarah Jane?'

'Yep.'

Despite the feeling in her stomach, the unanswered questions, Cathy's mind was already collating the information.

'Wait, the girl in the shop. Remember in Vijay's shop? She was sending money to Belarus – could she have asked Sarah Jane for help and Sarah Jane wrote her phone number down for her?'

O'Rourke didn't speak for a minute. She could almost hear the cogs turning. But Cathy didn't give him a chance to respond, adding quickly, 'I knew that security guy from The Paradise Club knew her better than he was letting on. Maybe he wasn't trying to pick her up at all, maybe she's being held there.'

O'Rourke's voice was low, full of suppressed anger, 'You could be on to something there. I'll get a team to keep an eye on The Paradise Club while we get confirmation from the owner of the phone. We need more than a hunch for a warrant.'

'The Paradise Club is on the next street but it backs onto the car park right behind The Rookery. Perhaps Daniella was working there too? It would explain the extra money she seemed to have that Jazz mentioned. Perhaps it wasn't from tips at all, perhaps she earned it in other ways.'

She could almost hear O'Rourke nodding.

The PM on the body they'd found had concluded asphyxiation was the cause of death. Her hyoid bone was intact, which suggested that she hadn't been strangled, but with semen in her oesophagus and bruising to her throat, Fanning – who seemed, rather worryingly to Cathy, to be an expert – had speculated she could have choked to death during some sort of sex game. She'd stopped him as he'd started to explain. There were times when she didn't need a diagram. She switched her attention back to O'Rourke, 'So what do you want me to do now?'

'Wait. We'll have the phone owner's details within the hour and get a team out to see if he knows who this girl is, and where she is.'

'And to see if he's seen Sarah Jane.'

'Absolutely.'

'And then?'

'And then we'll get down to this club, wherever it is – scope it out, see what we can see.'

'OK, OK,' Cathy felt like she'd been punched in the solar plexus. And things suddenly fell into place. She could have slapped herself. *Wait? Like hell.* Cathy didn't do waiting. She really wasn't very good at doing nothing, and he knew it.

O'Rourke continued, 'As soon as we've located the club the girl was calling from we'll organise a warrant. Farrell has given us permission to search The Rookery. He's being very helpful.'

Cathy's head was buzzing. The girl who had called Sarah Jane had sounded Eastern European? What had McIntyre said about Eastern Europeans? It had been about the mutilation to the girl's body, that it was a trademark of Eastern European gangs. Had Daniella got caught up in something? With so many non-nationals involved in prostitution, punters got impatient with girls who had little or no English. Good-looking girls who spoke English could command a much higher price – was Daniella involved?

There were brothels exploiting immigrants all over the country; when she'd first moved into the detective unit Cathy had worked a case where women were moved every week to a different part of Ireland, their trade plied through websites that gave punters the opportunity to review them. That had been what had chilled her to the core: the reviews. And girls who couldn't speak any English were often given lower scores. *What sort of men paid for sex and didn't think it weird that the girls didn't speak English?* Had Sarah Jane found out something about Daniella? Was that what this was all about?

'What's up, girl?'

Cathy looked up at the sound of Niall McIntyre's voice.

In a quiet housing estate on Dublin's north side Frank Gallagher and Jamie Fanning were sitting in the Dún Laoghaire DDU car watching number seventy-one. A two-year-old silver Nissan was parked in the drive, a child's scooter leaning against the porch door. It was mid-morning, a postman doing his rounds further up the street.

A black Ford Laguna pulled up.

Gallagher stopped drumming his fingers on the steering wheel and leaned forward to get a clearer look at the driver.

'That's him. Spitting image of his Facebook photo.'

Fanning pulled out his notebook. 'Steve Dolan. Thirty-three, married, one kid, another on the way. Warehouse manager, works shifts.'

'Family man.' Gallagher watched as Dolan locked his car and headed into his driveway.

'How long do you think?' Fanning pushed his notebook back into the inside pocket of his leather jacket. They'd both done this before. It was the lads' club approach, the *Listen, buddy, we know what it's like, everyone needs a bit of fun, but we know where you've been and what you've been doing, so can you help us with a bit of information?*

Gallagher pursed his lips like he was thinking about it. 'Fiver says two minutes.'

'You're on.'

It never ceased to amaze them how willing men were to talk when they'd literally been caught with their trousers down. As Gallagher had pointed out as they'd got into the car back at Dún Laoghaire Station, it always helped if you were sitting in their front room and the wife was in the house.

'Mrs Dolan?'

The woman who had answered the door of the tidy three-bedroom semi looked more than a little annoyed. Her long dark hair was caught back in a messy ponytail and she was carrying a toddler on one hip, the child's leg hooked around her pregnant stomach. The toddler was gripping a handful of her T-shirt in a less than clean fist, pulling the neck out of shape as he cuddled shyly into her shoulder. Emma Dolan's dark eyebrows knotted as she looked out at the two men standing on her doorstep.

'Yes?' The word was stressed at the end as if she was saying 'and who wants to know?'

Gallagher flashed his warrant card, 'Gardaí, Mrs Dolan. DS Frank Gallagher and Detective Garda Jamie Fanning. We were wondering if we could have a chat to Mr Dolan?'

'Why?'

Annoyance changed to suspicion as Emma looked from one man to the other, her eyes narrowed. She shifted the child up her hip a bit. He had brown eyes, his mother's dark hair, wispy in baby curls, a trail of snot heading for his upper lip.

'There's nothing to worry about. There was an incident early this morning that your husband might have been a witness to. We're just checking up.'

'Incident? Where? When he was out running?' She looked confused, 'He went straight to Woodie's afterwards. Had to get there when it opened so he'd have time to decide on paint for the baby's room. Apparently it's complicated.'

'We won't be a moment, really. Can we come in?' Gallagher's tone was soothing, calm, implicitly sympathising with the fact she'd been on her own all morning with a small child while her husband struggled with paint choices.

Emma glanced out of the door to either side, checking to see who was watching. Gallagher knew that they didn't look like double-glazing salesmen. Whether it was height or build he wasn't sure – it wasn't like Fanning was even wearing a suit – so maybe it was something about their posture, but they might as well have been wearing hi-vis jackets with Gardaí written in capitals across the back. And it wouldn't take long for the neighbours to start talking.

'I suppose you better.'

As Fanning followed Gallagher, sliding the porch door closed behind him, Emma Dolan threw open a door to the right. 'You can wait in here. I'll just get him.'

The living room was small but comfortable. A cream leather couch dominated one wall, and children's toys were scattered on the polished floorboards across a beige mat. Children's clothes were drying on an airer beside the radiator. The two men took it all in: the wedding pictures on the mantelpiece, the posed family portrait in a trendy black lacquer frame above the sofa. Glazed double doors linked the living room with some sort of dining room-cum-office behind it, papers spread across the dining table. Beyond it the window framed a small garden dominated by a trampoline and a large shed. Emma Dolan paused in the doorway.

'Excuse the mess. I won't be a minute, he's in the garden. Can I get you some tea?'

She sounded like she was saying it because it was expected rather than because she actually wanted to provide refreshments.

Gallagher shook his head, giving her a relaxed friendly grin. 'Don't worry yourself, we'll only be a few minutes.'

'OK. I'll get him.' She paused a moment longer, her dark eyes unsure, then she was gone, her footsteps loud on the polished boards in the hall. The two men exchanged glances as they heard the back door open and Emma calling her husband. Through the window, they saw the shed door open.

Fanning stuck his hands in his trouser pockets and rocked on his heels. 'Nice lady.'

Gallagher nodded, tight-lipped. There were lots of reasons men visited prostitutes, none of which would cut any ice with their wives. He didn't approve or disapprove once the women were in it voluntarily. In this job you saw all sorts, and one thing was for sure, every relationship had its stresses and strains. But when the girls were abused, or trapped into selling sex by violent pimps, then he got annoyed. Very annoyed.

A moment later the living room door opened.

'Mr Dolan?'

It took less than two minutes.

The moment Steve Dolan heard that his mobile had been tracked to a brothel he paled several shades and sat down heavily on the couch as if someone had put a pin in him and all the air holding him up had rushed out.

'What happens now?' His voice was hardly more than a whisper.

'Well that's up to you, Mr Dolan. We need you to tell us as much as you possibly can about the place you met this lady.'

His eyes darting about as if he was trapped by a searchlight, Dolan began to sweat. He pushed his fringe out of his eyes. 'And if I don't?'

'Then we'll have to have a chat down at the station and you might have a bit of explaining to do to Mrs Dolan.'

'OK, OK. But if I tell you, what happens then? Emma can't know about this.'

'We understand your problem, Mr Dolan, and we can't make any promises, but right now the most important thing for us to do it to get a bunch of trafficked women out of harm's way. That's our absolute priority. Once we know where to look, with a bit of luck you won't be hearing from us again.'

Steve Dolan nodded fast, 'Just don't say anything to Emma.'

'We won't, that's your business.' Gallagher paused, 'So where exactly were you between seven thirty and eight o'clock this morning?'

'Higher, girl. It's an axe kick, not bloody fairy football. Focus. You need to concentrate to win.'

Niall McIntyre held the pad Cathy was supposed to be kicking several inches higher, the sinews in his tattooed arms standing out like ropes. They were both sweating now, their vests stained, Cathy's black Lycra shorts clinging to her. Boxing was a full-on, full-body workout that tested every muscle and required a different sort of concentration from the norm. It was about attack and defence, attack and counter-attack. The gym was empty this early in the day, so they were alone in the ring, Cathy's feet echoing off the blue baize-covered boards with every kick, drowning out the sound of Spin FM.

He was deliberately working her hard trying to distract her, to stop her thinking about the girl who had tried to call Sarah Jane. He was doing the right thing by trying to keep her busy, and the sweat was running off her now, dripping off the end of her nose. She ran the back of her arm across her forehead, skipped back and tried to catch him by surprise: front kick, roundhouse, axe kick. The pad met her foot every time. *Christ, he was fast.*

'That's more like it.' He grinned at her, knowing exactly what she was up to. 'Water, then back on the bag.'

'Yes, Boss.' Bent double, Cathy leaned her gloved hands on her thighs, panting. *He was some bastard.*

As she grabbed her water from under the ropes her phone started to ring again. They both jumped. Ripping the Velcro off her gloves with her teeth, Cathy swung out of the ring and got to it before it went to voicemail. O'Rourke's name flashed on the screen.

'What?' She was breathless, panted out the word.

'We've got it. You were right. It *is* The Paradise Club. Frank's got chapter and verse. He's on his way back here now. Come in and we'll regroup.'

31

Even in the outer public office you could feel there was something happening in Dún Laoghaire Station. The desk was down to one man trying to deal with a growing queue of members of the public. They all looked at Cathy as she punched the code into the internal glass doors and headed for the stairs, her runners silent on the treads as she took the steps two at a time. But then she wasn't in uniform, had thrown on her black sweatpants and hoodie after training, pulled back her hair into a ponytail, and looked more like a cat burglar than a member of An Garda Síochána.

Her phone pipped with a message as she headed up the stairs. Pausing for a second at the top of the flight, she pulled it out. Aleksy again: *still trying number*; *no answer*; then more emojis, smiley faces and a pint of beer followed by a question mark. But she didn't have time to answer now. She stuck the phone back into her pocket – she'd answer later.

In the incident room O'Rourke was huddled over the conference table with Frank Gallagher and Jamie Fanning, a map spread out in front of them. Fanning, who had his back to her, turned as the doors swung closed behind her. O'Rourke looked up, flashing her a grin that did nothing to alter his frown.

'We've another development.'

Cathy caught her breath, 'What?'

'We're still waiting for a DNA match, but Daniella's medical records confirm she was AB negative. It's not an ID and it's not conclusive, but with the missing tattoo it's looking even more likely the body we found is hers.'

Cathy wasn't sure if that was good news or not. They'd found Daniella, but . . . Christ she hoped the same thing hadn't happened to Sarah Jane. She tried to keep her voice level, 'So what's the plan?'

'We've got a search warrant for The Paradise Club, but if we create a load of fuss at The Rookery, the girls being held in The Paradise Club could be moved on. We need to keep a lid on it, do them at the same time.' O'Rourke glanced at Cathy. 'What's the link between them?' Dumping her kitbag down beside the table she leaned over to look at the plan of the buildings on South William Street, the car park and the location of The Paradise Club on Drury Street.

Before O'Rourke had a chance to speak the swing door from the corridor burst open, J.P. barrelling through, a piece of paper in his hand. 'There's an R. Farrell on the board of directors of both companies. They are listed separately but . . .'

'That would explain his house,' Fanning cut in, glancing at Cathy.

'Sure would.'

O'Rourke's phone rang before anyone could comment further. His answers were clipped. 'Perfect, thanks.' He turned to them, pausing for a moment while he was clearly sorting the information in his head. 'That was Traffic: they've located the video of Daniella getting out of Farrell's car at the bus stop. He did just what he said: as soon as the bus came, he turned around and headed south; we're just waiting for Wexford to confirm he arrived in Gorey. Dublin Bus have come up with the tapes from the bus itself. She used her Leap card when she got on, and it looks like she was on her own for the whole trip, didn't speak to anyone, got off in the city centre. We're waiting for visuals from them both.'

'So that puts Farrell in the clear?' Fanning looked up from the map and pushed his blond fringe out of his face as he spoke.

O'Rourke stared at Fanning for a moment before answering, the cogs still turning visibly in his head. 'Not necessarily – assuming the body is hers, we don't have an exact time of death. He could have met her later. The DNA report on the semen will give us more information.' He turned to Cathy, 'What was your impression of him?'

Cathy shrugged, 'Rich, young, good looking. He could still be good for it unless we can conclusively rule him out.'

'And we can't do that yet. The tapes are on the way, we'll have a look at them ourselves as soon as they arrive.' O'Rourke stood up straight, 'Right, let's get organised. I want everyone in here.'

Ten minutes later the incident room was packed, all the focus on O'Rourke as he stood at the front of the room and brought them up to date.

'So Frank is going to lead the team going into The Rookery. I know you want to get in there, Cat, but we'll need you in The Paradise Club to help with these girls. Frank, I want all their CCTV tapes – check that Billy Roberts isn't holding anything back that we should be seeing. You'll have the Technical Bureau with you – empty the waitresses' lockers, go through every bloody drawer. We're looking for anything that can connect Sarah Jane and Daniella O'Connor.

'But you can't move in until we're ready to go into The Paradise Club, so it's going to be a late night.' He took a slug of the coffee that had materialised beside him on the edge of the snooker table. 'So here's the plan: myself, J.P. and 007 will go into The Paradise Club as if we're punters this evening.' He turned to 007 who was sitting in the front row, 'And don't get any ideas about ordering a load of champagne on the state – it's pints only, understood? If you order champagne you're paying for it yourself.' He paused, 'We'll suss the place out, see how many girls there are, what the security arrangements are. Then, coordinating with Frank's team, we'll raid it.'

'Not now? If we know the girls are in there?' J.P. was leaning against the back wall beside the door, his arms tightly crossed. He was wearing a denim shirt and chinos, but still looked too big for the room somehow. Cathy flashed him a smile.

At the front of the room O'Rourke was shaking his head, 'We need to catch them at it or we can't prosecute, so it has to be later when the girls are busy. We've done this elsewhere and come out with nothing – the girls are brain washed and so frightened of the traffickers that they deny they are there without their consent, it ends up a mess. Under the 1993 Sexual Offences Act the offence is in soliciting for prostitution and profiting from it. We can only prosecute the traffickers if we can prove that's what's going on, that the girls are being held against their will and forced into sex work that they are directly profiting from. Operations Hotel and Quest targeted trafficking and have been very successful, but The Paradise Club wasn't on their radar until now. Their team will be assisting this operation.'

Cathy had had several lectures on trafficking in a module on the psychology of hostages – it wasn't all about Stockholm syndrome. Often the girls lured into trafficking had been abused from a young age, came from homes they never wanted to return to; living like this, having sex many times a day with different men, was marginally better than home. They had somewhere warm to sleep, were fed and clothed. How bad did your life have to be to make this an alternative? Others were beaten and subjugated, terrorised into sex work by threats that their families at home would be harmed if they didn't cooperate. Cathy's tutor group had ended up debating the legalisation of prostitution, whether making it safe and looking after the girls just created another black economy for needs not serviced by the mainstream, for BDSM and bestiality, for stuff Cathy didn't even want to think about it. It was a no-win situation.

Cathy knew she wasn't like most cops, who operated in black and white – she saw all the shades of grey, could see that there might be women who wanted to work in the sex industry, women for whom the wins outweighed the losses, for whom regulating it had huge benefits. But with any big-money game there were vultures circling; the pimps and pushers would always be looking for their cut, and those types preyed on the most vulnerable and least able to defend themselves. That's the way the world worked and that's why she was in the job.

'And Sarah Jane?' Cathy's voice was louder than she'd anticipated. She was getting that anxious feeling she got before an important fight, that tension in her stomach that made her nervy.

'The punter the boys questioned didn't recognise her photo, reckoned it was the first time he'd been there.'

From the left of the room Frank Gallagher grunted. 'Isn't it always?'

O'Rourke acknowledged his point with a grimace, then continued, 'If Sarah Jane was working on a story about trafficking and she got too close, they could be holding her. They won't know who she has or hasn't spoken to, will want to find out so they can contain the information. For all they know she could be working undercover at The Rookery, could have a whole team backing her up.' He took another swig of his coffee. 'Whether that might mean she was grabbed when she got home on Sunday night and is being held on the premises, or elsewhere, we'll only know when we go in. We'll see if the girl who called her – Irina she said her name was – can tell us anything.'

Cathy nodded slowly, *if the girl wasn't too traumatised.* 'Do you think she could be there? Sarah Jane? At the club?'

O'Rourke met her eye. She could see he knew what she was really asking, could read her mind as well as she could read his: *Do you think she's still alive?* She couldn't say it out loud, couldn't even think it.

'Maybe.' He paused. 'It's a big building – four floors with the casino in the basement. We'll see what Irina can tell us.'

Cathy took a deep breath. For a moment no one said anything, and Cathy felt like they were trapped in some sort of vacuum, the murmur as the team absorbed the briefing continuing around them dulled somehow. Then J.P. was beside her, his hand on her shoulder. He gave her a squeeze.

'Cat, don't worry. We'll find her.'

Cathy threw him a grin and jostled him playfully with her shoulder.

'So it's all hands on deck, a pincer operation. We'll have armed back-up from the special detective unit and uniform from the B – South William Street is in Pearse Street's district. I've a call into Ruhama for one of their crisis teams to attend when we bring the girls in. They are an NGO specialising in assisting trafficked women and women in prostitution, and have lots of experience. They will bring spare clothes for them, emergency toiletries and the like.'

Cathy pulled her chain out from the neck of her hoodie, running the pendant nervously along its length. She'd done this before, it wasn't like a raid was a new experience. But she'd never been on one that was this close to her heart. She closed her eyes and took another deep breath, trying to still her stomach.

32

'Are you sure you've got everything now? I've put your tooth-brush in your washbag.' Rebecca picked up Jacob's Batman backpack from the end of the sofa and unzipped it, rifling through the contents again. *Washbag, phone charger, Minecraft magazine, T-shirt, clean underwear and socks. Ted bear.* She must have checked everything against his list at least three times already. She was sure everything was there, but the thought that something might be missing made her as anxious as it would Jacob. Something as simple as the wrong pair of pyjamas could send him into a meltdown; leaving something behind would throw his routine right out and could end in disaster.

'I've got a toothbrush at Daddy's, Mummy. I keep telling you.'

'Yes, but this one has soft bristles. You said the other one was too hard.'

Jacob's voice was stubborn, 'Daddy says mine's the same as his.'

I bet. Rebecca didn't say it. 'Just remember to use it, will you? And don't eat those jellies again. They make you go bonkers.'

Jacob picked up his new tablet computer from the coffee table. 'Daddy says his ones don't make me go bonkers, only yours.'

Great. Just great. Rebecca closed her eyes and counted to ten.

Outside a bitter wind was channelling down the main street of Enniskerry, bringing with it the smell of chips, setting the sign outside the pub swinging and squeaking noisily. Rebecca pulled the shop door closed behind them. At this time of the evening the village was winding down. Worry fluttered in her stomach; she had a nagging feeling they'd forgotten something. But she'd checked *everything*. What could it be? What on earth wasn't on the list? She went through the same process every time she dropped Jacob to his dad's. Thank God it was only once a fort-night, but each time it felt like the longest twenty-four hours of her life.

He was mad about Jacob, spoiled him rotten, but any eight-year-old could be a challenge, and one with Asperger's had his own set of complications. Once Jacob was given enough notice of change he actually coped very well; it was more often smells that set him off, or crowds, people bumping into him. Rebecca took a deep breath, tried to calm herself. *It would all be fine.* Sometimes something unexpected happened and he was com-pletely fine about it, surprising everyone. But she'd just seen too many times how her ex-husband failed to cope with situ-ations, and a small boy having what equated to a full-blown tantrum, whatever the reason, would test his patience, create an atmosphere that could go on for weeks – an atmosphere that an eight-year-old could never understand. It was so easy to avoid situations that were distressing for Jacob, but that required for-ward planning, and for her ex to focus on something other than himself, which was where things tended to fall down. At least when something went wrong Jacob's dad usually got straight on the phone to her, which was something. She pursed her lips . . .

Reaching for Jacob's hand to cross the road, she bobbed down in front of him, pulled up his hood and checked the zip was done up on his coat.

'Mummy, I'm eight.'

'I know, darling, but it's freezing. You won't forget to call to say good night, will you? You know I can't sleep until you do.'

'Yes, Mummy.' Jacob rolled his eyes, 'And I won't tell Daddy in case he gives out about the bill.'

'Good boy. We don't want Daddy to be cross, do we?' She kissed him quickly on the top of the head.

It was only twenty minutes to the house. Outside the gates she swung open the car door to press the intercom. He must have been watching for her. Just as she reached up to hit the button the gates began to open. *That would be right.* He'd seen her drive up and had waited for her to get out of the car before he'd opened the gates. It was only a tiny thing, but this was childish one-upmanship; like everything else he did, it was all a pointless power play.

She shouldn't be surprised. He'd been the same since she'd met him. But she'd been in love then, blind to the tell-tale signs. Now she knew better.

Climbing back into her red Golf as the gates opened fully, Rebecca began to feel sick. She'd done everything to contest his access, but the judge had bought his story that the stress of running such a successful business had been the reason for his lack of commitment to Jacob.

Pulling up outside the house Rebecca could hear the dog barking before she was even out of the car.

33

How long would it take the girl to get here? How quickly would she pick up her message? Leaning on the bar Irina glanced anxiously at the entrance to the club again. Someone was going to notice if she kept this up. She knew she needed to be more careful. But she was burning up with anticipation, had headed back downstairs as soon as she could when the guy with the phone had woken up. She'd smiled at him, had handed him back his phone with a look that told him he'd been the best she'd ever had. He'd been a bit groggy but had glanced over his shoulder at her as he'd left, his brown eyes hopeful. Lost. Irina knew he'd be back. But with a bit of luck she wouldn't be here.

She almost smiled. For the first time in months.

Hope was a powerful thing.

It was quiet this evening, with only a couple of men in the bar, both watching the floor show from opposite sides of the stage, studiously ignoring each other. It was still early, and most of the other girls were upstairs taking a break. Irina knew she probably should too – a big stag party had booked in later, would be arriving around midnight when they'd all be expected to be on the floor, persuading the men to spend €150 on a bottle of champagne and enjoy the free two-minute dance that came with each one.

But what if the girl came and couldn't find her? What if she was dancing or with a customer and they missed each other?

Irina pulled herself up onto the bar stool, glancing at the door again. The straps on her stilettos were cutting into her feet. *How long would she be?*

Behind her, Stacey, one of the pole dancers, was gyrating topless to the pop music that filled the club, her thong covered in sequins that caught the coloured lights that played across the stage. She was fit: her stomach rippled with muscle, thighs taut. All the men who watched her wanted a piece of her, but she was strictly hands off, had her own changing room out the back, was an 'artiste', as Irina had heard her saying to Nacek when he'd decided he'd try a piece of her himself. Actually Irina was pretty sure she was a he, that the breasts were fake, his dick taped up under the slinky thong that stayed firmly in place whenever 'she' was on stage. It made her laugh to watch the men's tongues almost hanging out, blissfully unaware. She half wished Stacey would make a move on Nacek; that would give him something to think about.

Irina pushed a strand of hair out of her face and tried to concentrate on anything other than the door. It was hours since she'd left the message. *Maybe the girl had lost her phone? Maybe the battery was flat and she hadn't even got the message?* Irina took an involuntary breath as a wave of hysteria threatened to envelop her. She couldn't think about that. She hadn't even considered what would happen if the girl didn't get the message. It had taken her so long to get a phone. A pain exploded in Irina's head and she suddenly found it hard to breathe. Grasping the back of the bar stool beside her until her knuckles went white, Irina fought for control. She couldn't lose it now. Not when she was so close.

She reached for images of Meti's face, his beautiful brown eyes, of sitting in the town square in the shade of a striped umbrella, sipping lattes, laughing. It was hard; her memories were fading, it felt like a different world, a different life. Was she even that girl anymore?

Irina fought back the sting of tears, holding on to the images like they were precious stones slipping through her fingers. The feel of Meti's stubble on her face, the sound of his laughter. It didn't matter what happened, she couldn't lose her memories, they were all she had left. And Meti would be waiting. She knew he would. He would be wondering why she hadn't got in touch, why she hadn't phoned, sent a postcard. He'd be waiting for her. He had to be.

Irina took a deep breath, trying to still her beating heart. The girl would help. Irina knew that for sure. She had understood the moment their eyes had met. But how could she know what was really happening, what the truth was? How could anyone imagine that a human sex slave trade was active in their city? Irina had read about trafficking and seen documentaries about organised crime. How had she been so stupid? Why hadn't she realised?

But it was going to be fine. Irina took a deep breath and fought to focus. She just had to get through tonight. It would all work out. She'd taken every day, every minute, one at a time since she'd arrived here, had focused on surviving, on getting through each increment without losing her mind.

The girl would come and she would get out of here ... She just had to wait a little bit longer ...

'You're wanted upstairs.'

Irina whipped around at the sound of Dog Face's voice, her eyes wide. She was sure the shock was written all over her face.

'Wh . . . why?' Irina stuttered, and the pain in her head started up again, throbbing like her skull was going to explode. Dog Face looked at her, her upper lip curled in a sneer.

'Nacek wants you.'

Irina felt herself sway, the bass beat of the music suddenly overwhelming. She clenched her teeth. She couldn't go back to the office. Not again. She couldn't go through that again. Last time she'd been terrified, but she hadn't known what was coming.

This time she did.

Struggling for breath Irina turned to look at Dog Face, grasping the back of the bar stool, trying to hide her fear.

'Now?' Her voice was weak.

Images of her last time in the office whirled in Irina's head. Unable to look at the woman beside her, focusing her eyes somewhere over her shoulder, on the other side of the club, Irina realised one of the doors of the booths had opened, the light thrown from inside illuminating a short, middle-aged customer in a three-piece suit who had just emerged from inside, his bald head, slick with sweat, catching the lights. She looked at him desperately – could she interest him in another dance? Buy herself some time?

Dog Face didn't seem to notice, but then she was used to the girls being stoned, to not being all there when she spoke to them.

'Well, what are you waiting for? Are you ill? He doesn't like to wait, you know. Get moving and make yourself presentable on the way.'

'I just . . .' Irina put her hand to her pounding head.

It was like it was all happening in slow motion. The dancer on the stage threw her leg around the pole.

'I—'

But Irina didn't get any further. The sound of laughter drew Dog Face's attention away from her for a moment. A group of men were coming in through the door of the club, three of them – new customers she hadn't seen before. One younger, blond, handsome. One a bit older – a big guy, his shoulders like a bull. The third, in a well-cut navy pinstripe suit and pink tie, seemed to be in charge, and was heading for the bar.

'Now boys, what are you having?' His accent was strange, different from the others she'd heard. Similar but softer. 'Pints all round?'

The moment he spoke Dog Face turned on the charm, her eyes lighting up, 'We have some fabulous champagne if you'd care for a glass. A bottle comes with the added bonus of the special attention of one of our girls.'

Smiling, she clicked her fingers, summoning the barman who had been washing glasses, his back to the club. 'I'm sure some of our girls can help you enjoy your evening.'

The guy who seemed to be in charge turned to her smiling. 'I hope so.'

As she looked at him properly Irina could see he was good looking too, not with the film star looks of the younger guy, but in a rugged, stubbly sort of way. Catching her eye he smiled at her.

Dog Face moved in immediately, clicking her fingers again for the drinks menu, 'We have a wide selection available. We cater for every taste.'

'I bet you do. Sounds good to me.' He leaned in close to Dog Face, his voice low, but Irina could just catch what he was saying, 'Mate of mine was here the other day, said he met a lovely girl, Irene was her name? Said she was very good company.'

Dog Face only paused for a moment, and glanced back at Irina. 'She did have an appointment, but I'm sure it can be delayed.' Dog Face beamed at him, 'This is Irina.' She took a step backwards, 'Irina, will you look after these gentlemen?'

34

As Irina pushed the door closed, shutting out the light from the club, the booth was plunged into semi darkness, the soft red up-lighting hiding the marks on the burgundy carpet. She gestured for the man to sit in the chrome and leather chair in the middle of the tiny room. Without looking at her, he put his champagne flute down carefully on the round smoked-glass table beside it.

For a moment Irina wondered who he was, what his story was. Was he married, single? She didn't really care, but he was going to get the dance of his life tonight, that was for sure. He'd paid for a full half an hour which meant she wouldn't have to go to the office – and if she could keep him entertained until the stag party came in, with a bit of luck she wouldn't have to go up tonight at all. Relief coursed through her.

Sitting down, facing her, the man leaned forward and opened his mouth to speak, but Irina didn't need to hear it. Instead she turned around, standing with her back to him, and picking up the bass beat of the music, a bluesy jazz number, began to dance, gyrating her hips, running her hands over her thighs, down over her butt. She turned around, smiling, taking a step towards him, but as she did so he put up both hands for her to stop. Confused, she paused.

'Is your name Irina?' He kept his voice low, barely more than a whisper.

Irina frowned, her eyebrows knitting, pretending she didn't understand.

He said it again, 'Is your name Irina? You speak English?' Still she pretended not to understand, stared at him blankly.

Then he reached inside his jacket pocket.

What was inside his jacket? A knife? In an instant Irina spun around, heading for the door of the booth, panic roaring in her ears. *He had a knife. He must have a knife.* Like the man who wanted to fuck Sabrina but hadn't wanted to pay. Nacek had sorted him out, but not before he'd cut her.

Irina tried to catch the door handle, panic making her blind, her hands suddenly sweating so much they slipped off it. Before she could open the door he had his hand on her arm, gripping her tightly. She spun around and, finally finding her voice, opened her mouth to scream. But the man held up his free hand, glancing up to check the camera in the corner of the room and turning his back to block its view as he flipped open a wallet, keeping it close into his chest.

He kept his voice low, little more than a whisper. 'It's OK. I'm police. Detective Inspector Dawson O'Rourke. I'm here to help you.' Then louder, 'Are you Russian? Talk to me in Russian, I want to hear how it sounds.'

Difficult to hear over the sound of the music, the first part of his sentence took a second to sink in, a second in which Irina felt her knees buckle and the lights in the room dance before her eyes as she sank to the ground. He moved fast, was there to catch her, a strong arm hooked under her shoulder as he eased her towards the chair, sitting her down, slipping off his jacket and slinging it around her shoulders, covering her up. Bobbing down on his haunches in front of her, O'Rourke leaned on the side table, trying to make eye contact with her.

Loudly he said, 'I love Russian girls.' Then, lowering his voice so she could barely hear him, 'I'm with the police. We're here to help you. But we're being watched, we need to make this look real. If you whisper they won't be able to hear over the music.'

Irina couldn't speak. Tears began to flow down her cheeks. She didn't try to brush them away, instead reached for his hand, holding it tight, her own so much smaller than his. He smiled, squeezed her fingers, rubbed the back of her hand. His fingers felt strong and warm and safe. *Police. He was police. The girl must have sent him.* Irina swallowed a sob, almost unable to catch her breath.

'Good girl. Now stand up and dance or they'll send someone in to see what's wrong.' It took all her energy but Irina stood up, his jacket swinging from her shoulders, then started to dance again. *She couldn't let this go wrong now.*

The man smiled, nodding encouragingly, then continued, his voice low, 'I doubt whoever is monitoring this can lipread, but act like I'm talking about you . . . We got your message. The one you left for Sarah Jane. We don't have much time, so I need you to tell me everything you can.' He paused, but Irina still couldn't speak. She swayed in time to the music and nodded to show she understood, took a deep shaky breath.

'The men I came in with are policemen too. They are looking at the security arrangements and getting an idea of the layout of the building. We're going to come back later this evening, and we're going to close this place down and get you out.'

His voice had taken on a hard edge. He understood. She knew he understood. She nodded again, 'I understand. Thank you. Thank you.'

Then it hit her. *Later tonight? Could she hold on?* What happened if she had to go back to the office? Irina could feel panic rising in her.

'How long? How long until you come back?'

'Another few hours – we need to wait until it's busy. But you'll be safe. One of my colleagues will stay in the bar and keep an eye on things. He'll make sure nothing happens to you.'

Her whole body shook as she exhaled, 'Thank you.'

He grimaced. 'Keep dancing, make it look real for the cameras.' Then, 'In your message, you said there were eight girls. Is that eight including you?'

Irina twirled her hair over her head, rotating her hips, her hands massaging her breasts under the jacket, putting on a show for whoever was watching. 'Eight plus me – we were ten, but one, a Slovakian girl, she got sick and they took her somewhere. Luisa is the youngest – she's Brazilian, she's only seventeen.'

His mouth was smiling, but she could see his eyes were hard, 'Do any of the others speak English?'

'No, only me, but they don't know.' She paused, her eyes meeting his, 'I've been listening. I know everything.'

'Good girl. We're going to have to interview you properly in a police station . . .'

'It will be my pleasure. You need to be careful, though, there are policemen who come here. I don't know their names but I think they are quite senior.' Turning around she ran her hands inside her G-string over her butt.

'Nothing's going to stop us coming back. Where are you from?'

She turned back to face him, 'Belarus, a village near Vitebsk. I answered an ad . . .' Irina could hear the desperation and despair in her own voice.

'It's OK. Tell me later. Where are the others from?'

'Nigeria, Romania, Bulgaria, all over.'

'We'll organise interpreters. There is an organisation who can help – they aren't police.'

Irina nodded, running her tongue over her lips, 'Pretend you just want to watch, that you don't want me to sit on your knee.' She moved towards him as if she was going to sit down and he held up his hands again. Taking a step back, twisting to the music, she slipped the jacket off her shoulders, laying it on the small round table, and continued, 'The girls are terrified of the police – the people in charge are always telling us how dangerous the police are here, that they shoot first and ask questions later. Lots of them have had bad experiences with that at home, they know you have weapons, think you will see them as filthy prostitutes. It would be better if they can talk to people outside.' Irina paused, 'Please don't be long. The head of security wanted me to go up to his office, he's . . .' She swallowed, 'he's very cruel.'

'Don't worry, we'll be back before midnight. Where are the others?'

'With clients upstairs. They have bookings and there's a stag party coming in later, a big one.'

'And when the other girls come down to the club they will be in the bar or in these rooms?'

'Both. There are doors hidden in the back of each of these rooms, they go to the bedrooms upstairs. But there are cameras everywhere. They will see you coming.'

'We'll be inside before they know we're here and we'll have men on all the exits. No one will be able to leave. How many of these rooms are there?'

Continuing to sway to the music she said, 'Eight. Some of them are bigger, there is room for more girls.'

'And how many on security?'

'There are always three men to guard us. They work shifts, change over at eight o'clock. They say they are there to protect us ...' She snorted, her lip curling. 'I think there are more on the main door and in the casino. I'm not sure how many. They change a lot.'

'And are there other staff here?'

'Bar staff, waitresses. Croupiers in the casino. We don't see them. We work here in the bar, dance and then take the customers upstairs.'

'And who's in charge?'

'Nacek is head of security. He's Albanian.' She shivered visibly. 'Then there's a bar manager – he has noisy shoes, you can always hear him coming. And the woman you met in the bar, she's the interpreter, she looks after us. She brought me to London. She works for the man who runs this place. I don't know his name, he's not here all the time.'

O'Rourke nodded, pointing as if he wanted her to turn around and keep dancing, 'Tell me about the girl you rang, Sarah Jane. Did you meet her here?'

Irina shook her head, 'No, outside. They pretend that we are earning a proper wage and we send it home using MoneyGram, but the men pay much more for us.' Her voice was full of contempt. 'Then our families think everything is OK and we are OK ...' She took a breath, contemplating the enormity of the implication that once money was flowing home, everyone was happy. Her voice caught as she continued, 'Each week a different girl gets to take the money. It's a power thing. We've been here for three weeks, the longest time anywhere. I took the money before, and then when they asked me again this week, I knew where I was going.' She paused, reaching to pick up his jacket again and pulling it around her, 'I knew I only had a second to find someone to help, and when she came into the shop, I knew it was my chance, she had a kind face. She might have just ignored me, but I had to try. Nacek went off to look at the magazines and suddenly she was standing beside me. I asked her for help, to please help me, and she wrote her number down on a piece of paper. I knew she'd know where to find us, I just needed to explain. I knew she'd help.'

35

It was starting to rain outside as the team gathered again in Dún Laoghaire's incident room, droplets coursing down the windows like tears. Inside it was hot and stuffy, and the room was packed, members from the SDU and Pearse Street Station swelling the numbers of the Dún Laoghaire team.

One of the key problems with an operation like this was finding enough female officers to balance out the predominantly male team. Looking around, Cathy could see that O'Rourke hadn't done a bad job – Aisling Kelly the detective sergeant from Cabinteely was here, girls from Blackrock and Shankill blended in with the lads, both detective unit and uniform. They were all the same out on the street, but with an operation like this female officers were key. The girls held at The Paradise Club would have been intimidated, threatened and violated, would be in fear for their own and their families' lives, and often too frightened to give evidence. Male officers could unintentionally make matters worse.

Thirsty had told Cathy stories from twenty years ago when it could take hours to track down a female officer to assist an arrest or question a suspect; now women still only represented a quarter of the force, but they were here, and just like in civilian life, they often had to work harder than their male colleagues to juggle careers and families.

'Thanks for coming in, everyone. We don't have much time, so listen up.' O'Rourke swung around to the incident board, a red laser pointer in his hand. 'To give you a bit of background, the team here have been investigating the disappearance of Sarah Jane Hansen from The Rookery restaurant in South William Street on Sunday evening. In the course of that investigation it has emerged that the premises that backs onto a shared car park behind The Rookery, The Paradise Club – I'm sure some of you are familiar with it – has been operating as a brothel with up to ten women who have been trafficked from Eastern Europe, Africa and Latin America. From a conversation I had with one of the women earlier this evening, the club appears to be part of a much bigger network, and these women have been moved on a weekly or monthly basis between flats and hotels starting in London. Obviously our colleagues in the UK will be interested to tie in from their end. It's a sophisticated operation using websites and mobile phones so the girls can be kept on the move.'

O'Rourke paused and the room shifted, every officer focused on him, 'From what we can gather from early recon at The Paradise Club, there are three key security staff keeping an eye on the door and the girls at any one time, and more in the casino. The girls dance for customers in the bar area, take them to booths for longer private dances and then up a back flight of stairs to the bedrooms above. The building has several floors, with the girls' accommodation right at the top.'

He paused again, looking around the room. He had everyone's attention. 'Obviously we can assume that there are other activities being conducted on the premises – the sale of narcotics et cetera – so keep your eyes open. And we will assume there are firearms and other weapons on the premises. I've never seen an operation like this that didn't have. You know the routine. The girls have been moved around and led to believe that we are the threat rather than their captors. They've been turned against each other and are in fear of their lives. One girl who was sick has apparently disappeared. None of the girls speak English except one, Irina, who is from Belarus – she speaks Polish and Russian as well, but we'll bring in female interpreters for the others as soon as we know what we need.'

Stepping back, O'Rourke glanced at J.P., who was hovering over a laptop which had been hooked up to a projector. Taking his cue he pressed a button and a map of the building appeared on the wall above the incident board.

'Public access to The Paradise Club is through the front entrance. There is a rear access here via the car park,' he waved the red pointer, 'and fire exits here, here, here and here. We need to cover them all and secure the perimeter. I don't want anyone leaving the building once we're in. That clear?'

A murmur of assent ran around the room.

'While the main team is at work in The Paradise Club, Detective Sergeant Gallagher,' O'Rourke nodded in Frank's direction, 'is going to take a team into The Rookery. There are definitely connections between the two premises. We've found an R. Farrell, whom we believe to be Richard Farrell, on the board of both companies. He's happy to let the world know he owns The Rookery, but he's been very quiet about The Paradise Club.'

A murmur ran around the room. Everyone knew Farrell from the newspapers. O'Rourke continued, 'A couple of our officers have been to his home to question him about the disappearance of another one of his employees, Daniella O'Connor, which we believe to be linked to the disappearance of Sarah Jane Hansen, and it's a very impressive pad in Foxrock, which would suggest he's doing extremely well in the restaurant business.' O'Rourke's tone left his opinions about Farrell's income stream in no doubt. 'Farrell was apparently one of the last people to see Daniella O'Connor before she disappeared, and we have reason to believe that the woman's body found in the Dublin mountains earlier this week will be conclusively identified as hers.

'We don't want any evidence, particularly documentation that might pertain to either business, to be compromised by raiding one premises and not the other, hence the two-pronged operation. And don't forget, we are looking for anything that can give us an indication of Sarah Jane Hansen's whereabouts.'

O'Rourke switched off the laser, 'Any questions?' He looked around the room, 'Great. You all know who your team leaders are?' A nod ran around the room. 'Then let's roll.'

Blue strobes reflected off the windows and damp pavements on South William and Drury Streets as several Garda vans pulled up. The back doors opened and uniform from Dún Laoghaire, Pearse Street and Blackrock poured out, silently heading up to The Rookery and The Paradise Club to assume their positions. With their navy and yellow jackets, baseball caps and body protection there was no mistaking who they were.

O'Rourke had swapped his overcoat for a bomber jacket and hat, had the warrant in his hand as he headed up the broad granite steps of The Paradise Club. The team behind him waited for the door to be buzzed open. A moment later they heard the electronic sound of the lock disengaging and he pushed open the highly polished front door, his ID and the search warrant in one hand, a radio in the other.

Speed was vital in an operation like this to prevent valuable evidence from being destroyed, and as the team flowed in a heavily made-up brunette in a very short fitted black dress stood with her mouth open behind the glass reception desk.

Cathy glanced around the hallway, trying to get a feel for the place, for the type of people who came here. The lighting was low, atmospheric with lots of dark corners. Like The Rookery, this building oozed Georgian splendour: handmade terracotta tiles flooring the wood-panelled hall, what looked like antique prints of burlesque dancers creating a patchwork of images on every vertical space. In the reception area, a huge velvet chaise longue was positioned under the window overlooking the street, while a spotlight fell on a lavish flower arrangement spilling out of a silver Romanesque urn at one end.

O'Rourke's radio buzzed. The team heading for The Rookery were in.

36

With all the lights on full and the music turned off The Paradise Club looked plastic and theatrical to Cathy. Plasterwork thick with gold paint surrounded huge mirrors and more antique prints of half-naked women. The upholstery on the banquette, red with a purple floral design, looked comfortably luxurious with the dimmed mood lighting, but bathed in bright light it looked massively over the top, like a stage set.

Her team, a group of female officers, had started at the top of the building, bringing everyone they found downstairs as they went. While they'd been busy, officers on the ground floor had started taking the customers' details, but first had moved the glass tables around in front of the stage, giving the girls somewhere to sit apart from everyone else, each with a female officer minding her. Several of them looked resentful, resisting attempts to seat them with a shrug of their shoulders.

The swing doors to the stairs, concealed from the public by thick claret flock wallpaper and panelling, sucked closed behind them as Cathy pointed the Romanian girl beside her towards an unoccupied table. She couldn't have been more than eighteen, her dark hair long and loose. She was sobbing quietly, had been completely confused when Cathy and a female officer from Immigration had arrived in the bedroom she was working in.

Not nearly as confused as her client, though.

The guy looked like a banker or perhaps an accountant: grey haired, jowly, late sixties at least. The shock on his face had been a picture. But then he'd been wearing a woman's pink nylon bra and stockings, and was busy hoovering the girl's room. His erection had vanished the moment he'd realised he had an audience.

The Romanian girl slid onto an upholstered bucket chair and crossed her arms, glaring at Cathy. Not for the first time this evening Cathy was beginning to wonder if all of these girls wanted to be rescued. She knew they were still in shock, would be terrified that they had somehow brought about the raid, frightened that the men who had held them would still be able to hurt them. But some of them really didn't seem to be too pleased with the disruption to their night.

Upstairs, doors to what were obviously the girls' bedrooms opened off a long corridor, a shared living room at the end. Some of the rooms were neat and tidy, comfortable but spartan. In others, clothes and underwear were strewn everywhere, the beds unmade.

On the way up Cathy had glanced into a utilitarian bathroom that looked a lot like the sports changing room at her school. At the turn of the stairs, a tiny kitchen contained not much more than a fridge, kettle and microwave with a two-ring hob set into the counter. Everything was practical, basic, a total contrast to the opulence below. She kept hoping she'd open a door and Sarah Jane would be there, waiting for her, slagging her about why it had taken Cathy so long to find her.

The Romanian girl safely seated, Cathy looked around the main bar and dance floor area for O'Rourke. Through the mass of people now filling the club – punters shifting uncomfortably,

their heads down, waiting to be questioned, detectives, uniform –
Cathy could see him holding court over beside the bar. He was
good at managing big scenes, at deploying the right people to
do the right jobs. The whole place had been sealed from the
moment they walked in, uniformed Gardaí on all the exits, the
street outside crowded with Garda vehicles. And everyone had
to be kept apart until they knew who was who.

Cathy caught O'Rourke's eye. He jerked his head marginally,
signalling for her to come over to him. She headed in his direction.

'How's Frank's team getting on at The Rookery?' She had to
raise her voice above the bursts of conversation and static coming over the radio in his hand. A flash of something dark passed
across his face and she felt her stomach flip. 'What? Tell me.'

'The boys have found Sarah Jane's laptop and her diary in an
unused locker in the staff room. You were right, it looks like she
used a different locker from her usual one, the one Billy Roberts
showed us.' With her deadlines looming, Sarah Jane would have
needed her laptop with her, would be using it every minute she
had to polish her articles, had probably been planning to work
during her breaks. But Cathy knew she would never have left it
there by accident. No matter how ill she was.

'I bet she forgot her locker key. She's hopeless with keys, she's
always losing them – she keeps her car keys and house keys on
two separate bunches so she'll never be totally stuck if one goes
missing.'

O'Rourke nodded, 'There don't appear to be any appoint-
ments listed in her diary – she had her shifts in the restaurant
marked but nothing else for last weekend.'

Cathy looked up at him, about to speak, but there was something else in his frown that made her stop. 'What else?'

He glanced away before he spoke. 'They've found traces of blood at the bottom of the stairs. It's been cleaned up but not well enough.'

'How much?'

'Enough to suggest someone received a blow to the head, or fell and whacked their head on the way down. Thirsty's looking at it now.'

'So not Daniella?'

He looked speculative, 'We can't say yet. It's possible Daniella was attacked there before she was dismembered, but there's not enough blood to suggest the hard work was done in that location.'

'So it could be Sarah Jane's?'

'You know we can't tell at this stage.'

Cathy shook her head; it was a stupid question. 'Sorry, I know . . . but . . .'. It came out as a whisper.

She'd been at scenes where splatter patterns had proved crucial evidence . . . Had someone caved in the back of Sarah Jane's head and then dumped her body? Cathy couldn't think about that. She didn't have room in her head. They were here to find Sarah Jane alive and they were getting closer, she was sure of it. Cathy felt O'Rourke looking at her hard. He brushed the top of her arm, 'As soon as I know anything, you'll know, perhaps someone just cut their finger and it bled badly.' She threw him a weak smile as he continued, 'Have you spoken to Irina yet?'

Cathy shook her head, forcing away the images of Sarah Jane lying unconscious at the bottom of the stairs at The Rookery.

'She's over there in the corner with Aisling Kelly. Is she the same girl on the video who was speaking to Sarah Jane?' He jerked his head to indicate a young blonde on the far side of the lounge area wearing an oversized grey sweatshirt and sweat pants with strappy high-heeled sandals. She was huddled on the banquette, her knees drawn up. Aisling was sitting beside her, her auburn hair pulled back, her notebook open as she jotted something down. They were deep in conversation.

Focusing on them, Cathy nodded her head slowly. She was definitely the girl they'd seen on the video talking to Sarah Jane in the shop.

Cathy replayed the video in her head. Sarah Jane reaching for the lottery slip, writing something down – her phone number, evidently – and giving it to the girl. It had been an instant reaction. But Cathy wondered if Sarah Jane had seen Irina before, had been investigating The Paradise Club. Maybe that's why she'd got the job in The Rookery in the first place? How much had Sarah Jane found out about what was going on here? And why hadn't she told Cathy? Cathy shook her head; she knew Sarah Jane, she was her friend, but surely she wouldn't have kept quiet because she was trying to get a story?

Cathy looked across at the two young women speaking, at Irina, and suddenly the storm of confusion that had been filling her head since Monday night began to clear. It was as if a light was trying to shine through the fog. Cathy rolled the videos they'd watched this afternoon through her mind; the traffic cam footage was top quality, they'd been able to zoom in on Daniella getting out of Farrell's sports car, fussing with her hair as she walked towards the bus which had pulled up behind the Aston Martin, her denim jacket embroidered on the back and shoulders with some sort of intricate pattern, sequins catching the light. The footage from inside the bus had been much poorer quality, grainy, but with her long hair and jacket she was easy to spot walking down to the back seat, looking out the window.

Cathy turned to O'Rourke. 'What do you see when you look at her?'

O'Rourke looked surprised, 'At Irina? Blond, young, slim?'

'Exactly.' Cathy looked at him pointedly, her eyebrows raised. It only took him a second. 'Like Sarah Jane and Daniella.'

Irina's hair was distinctive; like both Daniella and Sarah Jane's it was long, highlighted, blow dried straight. A lot of girls had the same look – Cathy saw them all the time in town, hanging out in Dundrum shopping centre, almost clones of each other.

Cathy turned to O'Rourke, putting her hand on his arm so she had his full attention. 'When you see a woman on a video or across a room, what do you notice first?'

O'Rourke looked at her, not answering, conscious it was a rhetorical question. Cathy continued, 'Her hair. Even if she's wearing something very distinctive. You notice her hair.'

37

Despite the noise and bustle of the club, the blasts of radio traffic, phones ringing, Cathy could feel O'Rourke focusing on her, 'What are you saying?' He looked at her hard.

'I'm not sure. I just have a hunch. Let me talk to her.'

'Aisling's getting background from her on the staff before we start interviewing them in the morning.'

'Any sign of that Nacek guy?'

O'Rourke shook his head, 'Went home earlier, apparently. There are six on security, but only three on at any one time. We'll round him up with the other two we're missing. We'll find him.' He paused, 'Go easy with Irina, she's had a tough time. She needs a break before we interview her at the station.'

They both knew she was under no obligation to give them a formal statement about the activity at the club, that in many similar situations they'd been unable to prosecute because the girls, understandably, just wanted to get home, to put the past behind them.

'I won't keep her.'

Aisling was closing her notebook as Cathy reached them. The corner she'd taken Irina to was out of everyone's way, a perfect place to let her talk. Their eyes met and Cathy could tell from the grim look on her face that Aisling had been getting many of the details O'Rourke had relayed to Cathy earlier. None of it was pretty.

'Thanks so much, you've been really helpful.' Aisling's voice was warm as she smiled at Irina and stood up. 'This is my colleague Cathy Connolly. She needs to have a quick chat with you, then we'll get you out of here to somewhere safe where you can rest.' Irina frowned. 'Tell me when you want me to go to your police station.'

Aisling smiled reassuringly as she answered, 'We will, don't worry. I'll just get you another glass of water.'

Irina smiled at her as Cathy sat down in Aisling's place. O'Rourke had said Irina wanted to help them all she could, but Cathy could see she was tense; it showed in her face and in the way she was gripping the hem of her sweatshirt, nervously fiddling with it, stopping and pushing her hair behind her ear. Cathy could see she was only just holding on. *She knew that feeling.*

'Are you with the police?' Despite her Garda baseball cap and jacket, Irina looked at Cathy's black sweatpants and hoodie, at her Nikes, obviously puzzled.

'Yes, I'm with the detective unit, like Aisling. Thank you for talking to me. The girl you telephoned, Sarah Jane, is my friend.'

Irina put out her hand, grasping Cathy's wrist tight, shaking her head, 'No, thank *you*. If your friend hadn't given me her number; if he,' she inclined her head towards O'Rourke, 'hadn't arrived, I might not be alive now.'

Her words were simple yet stark, said with total sincerity. She wasn't exaggerating. Cathy felt her anger rising. The men who had done this needed to be punished.

'He's a good guy.' Cathy rubbed Irina's hand. 'But it's you who has saved all these girls.' Cathy smiled, hoping it reached her eyes, 'I'm hoping you can help us with something else too. We're not sure what's happened, but Sarah Jane has disappeared. We're really anxious to find her.' Irina's hand shot to her mouth, her eyes filled with fear. 'Do you mind if I ask you about her?'

Irina shook her head, a dark cloud passing across her face. Cathy opened her mouth to speak, but before she could say anything Irina cut in, 'How did you get my message if she has disappeared?' Her eyes filled with fear and she started feeding the hem of her sweatshirt through her fingers again as if the feel of the fabric was centring her somehow. Cathy needed her to be strong now, and as she sat beside her Cathy's feeling that Irina was the missing piece of the puzzle was growing stronger. She needed to tread carefully.

'Her phone was with our technical people. The day she vanished she left it in her car.'

That still didn't make any sense. The phone had been dead when they'd found it, but if she'd forgotten it, why hadn't she gone back for it before she went home? Or had she not been able to collect it?

'Near here? Was her car left near here?'

'Yes, in Drury Street,' Cathy stopped herself. O'Rourke had said Irina hadn't been sure which city she was in – she wasn't going to know street names. 'Not far from here, in a car park.' Cathy paused, watching Irina. She knew she should be going in more gently, building Irina's trust, but time was against them. *How had she not seen this before?*

Watching Irina closely, Cathy continued, 'Sarah Jane worked next door in The Rookery restaurant. We know she felt ill on Sunday evening and the manager called her a cab to take her home. We've lost track of her when she arrived there.'

Irina froze, staring at a point on the floor not far from Cathy's foot, and Cathy was suddenly sure she was right. She pulled out her phone and texted O'Rourke: *NEED YOU*. Irina was obviously still fighting with her emotions, biting her lip as O'Rourke materialised silently beside Cathy from across the room.

Cathy knew she couldn't rush Irina, but she was bursting with questions now. O'Rourke hung back, his hands in his pockets. He pulled out his phone and switched it to silent. He was waiting.

'It was you, wasn't it? Getting into the cab, not Sarah Jane.'

It took Irina a few moments, then she looked up, her blue eyes meeting Cathy's, glancing anxiously at O'Rourke, her voice catching as she spoke:

'I didn't understand, I didn't know why. I was so frightened, the man with the cowboy boots . . .' Tears began to slide down Irina's cheeks. Then the words were tumbling out of her mouth, 'Nacek said I had to go with him.' In little more than a whisper, 'I didn't know.'

Cathy put her hand on Irina's arm, fighting to keep her voice calm, relaxed. She glanced at O'Rourke. 'I just need you to tell me exactly what happened.'

'The man who runs this place,' Irina's face clouded, 'he hurt me before, and then when they said to go in his car I was so frightened, I thought they were going to hurt me again.'

'His car?'

'Before – the day before I went in the taxi, they took me out to a big house and I had to get in his car and then catch a bus. I thought they were going to kill me, that it was some sort of game.'

Cathy took a breath, processing this information, trying to keep up. 'The man with the cowboy boots owns this place, and he hurt you before?'

Irina nodded wordlessly.

Richard Farrell. Had to be. The cowboy boots.

'Tell me in your own words exactly what happened when you went to the house.'

Irina began fiddling with her sweatshirt again. 'Nacek took me. He made me put on a jacket and denim skirt, to brush my hair over my face.'

'What was the house like?'

'Big, with gates and a long drive. There was this horrible dog. I thought he was going to rape me again . . .'

'Nacek or the man with the cowboy boots?' Cathy tried to keep her voice soft, empathetic.

'Both of them . . .' She stopped, obviously unable to speak about what had happened before.

'So tell me what happened when you got to the house?'

'Nacek took me into the living room, in the house, told me to put on the clothes. There was a swimming pool – through the window, I could see a swimming pool.'

'Where did he get the clothes from?'

She shrugged, 'They were just lying on the sofa. They weren't new, I could smell the girl's perfume on them.' Irina didn't meet Cathy's eye. 'Something really bad had happened to her, hadn't it? I knew, I knew. But I couldn't refuse in case it was me next.'

'I understand.'

Irina took a depth breath, 'So I got changed and then the boss arrived and took me though this big kitchen into the garage. His car was there. A sports car, black. I got in and Nacek said I just needed to get out of the car when the bus came. He gave me a green card like a credit card, I had to copy the other people and put it on a scanner just inside the door of the bus, then go and sit down. They told me I had to keep my hair over my face and keep looking at the floor.' The tears began to fall again, 'Nacek said he'd be following me in his car, that I had to get off the bus when I saw him pull in front of it. He said there were other people on the bus watching, that he would cut my throat if I spoke to anyone or tried to run.'

Cathy leaned forward, her heart beating hard, 'So you did what he said?' Irina nodded helplessly. 'When did this happen?'

'A few days ago, I'm not sure – the day after I saw your friend.'

'So then what happened?'

'The next day, the day after – after lunch . . . I knew something really bad had happened to the girl I had pretended to be. I saw the fire door open and I just ran. I got to the car park and then Nacek got me. I thought he was going to kill me . . . He hit me in the back of the head so there would be no bruises and then once in my stomach. It hurt so much.'

Irina bit her lip. Cathy reached forward and rubbed her arm. 'So tell me about Sarah Jane.'

'I didn't see her again after the shop, I didn't know anything had happened to her.'

'Tell me about the taxi, what happened that night?' Cathy could feel O'Rourke's presence, strong and silent behind her.

'Nacek came again. He had a pink scarf and a black coat, he told me to plait my hair and to put them on. Then he took me down to the fire exit and out across the car park to the bins. I didn't know what was happening. He made me wait behind the bins. Another man came out of a door. He made me pull the scarf over my face. Then Nacek said I was to go with him and get into the taxi, and I had to act like I was ill. He said he'd be driving behind, and when it stopped I was to get out and walk away from the taxi and he'd be there to pick me up again, like the time before. The man I didn't know put his arm around me and walked me around to the street, to the taxi.'

'Did he say anything? Anything at all?'

Irina frowned hard, 'I think he said something like, "She said she'd call." I wasn't really listening, I'm sorry. I was so frightened.'

Cathy moved forward onto the edge of the banquette and patted Irina's knee. 'I know. You've done brilliantly to tell us. I'll just be a sec.'

Standing up, she caught O'Rourke's eye and they moved a few metres away. Cathy was so angry she could hardly contain it.

'Billy Roberts is in this up to his neck. He knows what happened to Sarah Jane, he has to. Has done the whole time.' She drew in a sharp breath, her voice low, 'He or Farrell must have spotted the resemblance between Irina and Daniella and used Irina to make it look like Daniella got on that bus. Irina played her part so well they did it again to make us think Sarah Jane had got into the taxi.' She thrust her hands into the pockets of her hoodie, 'If I have to speak to Billy Roberts, I think I'm going to kill him.'

O'Rourke pulled out his phone. 'Gallagher's team are still in there. We'll see what Mr Roberts has to say for himself and bring him in. He's lied to us and he's probably edited those security tapes too – we'll get the techs in the Park to see if they've been tampered with.' Cathy stared silently at a distant spot on the ground, her hands balled in her pockets. 'You good to keep going with Irina for a moment?'

She nodded and turned to sit back down as O'Rourke's call connected.

If it had been Irina getting into the taxi, then the last definite sighting they had of Sarah Jane had been her getting into the car

with the guy in the combats. Who could have taken her anywhere.
Cathy thought about the information they had, her mind processing the detail. Had Sarah Jane realised what was happening? Had they confronted her and she said she'd call the cops, or her dad? Had she bluffed them into thinking she had back-up?

Cathy hoped so. With every particle of her being she hoped so. If they thought Sarah Jane had connections, maybe they were holding her while they got ready to move the girls from The Paradise Club, reckoned they could clean everything up, so if there was a raid the Guards wouldn't find anything. Or perhaps they were confident enough that the girls were so terrified they wouldn't talk. *They just hadn't bargained on Irina.*

Killing Sarah Jane would bring so much trouble down on them, but they'd already murdered Daniella. Perhaps Daniella's death *had* been an accident. It was looking more and more like Farrell was behind this; if he was rough with the girls at The Paradise Club perhaps he'd been a bit too rough with Daniella, and that was how all this had started?

Sarah Jane was different: she could bring way more trouble to their door. Cathy felt a shiver run down her spine. Sarah Jane's connections could equally make it essential she disappeared. Permanently. Cathy fought to focus on Irina, on what she could tell her. She needed to move forward, to keep moving forward.

'So you got into the taxi . . .'

'I thought I could tell the driver, ask him for help, but he was listening to something on the radio and then I thought he'd just tell Nacek. So I kept quiet. We went a long way, then got to some houses and he stopped. I did what I was told and got out and walked away. Nacek was right there, parked behind the taxi. I got into his car and he told me to wait.' Irina pulled a strand of hair from her face as she spoke, 'He locked me into the car and went up to this house. He rang the doorbell, but no one answered. He had a set of keys, and he let himself in. He wasn't there very long, came out with a suitcase, one of those ones on wheels, but he was carrying it.'

Cathy stopped her, 'What colour was it?'

'Pink, bright pink.' *Sarah Jane's hand-luggage case. Cathy had given it to her one Christmas – it was a perfect match with her phone case, Sarah Jane had loved it. Why hadn't they realised it was missing?* Irina continued, 'He threw it into the back seat and drove off, carefully, but I could tell he was trying to be fast. He kept looking in the mirror.'

'What happened then?'

'He called someone, said, "It's done", I think, and then took me back to the club. He told me to undo my hair and change back into my normal clothes. She shrugged, 'That was all.'

'Thank you, thank you for telling me.' Cathy's mind was reeling. Normally she distanced herself from the victim, they all did, focused on getting answers rather than dwelling on the emotion and fear that was inevitably tied up with violent crime. But this wasn't a normal situation. She moved as if she was about to get up.

'Please don't leave me.' Irina's voice was little more than a whisper, 'What happened to them? To the girl and your friend?'

'We don't know for sure . . .'

Cathy could see the fear in Irina's face, felt her own anger surging. This is what men like Richard Farrell and the other owners of The Paradise Club did.

J.P. had found out that the club was owned by a group of off-shore company directors, who probably had wives and mistresses and off-shore accounts, who lived in luxury while the women imprisoned here lived in constant, abject fear. Deep inside, Cathy felt like she was going to explode.

They were clever, there was no doubt about that. But not clever enough. They thought they had Irina so terrified she wouldn't give evidence, but they hadn't reckoned on the side of her she'd obviously managed to hide while she'd been here. They were used to destroying lives, taking advantage of women whose lives were already damaged by emotional or physical abuse. Women who couldn't fight back. Cathy gritted her teeth. If it was the last thing she did she was going to get justice for Daniella and Irina and the women like her.

O'Rourke had been resolute when he'd got back to Dún Laoghaire after his first visit here today, his own anger tangible. That was exactly how she felt now, and Cathy knew she couldn't let it go. The Boss called it her fight instinct. The raw emotion – aggression, if they were truthful – that made her a winner. Fight and win. Kill or be killed. And right now Cathy was ready to kill the evil bastards who were behind The Paradise Club and everything it represented.

38

There was no question in Cathy's mind that Richard Farrell was the cause of a whole heap of trouble.

Cathy glanced across the club at O'Rourke, the phone glued to his ear. He'd be putting out calls to get Richard Farrell and his sidekick Nacek taken into custody based on Irina's testimony. It was looking a lot like one or both of them were culpable in Daniella's death, and knew a whole lot more about what had happened to Sarah Jane than they'd indicated so far. Billy Roberts too.

She'd had a text from 007 to say they'd discovered the cameras in The Paradise Club were linked to the CCTV room in The Rookery, just before they'd found cocaine in Billy Roberts's office. They were bringing him in. She could imagine Roberts had been thrilled. *He hadn't seen anything yet.*

'We are going to the police station now?' Irina interrupted Cathy's thoughts, her voice betraying the strain she was under.

Cathy smiled encouragingly, 'Yes, you'll be completely safe there, and a woman from an organisation called Ruhama, who help women in your situation, will come and talk to you. They have safe accommodation they can take you and the other girls to.'

A flash of fear crossed Irina's face. 'I don't . . . the other girls . . . I don't trust them. If they realise it was me that caused all this they will get word to the men who were holding us.'

Irina sounded like a lost child. Cathy could see the tears welling in her eyes again.

'You'll be safe, I promise. I'll come down to the station with you. I just need a quick word with my inspector. Really, we'll keep everyone apart.'

'Will I be able to use a phone? I want to ring home.' Irina's voice cracked on the last word. Home must feel a very long way away right now.

Cathy pulled her mobile out of the pocket of her hoodie, 'Do you know the number?'

Irina nodded, taking the phone in her hand like it was made of gold. 'My mum keeps her phone switched off to save the battery, she doesn't really understand phones, only uses it to text, but . . .'

'Ring as many people as you need. Look, go over there,' Cathy indicated a dark corner of the club, 'No one will be able to hear you. I'll be right over here.'

Even with her back turned towards the room, Cathy could feel the emotion radiating from Irina. Her shoulders hunched, she curled up on the long padded seat that ran along the wall of the bar. It had to be the middle of the night in whatever place Irina came from, but Cathy could tell from her tears that someone somewhere was very glad to hear from her. She wondered if it would be the same for all the girls.

While Irina was talking Cathy headed straight for O'Rourke. He was leaning back on the bar, his mobile clamped to his ear.

'What?' He mouthed the word, still listening.

'Farrell set it all up, Irina was sure he was going to kill her unless she did what he wanted.'

He put his hand over the mouthpiece, 'Cabinteely are going to bring him in, and we've got an address for Nacek. I doubt he's got a work visa. The security guys and a couple of the bar staff all share a company apartment – uniform from Store Street are heading there now. We need an ID on him, though. You've met him – can you get a still from one of the surveillance tapes? A good clear shot in colour and we'll get it out everywhere. There's a good chance he's heard about the raid and will try to leave the jurisdiction.'

'I'll go and look at the footage now and drop Irina off at the same time.'

O'Rourke's nod was curt.

From across the club Cathy saw Irina click the phone off and take a moment before she turned to look for her. Not seeing Cathy, a look of panic paralysed her face. 'You're needed,' O'Rourke jerked his head in Irina's direction.

Cathy was back beside her a few seconds later, the relief clearly visible on Irina's face at seeing her crossing the club towards her. She handed her back her phone. 'Thank you.'

'You got through OK?'

Irina smiled, 'I've texted and left a message on my mum's phone. Then I rang Meti.' Then she suddenly broke down, sobbing like she was going to choke.

Cathy moved to her side, sitting down beside her, putting her arm around her. 'Who's Meti?'

Cathy could hardly hear the response, 'My fiancé. He's been waiting. He's been staying with my mum and my little brother so he woke them up so I could talk to them. He said he never gave up.' She gulped in a mouthful of air, 'He's been looking for me, trying to find out who placed the ad, to get the police at home involved. The money I wired to my Mum came from so many different places he didn't know where I was. I was moving about too fast for him to come and try and find me and the police were no help.' She paused, 'I don't know if he'll still want me after . . . after so many . . . I'm not the same.'

'You'll work it out. It'll be difficult for both of you. You've had a horrific experience.'

'When can I go home? I need to give you your statement, then I want to go home.'

'As soon as we have a statement from you about Sarah Jane, the bus and everything, you'll be free to go. You don't have to give a statement at all about working here straight away if you don't want to, you've got sixty days to decide.'

'But you need to prosecute them, Nacek and his men, for what they did to us. And the man with the cowboy boots, he raped me. I need to tell you.' She paused, 'It will be on one of the security tapes, they record everything.'

Cathy kept her face straight. Irina still had no idea what had happened to Daniella, how brave she'd been in contacting Sarah Jane, how much she'd risked. 'The sixty days is to give you time to recover. If you can tell us everything now it'll speed things up, but we'll get them. With your testimony and hopefully statements from the other girls we'll have lots to work with here – I'm sure there are work visa violations and revenue fraud as well. And the drugs team will come in and take the place apart.' She paused, 'The other investigations we're working on are extremely serious. Farrell and Nacek are looking at a long time inside if we can successfully prosecute. Your testimony is crucial to that.'

Irina closed her eyes for a moment, as if she was trying to get a grip on everything that was happening. 'They have drugs too. I've seen cars with bags of powder, they made us carry some when we went on the bus and the ferry. I wrote it all down, everything I could see, registration plate numbers, everything.'

'We'll get them, don't worry. We need to get down to the station quickly so I can get an ID on Nacek and notify all stations. Are you good to go now?'

Irina's eyes began to fill. She looked at the floor, then at Cathy, 'Yes. How can I thank you?'

'You don't need to. You've brought us here, closer to where Sarah Jane was last seen. Without you we'd have no idea what might have happened to her, or to Daniella O'Connor. I should be thanking you.'

39

In Pearse Street Station the CCTV viewing room wasn't much bigger than a broom cupboard. Cathy checked the time on her phone. She hadn't wanted to rush Irina, but she'd got here as fast as she possibly could; O'Rourke had sent the discs on ahead of her so they were ready as soon as she walked in. She stood behind the young Guard who had been volunteered to go through the footage. She could definitely think of more interesting jobs you could end up with in the Guards, like watching paint dry. It was stuffy in the small room, and he had his shirt unbuttoned and cuffs rolled up, which wasn't altogether a bad thing. At least the view was good. Cathy glanced at him, trying to still her heart. It had been racing since she'd spoken to Irina, but she knew she needed to keep calm, needed to focus and get this done.

Flipping the discs they'd burned in the club in and out of the machine, scrolling through the various cameras, the young Guard worked at lightning speed, she had to give him that. He'd said he was a gamer, that he was used to rapidly moving images.

Nacek had to be here somewhere – he worked in the damn place.

'Stop! That's him.'

The lad on the control panel touched a switch, changing camera.

'Better?'

The second camera showed Nacek's face clearly, his black T-shirt straining over his chest.

'Perfect. O'Rourke wants that sent over to Interpol, and circulated to all stations . . .'

Cathy started, her mouth open, the next sentence hanging. As the young guard had frozen the picture, Nacek had turned to speak to another man who had entered the frame. A fit-looking guy in a white T-shirt who looked like he had a cloth in his hand. A guy about six feet tall, his hair closely cropped, military style. A guy Cathy recognised, and not only from the clock tattoo on the back of his neck. What was Aleksy doing there? From the way they were talking, and judging by the cloth in his hand, it looked like he worked there.

'Oh holy feck.' It was out before she had time to get it back, and the lad swung around in his chair, one eyebrow raised. 'Know him?'

Cathy nodded slowly. She knew him all right.

O'Rourke was going to skin her. She'd given evidence, without authority, to someone who could be a material witness in a murder invesitgation. Cathy felt her skin chill, *and Aleksy had been at Johnny Fox's, close to where Daniella's body had been found, on Tuesday night.*

'I need to talk to O'Rourke. Can you get prints of those stills and get them out?'

'No problemo.'

Letting the door of the viewing room shut behind her, Cathy wished it was no problemo, but somehow she knew it was a fecking huge problemo.

Thankfully O'Rourke answered his phone quickly. Standing in an endless corridor, offices opening off both sides at regular intervals, the walls between crowded with steel lockers, Cathy leaned on the fire exit door, hoping no one would come up the stairs behind her. She kept her voice level, but she knew from his reaction that O'Rourke could hear the urgency in it.

'I need to talk to you.'

'Where are you?' His response was staccato, like machine-gun fire. Was it the way she said it? There was no point trying to hide anything from him: sometimes she thought he could read her mind.

'Pearse Street – meet you in the canteen?'

He cut in before she could continue, 'Is Irina OK?'

'Yep, she's fine.' Cathy reached for her necklace. 'It's something else. Something on the security tapes. We need to find the guy I was with in Flannery's the other night. Aleksy Janosik, he's Polish. I'll explain when you get here, but we need to find him fast.'

There was a pause, 'I'll get everyone on it. I'm on my way.'

As good as his word, O'Rourke appeared in the station canteen before her hot chocolate had cooled, his heavy navy overcoat flapping as he let the swing doors close behind him, his shoulders glistening with raindrops.

Fighting to keep calm, Cathy was nursing her cup, and had a coffee waiting for him. Thankfully the canteen was almost empty; a couple of the tables were occupied by the night shift, their navy bomber jackets slung over the back of the chairs, GARDA emblazoned in gold on the back. He strode over to the corner she was in and pulled out a chair, spinning it around so he was sitting astride it. He didn't take his coat off.

'So what's up? Who's this Aleksy?'

Cathy drew in a breath. 'It's complicated.'

'Shoot.'

Cathy bit her lip. *Where did she start? From the beginning was always the best place. Then she couldn't be accused of leaving anything out.*

'You know I went up to Enniskerry to question Jacob?'

O'Rourke interrupted, 'I thought this was about the security tape?'

Cathy held up her hand to stop him, 'It is, there's just a bigger picture. So when we'd finished the interview I was chatting in the shop with his mum,' O'Rourke rolled his hands like he didn't have all day, 'and this Polish guy comes in to collect some suits . . . Aleksy.'

'The guy from Flannery's?'

'Yes, he works for us translating, he speaks a load of languages. I recognised him from Pearse Street.' She cleared her throat, 'So, remember I got a look at those MoneyGram transfers that Irina was making home to Belarus? I wanted to get someone to find out where the money was going . . .'

'And I told you to focus on the case and leave it alone?'

Her smile of acknowledgement was weak, 'Well, we got chatting, me and Aleksy.'

O'Rourke raised an eyebrow, 'Did you know he worked at The Paradise Club?'

Cathy shook her head, 'No, he said he did painting and decorating, translating – odd jobs while he looks for a full-time job.

He's a mechanical engineer ... but I think he must be doing door or bar work too, I don't know.'

O'Rourke's face creased in a frown, 'Go on ...'

Cathy closed her eyes, 'We went up to Johnny Fox's for a jar.' *There were some details he didn't need.* This was the worst bit, the bit that had been making her feel physically sick since she'd left the CCTV room. *She was sure she was wrong, but O'Rourke had to know.* She turned her cup in her hands, 'It was Tuesday, the day Saunders thinks Daniella's body was dumped. He said he thought she'd been dead for about four days. If she was murdered on the Friday night when she went missing that all adds up.'

O'Rourke winced, and paused for a moment before he summed it all up. 'So now, on top of the head of security at The Paradise Club getting one of the girls to pose as Daniella O'Connor, we've got another member of staff – most of whom seem to be Eastern European ex-military thugs – in close proximity to the location of the decapitated body of a girl the same age and build as our missing waitress, within the crucial time frame? And you're telling me you might form part of an alibi for this guy?'

Cathy groaned inside; it sounded even worse when he said it than it had done in her head. O'Rourke tipped her chin and looked her directly in the eye. His look was hard but serious. 'You think he might have had her body in his boot while you went for a drink, and then dumped it when you left?'

She broke his gaze, 'No, honestly I don't. But it's a possibility.'

'You *have* been busy.' O'Rourke didn't attempt to keep the sarcasm from his voice. Cathy flinched. Ever since the whole business of her getting pregnant, he'd been fiercely protective of her – not that she'd had any proper dates in the past year, but she knew he was worried about her getting involved with the wrong type of guy. *He was worse than her mother.* She didn't mind, part of her hoping it was because he cared, in a more than a close friend kind of way. It was nice having him look out for her, although it had definitely been a bit awkward the other night. But maybe his instinct for trouble was better than hers – at least it wasn't confused by hormones.

'Really, he's a nice guy and he works for us – Pearse Street would have done background checks. He just wants to get a good job, get some experience and make some money, and get back home.'

'He's working in a brothel where a bunch of girls have been trafficked and were being held against their will. I'm not seeing "nice".' Cathy had to agree with him there. O'Rourke continued, 'And he had means, method and motive to dispose of Daniella O'Connor's body. It's some coincidence.'

It was more than a coincidence – what the feck had Aleksy been doing in Enniskerry the very same night Daniella O'Connor wound up a bit higher up the same mountain in a reduced state? And how could he have spent the evening with her if he knew something about Sarah Jane's disappearance? She'd been careful with the details when she'd explained it to him, saying it was an ongoing investigation; she hadn't mentioned The Rookery or the location of the newsagent's, but she'd told him Sarah Jane's name and it had been all over the news. A shiver went up Cathy's spine. Maybe she *was* a bad judge of character. *Maybe she was a total idiot.* Had she been totally taken in, her heart interfering with her head? Had he only been friendly because he wanted to know what she knew?

O'Rourke stared hard at the table and made a clicking sound with his tongue. She could see he was thinking. Fast. Cathy rubbed her hand over her forehead.

'How do you get yourself into these situations, Cat – I mean, how?'

Cathy couldn't meet his eye. She felt bad enough as it was. At least he wasn't shouting.

O'Rourke pushed his chair back.

'So we need to talk to your friend Aleksy rather urgently, find out what he knows about Daniella O'Connor and if he knows anything about Sarah Jane, and what his movements were when he left you at Johnny Fox's. I'll talk to Saunders, see if we can get a clearer time frame on when Daniella's body was dumped. He's sure she'd been dead for a few days before she was taken to the mountains, so she must have been somewhere – somewhere where there is a ton of forensic evidence.' He paused, 'But Cat, good work on piecing the bits together, on spotting Irina as a decoy. Let's hope between them, Billy Roberts and this Aleksy, it can get us to Sarah Jane.'

40

The car park behind Pearse Street Garda Station was quiet as Cathy headed back to her car. She had to leave it to O'Rourke now. She'd potentially compromised both herself and the investigation, and she had to give him space to fix it. Walking across the floodlit tarmac her head was a maelstrom of emotion, regret and anger combining into a dangerous cocktail.

She knew O'Rourke would head straight back to The Paradise Club to see if the team had tracked down Nacek or Aleksy while he'd been gone. Billy Roberts was in custody, but Farrell was a flight risk, and she was quite sure he knew that The Paradise Club had been raided and was being ripped apart by now.

Cathy hadn't wanted to leave, but she knew O'Rourke well enough to know that he was going to be pretty busy finding the pair of them, questioning them about Sarah Jane, and then about Daniella O'Connor, while at the same time trying to sort out the mess she was in without jeopardising her entire career. Which would be a challenge, she knew.

She'd gone directly against O'Rourke's orders pursuing the MoneyGram payments, and she'd managed to involve someone who was directly linked to the case.

In this job, you worked solo, even if you were working with a partner you didn't get time to confer when the shit hit the fan. You regularly had seconds to make decisions that could be the difference between life and death. Monumental errors of judgement, like disobeying direct orders and then ending up a a murder suspect's alibi, didn't do anything for your chances of promotion. Unless you were planning a career back in uniform in the arse end of Ballygobackwards.

She hadn't said anything to Aleksy about questioning Jacob, about The Rookery, about why she was in Enniskerry, but she'd mentioned that her friend was missing and he'd seemed so concerned. Was she that bad a judge of character that she'd ended up snogging someone who had hurt Sarah Jane, who might be implicated in Daniella's murder? The very thought made her want to heave.

Fighting to focus on the here and now, before she left the station Cathy headed downstairs to check on Irina. Her Nikes squeaking on the grey-flecked lino, she paused outside the interview room she'd left Irina in, her hand on the steel door handle. Irina had been amazing, but Cathy wondered how much she really knew; had she really not seen Sarah Jane again after meeting her in the shop?

Cathy knocked gently and pushed down the handle, sticking her head around the door. The conversation stopped. Wrapped in a dull, navy-blue blanket, Irina looked up. She flashed Cathy a smile, relief written all over her face. The Ruhama caseworker turned and gave her a reassuring nod.

'All good?'

'All good, Cathy, thank you.' Irina smiled at the case worker, 'I'm giving a statement and then I'm going home. They said they can organise an emergency passport if they can't find mine at the club.'

'But not tonight? I get to say goodbye to you in the morning.' Cathy knew she was smiling on the outside, but inside part of her she was thinking that the hours of darkness gave them time to verify Irina's story, to track down Nacek and . . . Aleksy. They might need to question Irina more closely before this was all finished.

Irina nodded, 'Yes, will you be here tomorrow?'

'I should be. I have to head now but just in case I don't get back, good luck.' Cathy meant it, 'You've been amazing through all of this, your bravery has saved those girls.' She paused, 'I'm sure it will all work out for you at home. I hope so.'

As Cathy reached her car, a part of her wished she could go to the gym. With everything in her head she knew she had no chance of sleep. Normally after a job like this the team all went out for a drink – even if it was six o'clock in the morning. Winding down, having a laugh, was what made them strong when they needed to be. They all knew each other like family.

But tonight she couldn't hang around waiting for them to wrap everything up: she needed to keep a low profile. She needed to get her thoughts in order. Cathy sighed. She did her best thinking while pumelling the punch bag, but if she went to the gym she'd have to go back to Dún Laoghaire first to leave her gun back at the station or go home and secure it in the wall safe Decko had had installed in the living room – there was no way she could leave it in her car. She had enough on her plate without being charged with neglecting her firearm. It was looking like home was her best option.

Christ, she hoped O'Rourke could find Aleksy fast, and find out what he knew. Cathy pulled her keys from her hoodie pocket and unlocked the car. After the explosion she had felt a wave of anxiety whenever she approached a car, not just her own. She was being irrational, she knew – who got blown up twice in a lifetime? She got herself into some shit, but really? She pushed the thoughts from her mind. Her kitbag was in the boot, and she had a key to the gym – would she be mad to go all the way back to Dún Laoghaire and then out to Ballymun now? After everything that had happened today, she knew a workout would be the only hope she had of winding down.

Before she could decide, her phone began to ring. She pulled it out, answering it as she swung the car door open.

'I'm really sorry to call so late. This is Rebecca Ryan, Jacob's mum.'

Cathy leaned in and checked the clock on the dash. Just after 12.45. Something must have happened for Rebecca to be calling in the middle of the night.

'How can I help?'

The words tumbled out, 'Jacob's gone. I don't know what to do. I think my ex-husband has taken him. He can be really violent. If Jacob has a meltdown, I don't know what he might do … I also think he might have something to do with your friend going missing too.' It took Cathy a second to process what she was saying. *What the feck?*

Frantic didn't even begin to describe the tone of Rebecca's voice, Cathy could feel her pain and panic like it was heat coming through her phone. And from what she knew of Rebecca Ryan, she was the type who only panicked when there was a very real reason to.

What else could happen tonight?

Cathy thought of the scar running down Rebecca Ryan's face; when she'd noticed it she'd thought fleetingly that it might have been from a car accident, but if her ex could be violent …

Had he done that? *And what on earth could he know about Sarah Jane?*

Cathy swung into her car and fired the engine, sticking the phone into its holder and switching to hands free. She fought to keep her voice calm, but her heart was thumping.

'Start at the beginning. Tell me exactly what's happened. Jacob first, then Sarah Jane.'

'Jacob just called me. He said he was waiting in the car for his dad, that he's taking him on a plane for a surprise. He can't do that without my permission. He's taking him out of the country, I know it.'

Cathy cut in, 'We'll stop him, don't worry.' Reversing out of the space, Cathy swung the car into a three-point turn and headed across the floodlit car park for the exit. 'Have you rung 999?'

'No, I didn't know . . .'

'Have you got another phone?'

'Yes, the landline, I've got the landline.'

Cathy swung around a Garda van and headed for the security barrier.

'I want you to dial 999, give them all Jacob's details and your husband's registration number – do you know it?'

'Yes, it's a private plate. It's a sports car.'

'Ring now, and when you've given them all the info, tell them I want a word, put the phones together.'

'OK, OK.'

As Cathy punched her number into the barrier at the car park entrance she could hear Rebecca asking the operator for the Gardaí, then, 'Jacob's eight. He's got Asperger's. My ex is Richard Farrell. He lives in Foxrock, Eyrie House. Jacob is with him tonight. He owns a restaurant in town, The Rookery. They could be going there, but from what Jacob said it sounded like they were heading straight for the airport. I think he's taking him to Spain.'

Cathy felt every hair on her body stand up. *Jacob's dad was Richard Farrell?* Oh holy God. Cathy wondered if Rebecca Ryan knew her ex-husband's business interests extended to running a brothel full of trafficked women. It wasn't exactly the type of thing you discussed over breakfast, and now wasn't the time to break the news to her. *Richard Farrell was Jacob's dad?* She could hardly believe it.

But that would explain why Rebecca was so familiar with The Rookery that she could get someone a job there, why she'd been dropping that girl's CV in when Jacob had seen Sarah Jane. And why Aleksy had been in her shop, of all the out of the way places he could have been collecting suits for his boss. She'd said she'd worked with Billy Roberts in Spain – perhaps she'd helped get him the job at The Rookery.

A moment later Rebecca had given her personal details and Farrell's registration plate to the controller. 'There's a Guard on the other line who needs to talk to you. Just a minute.' Cathy heard a click as Rebecca put the phones together.

Cathy tried to still her heart, to concentrate on the road. She needed to call O'Rourke, to get the troops out. Her mind worked fast.

'Thanks, Rebecca. Who's that?'

The voice was clipped, efficient, 'Sergeant John Fitzpatrick.'

'Fitzer? It's Cat Connolly. I don't have a radio. Richard Farrell is implicated in a double missing persons investigation and the trafficking gang O'Rourke raided tonight at The Paradise Club. He's there now. Can you update him?'

Fitzgerald didn't hesitate, 'I'm on it.'

'Thanks, Fitzer. We need to stop Farrell.'

'We will. Leave it with me.' Cathy knew from his voice he'd have every unit in the city looking for the car in seconds. The fastest way to get everyone on this was to go through Command and Control. A 999 call took priority over everything. And Fitzer was sound. They'd trained together, had got drunk together more than once.

'Keep me posted Fitzer?'

'Will do. You in the shit again?'

'I hope not, Fitzer, I hope not.'

The lights changed and Cathy focused on avoiding a pair of teenagers in hoodies who were intent on falling off the pavement into the road, as she switched back to Rebecca. 'You still there, Rebecca?'

'Yes, I'm here.'

'A call will go out to all mobile units in the city. We'll alert the airport and the airport police and all the ferry terminals. We'll stop him leaving the country. How long ago did Jacob phone?'

'I don't know, I've lost track of time – ten minutes, maybe?'

Cathy did some rapid calculations in her head. If they'd left Foxrock soon after Jacob called, they were probably on the M50 by now. If she headed west she could pick up the M50 at the Red Cow interchange, and if she really put her foot down, maybe arrive at the airport shortly after them. She knew Farrell drove an Aston Martin, but he'd be keeping to the speed limit to avoid getting noticed.

'Can they put out one of those missing child messages?' Rebecca's voice was starting to crack, the tears she was obviously holding back now on their way.

'A CRI Alert? Those are only used when the child's life is in imminent danger. Do you think your ex-husband would harm him?'

'Not intentionally, he's just totally unreliable – he drives too fast, and if he realises that I know and I've called you, anything could happen. Jacob can't do sudden changes of plan, he'll be having a meltdown.'

'We'll stop him, don't worry. I'm going to head towards the airport. You sure he'll take him to Spain?'

'He spends a lot of time in Marbella.'

The Costa del Crime – that would be right.

Cathy switched down a gear and skirted around a cyclist. She could hear Rebecca breathing heavily at the other end, knew she needed to keep her talking so she could hold it together. 'Tell me about Sarah Jane. Why do you think your husband could be involved?'

Cathy could hear Rebecca's voice fracture as she spoke, 'Jacob found some keys with her photo on them – he'd dropped something and they were under the sofa. When he rang he said everything was OK because the girl who'd got lost wasn't lost, she'd been to Richard's, and she'd left her keys there by accident and she probably just couldn't get into her house.' Cathy opened her mouth to speak but nothing came out.

Sarah Jane had her Facebook picture – the one taken at the Dún Laoghaire festival – on her car keys, a picture of all of them on a hot sunny day. So many questions fought their way into Cathy's head she didn't know which to ask first.

Sarah Jane had been to Farrell's house? Jesus. Before she could process the information properly, Cathy's phone pipped to indicate an incoming call. O'Rourke's name flashed up on the screen. Thank God for Bluetooth.

'Give me a sec – I need to put you on hold, Rebecca.'

She hit the button on the steering wheel, but jumped straight in before he could speak, 'Sarah Jane was in Farrell's house in Foxrock.' Cathy focused on keeping her voice calm, delivering all the information clearly, 'Rebecca Ryan, Jacob's mum, is on the other line. Richard Farrell is her ex-husband – he's abducted Jacob, they're heading for the airport. He must have heard about the raid and he's running. Jacob found Sarah Jane's keys at his dad's house. He told his mum. Sarah Jane's got a picture of a gang of us on her key fob. He recognised her.'

'OK.' There was a pause while O'Rourke pulled the strands together. 'Cabinteely have just called over to Farrell's house and there was no sign of him. Only some crazy guard dog.'

'Seems he has a lot of reasons to want to get out of Ireland.'

'What's your status?'

'Rebecca has called 999, Fitzer is getting Farrell's licence plate out to all units. He's driving an Aston Martin – black, private plate. Fitzer will keep you in the loop. I'm heading for the airport.'

'You'd be better off with Jacob's mum. You won't find him on your own and you don't have a radio.' O'Rourke was using the voice he seemed to save for Cathy: sort of annoyed but controlled.

'I know, but can you get on to Enniskerry to get someone out to Rebecca? I can't sit and wait. And I've met Jacob, I'll recognise him if I can get to the terminal.' *And when she got her hands on Richard Farrell . . .* She didn't say it. *Sarah Jane had been in his house? Like Daniella had been to his house?* She sure as hell hoped not.

Cathy could almost hear O'Rourke nodding. He knew she didn't do waiting.

'Be careful. We're still looking for this Aleksy character. Keep an eye out for him too. No heroics.'

'Cross my heart.'

There was a pause and he disconnected. She could picture him rolling his eyes.

Glancing in her rear-view mirror, Cathy switched back to the call with Rebecca. 'Rebecca, you still there?'

'Cathy? Yes.' Rebecca sounded excited, 'Listen, they're heading over the mountains. They've gone up past Glencree, looks like they're heading for Ballinascorney. Richard's taking the back roads, he knows you'll find him if he goes through the tolls on the motorway.'

'How do you know? Did Jacob call again?'

'No, the phone he's got is the one Richard gave him. It's an iPhone. I activated the Find My iPhone feature when he brought it home – I was really worried he'd lose it and Richard would go mad. I just remembered it. I can see them on my computer.'

'I need to catch up with them. They can't be going straight to the airport. Can you call the station in Dún Laoghaire, give them the new information, and get them to relay everything to Inspector Dawson O'Rourke? It's vital he's kept informed. I need to concentrate on driving. I'm almost at the M50, I can head up that way off the N7. It's a much faster road. If they change direction call me back.'

Cathy shifted in her seat, sitting up, her full attention on the road ahead. Rebecca's last update had put Farrell and Jacob turning left and heading for The Lamb and Manor Kilbride. The traffic had been light, and she'd flown out of town and across the Red Cow interchange, the lights in her favour all the way. That was a blessing. It was usually jammed bumper to bumper: there was a good reason that it was known as the Mad Cow. And, thank God, the N7 was empty at this time of night too.

She pressed her foot to the floor. After her last beautiful Mini had been blown up she'd taken her time choosing another one. Truth be told, she'd been worried about getting back behind the wheel, had done an advanced Garda driving course to get her confidence back. Not that she'd been actually driving when it had happened, but the trauma was all wrapped up with the car, and driving again had been a big hurdle.

When she felt she was ready she'd gone down to the Mini dealer and ordered the highest spec, most souped-up car Mini produced. Now she was glad for all of that, of the driving course and that her car was as fast as anything on the racing circuit. Heading down the unlit winding roads that crossed the Wicklow hills, her headlights on full beam, the Mini was earning the two black stripes that bisected its metallic paintwork.

Cathy hit dial on her phone.

Rebecca answered immediately. 'Where are they now?'

'It looks like they've stopped, just over the bridge after Blessington. The blip has been there for a few minutes.'

'I know it. Almost there.'

Cathy's mind worked fast. Blessington, a country town high up in the Wicklow hills, was one of the places she'd gone to run after the accident. Boxing had been out of the question while her ribs healed; instead she'd gradually got her fitness back pounding the damp sand around the Blessington lakes with only the moorhens and herons to hear her cries of anguish. Often blinded by tears, she'd kept running until she felt every muscle burning, until she'd got back on top physically and emotionally.

The lakes were a beautiful place to train – a bird sanctuary, the reservoir had been formed when a valley was flooded, a village submerged. It was lonely and unpopulated. And just over the bridge Rebecca was talking about, there was a car park overlooking the water. Cathy knew exactly where Farrell had stopped. But why there? Was he meeting someone?

'Can you contact Dún Laoghaire Station again? They'll let Detective Inspector O'Rourke know, and they'll notify Blessington Station – it's the nearest. I'm almost there. They need to know Jacob is there and it's a possible hostage situation.'

Rebecca's voice was strained as she replied, 'Thank you, Cathy.'

Why was everyone thanking her today? She hadn't done anything yet.

41

It was pitch dark as Cathy headed along the winding road into Blessington. With only the glowing cat's eyes to guide her this far, as she entered the town the lights of the broad main street that ran straight through the middle glowed bright. Shops lined each side of the road, deserted at this time of night.

Suddenly her phone lit up – Rebecca Ryan.

'Are you near them?'

Cathy could hear the strain in Rebecca's voice, kept her own deliberately level, 'I'm almost there.'

'Jacob just texted me.' Rebecca took a breath like she was trying to steady her voice; she was wavering on the edge of panic, 'He heard his dad on the phone. He's meeting someone called David Givens. Richard said he was in the army, like Action Man. I think he could be the man Jacob saw before, the man who met your friend.'

'Irish army?' Cathy could hear the confusion in her own voice. The Irish army was a small force of peacekeepers.

'No, Jacob says English. I'm not sure, his spelling isn't very good and he's very confused.'

British army . . . OK, that was different. Very different. 'Why are they meeting?'

'I don't know, but what if he's armed? And Jacob . . .' She sounded distraught.

'Don't worry, I'm almost there. I'm going to turn my phone to silent, though, so if I don't answer, don't worry. I'll call as soon as I have Jacob safe.'

Cathy clicked off the phone, her mind racing. British army? Why was Farrell meeting someone from the British army? What could he be doing here in the Republic? It didn't make sense, but she knew someone who might be able to help.

McIntyre picked up after one ring. 'Boss?'

'What's up, girl?'

'Name David Givens mean anything to you, British army?'

There was a split-second pause. 'Dave Givens? Christ, girl, where did his name come up? I trained him. Ex-special forces head. I heard on the grapevine that he went rogue and now he's for hire. He's normally based in the Middle East but I heard a rumour he was over here, had business in the North of Ireland.' McIntyre paused, 'He specialises in making people disappear. He's well known in army circles, Cat, and he's dangerous. What's going on?'

Cathy took a breath, focusing on explaining clearly in the shortest possible time. 'The Rookery, the restaurant where Sarah Jane worked, is owned by a guy called Richard Farrell. He was dating a girl who worked there too, and we think it's her body that was found in the mountains. He also owns The Paradise Club that we raided tonight – they've been trafficking women from all over the world into Ireland. Now Farrell's running, and he's got his son with him. I think he's meeting Givens.'

'Christ. He'd only be meeting Givens if he's contracted him for a job – maybe he's paying him?' McIntyre only paused for a split second as he absorbed what Cathy had said, 'But Givens definitely didn't kill that girl in the mountains – much too messy.' Then, 'Where are you?'

'Coming into Blessington. Farrell's ex-wife is tracking her son's iPhone signal. He's stopped by the reservoir.'

McIntyre didn't hesitate, 'That's an ambush. Dark lonely spot beside the water? Perfect location. I don't know what's going on, but Givens wouldn't work with traffickers – not his style. If he's found out what's happening he could be after Farrell. Luring him to a quiet location for whatever reason is a whole lot easier than trying to find him. You need to get there, girl. Whatever's going on, if Givens is planning to take out Farrell, that boy's in danger too.' McIntyre paused, 'Listen to me and listen good, Givens's unit was hit by a car bomb in Sierra Leone and he lost two of his team. He had to leave the army because the blast left him partially deaf in his right ear. His sight was affected too, maybe only his peripheral vision, but his right eye is the weak one. He's highly trained, but he must be in his fifties now and he's got a weak spot – that's it.'

'Got it. Call O'Rourke and fill him in? I'm almost there.' Her voice was steely.

'Keep safe, girl.'

Seconds later Cathy reached the other side of town and accelerated again. There was a short winding stretch of country road before the bridge that crossed the lake.

It was pitch black here, blacker after the lights of the town. There was no room for mistakes.

McIntyre's words ran through her head and she suddenly slowed. McIntyre was right: it was the perfect location for an ambush. And if they were in the car park, Cathy knew they'd see her car crossing the bridge. Granted they might think she was some boy racer, but she didn't want to spook them. She needed to take it slow like she was a local heading home from the pub. If Givens was intending to kill Farrell, he wouldn't hesitate to take her out if she blundered into the middle of it all. At least she was armed. She could feel her SIG hard against her side.

Jacob would be sitting in his dad's car, sleepy and frightened and wondering what the hell was going on. Maybe he'd fallen asleep on the back seat and Givens didn't know he was there. Maybe he was hiding like the night she and J.P. had gone to question him, curled up in the footwell in the back seat too terrified to come out. Maybe, maybe . . . Was there a saint of maybe she could pray to? In her head Cathy was with a small frightened boy in a car in a cold car park in the middle of nowhere without his mum. And right now, she was prepared to sell her soul to keep that little boy safe.

It took every part of her being to slow down, but her reduced speed gave her time to fully evaluate the scene. As she cruised across the bridge she could clearly see lights in the car park off to the left below her: two cars. The glow of one set of headlights.

She'd found them.

She would have punched the air if the circumstances had been different; instead she felt a surge of adrenaline that made her want to punch Richard Farrell so hard he never woke up.

The car park was set into the hillside beside the lake, the two vehicles parked opposite each other, parallel to the water. A Range Rover and a sports car.

The Range Rover had backed snug into the hillside, low scrub rising behind it to meet the fields. It was facing the entrance to the car park. A good tactical position, it had military written all over it.

The other vehicle, parked a few yards away, was sleek and low slung: Farrell's Aston Martin. The Range Rover was in darkness, lit by the Aston Martin's headlights which formed the only pool of light on the full length of the shore. The Aston Martin's driver's door was slung open, the interior light on. Was Jacob in the car?

Cathy only had a second to assess the rest of the picture as she crossed the bridge. Two figures, standing beside the cars, were facing each other. From his posture it looked like the larger of the two men, the one standing in front of the Range Rover, was holding a handgun. How much time did she have? From everything she'd heard about him, if Farrell had realised that the gun wasn't just for decoration he'd be trying to talk his way out of it. Which might buy her a few precious minutes.

Swinging past the entrance to the car park, Cathy hit the accelerator and headed up the hill. They'd be able to hear the Mini's engine; sound travelled remarkably clearly here over the water, but they wouldn't be able to see her, and she knew exactly where she could stop. Seconds later she flung the Mini into a driveway on her right. She'd driven past it a million times. It led to high entrance gates to what was probably a fabulous house set well back off the road. But this wasn't a house call.

Hauling on the handbrake, Cathy was out of the car in a second, her Nikes silent as she crossed the narrow country road. There was a two-bar fence bordering the field that ran down to the lake. The wood was rough under her hand, the ground sloping down steeply on the other side, but she didn't hesitate, vaulting the fence, dropping like a gymnast into the field. It was pitch dark but she headed fast diagonally downhill across the grassy field, praying no one had decided to move a herd of cows into it. She could feel herself gathering speed as she ran, her breath loud in the silence of the night. Short sharp bursts of intense activity were what she was trained for, and as she reached the corner of the field she vaulted the fence again effortlessly and landed in the scrub that edged the lake.

From here, she knew she could get to the sandy shore and head around the lake edge to the car park, approaching it from behind.

Her heart thundering in her chest, Cathy almost stumbled in the thick scrub. But this was ground she was familiar with. Notching it up a gear, she could hear the gentle lap of the water to her right, an owl calling in the distance as she ran around the edge of the lake. Ahead she knew the beach narrowed before opening into a spit below the car park, the sand grey, shining with mica. When she reached the car park, she'd be approaching the bank that separated it from the beach very slightly up hill, but she'd have the advantage of height when she got to the top. And if she was quiet enough, surprise.

Suddenly, over the sound of her own breathing and the lapping of the waves, she could hear snatches of voices. Swinging around the edge of the spit she slowed; she didn't want to be heard, and she wanted to hear what was going on above. Concealed by the waving couch grass and scrub, she knew she was invisible from the car park: her black hair, black hoodie and sweatpants blending with the landscape. The breeze switched direction and the men's voices came to her clearly.

'We were told you could do the job, Givens. You came highly recommended. How is your business going to fare if I put the word out that you can't be trusted, that you wanted more money to finish the job?' A south Dublin accent, arrogant, angry: Farrell.

'Oh I can be trusted, Mr Farrell, but I don't think loyalty is something you understand.' The other voice was educated, British army officer class.

There was a pause. 'Don't talk crap, you couldn't kill her because she's a woman. Just fucking admit it.'

'I get the job done – anyone, anywhere. But not this time.' Givens paused, his voice lowering, 'You're not here because I need more cash, you're here because you're a fucking idiot. You're here because I wanted you here.' Givens paused, 'You're a lowlife scum who doesn't understand the rules. You think you can buy my services? I work for governments, Mr Farrell, I specialise in removing parasites like you. I do odd jobs on the side, granted – I got a call from an old friend to solve a problem and it sounded clean, but you, Mr Farrell, you aren't clean, are you?'

Cathy hardly dared breathe as Givens paused. 'Two members of my unit owe their lives to a CNN journalist called Ted Hansen. He put his life on the line to help my boys get clear of enemy fire. He didn't have to, he didn't know them – he saw something going down and he acted. We have a code of honour in the army. His daughter has done nothing to you.'

'His daughter is threatening to wreck a big business, a business that is run by players who would give you nightmares.'

'Oh I doubt that, Farrell, I doubt that very much. I think you're the one running scared here. And your business associates aren't impressed. You fucked up once and they couldn't afford for you to fuck up again so they called me. I don't make mistakes, Richard, and I don't take risks.'

There was a pause, and Givens's tone went down a gear, deadly serious, 'So now my brief has changed. I was coming for you, but you have very conveniently come to me.'

From Farrell's silence, Cathy gathered he wasn't getting it. Givens must have realised too. He laughed, his tone of voice changing again. 'Christ, you're even more stupid than you look. You're a liability, Farrell. The people you work with have had enough, and so have I.'

This was ramping up. Givens was going to take Farrell out. *She needed to make her move or Jacob would be at risk. If Jacob was hiding and Givens fired, Jacob was bound to react and show himself.*

Jogging around to get a good position, Cathy eased out her gun. The SIG didn't have a safety catch, instead used double-action trigger pressure. It had been drilled into them from her first day on the range that you only fired if you warned the suspect first, or were in fear for your life. But she wasn't about to start yelling 'Armed Gardaí' into the night and make herself a sitting target. One thing she could be sure of was that Givens's reactions would be fast. He was combat trained. She'd been shot before, and it wasn't an experience she wanted to repeat.

But there was another way.

She needed to disable Givens before he got a shot off.

And to do that she needed as much power as she could to get over the bank. Her heart rate increased as she mentally calculated the distances.

Approaching this way, she'd be attacking from Givens's right, and, if McIntyre was correct, that was his blind side.

Givens started speaking again, and in that instant she knew she had to go, there was no time to be arsing about. Givens's voice was clear on the still night air.

'You don't understand how this works, do you? Sarah Jane has seen exactly who is involved in your little operation, and she's a bright girl, she's got it all worked out. She's going to spill your story, and both of us know you won't like that, so now you *really* need to take her out.' As he paused, Cathy took off, her toes digging hard into the soft sand, giving her the purchase she needed. 'And I can't let that happen. I don't take orders from people-trafficking scum like you.'

A shot exploded into the night as Cathy hit the top of the bank surrounding the car park. The flash from the muzzle was minimal, but enough in a split second to give her a clear location on the gun. As Farrell fell to the ground, his cry of anguish ripping through the still night air, Givens was taking aim to let off a second shot. But Cathy was already in the air, landing on the rough tarmac a few feet from Givens, Farrell's cries masking the sound. Givens was a big guy but using the powerful momentum she'd gained from her jump, twisting, she sprang into an axe kick. Even at this distance, moving, she could miss with the gun, but there was no chance she'd miss him with a kick.

His right side is the weak one. God Bless McIntyre.

As her right foot connected with the back of Givens's head he staggered and fired again, the shot going wide. She was used to fighting barefoot; wearing Nikes her kick would have knocked most people out for a week. Buckling under its force, Givens's knees hit the ground, and Cathy heard his gun, metal on tarmac, spinning away out of his hand to the edge of the pool of light cast by the Aston Martin's headlights.

Recovering from the kick in one movement, just like in the ring, she sprang in the direction of the sound and had kicked his gun into the scrub before Givens even knew what had hit him. In a fight, reaction was as essential to success as attack, avoiding the next punch crucial to winning. McIntyre had her well trained.

But despite Givens's age, he was fit and experienced. As Farrell writhed on the ground, crying out with pain, Givens was back on his feet, pausing for a second to get his bearings and assess the enemy before he lunged. It was all Cathy needed, catching her breath she blurted out, 'I'm Cat, Sarah Jane is my friend.' As soon as the words were out she saw his posture change a fraction. 'Thank you.' She meant it. He might have kidnapped Sarah Jane, but it seemed that he'd kept her safe and now he was making sure she would stay safe. It wasn't the way Cathy would have done things, but he operated in a different world.

'Help me! I need help. Oh my God.' Their eyes locked, Cathy and Givens were oblivious to Farrell.

'You're the cop?'

'Yes, and Richard Farrell's got a lot of explaining to do, not just about Sarah Jane.'

Givens glanced at Farrell. He'd suddenly gone quiet, his face drained of colour. Cathy couldn't tell if he'd just passed out or ... A movement in the Aston Martin distracted her for a split second as a small blond-haired boy appeared between the front seats from the rear of the car, his face tear stained, eyes wide.

Seeing his chance, Givens moved fast. As Cathy made eye contact with Jacob, wasting precious seconds frantically gesturing for him to duck down in the car, Givens was behind the wheel of the Range Rover and gunning the powerful engine. Cathy spun around, her gun raised to take out the tyres, but the vehicle was already accelerating. It was moving too fast, she didn't have a clear shot and couldn't risk a ricochet that might hit the Aston Martin. The wheels showered loose tarmac as he accelerated around Farrell's car, the sound of sirens coming from Blessington suddenly filling the night air. Back-up.

His lights off, Givens swung a left away from the bridge and Cathy could hear him accelerating up the hill.

'Feck it . . .' Muttering under her breath Cathy ran to check on Farrell. There would be plenty of time later for her to beat herself up about how she could have handled this better, but the registration number of the Range Rover was clear in her mind. Since he didn't change the plates he wouldn't get far.

Lying in the pool of light cast by the Aston Martin's headlights, Farrell was motionless, his chest soaked in blood. Cathy could feel Jacob watching her silently from inside the car as she checked for a pulse.

It was weak, but she could see a flutter as his chest moved. He was alive.

Looking up, she grinned at Jacob and pulled out her phone.

42

'Can't you keep out of trouble for more than two minutes, Cat?'

O'Rourke materialised out of the darkness, and Cathy realised she'd never been more grateful to hear his voice. Every muscle in her body was taut, her senses still heightened. She would have given him a hug if she hadn't been standing in a car park full of her colleagues and there hadn't been a small boy wrapped around her leg.

But he was here now, thank goodness. She couldn't relax yet, not until they found Sarah Jane, but at least she felt like her safety net was back in place.

O'Rourke had been the first person she'd called after she'd made sure Jacob was OK, although she knew her version of the events that had unfolded in the car park hadn't been entirely coherent – the key piece of information, the Range Rover's registration plate, was the only thing that had been completely clear. He'd gotten the gist of what had happened, though, his voice strained as he'd asked her if she was OK. Then she'd called Jacob's mum.

Now O'Rourke was glowering at Farrell's car, his hands buried in his overcoat pockets.

'You sure he didn't give any hints as to where he was holding Sarah Jane?' O'Rourke looked at her hard, his eyebrows raised.

He wasn't cross with her for not asking, she knew that; he was cross because she'd gone and landed herself in yet another situation that could have gone badly wrong, and she'd given him a fright. She shook her head.

'We've got search teams with dogs mobilising to check every building in a ten-mile radius from here.' He checked his watch, 'They will have started by now. This is an out of the way place to pick for a rendezvous – let's hope it's because he was holding her fairly close by.'

Jacob craned his head around Cathy's leg to get a proper look at O'Rourke. He had been holding on to her since the first cars had arrived and wasn't letting go. Cathy knew the noise and lights, all the activity were overwhelming. She'd been anxious to play down the shooting, had thought he'd be distressed at seeing his dad wounded, but then she'd remembered her brother Tomás saying something about kids on the spectrum being unable to empathise. And as Jacob had emerged from the back of the Aston Martin, she'd realised he wasn't seeing Farrell's injuries with the same eyes anyone else would.

The car park was full now, three patrol cars and an ambulance, a tech bureau van and O'Rourke's BMW filling the spaces normally occupied by tourists. The forensics team were just getting started, erecting arc lights and laying down markers on the tarmac indicating the trajectory of the bullet. Givens's gun, a Glock 9, the dull black metal hard to see in the dark, was still lying where she had kicked it.

Since they'd arrived, Jacob had been fascinated, watching the techs in their white forensic overalls, his stream of questions constant. Soon they would start work on the Aston Martin, lifting fibres from the interior while the others worked outside taking measurements. The flash from their cameras was already adding to the surreal, science-fiction-movie-set feel as they took preliminary shots

Across the car park, the paramedics were loading Farrell into the back of the ambulance. They'd taken a while to stabilise him. Admittedly getting shot in the chest wasn't on anyone's bucket list but, as one of the Blessington lads had muttered as he'd passed Cathy, there was 'no better man' more deserving of it.

The paramedics pulled the rear door of their vehicle closed with a bang that made Cathy jump. The second Givens's gun had discharged she'd been right back beside her Mini, the sound of the explosion that had shattered the windows around her, setting off every house alarm in the street, ringing again in her ears. Now every loud noise was testing her nerve.

She threw O'Rourke a weak smile. Maybe it was her nerves, or the sound of his voice finally sinking in, but she could feel herself going pale, starting to shake. As if he could read her mind, O'Rourke turned to face her, putting his hands on her shoulders, steadying her, ducking so he could look in her eyes, his voice calming.

'You're OK, Cat. Everyone that matters is safe. We'll find Sarah Jane. You did good.' Cathy could feel her eyes filling. For a moment she wanted it to be just them, with the sound of the breeze worrying the trees above them and the slap of the water on the shore, and to lean into his shoulder and curl up there.

Loosening his hold, O'Rourke reached out to ruffle Jacob's hair. Still managing to hang on to Cathy's leg, Jacob ducked out of reach and eyed O'Rourke suspiciously. It took Cathy a moment to catch her breath, tears burning her eyes. She brushed them away.

'This is my boss, Jacob, he's one of the good guys. You OK?' Still clinging to her leg, he looked up at her, his eyes huge, trusting. Before she could say anything more a patrol car appeared, travelling fast over the bridge, blue lights cutting through the night.

O'Rourke smiled down at Jacob, 'I think this might be your mum. She's going to be very pleased to see you.'

'Will she have chocolate?'

O'Rourke laughed, Jacob's innocence defusing the moment. He bobbed down to his level. 'If she doesn't I'll have a chat to her and see if I can organise some for you tomorrow, how's that?' Jacob's smile said it all.

A moment later the patrol car had swung into the entrance to the car park, the passenger door bursting open before it had even stopped. Rebecca Ryan jumped out and sprinted to Jacob, catching him in a hug that lifted him off his feet. He immediately started to struggle.

'Thank God you're OK. Thank God.' Her words were lost in his neck.

'Get *off* me, Mummy, you're hurting, and your fur's tickly.' Jacob pushed her arms away and rubbed his nose where the fur on her parka hood had irritated him. Rebecca pulled back, resting her hands on his shoulders instead, her eyes red. She took a breath, calming herself as she pushed a strand of hair out of her face where it had fallen from her hastily tied ponytail. 'What a brilliant boy you are for calling me and keeping your phone on.'

Jacob scowled, 'I fell asleep. Daddy said I couldn't call you, that it was too late, but you said—'

Rebecca interrupted him, smiling, her eyes sparkling with tears, 'I can't sleep until I've spoken to you. Thank you, my darling.'

Jacob wrinkled his face, frowning at her seriously, 'We've got a deal.'

'We have.' She hugged him quickly again, pulling away before he could push her. Turning, Rebecca looked up at Cathy, 'Thank you. Thank you so much.'

Cathy smiled, fighting to keep her voice level, hiding the emotion swirling inside her, 'No worries. He'll need to give us a statement in the morning, but take him home to bed. He's been brilliant, it's been a busy night.'

'A man shot Daddy, Mummy. Right there.' Matter of factly Jacob pointed to the front of the Aston Martin where Cathy suddenly realised the tarmac was stained with blood. A lot of blood.

'She flew through the air and stopped him. I saw her.' Cat smiled at him. He reminded her of Tintin, with his freckles and cheeky grin. Then his face changed, his voice completely serious, as he looked at her, 'You told me a big fib. You're called Cat because you're Cat Girl in real life.'

Cathy couldn't resist a smile, 'I'm not sure about that. And the doctor said your Daddy's going to be fine.' She turned to Rebecca, 'He got hit in the chest.'

'Gosh, that must have been painful.'

Rebecca's sarcasm was lost on Jacob, who nodded, 'He was yelling a lot.'

'I bet.'

'Can I look at the police car?'

O'Rourke smiled, 'Be our guest, it'll be taking you home in a minute, but the boys can show you how everything works first.'

Not waiting to be told twice, Jacob dragged Rebecca by the hand towards the car. She smiled at O'Rourke over her shoulder, shaking her head.

'Look, Mummy . . .'

Once they were out of earshot Cathy turned to him. 'Have you spoken to McIntyre?' Cathy could hear the exhaustion in her own voice. *Christ, what a night.*

O'Rourke kept his voice low, conscious of the activity around them, 'Briefly. I'm still not completely clear on the order of events, but I do know you've just apprehended a major suspect in a pan-European sex-trafficking gang that has a strong relationship with some big players in the drugs and gun-running worlds.' He paused, 'Would have been better if you'd got the hitman too, but we can't have everything.'

Cathy half smiled, 'Is that enough to get me out of the shit for potentially being the alibi for a murder suspect?'

O'Rourke rolled his eyes, 'Your friend Aleksy came in voluntarily earlier tonight when he heard The Paradise Club had been raided. It seems he was doing bits of bar and maintenance work for them, but he hasn't been there long.' O'Rourke paused, 'Apparently he's been working covertly with the Criminal Assets Bureau who have an active interest in Farrell and his associates. He couldn't say anything to you as Internal Affairs are all over it. There could be a few senior officers involved who are about to get shot down in flames by the sounds of it. And we're not exactly flavour of the month with CAB as we've virtually blown his cover – when he started working there Nacek found out he did a bit of translation for us, and apparently thought it was very handy to have one of his guys working with the police so he was encouraging it. He thought Aleksy would let him know if we ever started to get interested in the place. That gave Aleksy an opportunity to liaise with CAB without exposing himself.'

Her eyes fixed on the rough tarmac of the car park, Cathy nodded slowly. *The guy in the jacket who had spoken to Aleksy in the bar was CAB, she was sure of it.* It would have been helpful for her and O'Rourke to know The Paradise Club was under investigation, but she knew how these things worked. Protecting a valuable source and nailing someone like Farrell necessitated the highest level of secrecy. And she was sure CAB were saying the same thing about their investigation.

O'Rourke continued, glancing around, making sure no one could hear him, 'CAB have him in a safe house. He's more than likely going to go into witness protection. From the sounds of it, Farrell's operation was the linchpin in an international network.' O'Rourke paused, 'And from what I can gather, it sounds like he's been looking out for Irina.' Cathy raised her eyebrows. She knew Irina's story had affected him. 'But the good news is that he was clocked speeding on the N11 at 11.17 p.m. that Tuesday night. It looks like he left shortly after you did. It's not an alibi yet, but at least he couldn't have been in the mountains burying a body at the same time.'

Thank God. But before Cathy could respond her phone began to vibrate in her pocket. McIntyre.

He spoke before she did, 'You OK, girl?'

Cathy glanced at O'Rourke, mouthing 'The Boss', before replying, 'I'm good. You missed the best axe kick I've ever done.'

She could almost hear him smiling, 'You're a champion, girl, I keep telling you. What happened?'

'Let's just say Dave Givens is fast. I stopped him shooting Farrell dead, but he made a run for it. We've an alert out for his vehicle.'

O'Rourke raised his hand, indicating that Cathy needed to be careful what she said. On the other side of the car park Jacob had finished inspecting the car. Rebecca grabbed his hand and bent down to whisper in his ear. He smiled happily and they both headed back towards Cathy, skirting Farrell's Aston Martin.

'I've got to go, can I call you later?'

'Keep me posted, girl.'

Cathy clicked off the phone as Rebecca and Jacob arrived beside them. O'Rourke smiled at Jacob, 'I think your ride is ready, young man – must be time to get home to bed?'

Rebecca ruffled Jacob's hair, but he ducked out of the way, 'It certainly is. Come on, soldier, I've got a mug of hot chocolate with your name on it at home.'

'What about the plane, at the airport? It's waiting for us.'

'I've sorted that out, don't worry. How about you and I go on a plane another time?'

Jacob nodded and slipped his hand into Rebecca's. 'I told Daddy it was silly to go at night. Can we go in the police car now?'

O'Rourke grinned, 'You certainly can.' He gestured to the driver, calling over to him, 'The full service.'

The Guard tipped his hat in response and held the rear door open ceremoniously for Jacob to jump in. Glancing at them, Rebecca paused before she headed back to the car. She turned, her eyes meeting Cathy's, 'Thank you, really.'

Cathy held up her hand, 'Without Jacob's skills of observation we'd have been in the dark on a lot of things. He's the one I should be thanking.'

A moment later the blue strobes were flashing and the driver flipped the siren into a wolf whistle as he pulled away.

O'Rourke turned to Cathy and rubbed her shoulder again like he was checking she was still there. His touch was like electricity. 'You sure you're OK?'

'Better now.'

'Come on, it's cold, and we still need to find Sarah Jane. The boys can bring your car back – I'll drive you home.'

43

O'Rourke's phone started to ring almost the moment they got into his car. Pulling it out of his jacket pocket, he stuck his keys in the ignition and sat back in the driver's seat as he answered. Buckling her seatbelt, Cathy glanced across at him. His face was partially lit by the cold hard light the technical bureau were using to illuminate the scene around Farrell's Aston Martin. He looked exhausted. They all were. But they still needed to find Sarah Jane.

She looked out of the window across the lake, the moon reflecting off the brooding, rippling water for a moment before the clouds closed around it.

'Say that again slowly for me.' There was something about the tone of O'Rourke's voice that made Cathy swing around to look at him. He glanced across the car, his eyes meeting hers with a look that had Cathy immediately alert and sitting forward in her seat.

'Northern Irish accent? And he said Hollywood? Definitely Hollywood, County Wicklow, not County Down?' He paused as the caller answered, 'Got it, I'll put a call in to Assistant Commissioner Connolly, we'll need the Emergency Response Unit up here with a crisis negotiator. All roads in and out of the location closed. We're only about ten minutes away. Nobody moves till I get there.'

He clicked off the phone and immediately dialled another number. Cathy held her breath, desperate to ask what was going on, but this wasn't the moment. She kept quiet. He glanced across at her as his call connected.

'Niamh? It's O'Rourke.' He paused while she answered, 'Yes, Cat's safe, she's here with me. We've had a tip-off that Sarah Jane's being held in a cottage near Hollywood. Caller described her in detail, it sounds kosher. The guy in the middle of this is ex-British special forces. I need the ERU to attend.' Cathy couldn't hear her sister-in-law's reply but she could see from O'Rourke's face that it was an affirmative.

'Thanks, Niamh, I'll keep you briefed.'

Passing Cathy his phone, he gunned the engine, swinging the car around in a spray of gravel, accelerating to the mouth of the car park. He paused for a split second, flicked on the high beams and, leaning forward in his seat, his focus fully on the junction ahead, pulled out onto the road. Cathy couldn't wait any longer.

'What's happened?'

'Sorry,' his eyes back on the road, he hit the bend and accelerated up the hill past Cathy's Mini. 'Command and control just got a call from a call box in Northern Ireland. Caller said there's a girl being held in an old cottage up in Hollywood. It's not far from here – off the main road in the middle of farmland. He seemed very sure, said she had purple streaks in her hair. When our lad looked for a personal detail to verify it, the caller said she was wearing an amethyst bracelet. Then he gave coordinates and rang off. They're texting them through.'

'Christ, that's her, and she wears that bracelet all the time. But who gives coordinates to a scene?' Cathy's tone was incredulous.

'The British army.'

He had a point. 'Is she OK?'

'Let's hope so, and that it's not a hoax to throw us off Givens's trail.'

A second later the text arrived. 'Put the coordinates into the GPS. I've a fair idea where it is. We found an arms dump up there years ago.'

'IRA?'

'Dissidents.'

'McIntyre said he'd heard Givens was in the North – maybe his friends up there know this area?'

'That would make sense. Irina said she thought they'd been taken somewhere near Belfast after the ferry . . .' he pursed his lips. 'Farrell needed help with a problem so he phoned a friend? It only takes two hours to get down here from Belfast.'

'But McIntyre said Givens wouldn't work with traffickers.'

'In my experience these guys work for whoever is paying the most. Maybe he was in the North doing another job for someone Farrell knows and this came up as a handy nixer on the side, but he didn't get the whole story.' O'Rourke's voice dripped with sarcasm. As he spoke the GPS pinged.

'It's found it. Says seven minutes.'

'ERU should be there in forty, less with luck. Uniform from Tallaght will set up the road blocks.' Cathy took a breath, her heart beating hard. The Emergency Response Unit were permanently on alert to scramble anywhere in the country in two hours. From their base in Harcourt Square in the city centre they'd have a clear run at this time of night.

If Cathy had thought the drive up to the mountains to identify the girl's body was stressful, the drive to Hollywood was ten times worse. Granted it was faster, but it was pitch dark, and every minute they were on the road her stomach felt sicker, adrenaline coursing back through her system making her more alert than she was physically able for after everything that had happened tonight. It was 2 a.m.; she'd hardly slept last night and had woken up at six. She knew she needed to calm down and pace herself. Like when she was running after the blast, it was going to be a long night and she needed to keep everything on the level or her emotions would start seesawing and she'd be useless to everyone, most of all herself.

She pulled out her phone, clicking through to Google, copying the coordinates off the screen on O'Rourke's iPhone into Google Maps. She clicked through to Street View, zooming in on a single-storey whitewashed cottage that looked like it had last been inhabited in 1950. The Street View shots had been taken during the summer, the faded pale-blue front door peeling, windows dark with dirt. Set back in a garden overgrown with wild roses and brambles, a hand plough was leaning against the wall, rusted beyond use. Cathy rotated the image. Immediately opposite the cottage a corrugated steel hay barn, its red paint worn, looked like it had been built more recently. She played with the view, trying to see behind the cottage. No good. She zoomed out.

'It's literally in the middle of nowhere. Like the nearest house is miles.'

'Perfect place to hold someone. Easy enough access from the city, but way off the beaten track.'

He was right. It was a natural place for Givens to choose: its location gave him the tactical advantage.

But who had called them? Did Givens have a team on this? Cathy guessed that's what O'Rourke was preparing for.

O'Rourke's phone rang again, and he depressed the button on the steering wheel to patch it through to the speaker. The voice on the other end was clear, practised.

'ERU are on the way, ETA thirty-four minutes. A full crisis team plus hostage negotiator and snipers. Surrounding roads will be closed in fifteen. Paramedics en route.'

'Excellent, we'll be there in five.'

Cathy rested her elbow on the door and ran her fingers through her hair. Her head was starting to pound. *What would they find? Had Givens gone back there? Or had he run and left an accomplice holding Sarah Jane? How many people were involved in this? He'd protected her so far, would he put her in danger now?* The questions danced in her head.

'You OK?'

'I'll be better when we get there.'

O'Rourke hit his indicator, glancing in his mirror as he swung right off the main road and down a narrow lane, his high beams bouncing off steep banks on either side of the road. Outside the reach of the headlights it was pitch dark, darker than Cathy could imagine. She felt like they were going through a tunnel. Suddenly, approaching a bend, he slowed. To her left Cathy saw a break in the steep-sided bank and a tubular steel farm gate, pinned open. O'Rourke pulled through the gate, his lights momentarily lighting a track that stretched across a lumpy field. He swung in hard to his left, tucking the car into the hedge.

'Come on, I've gear in the boot.'

Popping the boot release, he was out of the car, slipping off his overcoat and balling it up before Cathy had moved. She didn't hang about, though. As she got out of the car she immediately felt the drop in temperature. They were up the hills, higher than the reservoir, and O'Rourke had had the car's heating up at full blast, knowing she was always cold. She shivered as she moved beside him, glad of her Nikes on the uneven grass. He passed her a navy Garda jacket and baseball cap.

'I've your body protector in here somewhere.' He turned to grin at her, 'Better late than never.' He rooted in the boot, shifting white forensic suits and his own body armour out of the way, 'Here, get this on.'

As she pulled on the heavy navy jacket and Kevlar vest, he grabbed a pair of boots, dropping them on the grass and slipping off his shoes. 'Let's just hope this evening isn't the ruin of a very good pair of Armani trousers.'

She grinned, adjusting the clip on the back of the baseball cap to make sure it was a snug fit. He shouldered off his suit jacket and pulled off his tie, tossing them into the boot before putting on his own bomber jacket, GARDA emblazoned in yellow across the back.

'Let me have a look at your phone. We need to get a feel for the layout of the place. I doubt anything's changed since I was last here, though.'

Cathy pulled out her phone, finding the Google Street View image. It was amazing Google had made it up here and found the place, but Cathy had once seen a Street View shot of the desert, the shadow of the camel that was being used to take it dominating the picture. Anything was possible if you had a big enough budget.

O'Rourke leaned to look at it, the weight of his chest pressing into her shoulder, his aftershave masking the night scents of the field. But she didn't have time to think about that now. She turned the image so he could see the approach to the building. It was as if the cottage had been frozen in time. Before he could comment, O'Rourke's phone vibrated. Moving away from her slightly, he picked up the call.

Cathy scanned the field while he was listening to the caller. It looked like grazing land for sheep or cattle, and fell away gently down the hillside. Bisecting it, running from the gate they'd entered by to another in the opposite corner, she could just see a track, illuminated here by the BMW's rear lights, the grass newly flattened by the wheels of a heavy vehicle. *Givens's Range Rover?*

O'Rourke clicked the phone off, 'Tallaght have done a recon – there's signs of recent habitation and a light on in the cottage. Apparently it's not been occupied since the late seventies – farmer hardly ever gets up here, keeps his herd lower down.'

As he spoke, they heard the distant sound of a vehicle on the road. The hairs stood up on the back of Cathy's neck as O'Rourke threw a meaningful glance at her and pushed the boot silently closed. He indicated she should get back in the car. This *should* be the ERU team, but there had been enough surprises tonight already.

O'Rourke switched off the lights and swivelled around in the driver's seat, waiting. Then, fighting a smile, he glanced at her, 'You know, if this turns out to be Givens we're going to have to pretend we're up here having a shag.'

She glared at him, praying he couldn't see her face glow bright red in the darkness, *Christ, he picked his moments.*

'I don't think that would do your back a whole lot of good.'

Before O'Rourke could respond, a pair of headlights swung into the gate. Still smiling, he raised his eyebrows. 'Looks like you're off the hook.'

44

Sitting in the darkened car, Cathy was almost blinded by the lights of three unmarked and blacked-out Land Rover Discoverys that swung through the gate into the field beside them. O'Rourke glanced at her as he pushed his door open. This was it.

The passenger in the lead vehicle climbed out to meet O'Rourke. He was little more than a shadow in the dark in his black uniform and helmet, night-vision goggles already in place. Anonymity was key with the Emergency Response Unit. The most highly trained tactical response unit in An Garda Síochána, specialising in counterterrorism, crisis negotiation and hostage rescue, members were protected in court, giving evidence on camera. But it didn't matter to Cathy right now who they were, they knew their stuff and they were damn good. And they were going to help find Sarah Jane.

O'Rourke's conversation with him was brief. Then he turned to Cathy and gestured that she should join them. She slipped out of the car.

The ERU Inspector grinned at her as she came around the bonnet of O'Rourke's BMW. At least she thought he did; under his matte-black helmet and goggles he wore a balaclava. It was hard to tell what his face was doing.

'So this is Cat Connolly, the kick-boxer?' Cathy raised an eyebrow in surprise as he put out his hand to shake hers, his grasp firm. 'Have you worked with us before?' She could hardly hear him, his voice was so low. She shook her head.

'How about we get you into the loop so you can see exactly how we operate? We need more women like you.'

Surprised, Cathy nodded. She'd thought she'd be wallpaper in this operation, that the last thing they'd want was to be falling over her. These guys were as highly trained as they came.

The inspector continued, 'I heard you'd been over to the Met, you've done their anti-terrorism course?'

'It was a while ago now, it was only an introduction.'

He shrugged, 'It's all good, it all adds up. You never know what will come in useful out on the job. But I don't need to tell you that.'

Despite the sick, nervous feeling in her stomach, or perhaps because of it, Cathy felt a surge of excitement. She'd often seen reports of this elite unit in action, and wondered if they had any female members; whenever she'd asked, the general feeling had been that the two-week commando-style induction that had ninety-five per cent of applicants in a heap on the floor before it was finished reduced the appeal somewhat. It wasn't all rushing about dressed in black with sub-machine guns.

The inspector leaned into the vehicle he'd climbed out of, speaking to someone inside, 'Can we have eyes and ears here?'

He turned back to Cathy and O'Rourke, his voice little more than a whisper, 'We're going to set up an ops base in the barn opposite the cottage. The guys will surround the building, see how the land lies.'

O'Rourke looked at Cathy, 'You ready?'

Cathy nodded. Her exhaustion had slipped away as she'd sat in the car, the few moments of quiet enough for her to re-centre herself and focus. Now she felt an overpowering need to get moving. Well, most of her did. This was the best lead they'd had, but despite her excitement, she was still nervous about the timing. Cathy knew Givens was an experienced player, he didn't make mistakes. They were clearly meant to get this information now. But it felt like he was playing a game with them, keeping them busy so he could slip out of the country more easily.

There wasn't time to wonder. The driver's and rear doors of the first Land Rover opened and three more officers dressed from head to toe in black spilled out, one of them carrying a large black holdall. As the doors in the other vehicles opened, the guy with the bag pulled out earpieces and radios and proceeded to wire Cathy and O'Rourke up. The earpiece felt just like the ear phones she used when she was running. Night-vision goggles, though, took a few more minutes to get used to. She knew they were in a field, but everything looked green. It took her a moment to realise that despite the unusual shading, she could see quite clearly.

She pulled her baseball hat back on. The ERU's tech was certainly impressive.

The ERU inspector gestured for her to join them as eight heavily armed officers gathered around for their briefing. He brought them up to speed quickly, efficiently and quietly. They looked like storm troopers, radios strapped to their shoulders, balaclavas, helmets and night-vision goggles in place, GARDA emblazoned on their breast pockets in gold, POLICE written across their backs. *No chance of any confusion there.*

Then they were on the move. Single file, not speaking, scanning the surrounding countryside as they headed for the cover of the hedge.

Staying close in, ducking down to avoid being silhouetted against the landscape if the moon did decide to appear, Cathy slipped into line right behind the ERU inspector, his weapon invisible against his black uniform.

At the opposite end of the field the track turned through a wide set of double gates, one hanging open, and crossed the corner of another field before disappearing through more gates into a rough concrete yard. Tucked into the apex of the hedges surrounding the fields, a hay barn rose on the left, a patchwork of corrugated steel sheets closing its sides to the elements.

Opposite it, separated from the yard by a low drystone wall, was the single-storey cottage.

They passed through the gates silently. Reaching the second set, O'Rourke indicated Cathy should follow him as the rest of the team melted into the darkness. The narrow path between the hedge and the near side of the barn was out of sight from the cottage. The grass was longer here, brambles catching at her ankles. Ahead of Cathy and O'Rourke, the ERU inspector and two of his team – the man with the bag and another one – walked in single file, disappearing around the far corner of the barn. As Cathy reached the corner an old tractor loomed out of the darkness where it had been abandoned, the grass around it knee high. The night was unbelievably dense and silent this far up in the hills, heavy clouds obscuring the moon. Somewhere, a long way away, she thought she could hear the sound of water. The smell of cats was strong. She adjusted her goggles, trying to make them more comfortable.

A bat swooped above her, the sudden movement making her start.

At the end of the barn, the ERU inspector indicated a gap in the corrugated steel wall, a makeshift doorway. They hardly needed to use it as the whole wall on the long side was open to the elements, allowing the wind to keep the hay dry when it had been in use. Inside their footsteps were quiet, soft soles on concrete.

Cathy looked around. The barn obviously hadn't been used in a while, and seemed to have become a dumping ground for old machinery. Around the edges of the structure was what looked like ancient farm equipment, bits of a plough, a battered car, a feed bin.

The four men moved into the corner nearest the cottage, a gap in the steel sheeting giving them a narrow but clear view. Bobbing down, the man with the bag unzipped the holdall and proceeded to pull out a laptop and several devices that Cathy couldn't identify. He laid everything out on the ground, silently powering the laptop up and inserting several USB sticks. Within minutes he'd created a command centre.

The ERU inspector bent forward, listening to his earpiece.

And suddenly, through her own earpiece, Cathy could hear the team reporting in, taking up their positions to surround the house, calling in as they found cover. She put her hand on her earpiece too, straining to hear their low voices. The ERU was a one-hundred-strong elite tactical team trained in the use of a huge range of weapons from the SIG P226 she carried to Heckler & Koch assault rifles and sub-machine guns. They trained with the FBI in Quantico, and were part of the ATLAS group, a team drawn from thirty-two European nations on alert and provisioned to attend incidents in any part of Europe.

The inspector gestured for her and O'Rourke to come in close; he mimed shooting a gun and pointed at her. She nodded, understanding: she needed to check her weapon. It held nine 19-millimetre rounds. She'd knocked the unused round out of the chamber when the troops had arrived earlier. Thank goodness she hadn't fired on Givens or she would have had to turn her gun in as evidence. It felt familiar in her hand, the weight exactly right, the curve of the stock comfortable. She just hoped she wouldn't have to use it. Tactical assault to rescue hostages carried the highest casualty rate, and was only used when all reasonable attempts to resolve the crisis by negotiation had failed. She slipped it back into her holster.

They'd try talking their way in first.

45

Ten minutes in her normal life felt like a blur. Ten minutes when you're huddled in a freezing barn waiting to see if your best friend is still alive and uninjured takes for ever. Cathy could understand that it was essential that the team were briefed, that the inspector fully understood the layout of the area, that they established a command and control centre . . . She could hear them working fast, preparing their equipment, assessing the options open to them, *but bloody hell*.

Cathy's heart was beating hard, echoing so loud inside her head she was sure the rest of the team could hear it. She stuck her hands in the pockets of the blue bomber jacket, trying to focus, to blank out everything going on around her. Beside her, O'Rourke and the negotiator had their heads together, but their voices were so low she couldn't catch anything except Sarah Jane's name.

She knew they needed to work out the best means of establishing communication. If whoever was in the house didn't have a phone, the team had a throw phone, a secure private line that connected hostage taker with negotiator. She just hoped they'd be willing to talk.

Cathy shifted her position, her legs getting stiff from her exertions earlier. Taking a step forward she peered out through the gap in the sheeting. It was still pitch dark, but a light in the far end of the cottage glowed dimly.

Someone was in there.

Was it Sarah Jane? Part of her wanted to haul open the front door to see.

But that could be fatal. For both of them.

The ERU inspector put his hand to his ear again, holding a tiny microphone close to his mouth with the other hand. Their dialogue relayed through Cathy's earpiece as each of the team checked in again.

Immersed in her own thoughts, Cathy peered again through a gap in the barn wall, everything tinted green through the goggles. Then a voice filled the farmyard and she almost jumped.

The tone was firm but calm. The negotiator. She glanced behind her. Speaking into a loudhailer he was watching the cottage closely through the gaps in the sheeting, looking for a reaction from inside.

'This is Colm Hayes, I'm part of the Garda Síochána Crisis Unit. I'm here to listen to you and to try to make sure everybody stays safe. Can you indicate that you can hear me?'

Whoever was in the house couldn't *not* hear that, even if they were asleep. Cathy could feel her mouth go dry. *Who was in there?*

But the silence gaped as they waited for a response. Long minutes.

At the far end of the cottage, in what Cathy guessed was the bedroom, the only light they could see was weak. Cottages like these were scattered all over the country, traditionally built with the front door opening directly into a stone-floored living area with a huge fireplace used for heating and cooking. In former times this space would have doubled as a sleeping area for big families. If they were lucky, a second room opened off it into a bedroom. Looking at the size of it, Cathy was pretty sure this was a two room cottage. Cathy strained her eyes to see through the tiny windows. Even with the night-vision equipment it was impossible to see inside, the glass darkened with layers of dirt, no doubt the frames fused shut, thick with a hundred years of paint.

Why was it taking so long for anyone inside the house to respond?

But she wasn't going to let her imagination work on that one.

The negotiator tried again, his amplified voice reverberating off the concrete surfaces in the yard, off the steel walls of the barn, 'Can you tell me if you are you OK? Does anyone need medical attention?'

No response.

What was happening in there?

'Can you indicate you can hear me? Is everybody safe?'

Nothing.

Maybe it was a hoax. But how could anyone who wasn't directly involved know what had happened tonight? How could they have known about the proximity of this location to the car park at the reservoir? Had Givens left Sarah Jane alone and another one of Farrell's gang got to her? Cathy pulled her pendant out from the neck of her hoodie and ran it nervously along the chain.

Still calm, his tone indicating he was in complete control, the negotiator repeated his first request.

Across the yard, the light in the cottage flashed.

Cathy started, swung around to the inspector. He'd seen it. He raised his hand, signalling to the negotiator.

Glancing back at them, the negotiator nodded sharply. Then his voice echoed around the farmyard again, 'Can you tell me if you are you OK? Does anyone need medical attention?'

The light flashed again: dark, light, dark, light. Nine times. Different lengths.

Cathy turned to grab O'Rourke's arm. He leaned forward so she could whisper in his ear, her chin brushing his stubble. 'That's Sarah Jane – it's Morse code.'

He nodded, .

The ERU inspector turned to her and nodded too, unspeaking.

Morse code wasn't widely used anymore but last summer they'd gone to the National Maritime Museum in Dún Laoghaire: Cathy, Sarah Jane, Decko and J.P. Sarah Jane had been fascinated by the huge lighthouse lenses suspended above the pulpit and a Morse code machine. It had been freezing, but they'd gone to Teddy's afterwards for ice creams, and she'd had them all tapping out their names and the SOS sequence as they sat and shivered in the park.

It was Sarah Jane, it had to be. And the fact that she was trying to communicate with the negotiator implied she was on her own in the bedroom, that she was hoping whoever was hidden in the main section of the house would be so busy concentrating on what was going on outside they wouldn't see what was happening inside.

The comms in her ear were staccato, each officer radioing in. Then she heard the inspector say, 'Keyhole, front door. Move in now – over.'

'Affirmative – out.'

The response was instantaneous and, as the negotiator tried again, Cathy could see a black figure slip around the far corner of the cottage and drop to the ground, crawling towards the front door.

Cathy heard O'Rourke's voice in her other ear before she realised he was still standing right behind her. 'They've a night-vision keyhole camera. If they can get it through the door, with a bit of luck they can see who is in the main room.' She nodded silently.

The figure spent a few moments beside the door, then raised his hand.

O'Rourke turned to look at the inspector , who gestured for them to join him. He pointed to the laptop screen. The camera was transmitting a black and white night-vision picture of the inside of the cottage – close to the floor, admittedly, but it was far crisper and clearer than Cathy could have imagined. She could see the uneven stone floor, a table and chairs. As they watched, the operative rolled the camera around to try and get a clear shot of the whole room. From his position beside the cottage and the view they had of the room, Cathy guessed he'd managed to get it through a gap in the door about two and a half feet from the floor. A fire glowed white hot in the huge fireplace. They didn't have a full three-sixty of the room, but it looked deserted. Was whoever was holding Sarah Jane just out of view?

Cathy turned back to the crack in the sheeting. And the light began to flash again, irregularly this time. Flash, flash, flash.

They had to do something. Cathy focused on an image of Sarah Jane's face, willing her to be OK, but she had a strong sense that whoever was in the bedroom was getting more distressed as the minutes ticked past. Was she injured? Cathy's palms began to sweat.

Cathy touched the ERU inspector on the arm, whispering to him, 'Have you got a heartbeat detector like the ones they use in earthquakes?' She knew it was a longshot but she'd read somewhere that a group of scientists had developed a device that used microwaves to detect human heartbeats in piles of rubble; that's exactly what they needed now to establish how many people were on the premises. He turned to look at her, giving her a negative with a shake of his head. They had one, but it wouldn't work in these conditions? Good idea, but they didn't have one? Cathy wasn't sure. Ireland wasn't exactly an earthquake zone, so she was pretty sure it wouldn't be standard issue.

Cathy took a step backwards and looked at O'Rourke, raising her eyebrows. He understood her unspoken question and shook his head, 'They can't go in yet – too dangerous in the dark. They need to wait until first light.'

'But dawn's not for another three hours – they have to go in, the last flashes . . .' Cathy could hear the desperation in her voice, but before O'Rourke could react the ERU inspector raised his hand. Through the earpiece Cathy heard it too,

'We're in. Contact made.'

Contact with Sarah Jane? Cathy felt an overwhelming surge of emotion engulf her, threatening to drown her.

The ERU inspector indicated the laptop again. A new screen opened to reveal another shot. The camera angle was higher this time, halfway up the wall, they must have pushed the camera through the window frame. The room was a bedroom, a high, old-fashioned bed in the middle of the room, a military-style camp bed and sleeping bag on the floor beside it. The walls were whitewashed, uneven, a holy picture askew on the far wall.

And, huddled on the floor between the bed and the camp bed, as far away from the door as she could get, was a figure with pale hair. Her head was tucked into her knees, her arms around them as if she was trying to make herself as small as possible. Beside her on the floor a camping lamp glowed.

And Cathy felt every hair stand up on the back of her neck. Relief blending with fear in a potent cocktail that made her feel physically sick.

Sarah Jane.

Now they just had to get her out.

46

The ERU inspector's voice was calm and practised as he drew Cathy and O'Rourke in close, keeping his voice low. The cottage was at least thirty yards away, and the door firmly closed, but the long side of the barn was open. And sound travelled easily at night.

'The lads are happy she's on her own in the bedroom, but we have to assume whoever is holding her is in the main part of the house out of range of the camera. The boys think they can remove the bedroom window, but it's very small.'

Cathy ducked to look out of the crack in the corrugated steel wall facing the cottage, assessing the size of the window on this side of the building. The one at the rear would be the same size. It was small – just four tiny panes – but Sarah Jane was slim and fit. Cathy reckoned she could manage it.

'She'll get through.'

The inspector nodded. 'Colm's going to start talking to create a bit of noise out the front here while the boys remove the window frame at the rear of the house. It's rotten as hell – they reckon it'll come away easily. The lads are all too big to get through so we need her to come out on her own as quietly as possible. The second she moves, we'll create a distraction and a bit of noise to give her the chance to get clear.'

He looked at Cathy to see if she understood. She nodded. 'I want you around the back. She knows you, she'll respond to you. We will only have a few seconds to make this happen.' Cathy nodded again as the inspector spoke into his mouthpiece, 'Good to go – she's on the way.'

O'Rourke squeezed Cathy's shoulder as she turned to head out, back the way they had come. She followed the side of the barn around to the gate. Above her, thick cloud blocked out the stars and the ghostly smudge of the moon. *Christ, it was dark.* Without the night-vision goggles she wouldn't be able to see her hand in front of her face.

Reaching the gate Cathy could see a figure in black waiting for her across the field. He signalled for her to get down low. Glancing at the cottage, Cathy crouched down as low as she could and covered the gap between the corner of the barn and the gate. Then around the hedge and into the field. Looking at the size of the windows and angle of the cottage she was sure she was out of view here, but still keeping down, she jogged to the officer waiting for her.

The night air was freezing but Cathy was sweating now, the wind whipping across the field stinging her face as she reached the officer and followed him to a gap in the hedge. Pulling her jacket around her to protect herself from the brambles, she pushed her way through.

Givens had said he wouldn't kill Sarah Jane, that he knew her dad, that he owed him; and then they'd had the tip-off about her location. So they'd found her, but they couldn't take the risk that whoever he had left her with felt the same. Then it dawned on Cathy – Givens wouldn't expose one of his team. Someone had given them Sarah Jane's coordinates, and Cathy was sure it was one of Givens's associates who had called, presumably on Givens's instruction, but he wouldn't leave one of his guys out on a limb. What if he'd left Sarah Jane on her own? Was there anybody in the house at all with her? Was that why they couldn't see anything on the camera in the main part of the house? From the way she was behaving it looked like *she* thought there was someone there, and therefore they had to assume there was, but was there really?

Pushing through the hedge immediately behind the cottage, they came to a small clearing, what must have once been the cottage's back yard, where another officer was waiting. A rusted pulley stood in the middle: what was left of a well. The sound of water trickling was louder here, and Cathy could hear the distant lowing of a cow somewhere across the fields. The area was waist high in brambles and overhung by trees, but Cathy could see the back wall of the cottage, the officer operating the camera they had fed through the window frame hunkered down against the wall. As Cathy reached him an owl suddenly hooted somewhere overhead, making her start.

The two ERU officers indicated she should sit back while they worked on the window. The wooden frame was like cardboard, completely rotten under the layers of paint. They slipped what Cathy presumed was a blade in between the main frame and the wall, sliding it around as quietly as possible. From the front of the house Cathy could hear the negotiator again, his voice drowning out any sounds they might be making. *'We have supplies of food and water, can you tell me if anyone requires medical assistance?'*

Then the two men paused, as if they were counting the minutes before the negotiator started speaking again. Right on cue he did, and a moment later, suction cups on the glass, they wriggled the entire window out. Lowering it against the wall of the cottage, they signalled for her to move in, one of them cupping his hands to give her a boost up to look through the window. Cathy pulled off her baseball cap and goggles and vaulted up.

The walls were cold and rough under her hands, the opening tiny, bits of wall and wooden frame crumbling down on her as she leaned in over the deep window sill. Sarah Jane, only a few feet away, was looking up at the window, her face paralysed by shock. Cathy grinned and, without speaking, Sarah Jane hauled herself up and came towards her. Cathy put her fingers to her lips and signalled that she should climb out. But the window was a fraction too high for her to jump up. Peering up, her face desperate, Sarah Jane gestured to Cathy that she couldn't get out.

Silently she indicated that Sarah Jane needed to move away from the window. Cathy hopped back down, unclipped her kevlar vest and pulled off her jacket – they were too bulky to allow her to fit through the space,. She threw them onto the ground. The officer cupped his hands again, and a second later Cathy was wriggling through the window, hands out, landing on the camp bed below it in a forward roll. As she stumbled up, Sarah Jane threw her arms around her. For a second they hugged, then Cathy pushed Sarah Jane away, bending to give her a boost up out of the window. On the other side the two ERU officers waited.

Sarah Jane didn't hesitate, was up and through the window, landing, Cathy hoped, in their arms.

Cathy next.

Backing across the room, getting as far from the window as she could, she ran at it, springing up to grab the edge of the sill, making way more noise than she'd intended. But a second later she was out, the second officer standing beside the window so she could grab his shoulder and haul herself through. Stumbling, Cathy grabbed her jacket and vest and followed the officer through the hedge. Then they were both running across the field, the ERU officer's arm over Cathy's shoulders protecting her, keeping his body between her and the cottage. Cathy's chest was bursting with the cold air. Beyond them, the first officer and Sarah Jane were almost at the parked vehicles; vehicles that had now been joined by an ambulance.

47

It was almost five thirty in the morning and the lights of the interview room in Dún Laoghaire Station were harsh, bouncing off the cream walls and polished grey surface of the tower recording system bolted onto the wall. Cathy knew Sarah Jane was exhausted, they all were, but it was vital to get everything she could remember on tape as soon as was humanly possible, before her memory started to fade, to obscure the facts. It happened to everyone, perception – what people thought they'd seen – and what had actually happened could be quite different places.

Wrapped in a Garda jacket, her hair tied in a knot, Sarah Jane put her elbows on the table and ran her hands over her face. Across the table, O'Rourke activated the equipment to record the interview – visuals and audio from the camera above them. Cathy reached across the table and rubbed Sarah Jane's arm.

Listening to the whirr and click of the machine, Sarah Jane took a sip from the steaming cup of hot chocolate in front of her, warming her hands as she held it. A high-pitched bleep indicated everything was ready to go.

'Now start at the beginning and tell us everything you can remember.' O'Rourke's voice was warm, encouraging.

Putting her cup down, Sarah Jane smiled weakly and drew in a breath, her voice husky, little more than a whisper. 'I really don't know how I could have been so stupid.'

'Just take it one step at a time. Try and remember everything.'

'It started in the shop, in Vijay's shop ... Oh ...' Having hardly started, Sarah Jane stopped suddenly, her eyes open wide, 'Does Vijay know? Was it in the papers?'

Cathy smiled. She knew exactly what was on Sarah Jane's mind, 'You've been all over the news, but don't worry, we'll notify him as soon as we can. You can give him a call yourself a bit later – he'd definitely like to hear from you.' Sarah Jane shook her head, blushing, understanding Cathy's tone. 'You'll have loads to talk about – getting kidnapped is as good a starting point for conversation as any.'

O'Rourke leaned forwards in his seat. 'So tell us what happened in the shop?'

'OK, so it started on Friday. I was a few minutes early for work, so I popped into the shop to see if Vijay was there. There was a girl standing in the queue in front of me – very nervous, Eastern European, I think. She was filling out some form and I was just standing there, and she turned around and whispered, "Help me."' Sarah Jane paused, her eyes fixed on her takeaway cup, turning it slowly. 'I didn't know what she meant, but she looked so terrified, kept glancing at the guy she was with, so ...' Sarah Jane paused again, 'I didn't know what to do. I couldn't talk to her with him there, so I scribbled down my phone number on a lottery slip. I didn't know if the guy was her husband and was beating her up or what.' Sarah Jane's eyes met Cathy's. She'd heard the stories of domestic violence that featured almost every week in Cathy's job. Sarah Jane sighed, 'I waited for them to leave and I thought I'd just keep an eye out to see where they went. I saw them go into the car park behind the restaurant.' Sarah Jane pushed her fingers into her hair, her eyes fixed on the cup as she relived the events of Friday, 'But then one of those street-cleaning trucks came past, and by the time I'd gone around it to cross the road they'd disappeared.'

O'Rourke shifted in his seat. Cathy could feel he wanted to interrupt, to ask questions, but he knew they had to let Sarah Jane talk first. Sarah Jane screwed up her face in a frown, 'It was really bugging me. It was the girl's eyes – she was so desperate, so frightened. So when my dad rang on Friday evening I told him about it. When I described the guy she was with, explained that I thought she was Eastern European or Russian, he told me to be careful, that it could be anything – drugs, prostitution, anything. I thought it sounded a bit mad, to be honest, but apparently there are lots of trafficking gangs operating in Ireland, bringing people through here to the UK. It was something he'd started working on – the organised crime angle – but then the Syrian thing happened and CNN wanted him to go there.'

'*Why* didn't you call me?' Cathy gave her a meaningful glare, half joking, but she meant it.

'I don't know, I was working on my assignments all day Saturday and I had other stuff on my mind – I didn't want to create an international incident over a girl and her boyfriend. I thought I'd keep an eye out, and if I saw her again or if she called, I'd tell you. You know what my dad's like, he sees the worst in every situation.' Sarah Jane took a sip of her hot chocolate, 'So then on Sunday, I was on my way to work and I was pulling into the car park on Drury Street and I saw the guy again, the one from Vijay's shop. So I parked as fast as I could and flew down the stairs to see if I could see where he was going. I thought he might be meeting the girl again and I could talk to her . . .'

'You know you didn't lock your car?'

Sarah Jane looked confused, 'Didn't I? I thought I'd done the central locking thing? I grabbed my laptop but I forgot my phone too – the damn battery died so I stuck it in the glove box. I only realised when I got to work. I was planning to go back during my break and pick it up, see if I could borrow a charger.' Sarah Jane grimaced, 'But *that* didn't happen . . . I was just so keen to see where the guy was going, I guess I didn't think . . . Managed to forget my locker key too – when I got to work I realised I'd left it in my denim jacket at home . . .'

O'Rourke smiled sympathetically, 'Don't worry, what happened next?'

'Well, I got to the ground floor of the car park but I couldn't see him. I've no idea where he went, so I headed to work. *Then*, everything was fine until I went upstairs to get fresh table linen. The window was open and I heard this scuffle outside in the car park. It was that same girl from the shop, dressed like a hooker and running out of the fire exit of one of the buildings that backs onto the car park. Before she'd got more than about six feet, the guy I'd seen appeared and grabbed her and punched her so hard she collapsed.'

Sarah Jane bit her lip, the shock at the memory obvious in her face, 'I went running straight down the stairs, calling for Billy to call the Guards. I started saying about girls being trafficked and about the girl being beaten up, and then he slapped me. I must have fallen and hit my head. I don't remember anything then until I woke up in his office. He asked me if I was OK, and said he was really sorry for slapping me, but I'd been hysterical and he gave me a tablet for my head.' Sarah Jane sighed, 'I thought he was being nice. I'm so stupid.'

'It wasn't paracetamol?' Cathy could hear the suppressed anger in O'Rourke's voice. He'd been deeply unimpressed by

Billy Roberts's concern for his missing employees – or lack of, to put it more accurately.

Sarah Jane leaned her head against her hand. 'I've no idea what it was, but it made me really, really groggy.'

Cathy leaned across the table, rubbing her arm, 'You're doing great, and you're safe now, nothing can hurt you.'

Sarah Jane's smile was weak, 'So I'm totally zonked from the tablet – I've no idea how long I was there for – but then I can hear voices around me. I couldn't really focus. Then this guy appears, who Billy says is going to take me home. He had to half carry me to his car.'

'Dave Givens?' Cathy interrupted.

'Yes, but I didn't know who he was then. And he didn't take me home. He took me to this guy Richard Farrell's house. He owns The Rookery. I'd only met him a few times before, he's not there a lot. He's some sort of society playboy, is in the magazines the whole time. There's a girl in work called Daniella, she fancies the pants off him and I think she's been dating him secretly – anyhow, she'd told me all about him.'

Cathy felt her stomach lurch but didn't say anything. Sarah Jane needed to get a good night's sleep and to feel safe again before Cathy told her about Daniella. Knowing now, rather than tomorrow, wasn't going to bring her back.

Sarah Jane continued, 'So Farrell is all smiles when he opens the front door. I was still out if it; I couldn't work out why I was there. He showed me into the living room with this huge widescreen TV and the fire lit, and there was this pool . . .' Sarah Jane drifted off for a moment, remembering, then said, 'I sat down on the sofa, and tried to put my bag down, but I dropped it and everything fell out. Whatever Billy gave me made me feel really heavy and in a sort of fog. Then Farrell turns around, and

I knew ...' She glanced at Cathy, 'The look on his face. I still didn't understand why, but I knew I'd really fucked up ... I really thought he was going to kill me there and then, and leave me floating in the pool and pretend it was all an accident.'

Cathy reached across the table and rubbed her arm again as Sarah Jane took a breath, her eyes fixed on her cup, 'He asked me who I'd been talking to and said that he didn't like journalists sneaking around his business.' Sarah Jane shook her head, 'And then Givens, the guy who'd brought me there, comes into the room. He's like about seven feet tall and in a paramilitary canvas jacket and army boots and he stands with his hands behind him and his back to the wall just staring at me. It was terrifying.'

'You're safe now – neither of them can hurt you.'

Sarah Jane smiled at O'Rourke, 'I know.' Then she stared back at her cup as if she was reliving the scene, 'So then Farrell asked me about my dad ... I said he was in Syria, so he says, "And what's the famous Pulitzer Prize-winning Ted Hansen doing in Syria, Sarah Jane?"' She paused, 'Which, as it turned out, was the best thing he could have said, because at that point Givens didn't know who I was. He told me afterwards that he'd been called in to "remove me cleanly" – those were his words. There had been some previous cock-up, some guy who worked for Farrell had had to get rid of someone and had made a mess of it.' Sarah Jane's face paled, 'It's like killing people is normal for them.' She took a slug of her hot chocolate, 'So then Farrell says, "This is the same Ted Hansen that found evidence of Hezbollah working with the cartels in Mexico?" I just looked at him – Dad won his Pulitzer for his work on the links between organised crime and terrorist organisations. That's when I realised what was happening. Dad had been right on the phone – human trafficking is one aspect of transcontinental organised crime. These are the type of people who are involved in drugs and guns. Dad had been looking at the covert movement of people and weapons.'

As Sarah Jane paused, Cathy suddenly became aware of the sound of O'Rourke's watch ticking loudly. But Sarah Jane was oblivious to it, and shook her head as she continued, 'Then Farrell starts asking me about Daniella. I said she was helping me with my thesis – I couldn't see what that had to do with anything.' Sarah Jane paused, catching a look that passed across Cathy's face, 'Is she OK?' Sarah Jane's hand shot to her mouth, 'Oh my God, what's happened?'

Cathy didn't reply, instead shifted in her chair, trying to find the right words. 'Don't worry about that now, a lot's been happening since you vanished. The girl you met in the shop is called Irina, she's from Belarus. That back door you saw her come out of leads to The Paradise Club on Drury Street. We raided it last night. She's safe.' Cathy paused, 'You were bang on about her being trafficked. But it wasn't just her, there were girls there from Romania, Nigeria and Brazil too. They're all safe now.'

'And Richard Farrell? Have you arrested him?'

Cathy rolled her eyes, 'Let's just say he met your friend Dave Givens again and he's still alive, but he won't be going anywhere for quite a while.'

48

The next morning, sitting on one of the desks in Dún Laoghaire's otherwise empty detective office, her feet resting on a hard stacking chair, Cathy tried to look relaxed. It wasn't easy. O'Rourke was interviewing Aleksy downstairs, and she knew it was part exhaustion, part nervous energy generated by the fact that Sarah Jane was safe, but she felt like someone had wound her up and was holding the key.

Had she alibied a murder suspect? Surely with Aleksy's involvement with CAB, everything would be fine, besides, his dad was a cop, according to O'Rourke. And he'd been photographed by a speed camera on the N11, so the chances of him being involved in Daniella's murder and the subsequent disposal of her body looked increasingly unlikely. Cathy bit her lip. But there was still the possibility that they'd got it all wrong here, that things weren't as they seemed.

Her stomach knotted with tension, Cathy tapped her fingertips on the edge of the desk, beating out the tempo to the song going around inside her head: Katy Perry's 'Roar'. She was a champion, but she wasn't doing much roaring this morning.

She'd caught a glimpse of Aleksy earlier with O'Rourke, looking just as gorgeous as he had the other night, a clean white T-shirt showing off his ripped arms and tattoos. But she couldn't get involved. He was trouble in so many ways: super dreamy delicious trouble, but trouble nonetheless.

Cathy yawned. When they'd finished taking Sarah Jane's statement, a patrol car had been ready to take her home, and Cathy had accompanied her back to her own house, where she knew Sarah Jane would feel safer for the moment. Cathy had settled Sarah Jane into her own room, dug out the blow-up mattress the lads used when the house was at capacity after a party, knowing she'd be fine sleeping on the floor for a few days. It was a tiny room, but there was just enough space for both of them.

Her car had been in the drive when they'd arrived, the keys on the doormat, so when O'Rourke had texted to say Aleksy was being moved to Dún Laoghaire, Cathy had had the world's fastest shower and headed straight back to the station.

She had been lurking at the end of the corridor, trying to stay invisible as O'Rourke had turned the corner heading for the interview room with Aleksy. Aleksy hadn't seen her, but she'd caught O'Rourke's eye as he held the interview room door open. Half frowning, he'd shot her a 'keep away' look.

So now she was keeping away and it was killing her.

And she was feeling sick.

This was almost as bad as the feeling she'd had when Sarah Jane had first disappeared, a sort of dread mixed with she wasn't sure what. And on top of that she was as stiff as hell, her forearms bruised from vaulting through the window of the cottage.

But Sarah Jane was safe now, she'd been checked out by the duty doc, had had a long bath at Cathy's and had slept well. She'd said she'd be back over to the station later when she'd had

some breakfast and sorted out her clothes – there was still information they needed to check and Sarah Jane needed to share.

Over at the Bridewell, Frank Gallagher and Jamie Fanning
were interviewing the security staff from The Paradise Club, all
Eastern European; none of whom had visas.

Cathy's head was so busy she didn't notice J.P. appear at the
door of the detective office, his raspberry crew neck jumper
almost as crumpled as his shirt collar. He was holding a couple
of mugs of coffee. Pausing in the doorway, watching her for a
moment, he put his head on one side.

'What's up, miss? You're like a cat on a hot tin roof.'

'Ha ha, very funny.'

'Sarah Jane will be fine, you know. She's a tough one.'

Cathy threw him a grin; she'd thought she'd never worry
again after she'd hugged Sarah Jane last night, but this morning
there were still a whole heap of things she needed answers to.

J.P. came into the office and passed her the cup, 'Two sugars –
figured you needed it. Heard anything more on Givens?'

'Nothing solid. He was fast – he slipped passed Traffic's patrols.
The Range Rover was left in the short-stay car park at Dublin airport. His passport is flagged, but I doubt he'd use his own.'

'Reckon he's gone?'

'Seems likely. According to McIntyre he's used to keeping
below the radar.'

'So what's the story with Sarah Jane's dad – he knew him?'

'Yep, Givens was in some elite unit in the British army – part
of a team the Brits had in Sierra Leone retraining the army after
the civil war. A bomb was set off by dissident rebels. It was pretty
shit by all accounts.'

'Sounds it. Did I hear her dad's on his way over?'

'You did. Someone got a message to him that Sarah Jane was in trouble. I have a feeling that must have been Givens too – CNN drew a total blank trying to track him down. He's on a plane now.'

'Givens seems to be some operator.' J.P. took a sip of his coffee and yawned. 'Heard ERU were pretty impressed with you, though.' Cathy nodded, half smiling. The ERU inspector had called O'Rourke while they'd been in the interview room with Sarah Jane this morning, leaving a message to say Cathy had been right about the cottage being empty.

She sipped her coffee. And started tapping her foot.

'Can you keep still?' J.P. moved from leaning on a filing cabinet to sitting at one of the empty desks. It was rare for the office to be totally empty, but Cathy was grateful for it today. She drew in a breath and grimaced at J.P., 'Sorry, I . . .'

Before she could finish O'Rourke appeared at the door. He jerked his head in the direction of the corridor and vanished.

J.P. looked a her half teasing, 'You're in the shit again.'

Cathy rolled her eyes, 'Back in a minute.'

Outside in the corridor O'Rourke was waiting for her, leaning on the end of a wall of dark blue steel lockers, each one numbered in marker pen on a white sticker. He had his hands in his trouser pockets and was jiggling his change. *Pink tie again today, he must be in a good mood.*

'Turns out your friend Aleksy is very helpful. He said he was up in Enniskerry that night to collect some suits for Richard Farrell. As we know, Farrell's ex runs the shop there. He confirms he met you, you both went to eat and then up to Johnny Fox's. He drove back into the city a bit quick and, as we also know, got clocked for speeding down by UCD.'

Cathy nodded silently. Beside University College Dublin the road dipped and the speed limit dropped inexplicably from eighty to sixty. He wouldn't be the first to have been caught out there. *Thank God.*

'Then he said he went home.' O'Rourke glanced at her, his eyes meeting hers. 'This is where it gets interesting. Apparently he lives in an apartment off Gardiner Street with some of the other bar and security staff from The Paradise Club. It's a temporary thing while he finds new digs – his previous landlord is selling up, and he was stuck. It was supposed to be his night off, but shortly after he got home, the head security guy, that Nacek character you met, texts him to say he needs him to go into The Paradise Club to cover for him. Aleksy says a lot of people would have seen him there from about twelve onwards.'

Cathy felt a surge of relief. *Good, that was good.* But she could feel O'Rourke's disapproval radiating from him like a heat lamp, sucking the air from the corridor. Cathy glanced anxiously at him. *What was coming next?*

'When did he finish work?'

'Ten in the morning, apparently. Long shift, it was a busy night.' O'Rourke's tone was clipped, 'He said he started working there doing a painting job, and when he got chatting to Nacek he hired him to do some maintenance and door work. He helps out behind the bar too when it's quiet.' O'Rourke looked at the floor and rattled the change in his pocket again, 'When he got back to the flat the next morning, it was about ten fifteen. Nacek was in his room, but he had the washing machine going on a hot wash. Your friend thought it was a bit weird, because he only seemed to be washing one lot of clothes – jeans, a T-shirt and a hoodie, and his trainers. And as soon as it was finished he got up and ran everything through again.'

'Very odd.'

O'Rourke's expression was serious, 'And there were traces of dirt all the way up the hallway like someone with muddy shoes had walked in. I've briefed Gallagher and 007. We caught up with Nacek heading for the ferry but so far he isn't saying a word. He reckons the muck has nothing to do with him, that he was working in a different part of the club all night, so Aleksy didn't see him, and he reckons the girls will say he was there.'

'Bet they will. No pressure.'

O'Rourke pursed his lips, 'We've a search warrant for the flat. The lads should be starting any time now – we'll see what they can find. If the clothes are still there it doesn't matter how many times he's washed them, we'll find traces if they were blood-stained.'

'If he dismembered Daniella there would have been a lot of blood.'

'That's what Saunders said. And it won't matter who said they saw him if we have forensics that put him at the scene. The soil samples will be the final nail, with a bit of luck. And in the meantime, guess what's turned up?'

'What?' Cathy glanced at him, her stomach doing a flip. *What now?* She pulled her necklace from the neck of her sweater.

'The fingerprint guys have identified a partial print on the bottom of the banister in Sarah Jane's house belonging to Nacek. Once we brought him in and ran a check it showed up. And he's all over the European databases. He's got a list of previous convictions as long as your arm – GBH, ABH, you name it – and a pile of outstanding warrants.'

Cathy ran her pendant along its chain, 'That corroborates Irina's testimony that he followed her cab to Sarah Jane's and then went into the house before he took her back to the club.'

'That's it. She's been very brave to confess to her involvement.'

'But she won't be prosecuted for assisting, will she, seeing she was under duress?' Cathy could hear the anxiety in her own voice.

'I'm not seeing the state prosecuting her as an accessory under these circumstances. We've got Nacek at Sarah Jane's house now, which is excellent. There's a lot more work to be done to tie him to Daniella, but it's looking like he was involved at every stage.'

'Sarah Jane's old desktop must be somewhere – Irina said he came out with her suitcase?'

'We're looking. He's probably dumped it, along with her keys, but it sounds like he let himself in, tossed her room and walked right out again. Her housemate is some plank, isn't he?' Cathy pulled a face. That about summed Slug up. He hadn't told them outright, but she reckoned he'd been high as a kite that Sunday night. He hadn't even been sure what time he'd got home from the pub after lunch. O'Rourke continued, 'It's looking like Farrell must have sent Nacek to search Sarah Jane's room. I'm guessing he wanted to question her to find out how much she knew about their little operation – they were worried she was working on a story and had been gathering evidence, photographs, whatever, since she started working at The Rookery and had it all stored on her computer. I think he used her suitcase to take it out so it looked less suspicious if anyone saw him.'

'And Aleksy?'

'He's being very helpful, and his work visas are all in order which is always a good start. He's been compiling information on Farrell's network since he got the job at The Paradise Club. He knew there was a lot wrong from the moment he walked in and he'd already made some friends in Pearse Street because he'd painted someone's sister's living room or something. Then Pearse Street needed an interpreter and none were available so they called him.'

'So when he got the job at The Paradise Club, he had a chat to his mate in the station and the rest is history?'

O'Rourke rocked back on his heels, 'That's about it. The Criminal Assets Bureau were already sniffing about – looking at The Rookery, apparently, had their eye on Farrell. He's got some dubious business contacts and the restaurant seemed to be making a lot a money. He popped up on their radar. Aleksy was a gift.' He raised his eyebrows, 'And he was helping Irina – she had some pretty heavy clients, and he gave her some sort of narcotic to knock them out so she didn't get hurt. He had trouble sleeping himself apparently, got it from the internet.' O'Rourke paused, 'He thought she was Russian. He was worried about being watched so he didn't get a chance to talk to her properly. He was quite surprised to find out she was from Belarus.' O'Rourke raised his eyebrows meaningfully.

Aleksy had told him about her scheme to contact the Money-Gram recipient. Cathy looked at him deliberately innocently, 'Really?'

She left it hanging there. It didn't matter now. A part of Cathy started to relax. Perhaps her judgement about Aleksy wasn't utterly flawed after all. But there was still a bigger question in her mind. 'What about Sarah Jane? Did he know anything about her kidnap, or about Daniella?'

O'Rourke looked non-committal, 'Apparently not. Nacek is the cagey type, didn't let anything out.' Cathy ventured a smile. 'But Cat?'

'Huh?'

'Keep clear until the dust settles, yeah? You're damn lucky.'

'Yes, boss.'

'I mean it.'

O'Rourke pulled away from the wall and gave her one of his looks. He was her guardian angel. He'd once said she'd been his. His eyes met hers and held them for a moment. He cleared his throat and chucked her under the chin.

'Aren't you due in court this afternoon? Nifty Quinn?'

'Ah feck. Totally forgot.' She shook her head. They'd finally caught local burglar Nifty almost red-handed, and she'd been the toast of the station. Thirsty would be waiting for her.

He checked his watch, 'Have a word with Thirsty now and the two of you seek an adjournment – you want to be fully focused in front of Judge McKenna. I'm going to talk to Billy Roberts, we've got him over in Pearse Street. When you're finished come into town and we'll head into Tallaght Hospital for a chat with this Richard Farrell character.'

Cathy felt a sense of relief as she left Thirsty's office. But it was relief mingled with something else. Something was niggling her. She paused for a second as she pushed open the swing door to the recreation-cum-incident room, heading for the coffee machine. There was something about all of this that didn't quite fit, something that didn't feel right.

But Sarah Jane was safe and they had Farrell in custody. And it looked like she was in the clear with Aleksy. So why was she feeling like this?

The District Court was right next door to the station. Two coffees later Cathy grabbed a black tailored jacket from her locker, slipped it over her polo neck and pulled her hair back into a ponytail. Judge Justin McKenna was a stickler for his court running like clockwork. Thirsty was waiting for her in the public office. They were in and out in half an hour.

As Cathy pushed open the front door of the station, she saw Sarah Jane was waiting for her in the lobby. Her hair, clean and shiny, was plaited over one shoulder, and she was wearing Cathy's denim jacket over her black skinny jeans. Last night, on their way home, Cathy had got their driver to call over to Sarah Jane's and had fished the jeans, a couple of T-shirts and enough underwear to last her for a few days, out of the mess of her room. She planned to get back to tidy it up properly as soon as she got a chance. Cathy had made Sarah Jane wait in the car; she could live without seeing her personal space violated on top of everything else.

'Everything OK?' Cathy kept her voice low, avoiding the inquisitive looks from the gurriers hanging about trying to look like they weren't there for anything specific. Like signing in to satisfy their bail conditions. Sarah Jane nodded, her face grim, pale with exhaustion. 'More questions to double-check everything, and I had to identify everyone from photographs. I just feel like such a total idiot, but it all happened so fast. Now I can see there were signs that something weird was going on.'

'O'Rourke always says hindsight is a wonderful thing.'

'He's right.' Sarah Jane grimaced, 'Do you think they'll need to keep my laptop for long?'

Cathy shook her head and yawned. Apart from her lack of sleep, at the end of any investigation she always felt burned out, and this one had used up all her emotional energy. 'Not for too much longer. I'll have a word and see what the story is.'

Sarah Jane bit her lip, 'I didn't know if he was telling me the truth – Givens, I mean. He told me how Dad had saved his men. They hit a landmine or something, but Dad helped them and they were all OK.' Cathy put her hand on Sarah Jane's arm.

'I know, I heard Givens tell Farrell before he shot him. That's not the sort of thing a soldier forgets. It's way above and beyond. Your dad could have run with his cameraman and they would have both been safe. But he didn't. He stayed. Givens will protect you and your dad for ever, you know that?'

Sarah Jane's eyes filled with tears, 'I know.'

'He was going to kill Farrell for you. Farrell's not at all happy this morning, from what I hear.' That brought a weak smile from Sarah Jane. As one of the lads had said last night, Farrell had everything coming to him.

'I can't forget her face, the girl in the shop – Irina did you say her name was? Her eyes were so intelligent, so hurt. And then when I saw her trying to run out the back door of that building . . . that guy just hit her so hard.'

'She's safe.' Cathy could feel her own eyes stinging; a lot had happened in the past few days. 'She's safe now and she's got people helping her.' Cathy paused, smiling, 'Have you called Vijay?'

Sarah Jane blushed, 'I haven't had a chance yet. I'm going to do it as soon as I get back to yours. I thought I'd see if he wanted to meet for coffee . . .'

'Or a drink maybe?' Cathy opened her eyes wide, feigning innocence.

Behind them they heard the door to the interview room swing open and Jacob's voice. 'But why doesn't he wash his clothes or go in the shower, Mummy? Then he wouldn't smell.'

Cathy and Sarah Jane smothered laughter at Rebecca's eye roll as she steered him into the large tiled hallway. 'Why don't we talk about this at home, darling? Look, here's Cat.'

'Hello, soldier. Have you and your mum been talking to my colleagues?'

'They've got a digital recording system, it does three discs at the same time. Aren't you the girl who got lost? Your hair's different from the picture.' Jacob looked critically at Sarah Jane's lilac streaks, 'You left your keys at my dad's. You should be more careful with keys.'

Rebecca interrupted him, 'Come on, darling, we need to be quick – we've lots to do.'

Sarah Jane smiled at Jacob, 'I will be, don't worry.'

Jacob cut in, 'Are we going to see Daddy now?'

Rebecca's smile was less than enthusiastic, 'We'll see, darling. Let's get home first. Ciara's coming over to do some baking with you – she says you make better chocolate cake than she does.'

Cathy almost laughed as Jacob's face lit up, 'Will you save some for me?'

'Of course. Come on, Mummy, we better not be late.'

'Let me just do up your coat, it's cold outside.'

Jacob started to pull Rebecca through the crowded hall just as a man with a golden Labrador puppy walked in. Jacob immediately stopped to pet it. Rebecca stood back to let him, their hurry forgotten.

Cathy turned to Sarah Jane, 'What are your plans for the day?'

'Mum's on her way up. I think she's going to be here about nine. I want to go and see Jazz, but he said he won't be up at Keane's Field until about six.' Cathy nodded. She'd finally told Sarah Jane about Daniella this morning, and it had been one of the hardest things she'd ever had to do. They were still waiting on the DNA reports that would prove conclusively that the body was hers, but with the mutilation that appeared to be a deliberate attempt to hide her tattoo and the match with her rare blood group, it was looking increasingly likely.

Sarah Jane continued, stretching, 'Right now I'm going to go back to yours and have a lie down.'

'Pop over to the gym after you've seen Jazz? The Boss wants to see you, and I'm way behind with training – the semis start at the end of the month.' Cathy grinned, 'And you owe me a session.' She paused, glancing at Jacob and the puppy, choosing her words carefully, 'O'Rourke wants to interview our suspect this afternoon before he "forgets" anything. I'm going with him – we'll see what he has to say for himself. And then I'm going straight to the gym.'

Cathy doubted Farrell would confess to anything – it would be down to them to gather the evidence. There was a forensic team starting on his house, but if they got a DNA match on the semen in Daniella's oesophagus he'd have a hard time explaining his way out of it. And after Aleksy's testimony, Nacek's clothing was being examined. If he had disposed of her body, and it was looking very likely that he had, the forensics would be irrefutable. The soil samples from his flat were already being analysed and cross-matched with the area where the body had been found.

No doubt Farrell's story would be that it had been all Nacek's fault.

She turned to Sarah Jane, 'How are you getting home?'

'Taxi now, but J.P.'s lent me his car until I get mine back – he's sorting out the insurance today.' She smiled, 'And Decko's lent me his old phone. I got a temporary SIM card for it – I'll text you so you've got the number. So I'm sorted. See you later?'

49

O'Rourke was quiet in the car on the way out to Tallaght Hospital. Farrell had regained consciousness last night once he'd been hooked up to a drip, and was, according to the doctors, sedated, but not enough that he wasn't causing trouble with the nurses. Farrell was in a private room away from the general hospital population, an armed Guard in his room just in case he decided to do a runner, which would be a challenge given his condition, but O'Rourke wasn't taking any chances that someone could come after him.

It had taken O'Rourke longer to get out of Pearse Street Station this afternoon than he'd expected. He'd gotten the superintendent's permission to extend Billy Roberts's detention and questioning; Irina's statement indicated that he'd been complicit in creating a smokescreen to hide Sarah Jane's disappearance, and knew more than he was letting on. Just getting him to admit it was proving time consuming.

O'Rourke glanced in his rear-view mirror and eased the car into the bus lane as they swung out of Pearse Street. He was looking as tired as Cathy felt. He obviously hadn't had time to shave since yesterday, and the day's growth made him look rugged rather than exhausted. Rugged and very sexy. Cathy tried to focus on the traffic. Maybe it was the relief that Sarah Jane was safe and that they had a suspect in custody that was causing her hormones to start hopping. She wasn't sure – one day they would actually be in line with the appropriate moment, and this wasn't it.

As she looked at him out of the corner of her eye, O'Rourke scowled, focusing on the back of the blue and yellow bus ahead of him, his mind obviously processing the information they'd been gathering.

'Roberts have anything interesting to say?' She interrupted his thoughts and it took him a moment to answer. When he did, he made a snorting noise that summarised his feelings towards Billy Roberts.

'Billy Roberts reckons he only runs The Rookery, doesn't know anything about The Paradise Club. Said Farrell owns them both, that he's the boss. He claims Farrell sent Givens to collect Sarah Jane when he found out she wasn't feeling well. Roberts thought he was taking her home.' O'Rourke raised his eyebrows in disbelief.

'And he thought we'd swallow that? Really?'

'He says Farrell told him to get a cab for Irina on Sunday evening – he didn't know who she was or why. Was too busy to ask. He reckoned that he'd got mixed up when we questioned him the first time – he has a lot to think about, apparently, and organising cabs for people isn't a high priority. It had been a busy day, he was under pressure with Sarah Jane being sick and he was a bit under the weather himself. He got mixed up about who went in which car.'

'Confused? Right . . .' Cathy's tone said it all.

'What I don't get,' O'Rourke measured his words, 'is how Farrell managed to keep The Paradise Club and The Rookery going with no one realising his involvement in them both. It's a big operation, and from all accounts he spends half his time in the bar or schmoozing at celebrity events. Did he come across as a criminal mastermind when you questioned him with 007?'

Cathy shook her head. That bit had been bothering her too. 'Far from it. He's a pretty boy, but his brains are in his trousers.' She wrinkled her nose, 'Maybe Billy Roberts was the one pulling the strings? I think he's a damn sight sharper than he looks.' O'Rourke frowned as she continued, 'I reckon Farrell was the face all right, but remember J.P. said there was a board of directors – perhaps Farrell's just a front man?'

'I think you're right. And you could be right about Roberts. I've got the team doing searches through the Companies Registration Office now, we'll see what they turn up. The other directors all seem to be non-resident, but this type of operation is international so we shouldn't be surprised by that.'

'Rebecca said Farrell had a place in Spain, and that's where he was taking Jacob. Maybe start there?' Cathy shifted in the seat, thinking hard, 'And someone put Farrell in touch with Givens. McIntyre heard on the grapevine that Givens was in the North, so perhaps that's it. Someone up there is controlling things here. The Rookery and the casino at The Paradise Club are the perfect places to launder cash – nice little businesses, especially with Farrell providing the gloss to keep prying eyes away.'

O'Rourke slowed, glancing into his mirror as he filtered into the lane that would take them onto the M50. 'That could be exactly the place we need to look. I think we need to have a chat to the PSNI.'

Cathy hated hospitals. The moment she walked through the doors and was hit with the too-bright lights and clinical smell she was right back to those weeks after the explosion that had felt like years. Trapped in a bare room, all hard edges and hard surfaces, when she'd first come out of sedation she'd stared at the wall trying to get her head around what life would be like if she couldn't box, if she couldn't get back to the job.

Desperate to escape herself as well as the four walls of her room, she'd discharged herself early but still had to come back to be checked out, to have her pain medication monitored, her scars and skin grafts examined. She found hospital a tough place to be, meeting people daily who were in a much worse state than she was . . . She was a fighter, and once she'd been given a road map to recovery she'd astounded her doctors. It didn't heal the mental scars, though, the sleeplessness, the nights spent lying alone grieving for her past self, for her baby, for everything that could have been. The memories were still raw – she'd done the obligatory counselling to get back on the job, the bare minimum, but every time she walked back into a hospital she was right there, all over again.

As if O'Rourke sensed her mood change, he rubbed her shoulder. She threw him a weak smile. He'd been through it with her.

Before O'Rourke could say anything his phone began to ring in the depths of his pocket. He stopped walking, grimacing as he listened to the caller. Cathy crossed her arms tightly and took a deep breath to still her anxiety, trying to focus on him and blank out everything around her.

'Thanks, keep me posted.' He turned to Cathy, 'The tech lads are over at Farrell's place. They've found traces of blood in his garage. It's been hosed down and bleached, but they reckon there was a lot of it.'

'Daniella's?'

'It seems a strong possibility. From Saunders's report it's looking like she died during some sort of sex game. I reckon Farrell panicked and called Nacek to get rid of her. There's a strong chance that her head and hands are in a weighted sack at the bottom of one of the lakes, but unless we get a confession we may never know. Come on, lift is this way. We'll see what Farrell's thoughts are on the matter.'

As they arrived at the lift O'Rourke's phone began to ring again. Cathy heard him exhale like a bull about to charge.

'What the fuck?'

An elderly nun, who had appeared beside him, glared. He didn't notice. Staring at the phone in disbelief for a moment, he slipped it back into his inside pocket and said calmly, 'Farrell's dead.'

Cathy swung around, looking at him, shocked. She opened her mouth but nothing came out. Farrell had been fine when they'd last checked: how long ago was that, an hour? His injuries weren't life threatening.

Finally she found her voice: 'How?'

'Doc won't comment, could have been an aneurism, reaction to the drugs. They've only just found him. We'll know more from the PM.' He glared at the lift indicator as it clicked through the floors, his lips pursed in a hard line.

'Has anyone been in to see him?' Her eye met his. This wasn't death by natural causes. Someone had taken him out, they both knew it. *Could Givens have doubled back and still be in Dublin?*

'Only the medical staff, apparently. There's been an armed Guard in the room since he arrived, for Christ's sake. Obviously there are people out there who are very determined he doesn't talk to us.'

Upstairs they weren't able to get much more information. Beside the nurses' station a group of medics had gathered, two doctors at its centre. As O'Rourke strode out of the lift one of the doctors broke away and held out his hand, 'Inspector, Dr Murray.'

'What can you tell us?'

'Not much at this stage. His vital signs were being monitored, we were checking him at regular intervals. Everything seemed to be stable. I'm not very happy with his drip line, though, there's a possibility it's been tampered with.'

'We'll need to seal his room.'

'Already done.' Dr Murray was familiar with the procedure. 'It's this way.' Reaching a door on the left, the doctor indicated that they could look through the glass. O'Rourke took a glance and pulled his phone out. Cathy slipped in behind him. Farrell looked like he was asleep, the only indication that something was wrong the fact that the machines surrounding him were all switched off. 'We shocked him but . . .' Murray shrugged.

Cathy waited while O'Rourke called in the techs and uniform to secure the scene. Leaning on the sill staring out of the huge window at the end of the corridor, rain forming droplets that coursed down the pane, her mind was clicking through all the information.

They'd raided the club – they had physical evidence as well as what must be hundreds of witness statements, had Irina's testimony about what had been going on there. As the investigation continued they'd go through all the paperwork, the bank statements. So what was it that someone thought Farrell could have told them that they didn't have evidence of already? What weren't they seeing? Did he have information on arms, or drugs, on who was supplying them? Sarah Jane had said that Farrell had been sure her dad was invesitgating his operation, was looking for information on the connections between organised crime and terrorism. Was that it? Was there something much bigger going on here?

The Guard on duty hadn't even left his post to take a piss. Which meant if someone had come in and done Farrell harm, they must have been dressed very convincingly as a member of the medical staff. Maybe the CCTV tapes would reveal something.

Her forehead on the cool glass, Cathy looked down on the tarmacked road that snaked through the hospital grounds and landscaped gardens. It was never quiet here, visitors constantly criss-crossing the car park, patients in dressing gowns and slippers hanging out, smoking. Behind her, Cathy could hear O'Rourke pacing the corridor. She could see his reflection in the glass – her own face pale, her crazy hair like a dark halo. Over her shoulder O'Rourke was a blur of navy blue, ghostlike. She glanced behind her; he still had his phone clamped to his ear. Turning her attention back to the limited view outside, she could see the rain was getting lighter, and those who had been sheltering, having a quick smoke break, were now making a run for it. A woman pushing a buggy appeared around the corner of the building heading for the car park.

Who knew Farrell was here? They hadn't exactly made it public. Who would have easy access? Who would be sharp enough to mastermind something like this?

Then it hit her.

Rebecca.

It had been obvious from the second she'd mentioned Farrell to Cathy that she hated her ex; would she have done this to punish him for trying to take Jacob? Was she more involved in the restaurant than she'd let on? She ran her own business, was obviously in control . . . Billy Roberts had said he knew her from Spain, from before she'd met Farrell.

And Roberts was up to his neck in this.

The idea gathered momentum. The PM had suggested that Daniella had been asphyxiated during sex. Had Farrell called Billy Roberts first in a panic to help him dispose of Daniella's body? Had Roberts called Rebecca? If Rebecca was the brains behind the business, that would make sense. Farrell sure as hell wasn't. And Cathy would bet he'd not mentioned the semen . . .

Cathy thought back through all her interactions with Rebecca, starting with interviewing Jacob. What had Rebecca said? That Jacob didn't lie? Had her reporting his sighting of Sarah Jane been a damage-limitation exercise? The information she'd provided had been sketchy, potentially misleading, but maybe that was deliberate? Givens drove a Range Rover, how could you forget that? Cathy's mind went back to their chat, to Rebecca's living room with the brass shell cases on the mantelpiece, to Rebecca's African rug. Did she know Givens? Had she met him in Africa? The only people Cathy knew who had shell cases like that were operational in theatres of war, guys who had served with the UN.

And this morning with Sarah Jane, Rebecca had said she was in a hurry and then had been hanging about letting Jacob pet that puppy. Listening to their conversation.

And Jacob . . . Jacob was eight. He played Minecraft all the time. On the phone, when Rebecca had told her Jacob had texted her from his dad's car, he'd said the man Farrell was meeting was like Action Man – how did he even know who Action Man was? That wasn't his generation, it was Rebecca's. Christ, *she'd hired Givens*, she must have done. And then when he'd found out what was really going on, Givens had gone after Farrell not knowing he had Jacob with him. That's how Rebecca knew he was British army, not Irish – Jacob couldn't have heard his voice on the phone from the back of the car, he couldn't have told her – she already knew. And he'd hardly have fitted all that information into a text. Jacob must have called her all right, and then she'd panicked when she realised what was happening. Perhaps she'd tried to call Givens to stop him, but he was hardly going to answer his phone to her if he was about to murder her ex-husband.

Breathless, Cathy swung around to face O'Rourke. 'It's Rebecca.'

He looked at her in surprise, stopped speaking into his phone for a moment. And, as Cathy said it, another thing fell into place. 'She's the R. Farrell on the company directors list, not Richard. When they were married she would have been Rebecca Farrell. She must have reverted to her maiden name when they divorced.'

Before he could object, she was halfway down the corridor. 'Come *on*.' She spun around to face him, 'Rebecca is the only one who knows Farrell is here – she's next of kin. She needs to erase all her links to The Paradise Club and its operations. When Jacob saw Sarah Jane with Givens, Rebecca was *in* the restaurant, she must have spoken to Billy Roberts. Sarah Jane was drugged, but she's starting to piece things together. I'm sure of it. Rebecca will be after Sarah Jane next, she can't risk her remembering her being there.'

O'Rourke stared at her for a split second. 'You sure?'

'I know it. We need to find Sarah Jane. She's meeting Jazz O'Connor at Keane's Field at six. Rebecca was there when she told me. We need to get out there.'

The blue strobe light on O'Rourke's dash illuminated their faces as he cut through the evening traffic. It was getting darker earlier every evening, and with the fine rain now falling the roads were a blur of moving lights. This was the worst time to try to get anywhere in Dublin, but they were only twenty minutes from Ballymun.

'She's not answering her phone.' Cathy clicked out of the call. 'Decko lent her an old one of his, but maybe the battery died. I'll try J.P.' Moments later J.P. answered. Cathy relayed it to O'Rourke, 'She's got his car, he doesn't know when she left.'

'Get him to contact Ballymun with the make and model. As soon as they spot it get them to call us.' O'Rourke paused, 'You're *sure* about this?'

'Absolutely. Rebecca said she'd do anything for Jacob. She'll be terrified of losing him if anyone finds out about her connection to the club. I'd guess it's only Billy Roberts and Farrell who know she's behind everything. She goes back a long way with Roberts, and if he's not been directly involved with The Paradise Club the only thing we can prove is that he helped Irina into a cab. He's got nothing to gain by implicating her.

'Farrell would have been the opposite, though – the minute he saw he was going down for everything he would try to bury everyone around him. I think she's the puppet master, she's controlling every-thing, came up with the idea of using Irina to impersonate Daniella, and then when it appeared to work, decided to try it again to direct suspicion away from the restaurant over Sarah Jane's disappearance.' Cathy stopped speaking, pulling at her necklace, 'We should have realised it wasn't Sarah Jane when Vijay didn't recognise her – do you remember he was surprised when we told him that it was her getting into the taxi? He knows her but he didn't recognise her. How big does the writing have to be for us to read it?' She shook her head.

O'Rourke listened silently, nodding, concentrating on driving up the hard shoulder. The northbound traffic on the M50 was heavy but moving. On the southbound side it was parked. Cathy glanced over the central reservation. If they'd been heading the other way they'd need a helicopter.

50

'Oh shit.' Cathy leaned forward in the passenger seat, her eyes fixed on a fire engine-red Golf parked at an erratic angle beside the flat scrub at the edge of Keane's Field.

'What?' O'Rourke swung the powerful BMW off the road. Huge rocks littered the verge, an attempt by the Dublin City Council to keep traveller caravans off the land.

'That's Rebecca's car. Look at the number plate. 161-D-2. Jacob told me.'

'First car issued this year, after the Lord Mayor's. Expensive. I can't see J.P.'s car?'

'If Sarah Jane's here already she would have parked beside Tesco's and walked over – she wouldn't take the risk J.P.'s car would get keyed.' Cathy swung the door open.

'Hold on, Cat, we need back-up. If you're right about Rebecca killing Farrell, she could be armed.'

'No time. I've got a feeling.' She pushed the car door fully open.

He swung his own door open, about to get out. 'Not on your own.'

'You're wearing a suit and leather shoes. It's muddy, the grass is like an ice rink. This one's mine. We don't have time to wait. I can do it.'

Before he could argue she was out of the car and running up the narrow slippery path worn in the patchy grass to the top of the slope. *How long ago had she been here looking for Jazz? It felt like a lifetime.*

A lot had happened since then.

On the other side of the hill Cathy knew the horse trough was the only focal point, nestled in a dip in the hills. Jazz had said there were stables on the far side of the field, out of sight, but the trough would be the place where Sarah Jane would meet him, Cathy was sure, and there was a good chance that's where Rebecca was headed too.

Running silently Cathy reached the top of the hill, her black leather jacket, black sweater and combats blending in with the night. She'd grabbed her Nikes this morning when she'd got dressed, hadn't had the energy to find her boots, and was very glad of them now.

As she reached the brow of the hill she realised she'd be silhouetted against the sky if she wasn't careful – anyone could see her for miles. She threw herself onto the cold muddy ground using her elbows to shimmy up to the very crest of the hill.

Then she saw them.

Below her, two women, approximately the same height and build, one blonde, one darker, were standing twenty feet apart. Sarah Jane had her hands open wide, as if she didn't understand what the other was saying. Even from this distance Cathy recognised the other woman as Rebecca Ryan, or Farrell as she had once been. She was holding a gun, two handed like she'd had experience, aimed directly at Sarah Jane.

Cathy's mind switched up a gear, just like it did before a fight, like she had the other night at the reservoir and later at the cottage. It was something The Boss had taught her – a mindset that enabled her to filter out the background noise, the extraneous detail, so that she could coolly assess her opponent, calculate odds, assess angles of attack. It was a crucial ability that enabled her to centre herself, to bring all her skills into one place and focus on her target. Winning.

From up here Rebecca was way out of the range of her own SIG. The P226 was developed to use higher-capacity, double-stack magazines, but she'd need a rifle to ensure accuracy at this distance. She'd have a chance if she could get closer, but it was a long run across open ground. Rebecca might not be facing this way, but she'd be sure to catch Cathy in her peripheral vision and would have plenty of time to aim – even if Cathy kept moving she'd be a clear target with zero cover. Cathy pulled her gun from its holster.

How good a shot was Rebecca? It looked easy in the movies, but hitting a target of any sort took practice. Especially a moving one. Cathy knew she consistently hit ninety-eight per cent accuracy at the Garda range – she was good, but she wasn't any use to Sarah Jane if she was lying wounded on the side of a hill.

The wind was buffeting across the hillside, changing direction, carrying snatches of their conversation towards Cathy and then out across the fields. Cathy could tell from Sarah Jane's body language that she was talking to Rebecca, pleading with her.

'You knew? You knew he'd killed Daniella?' Sarah Jane's voice suddenly reached Cathy – high, incredulous, Rebecca's answer snatched away in the opposite direction.

'He's an idiot, always has been . . . needs someone to think for him.' No prizes for guessing who she was talking about. *Damn the wind* – the horses in the stable at the back of the field were getting more of this conversation than Cathy was.

Then Cathy saw Sarah Jane take a step backwards, caught part of her next sentence, 'You were there, you were in Billy's office . . . I heard you talking to Givens, you knew him, you . . .' Cathy lost the end of it, but she'd heard enough to confirm her suspicions. Sarah Jane was the crucial witness who could directly link Rebecca to Givens, to her kidnap. And now Rebecca had confessed to concealing Daniella's murder. Had she organised for Nacek to dispose of the body?

Jesus, she needed to move now. If she stayed on her stomach, how far down the hill could she get without being noticed?

A moment later Cathy's decision was made for her.

The sound of a shot ringing out across the Keane's Field sent Cathy mentally spinning back to the car park beside the reservoir, to Farrell crying out in pain, back to pressing the central locking on her Mini, an explosion lighting up the night.

But she didn't have time to deal with any of that now. Cathy watched in what felt like slow motion as Sarah Jane's hand moved to her shoulder and she fell backwards, her body bouncing on the hard ground like a dressmaker's dummy.

In that same moment Cathy took off so fast she felt like she was flying down the hill, realising that as each foot connected with the ground she could hear or feel something else, a deep rumbling vibration. The vibration of hooves pounding across the field.

She was still thirty yards away when a huge piebald horse with a rider appeared over the brow of the hill, ears back, mane flying, nostrils flared. Rebecca swung around, her attention on the horse, the sound of its hooves drowning the sound of Cathy's Nikes on the grass. In a blur the horse was almost on top of her, a scream ripping through the night air as another shot rang out.

The horse stumbled and fell, landing heavily, throwing its rider like a rag doll, but Cathy had stopped running, and now within range, fired two handed. She could hear her heart thundering in her ears as Rebecca fell forward, her gun flying out of her hand, and then Cathy was on the move again, crouching beside her. She was conscious, rolling on the ground, her face contorted with pain and anger.

Cathy couldn't see where she'd hit her, but shoving her own gun in the back of her combats, she unclipped her handcuffs from her belt, opening the metal ratchet. Roughly, she flicked them onto Rebecca's wrists, disabling her. The moment she had both of Rebecca's hands secured, Cathy ran to Sarah Jane.

Beside them Krypton lay panting, tongue extended, his flank heaving. A few metres away, covered in mud, Jazz staggered to his feet.

But Sarah Jane was her first concern.

Running over to her, Cathy met her eyes. The confusion, the pain, was clear as Sarah Jane searched Cathy's face for an explanation. She was barely conscious, the shoulder of her denim jacket soaked in blood. Cathy hauled off her jacket, balling it inside out, pressing the padded lining into Sarah Jane's shoulder to stop the flow. *It was a flesh wound; once she could stop the bleeding, Sarah Jane would be OK.*

'She said . . . about Daniella . . . that she'd made sure no one knew . . . Is it true?' Before Cathy could answer, Sarah Jane continued, her voice little more than a whisper, 'She said that I knew too much about her business, that it's bigger than one shop or one club, that I was putting Jacob's future in jeopardy.'

Cathy leaned over her, about to speak, when she froze at an explosive sound behind her.

Another shot.

She half turned to see Jazz standing over Rebecca, her gun in his hand. Her arms still trapped behind her, her face was turned towards Cathy, her eyes open but lifeless, a trickle of blood sliding from the corner of her mouth. Her chest was a bloodied mess where he'd shot her at point-blank range. Dazed, Jazz turned to Cathy, his face muddy and tearstained, full of anguish. 'She knew. I heard her say it. She knew what happened to Daniella. She helped, and she was going to kill her too.' He motioned to Sarah Jane.

'Drop the firearm.' Cathy didn't know how loud she said it, but it fell from his hand, and Jazz stood swaying for a moment before he turned to stumble over to the horse, wrapping his arms around it as his face fell against its neck, the sound of his sobs tearing the air.

Cathy turned back to Sarah Jane, 'Hang in there. It's going to be fine. Just hold on.' Still conscious, Sarah Jane nodded weakly. She closed her eyes as if she was summoning all her reserves of energy, 'He was protecting me, you know that – he shot her to protect me.'

'I know . . . Try and keep your eyes open, you can't sleep.' With her free hand Cathy reached for her phone, but before she could dial there was a movement beside her and Cathy felt O'Rourke's arm around her, his face brush her hair as he hugged her.

'Christ, Cat, how many lives have you got left?'

Acknowledgements

Bringing a book to the bookshelf requires a huge number of dedicated people and many hours of their time. I am blessed with a truly wonderful team who make the whole process seamless – from my incredible agent Simon Trewin to my brilliant editor Katherine Armstrong at Bonnier Zaffre, they are a total pleasure to work with and have my undying gratitude. Simon, Declan and Helen at Gill Hess, who look after PR in Ireland, and the Bonnier PR team in the UK, are a joy to work with and an integral part of the machine.

My family get to see behind the scenes and put up with a lot to support me in all that I do – huge thanks and love to my children Sophie and Sam and my husband Shane.

Part of creating fiction is pulling together many diverse strands of information, ideas and research and blending them to deliver a credible story that while it is all part of my imagination, feels real. I am very lucky to have great help and expert guidance in doing that – huge thanks go to Eugene Roe of the National Rehabilitation Hospital who helped with the physical and mental impact of the aftermath of Cathy's car bomb blast. Thanks too to my Garda experts, retired Garda Colm Dooley, Garda Joe Griffin and to Assistant Commissioner Fintan Fanning who was invaluable in clarifying detail. Glen Heenan at Elite Marshall Arts ensured the boxing sequences made sense and Jane Alger's eye for detail avoided a major transport issues. Any mistakes are entirely my own – I don't think I've transplanted a major department store in this book, but for anyone looking around Dublin for The Paradise Club, The Rookery or the connecting car park, these are entirely fictitious, although they are set in real streets amid the shadows of real stories.

The team who run Ruhama in Ireland are an incredible group of dedicated women who helped hugely in the research for this book, thank you so much for your time and compassion Sheila Crowley. Ruhama is a Dublin-based NGO which works on a national level with women affected by prostitution and other forms of commercial sexual exploitation. A voluntary organisation, Ruhama is Hebrew for 'renewed life'.

The organisation is predominantly a frontline service and began its work in 1989, as an outreach service to women in street-based prostitution. Adapting since then, to a trade that has become more globalised, predominantly indoors and controlled by organised crime.

Ruhama's services are extensive in breadth and have a unique model of work which is not replicated by any other agency in Ireland. In 2014, Ruhama celebrated its 25th anniversary of providing services to women affected by prostitution. Their records show that they have assisted over 2,500 women from over 60 countries during those 25 years. They are amazing.

My writer friends keep me sane day to day and help so much in the creative process. Niamh O'Connor puts up with my rambling, Andrea Hayes keeps me positive, and Alex Barclay helps me kill people. Sarah Webb is always there with support and good sense. There are so many more – you know who you are! Thank you ALL for all your support and help. Without you there would be no magic.